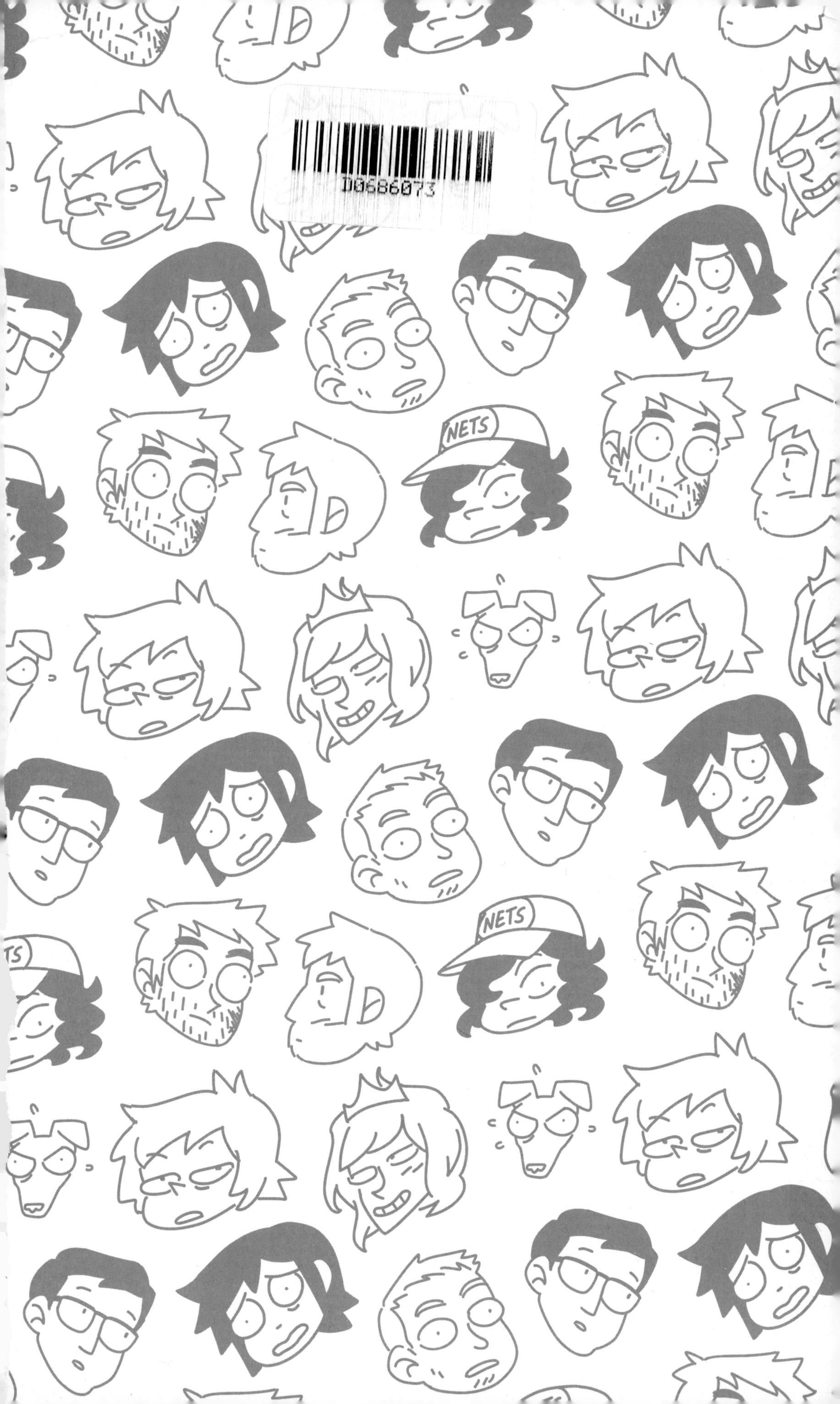
NETS
NETS

octopus pie

volume 4

by Meredith Gran

IMAGE COMICS, INC.
Robert Kirkman – Chief Operating Officer
Erik Larsen – Chief Financial Officer
Todd McFarlane – President
Marc Silvestri – Chief Executive Officer
Jim Valentino – Vice-President

Eric Stephenson – Publisher
Corey Murphy – Director of Sales
Jeff Boison – Director of Publishing Planning & Book Trade Sales
Jeremy Sullivan – Director of Digital Sales
Kat Salazar – Director of PR & Marketing
Emily Miller – Director of Operations
Branwyn Bigglestone – Senior Accounts Manager
Sarah Mello – Accounts Manager
Drew Gill – Art Director
Jonathan Chan – Production Manager
Meredith Wallace – Print Manager
Briah Skelly – Publicity Assistant
Sasha Head – Sales & Marketing Production Designer
Randy Okamura – Digital Production Designer
David Brothers – Branding Manager
Ally Power – Content Manager
Addison Duke – Production Artist
Vincent Kukua – Production Artist
Tricia Ramos – Production Artist
Jeff Stang – Direct Market Sales Representative
Emilio Bautista – Digital Sales Associate
Leanna Caunter – Accounting Assistant
Chloe Ramos-Peterson – Administrative Assistant
IMAGECOMICS.COM

OCTOPUS PIE, VOL 4 First printing. May 2016. Copyright © 2016 Meredith Gran. All rights reserved.

Published by Image Comics, Inc. Office of publication: 2001 Center Street, Sixth Floor, Berkeley, CA 94704.

Printed in the USA. For information regarding the CPSIA on this printed material call: 203-595-3636 and provide reference #RICH–679810.

For international rights, contact: foreignlicensing@imagecomics.com.

ISBN: 978-1-63215-755-3

www.octopuspie.com

Interior designed by Meredith Gran. "Vacation Day" pixel art by Lacey Micallef.
Colors by Sloane Leong, with flats by Gisele Jobateh.
Cover art colors by Valeria Halla.

For Mom.

Thanks to Lacey Micallef for her collaboration and friendship. Thank you to Sloane Leong for thoughtfully visualizing *Octopus Pie* in color for the first time.

And a big thanks to the readers on Patreon, whose pledges have funded O.P.'s switch to color, and its existence in general. It's a gift to make comics with your support.

All right, here we go: the book where *Octopus Pie* "gets good." That's what the literary snobs will tell you before they graduate college and find a shirt/jacket combo that fits their body. Or what I've sometimes told myself in those narrow moments of judging my and others' art in a vacuum. Don't listen to me or the snobs, though. We'll someday join the rest of civilization in enjoying those first, second, and third volumes at the Library of Congress' prestigious webcomic bin.

But, look — the series took a big step in this book, and I'm proud of that. I feel validated by these pages. There was an already-established clarity to the series that allowed me to speak more freely, at a time when I needed to most. By defining moments of longing and sorrow on the page, I could face them more directly in life.

That said, it's not always easy to be clear. Until I experienced it, heartbreak looked different written down. I grasped that it was super sad, a wound to be healed, an undeniable reality or whatever. But the obsession, the depth of longing, the cyclical, incommunicable nature of the pain... Well, those are just words to accompany pictures. If you know what I mean, you **know**, and will hopefully see it reflected here. (And if not, there's also a dece amount of sex and seduction in these chapters, of which I am equally proud.)

I think recovery is also particularly hard to convey in writing. It's an eventless event, seemingly too gradual and invisible to weave into fiction. Getting better never looked like a "light" at the end of a man-made underpass for me, desperate as I was for one. It was a moment of curiosity, a brief bit of hunger, a glimmer of interest followed by long (but subtly, arbitrarily decreasing) expanses of misery. Between those hopeful and miserable points there was an endless amount of searching.

Anyway, I'm happy with this collection because it's the culmination of that search. But I change my mind a lot, so you really shouldn't listen to me.

-Meredith Gran
April 2016

Contents

39

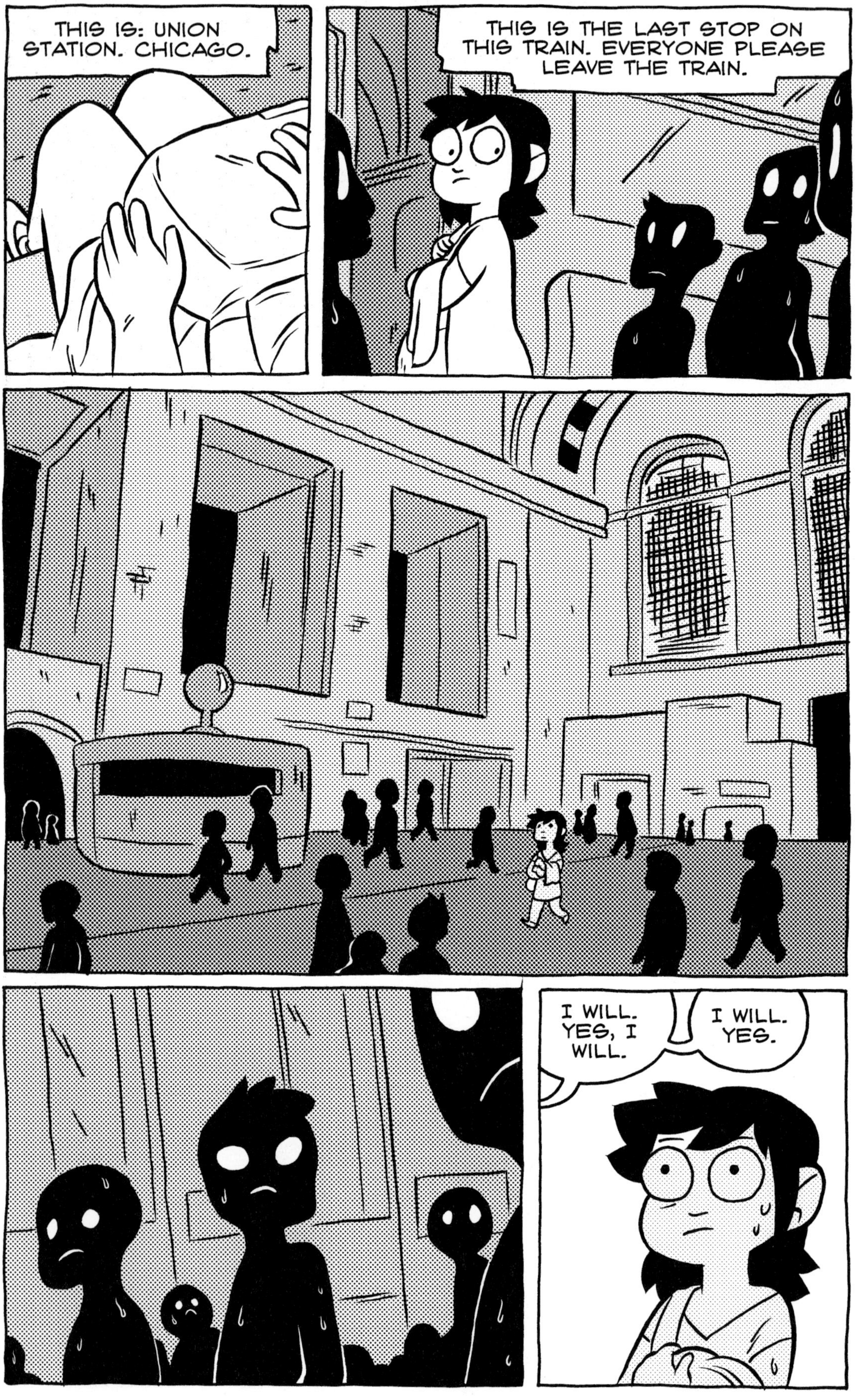
THIS IS: UNION STATION. CHICAGO.
THIS IS THE LAST STOP ON THIS TRAIN. EVERYONE PLEASE LEAVE THE TRAIN.
I WILL. YES, I WILL.
I WILL. YES.

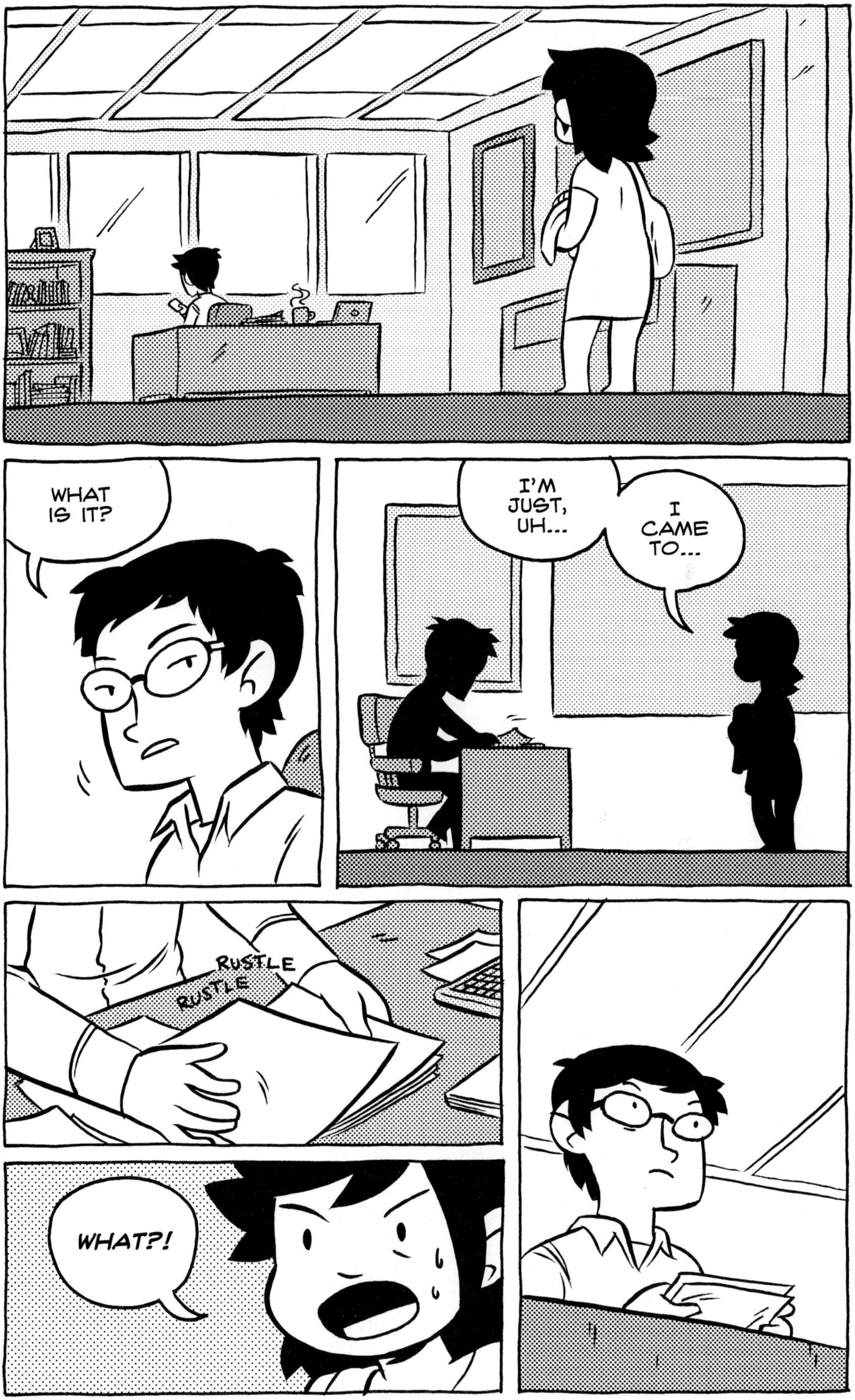
WHAT IS IT?
I'M JUST, UH...
I CAME TO...
RUSTLE
RUSTLE
WHAT?!

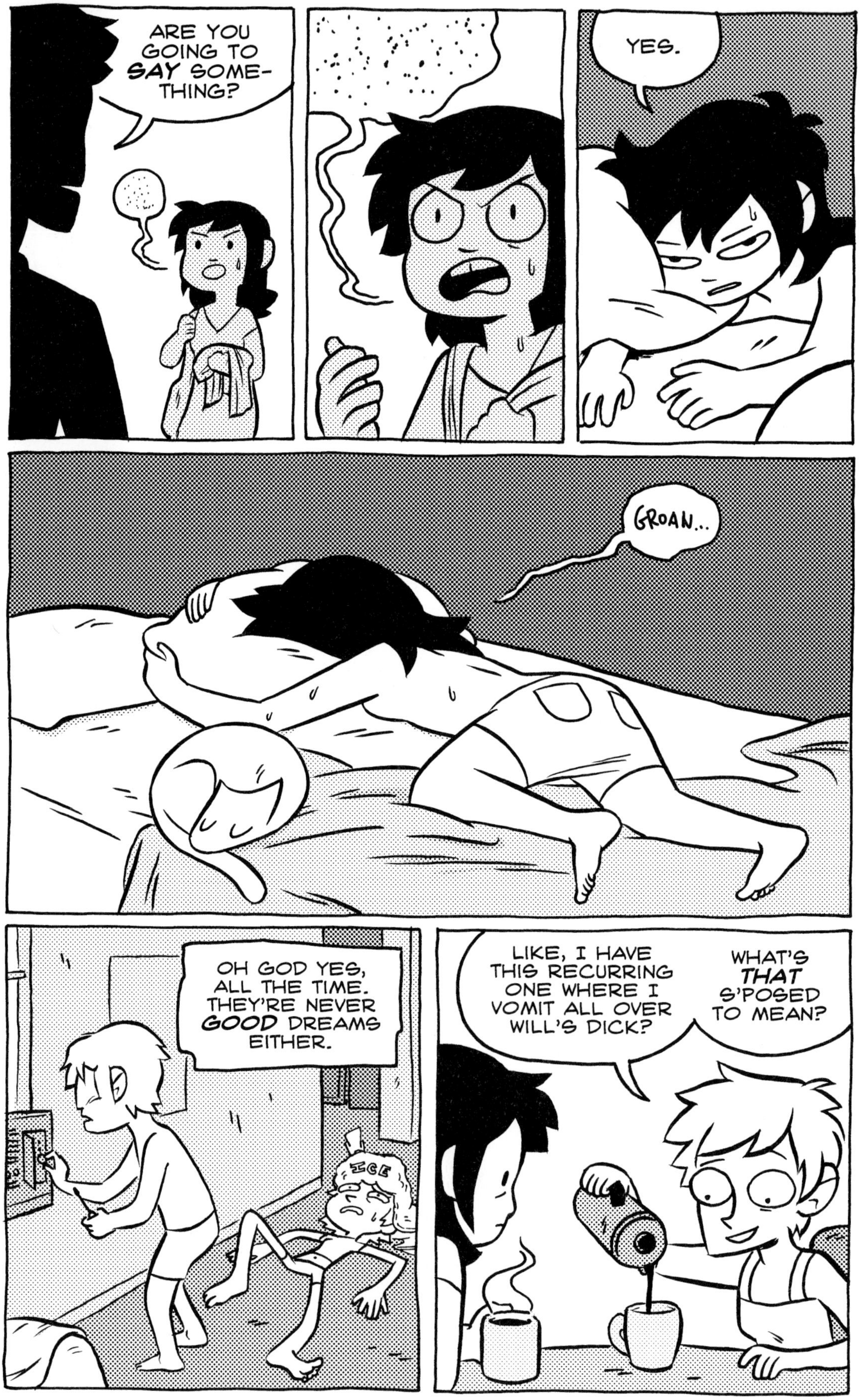
ARE YOU GOING TO SAY SOME-THING?
YES.
GROAN...
OH GOD YES, ALL THE TIME. THEY'RE NEVER GOOD DREAMS EITHER.
ICE
LIKE, I HAVE THIS RECURRING ONE WHERE I VOMIT ALL OVER WILL'S DICK?
WHAT'S THAT S'POSED TO MEAN?

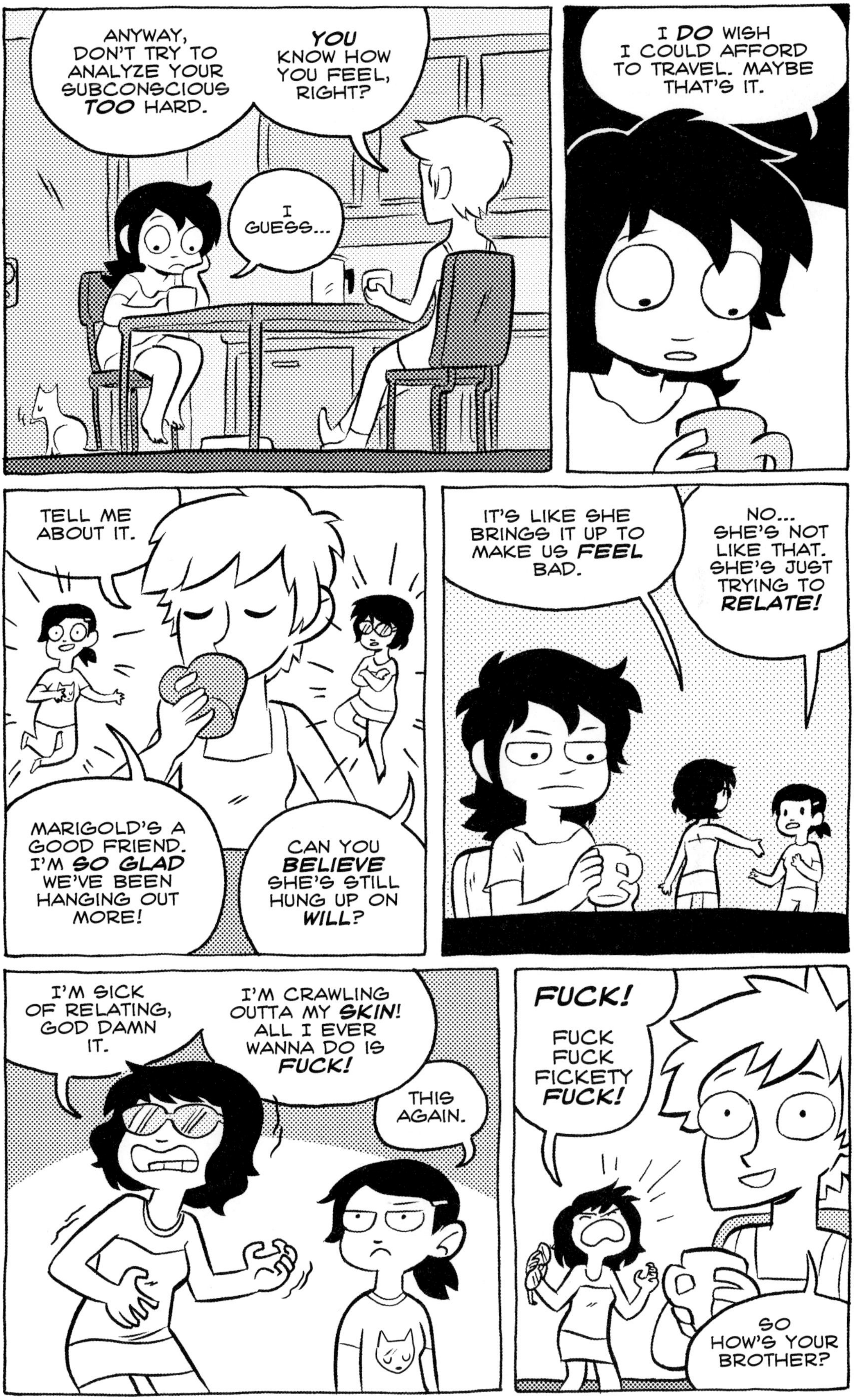
ANYWAY, DON'T TRY TO ANALYZE YOUR SUBCONSCIOUS *TOO* HARD.
YOU KNOW HOW YOU FEEL, RIGHT?
I GUESS...
I *DO* WISH I COULD AFFORD TO TRAVEL. MAYBE THAT'S IT.
TELL ME ABOUT IT.
MARIGOLD'S A GOOD FRIEND. I'M *SO GLAD* WE'VE BEEN HANGING OUT MORE!
CAN YOU *BELIEVE* SHE'S STILL HUNG UP ON *WILL*?
IT'S LIKE SHE BRINGS IT UP TO MAKE US *FEEL* BAD.
NO... SHE'S NOT LIKE THAT. SHE'S JUST TRYING TO *RELATE!*
I'M SICK OF RELATING, GOD DAMN IT.
I'M CRAWLING OUTTA MY *SKIN*! ALL I EVER WANNA DO IS *FUCK!*
THIS AGAIN.
FUCK!
FUCK FUCK FICKETY *FUCK!*
SO HOW'S YOUR BROTHER?

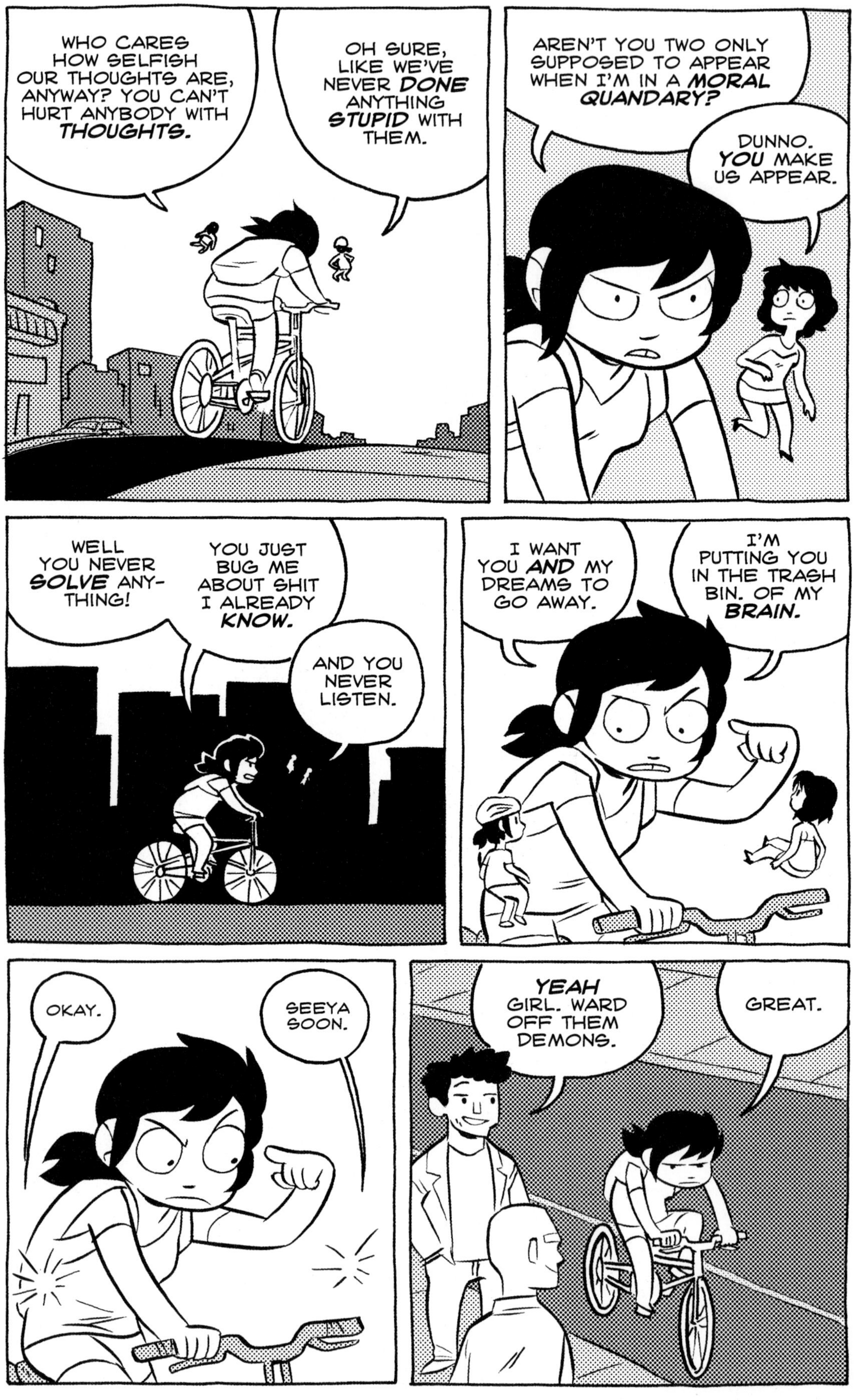
WHO CARES HOW SELFISH OUR THOUGHTS ARE, ANYWAY? YOU CAN'T HURT ANYBODY WITH THOUGHTS.
OH SURE, LIKE WE'VE NEVER DONE ANYTHING STUPID WITH THEM.
AREN'T YOU TWO ONLY SUPPOSED TO APPEAR WHEN I'M IN A MORAL QUANDARY?
DUNNO. YOU MAKE US APPEAR.
WELL YOU NEVER SOLVE ANY-THING!
YOU JUST BUG ME ABOUT SHIT I ALREADY KNOW.
AND YOU NEVER LISTEN.
I WANT YOU AND MY DREAMS TO GO AWAY.
I'M PUTTING YOU IN THE TRASH BIN. OF MY BRAIN.
OKAY.
SEEYA SOON.
YEAH GIRL. WARD OFF THEM DEMONS.
GREAT.

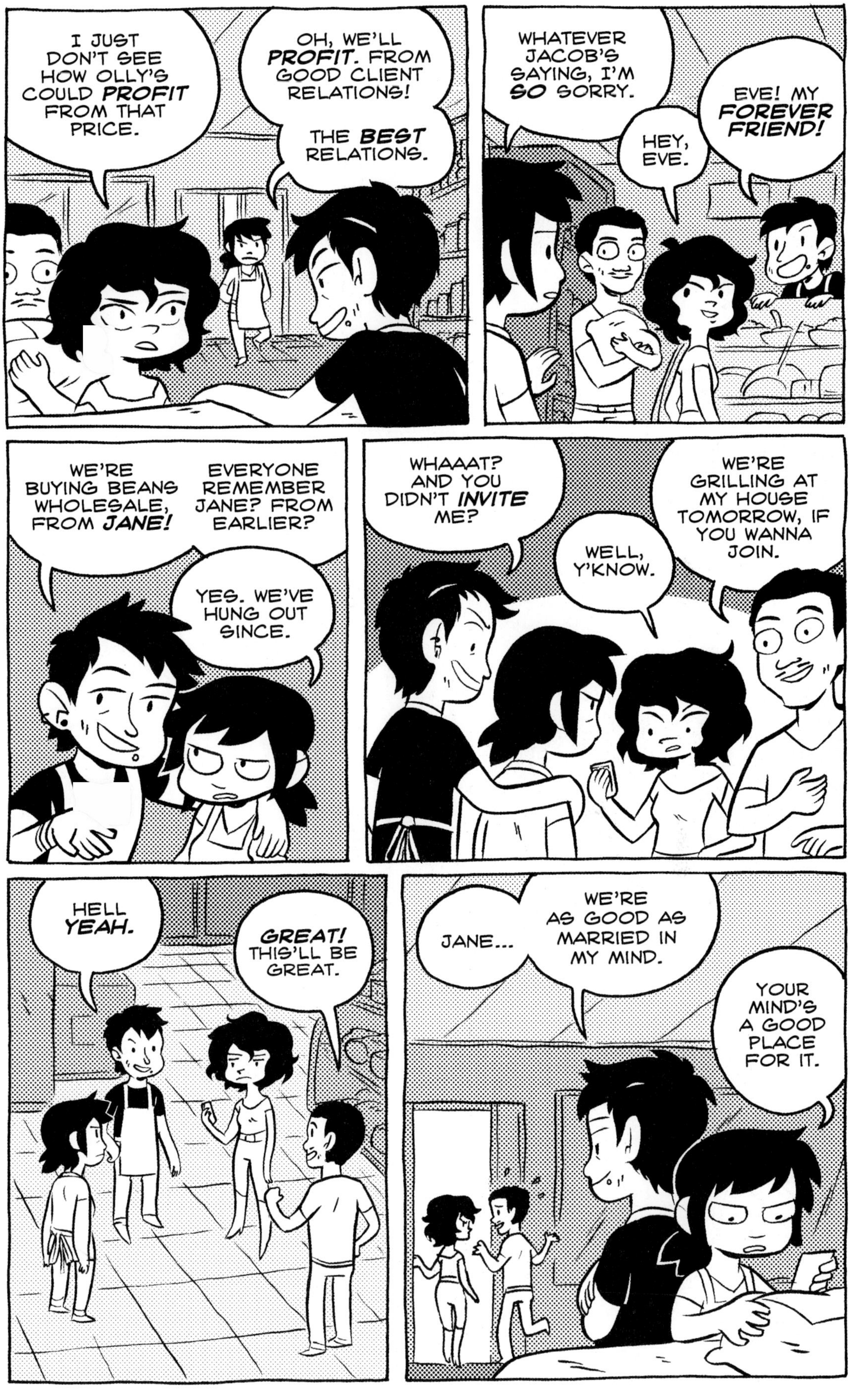
I JUST DON'T SEE HOW OLLY'S COULD **PROFIT** FROM THAT PRICE.
OH, WE'LL **PROFIT**. FROM GOOD CLIENT RELATIONS!
THE **BEST** RELATIONS.
WHATEVER JACOB'S SAYING, I'M **SO** SORRY.
HEY, EVE.
EVE! MY **FOREVER FRIEND!**
WE'RE BUYING BEANS WHOLESALE, FROM **JANE!**
EVERYONE REMEMBER JANE? FROM EARLIER?
YES. WE'VE HUNG OUT SINCE.
WHAAAT? AND YOU DIDN'T **INVITE** ME?
WELL, Y'KNOW.
WE'RE GRILLING AT MY HOUSE TOMORROW, IF YOU WANNA JOIN.
HELL **YEAH.**
GREAT! THIS'LL BE GREAT.
JANE...
WE'RE AS GOOD AS MARRIED IN MY MIND.
YOUR MIND'S A GOOD PLACE FOR IT.

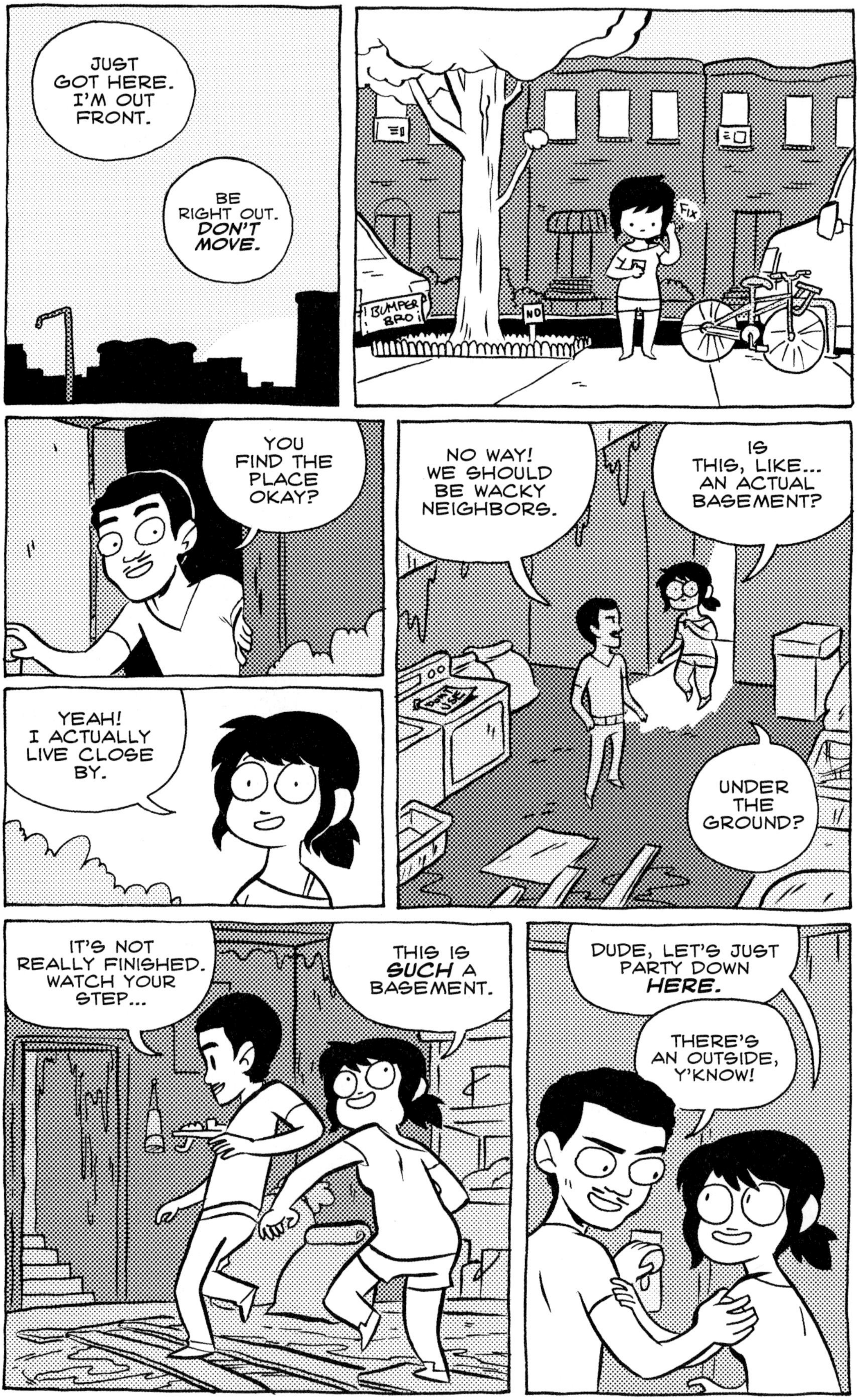
JUST GOT HERE. I'M OUT FRONT.
BE RIGHT OUT. *DON'T MOVE.*
FIX
BUMPER BRO
NO
YOU FIND THE PLACE OKAY?
YEAH! I ACTUALLY LIVE CLOSE BY.
NO WAY! WE SHOULD BE WACKY NEIGHBORS.
IS THIS, LIKE... AN ACTUAL BASEMENT?
UNDER THE GROUND?
IT'S NOT REALLY FINISHED. WATCH YOUR STEP...
THIS IS *SUCH* A BASEMENT.
DUDE, LET'S JUST PARTY DOWN *HERE.*
THERE'S AN OUTSIDE, Y'KNOW!

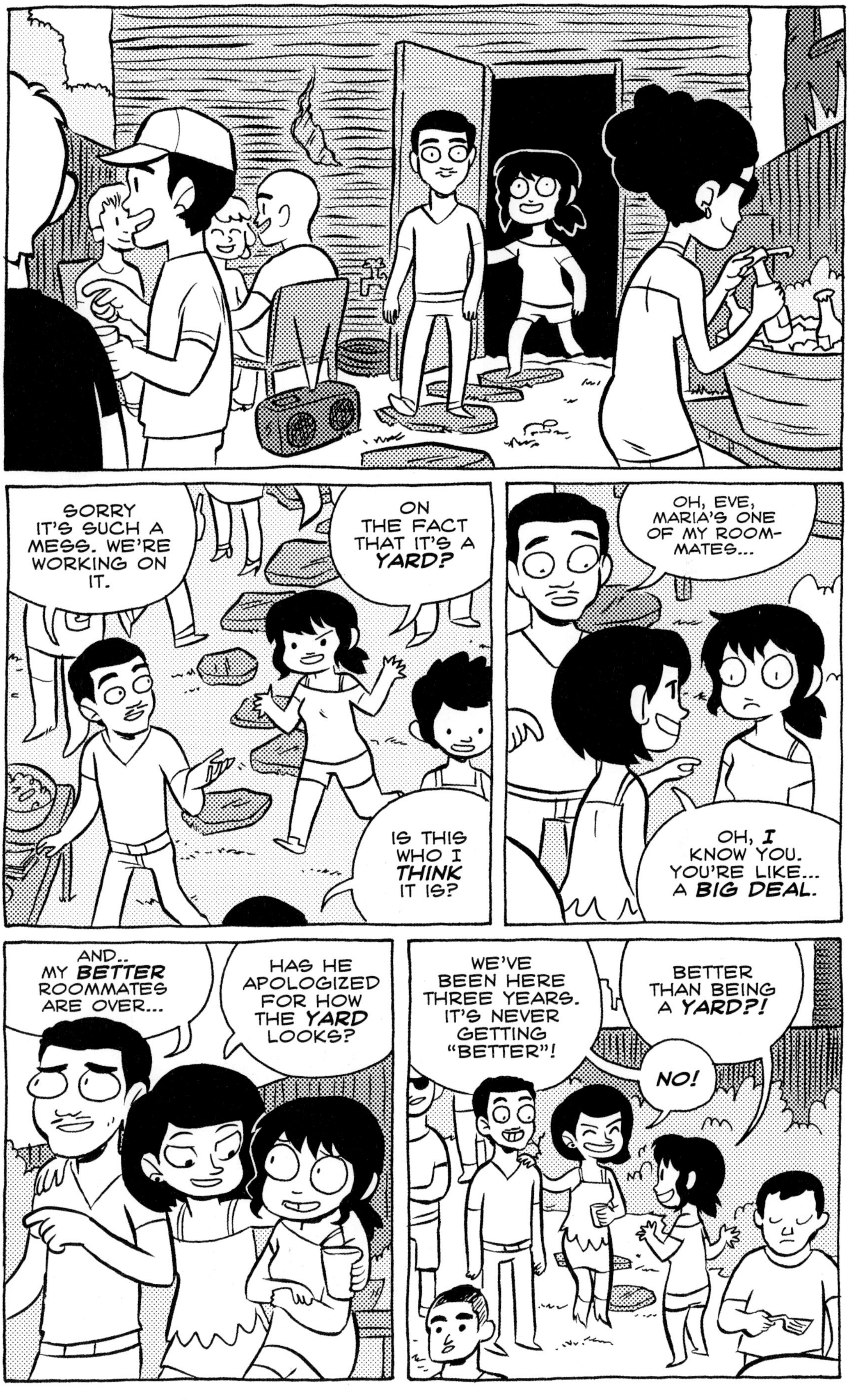
SORRY IT'S SUCH A MESS. WE'RE WORKING ON IT.
ON THE FACT THAT IT'S A *YARD?*
IS THIS WHO I *THINK* IT IS?
OH, EVE, MARIA'S ONE OF MY ROOM-MATES...
OH, *I* KNOW YOU. YOU'RE LIKE... A ***BIG DEAL.***
AND.. MY ***BETTER*** ROOMMATES ARE OVER...
HAS HE APOLOGIZED FOR HOW THE *YARD* LOOKS?
WE'VE BEEN HERE THREE YEARS. IT'S NEVER GETTING "BETTER"!
BETTER THAN BEING A *YARD?!*
NO!

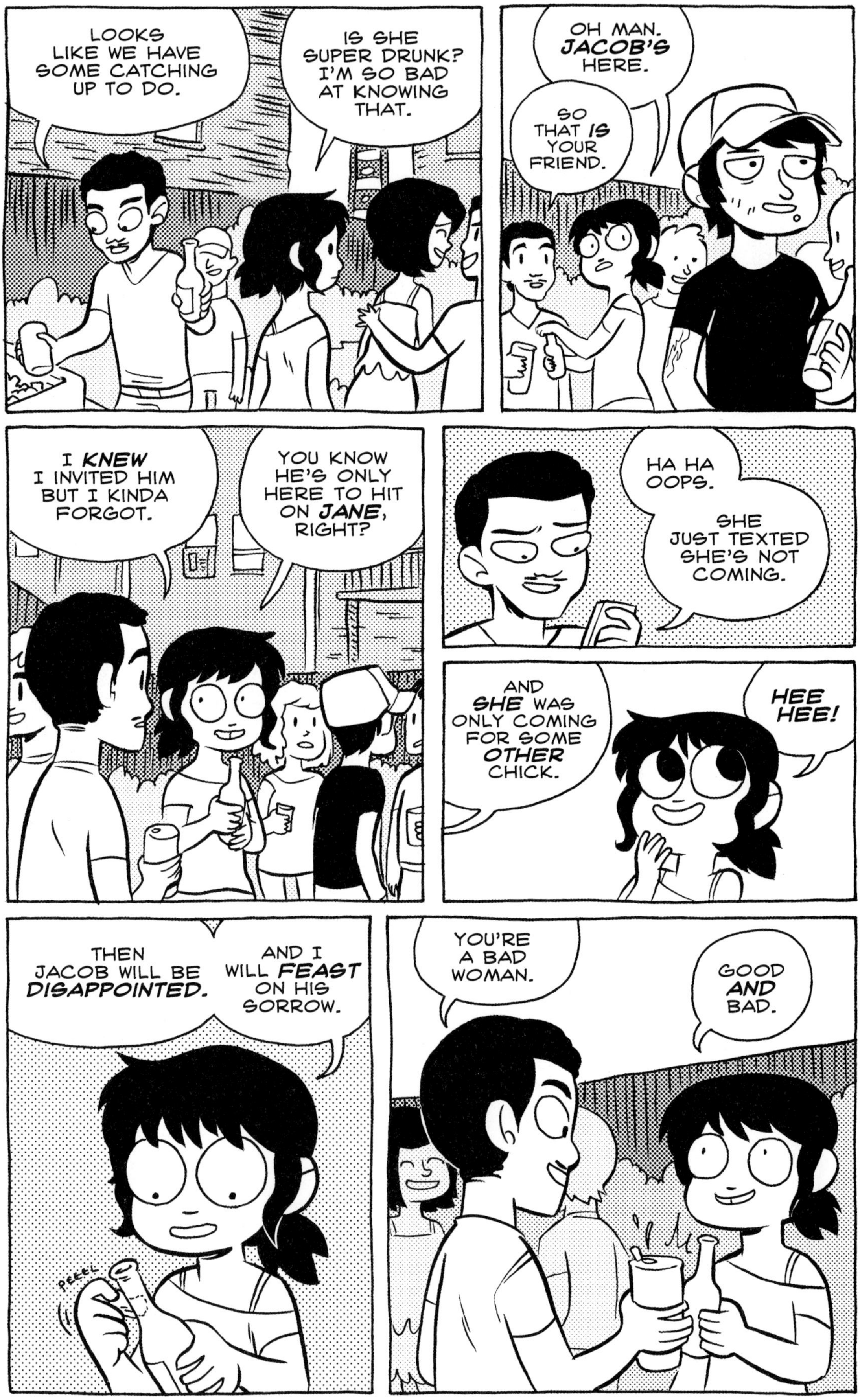
LOOKS LIKE WE HAVE SOME CATCHING UP TO DO.
IS SHE SUPER DRUNK? I'M SO BAD AT KNOWING THAT.
OH MAN. JACOB'S HERE.
SO THAT IS YOUR FRIEND.
I KNEW I INVITED HIM BUT I KINDA FORGOT.
YOU KNOW HE'S ONLY HERE TO HIT ON JANE, RIGHT?
HA HA OOPS.
SHE JUST TEXTED SHE'S NOT COMING.
AND SHE WAS ONLY COMING FOR SOME OTHER CHICK.
HEE HEE!
THEN JACOB WILL BE DISAPPOINTED.
AND I WILL FEAST ON HIS SORROW.
PEEEL
YOU'RE A BAD WOMAN.
GOOD AND BAD.

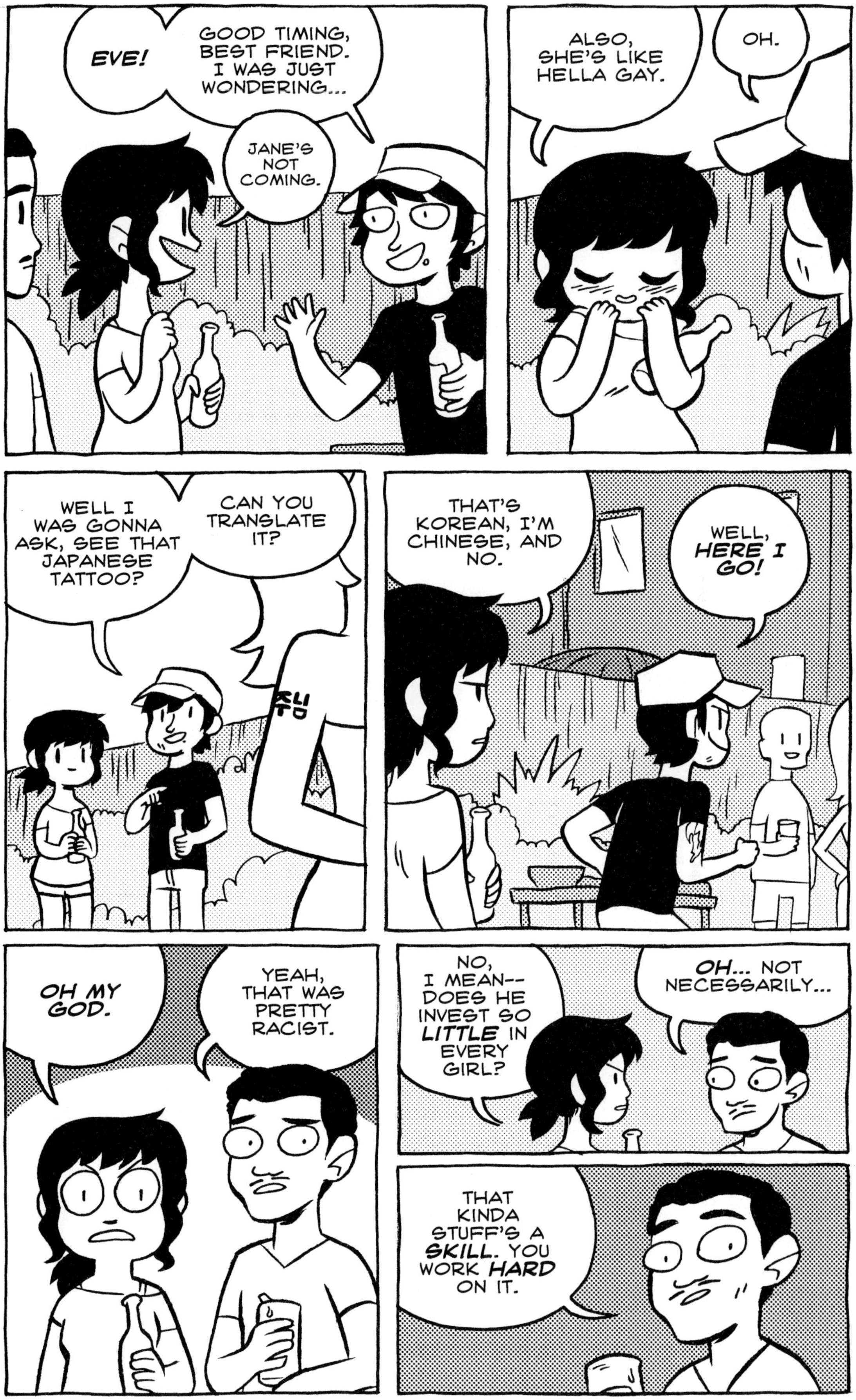
EVE!
GOOD TIMING, BEST FRIEND. I WAS JUST WONDERING...
JANE'S NOT COMING.
ALSO, SHE'S LIKE HELLA GAY.
OH.
WELL I WAS GONNA ASK, SEE THAT JAPANESE TATTOO?
CAN YOU TRANSLATE IT?
THAT'S KOREAN, I'M CHINESE, AND NO.
WELL, HERE I GO!
OH MY GOD.
YEAH, THAT WAS PRETTY RACIST.
NO, I MEAN-- DOES HE INVEST SO LITTLE IN EVERY GIRL?
OH... NOT NECESSARILY...
THAT KINDA STUFF'S A SKILL. YOU WORK HARD ON IT.

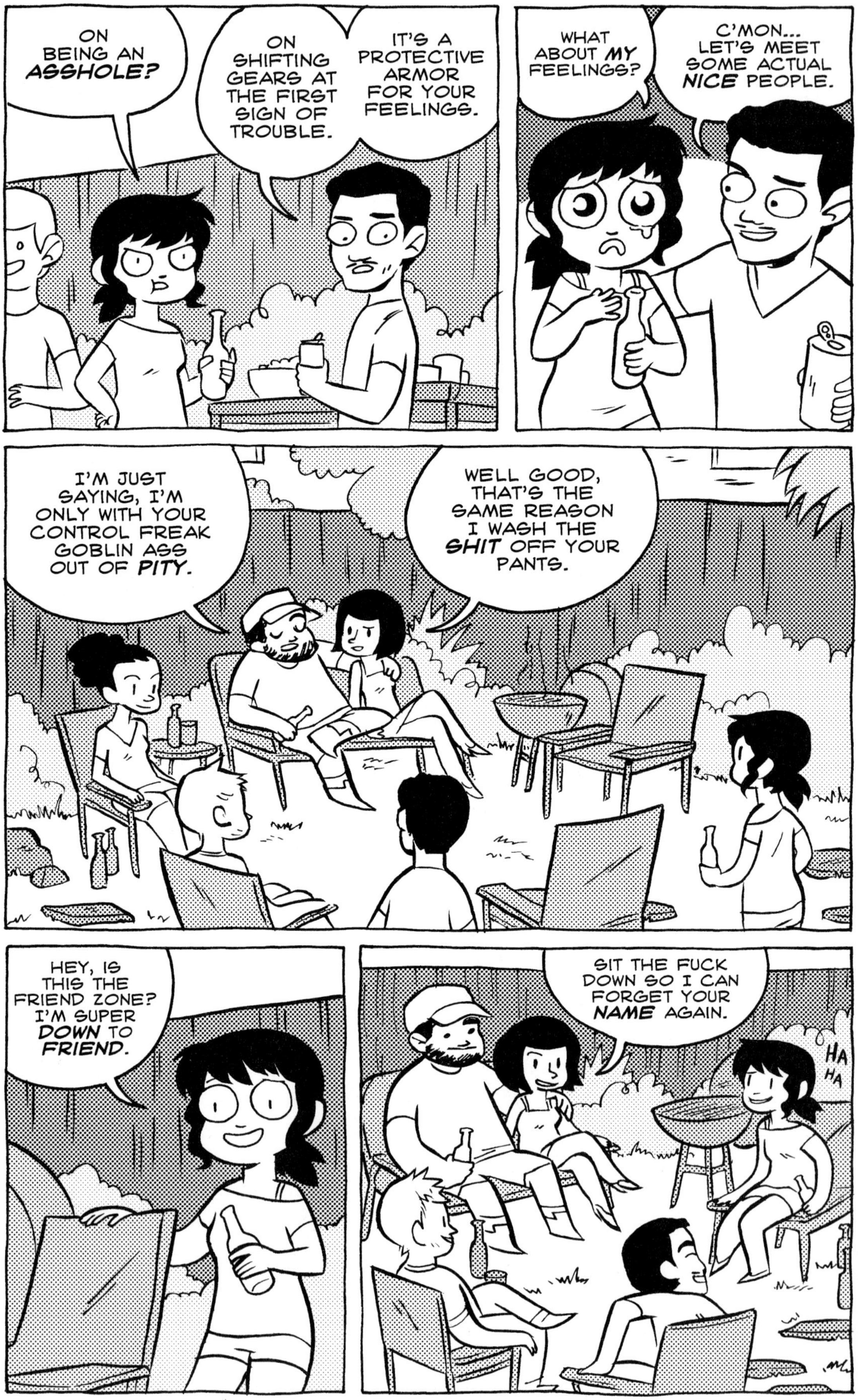
ON BEING AN ASSHOLE?
ON SHIFTING GEARS AT THE FIRST SIGN OF TROUBLE.
IT'S A PROTECTIVE ARMOR FOR YOUR FEELINGS.
WHAT ABOUT MY FEELINGS?
C'MON... LET'S MEET SOME ACTUAL NICE PEOPLE.
I'M JUST SAYING, I'M ONLY WITH YOUR CONTROL FREAK GOBLIN ASS OUT OF PITY.
WELL GOOD, THAT'S THE SAME REASON I WASH THE SHIT OFF YOUR PANTS.
HEY, IS THIS THE FRIEND ZONE? I'M SUPER DOWN TO FRIEND.
SIT THE FUCK DOWN SO I CAN FORGET YOUR NAME AGAIN.
HA HA

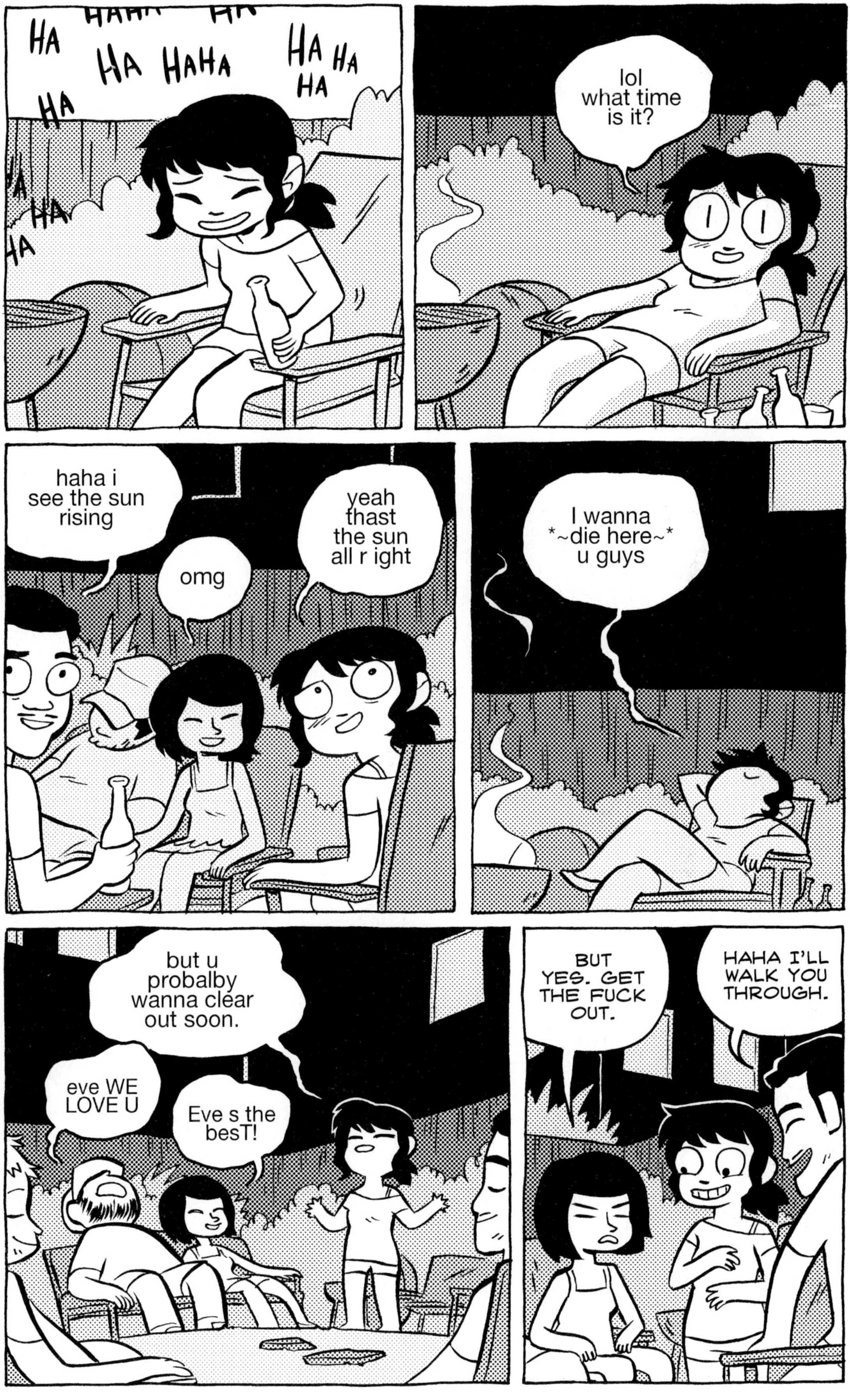
HA HAHA HA
HA HA HAHA HA HA HA HA
HA
HA HA HA
lol what time is it?
haha i see the sun rising
omg
yeah thast the sun all r ight
I wanna *~die here~* u guys
but u probalby wanna clear out soon.
eve WE LOVE U
Eve s the besT!
BUT YES. GET THE FUCK OUT.
HAHA I'LL WALK YOU THROUGH.

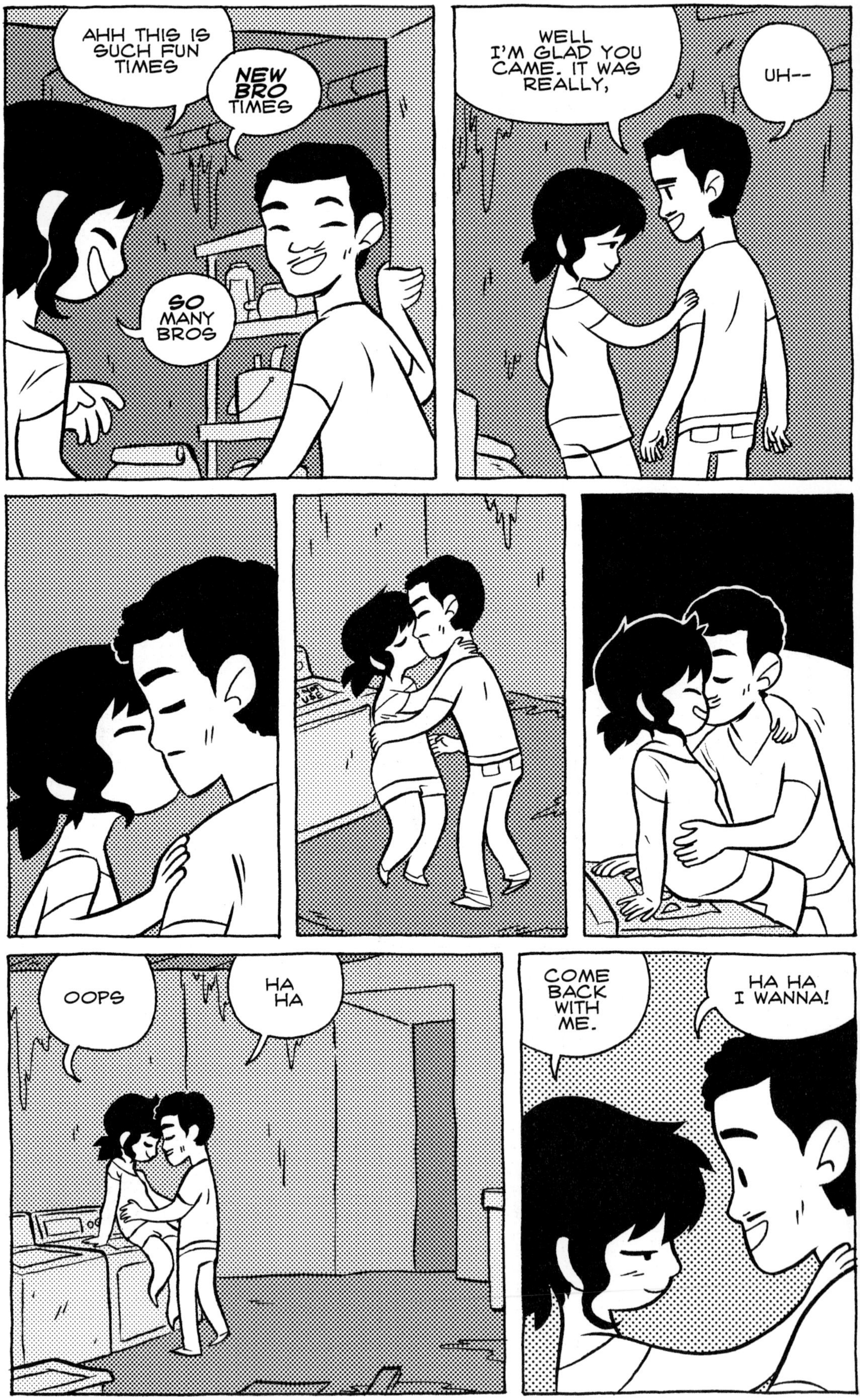
AHH THIS IS SUCH FUN TIMES
NEW BRO TIMES
SO MANY BROS
WELL I'M GLAD YOU CAME. IT WAS REALLY,
UH--
OOPS
HA HA
COME BACK WITH ME.
HA HA I WANNA!

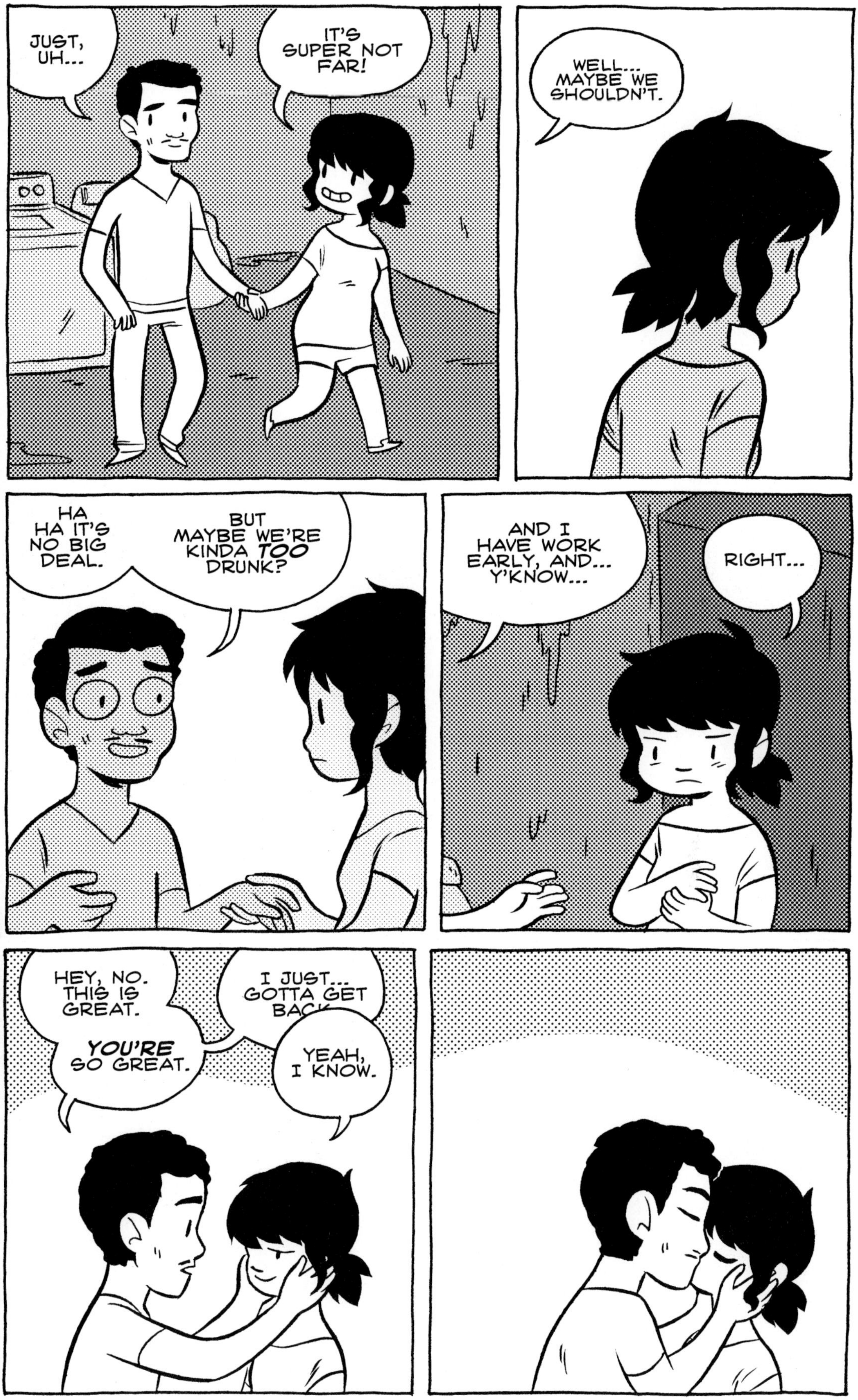
JUST, UH...
IT'S SUPER NOT FAR!
WELL... MAYBE WE SHOULDN'T.
HA HA IT'S NO BIG DEAL.
BUT MAYBE WE'RE KINDA *TOO* DRUNK?
AND I HAVE WORK EARLY, AND... Y'KNOW...
RIGHT...
HEY, NO. THIS IS GREAT.
YOU'RE SO GREAT.
I JUST... GOTTA GET BACK
YEAH, I KNOW.

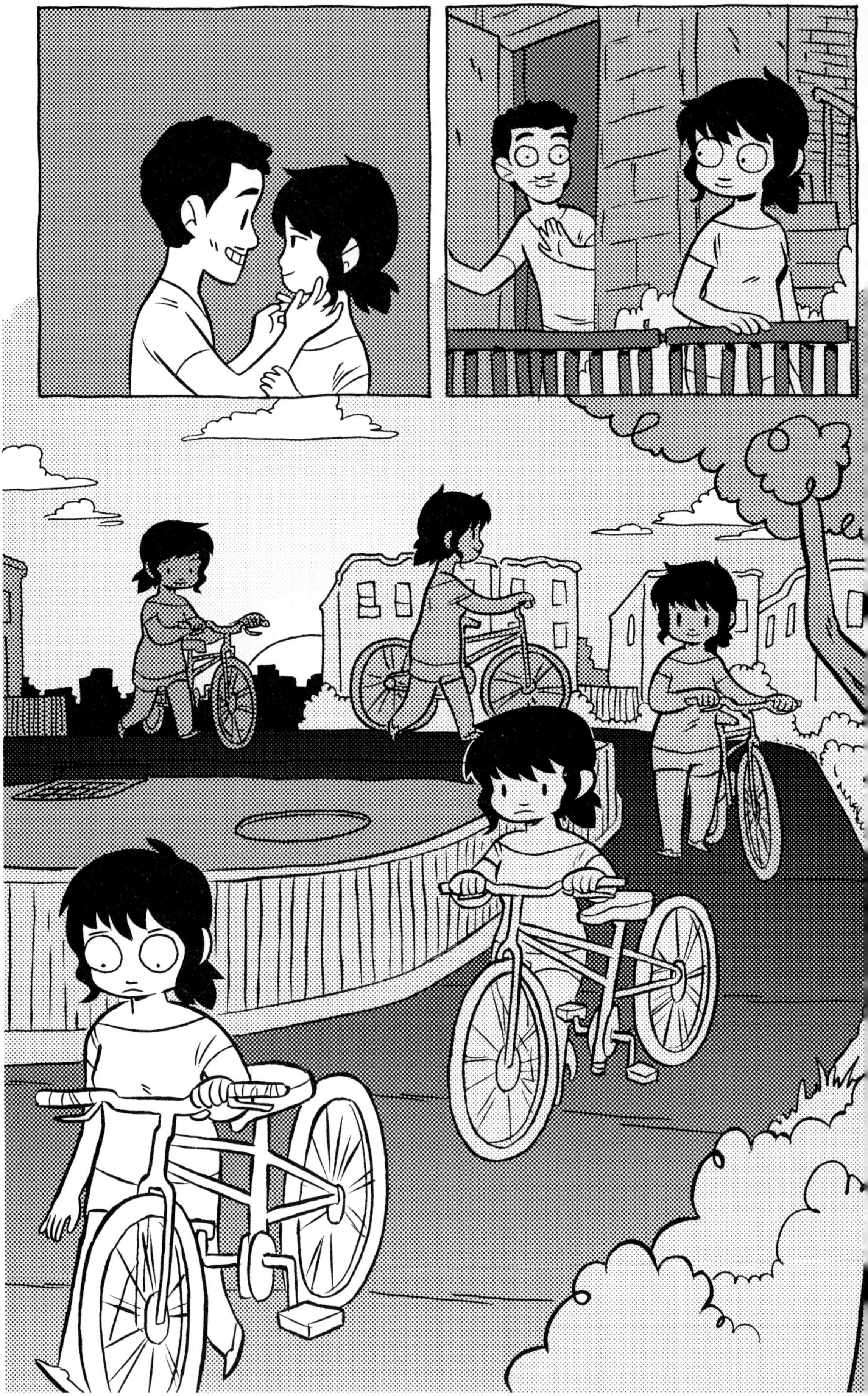

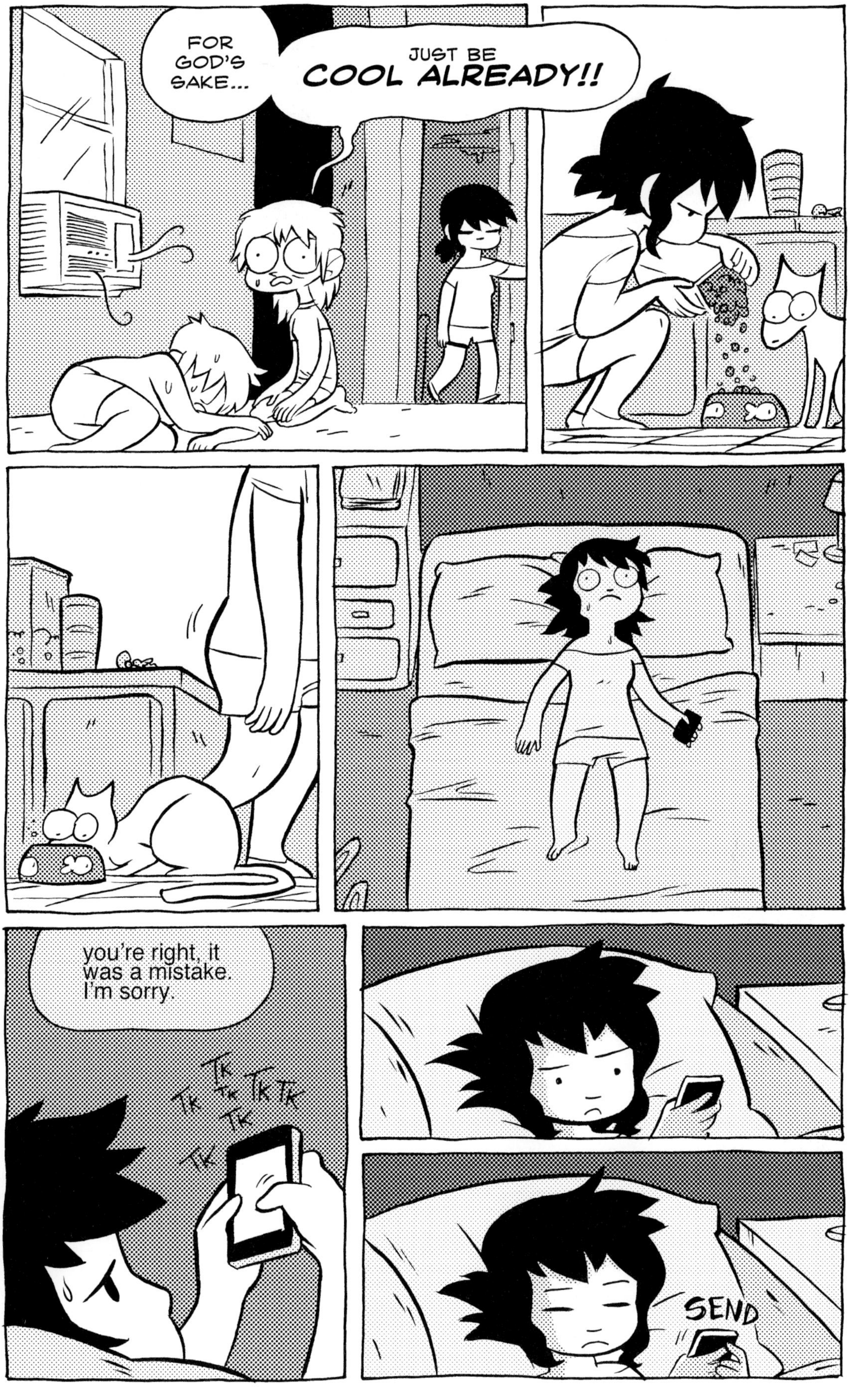
FOR GOD'S SAKE...
JUST BE COOL ALREADY!!
you're right, it was a mistake. I'm sorry.
TK TK TK TK TK TK TK
SEND

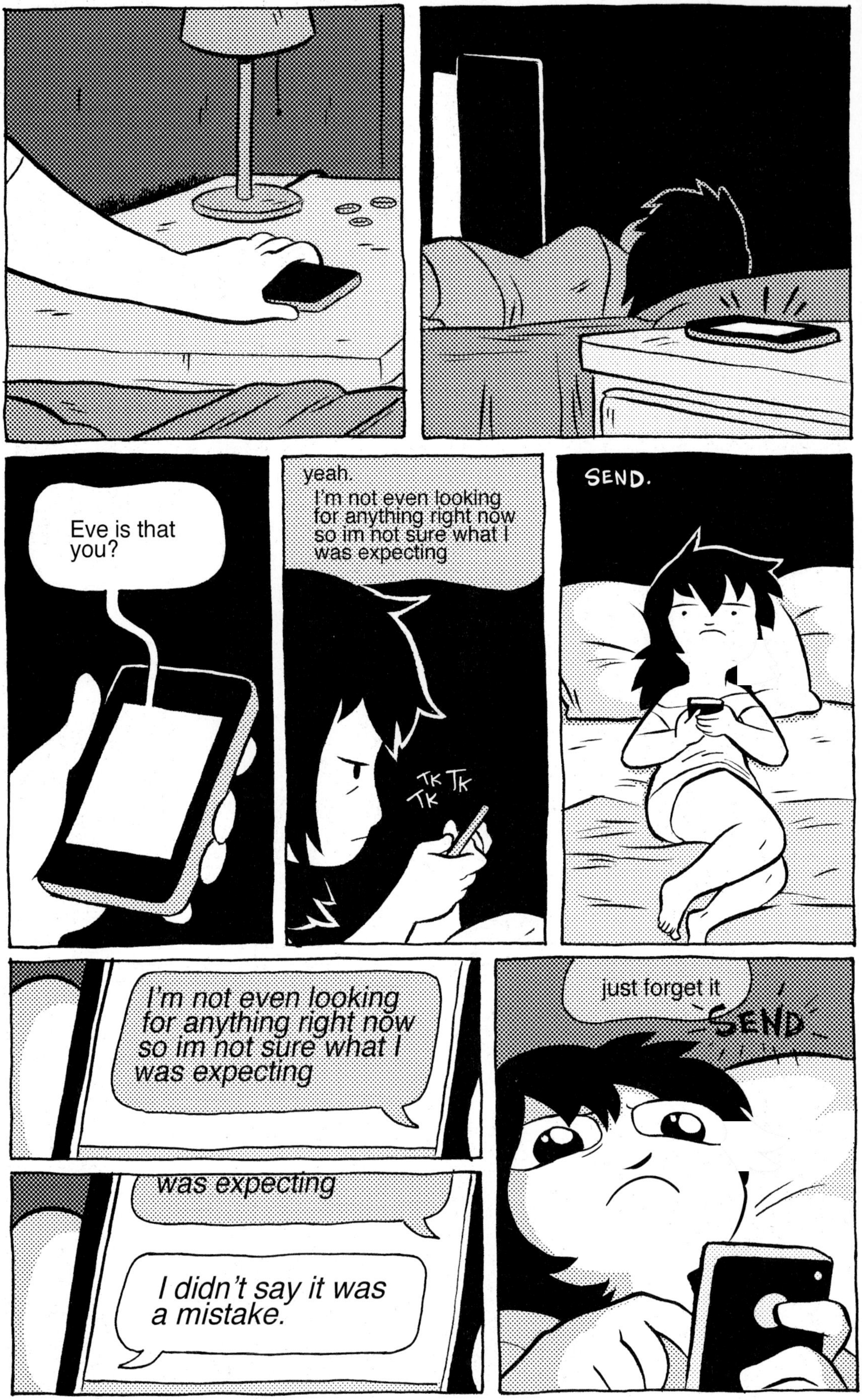

Eve is that you?
yeah.
I'm not even looking for anything right now so im not sure what I was expecting
TK TK TK
SEND.
I'm not even looking for anything right now so im not sure what I was expecting
was expecting
I didn't say it was a mistake.
just forget it
SEND

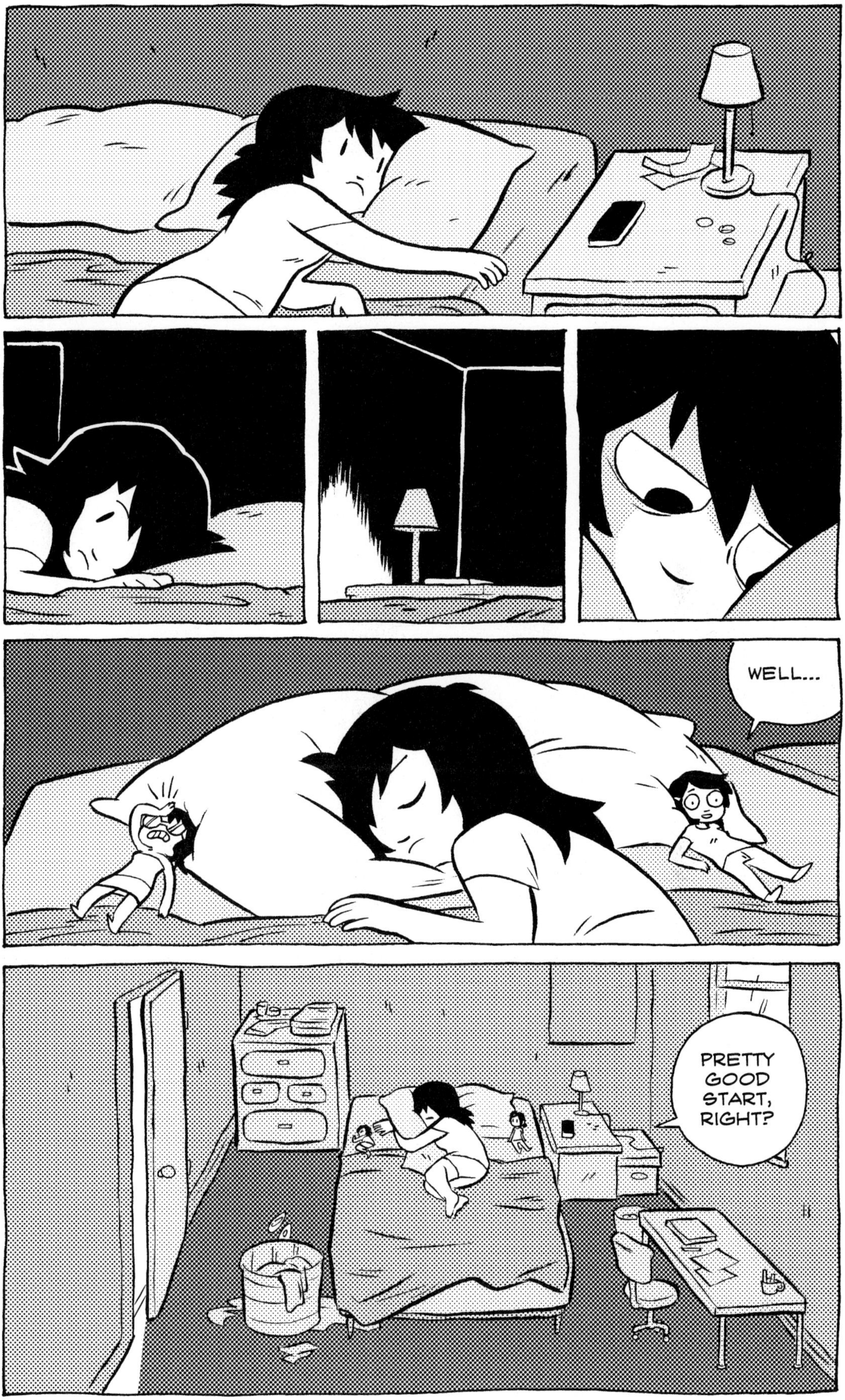
WELL...
PRETTY GOOD START, RIGHT?

40

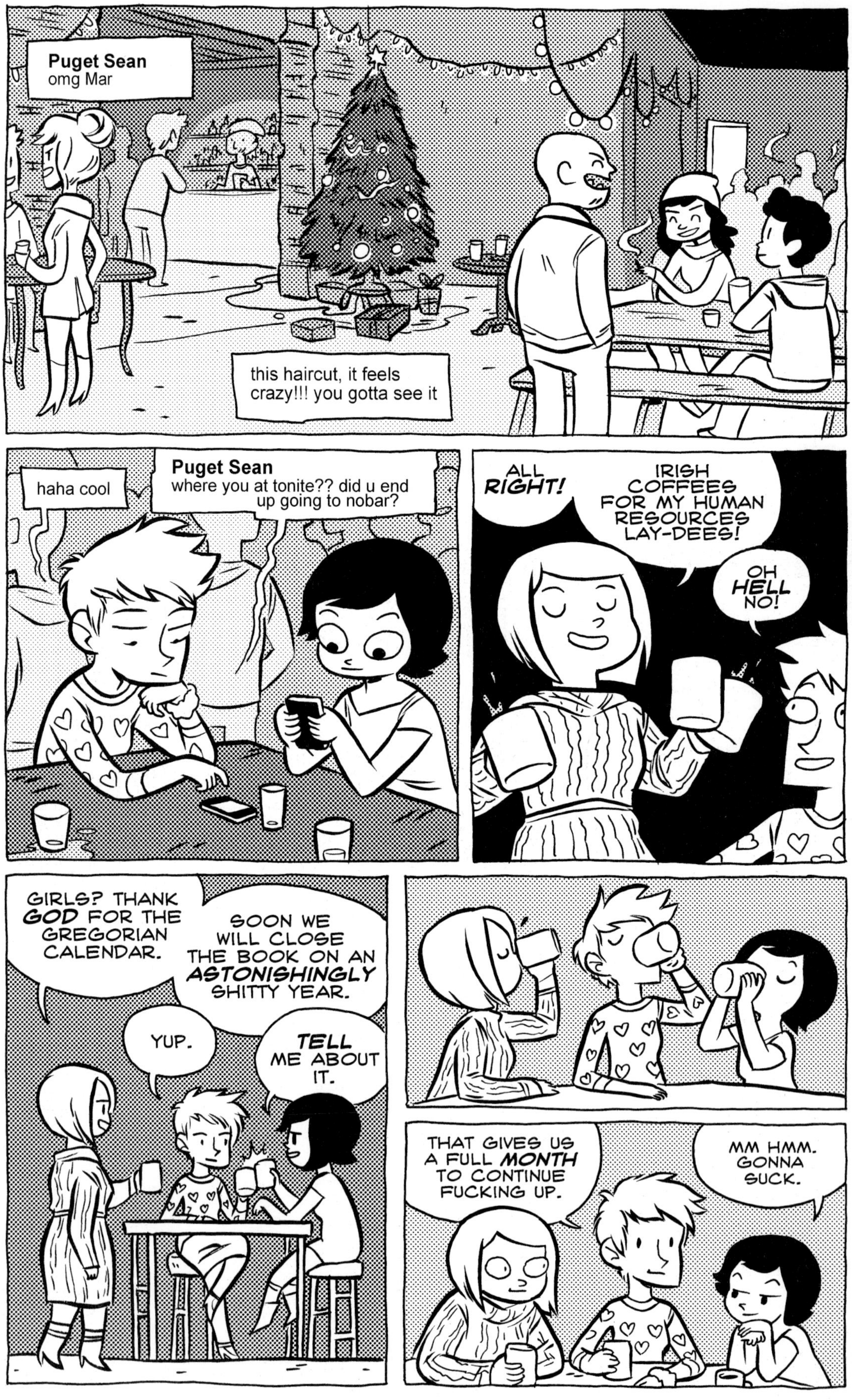
Puget Sean
omg Mar
this haircut, it feels crazy!!! you gotta see it
haha cool
Puget Sean
where you at tonite?? did u end up going to nobar?
ALL RIGHT!
IRISH COFFEES FOR MY HUMAN RESOURCES LAY-DEES!
OH HELL NO!
GIRLS? THANK GOD FOR THE GREGORIAN CALENDAR.
SOON WE WILL CLOSE THE BOOK ON AN ASTONISHINGLY SHITTY YEAR.
YUP.
TELL ME ABOUT IT.
THAT GIVES US A FULL MONTH TO CONTINUE FUCKING UP.
MM HMM. GONNA SUCK.

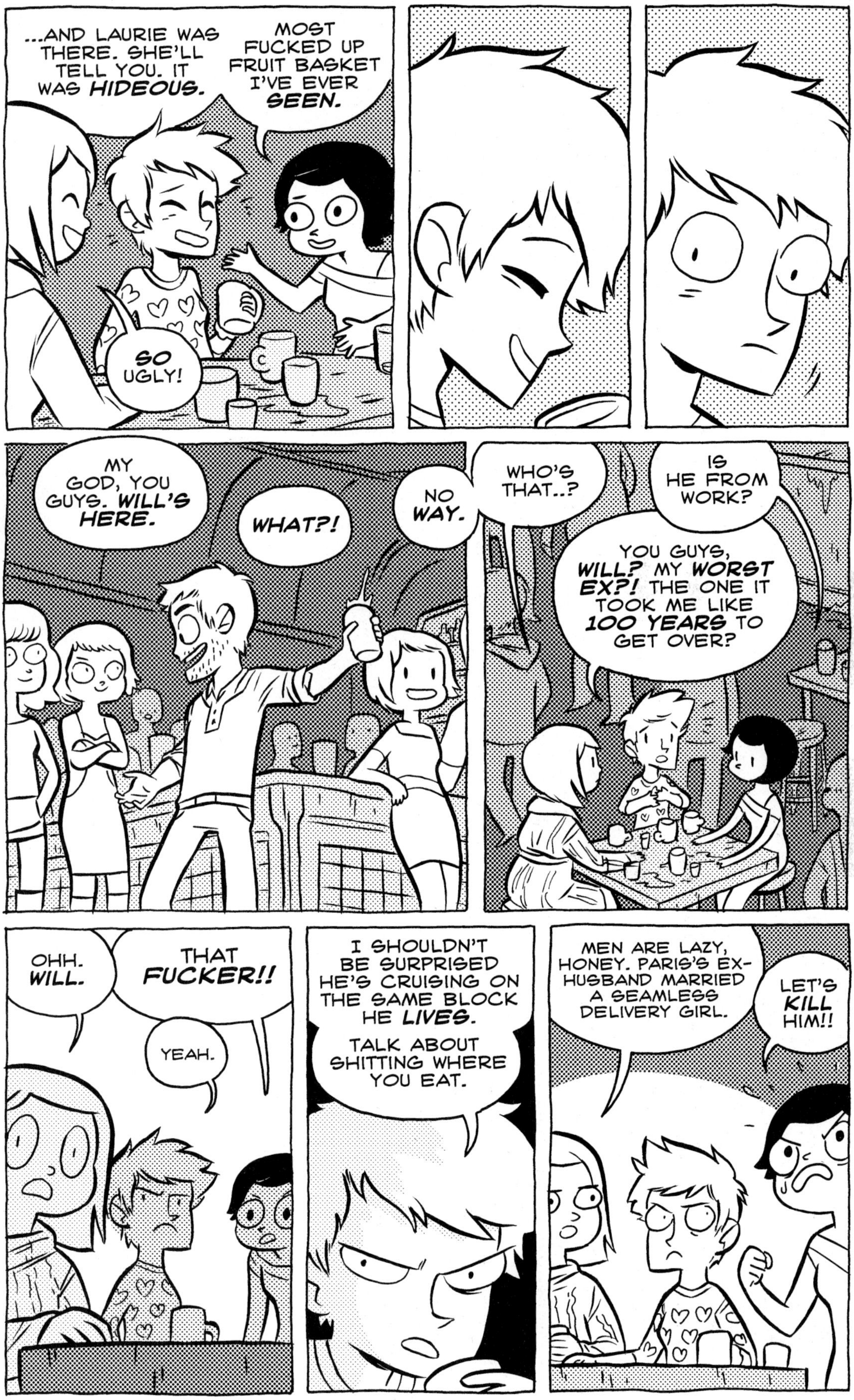
...AND LAURIE WAS THERE. SHE'LL TELL YOU. IT WAS *HIDEOUS.*
MOST FUCKED UP FRUIT BASKET I'VE EVER *SEEN.*
SO UGLY!
MY GOD, YOU GUYS. *WILL'S HERE.*
WHAT?!
NO *WAY.*
WHO'S THAT..?
IS HE FROM WORK?
YOU GUYS, *WILL?* MY *WORST EX?!* THE ONE IT TOOK ME LIKE *100 YEARS* TO GET OVER?
OHH. *WILL.*
THAT *FUCKER!!*
YEAH.
I SHOULDN'T BE SURPRISED HE'S CRUISING ON THE SAME BLOCK HE *LIVES.*
TALK ABOUT SHITTING WHERE YOU EAT.
MEN ARE LAZY, HONEY. PARIS'S EX-HUSBAND MARRIED A SEAMLESS DELIVERY GIRL.
LET'S *KILL* HIM!!

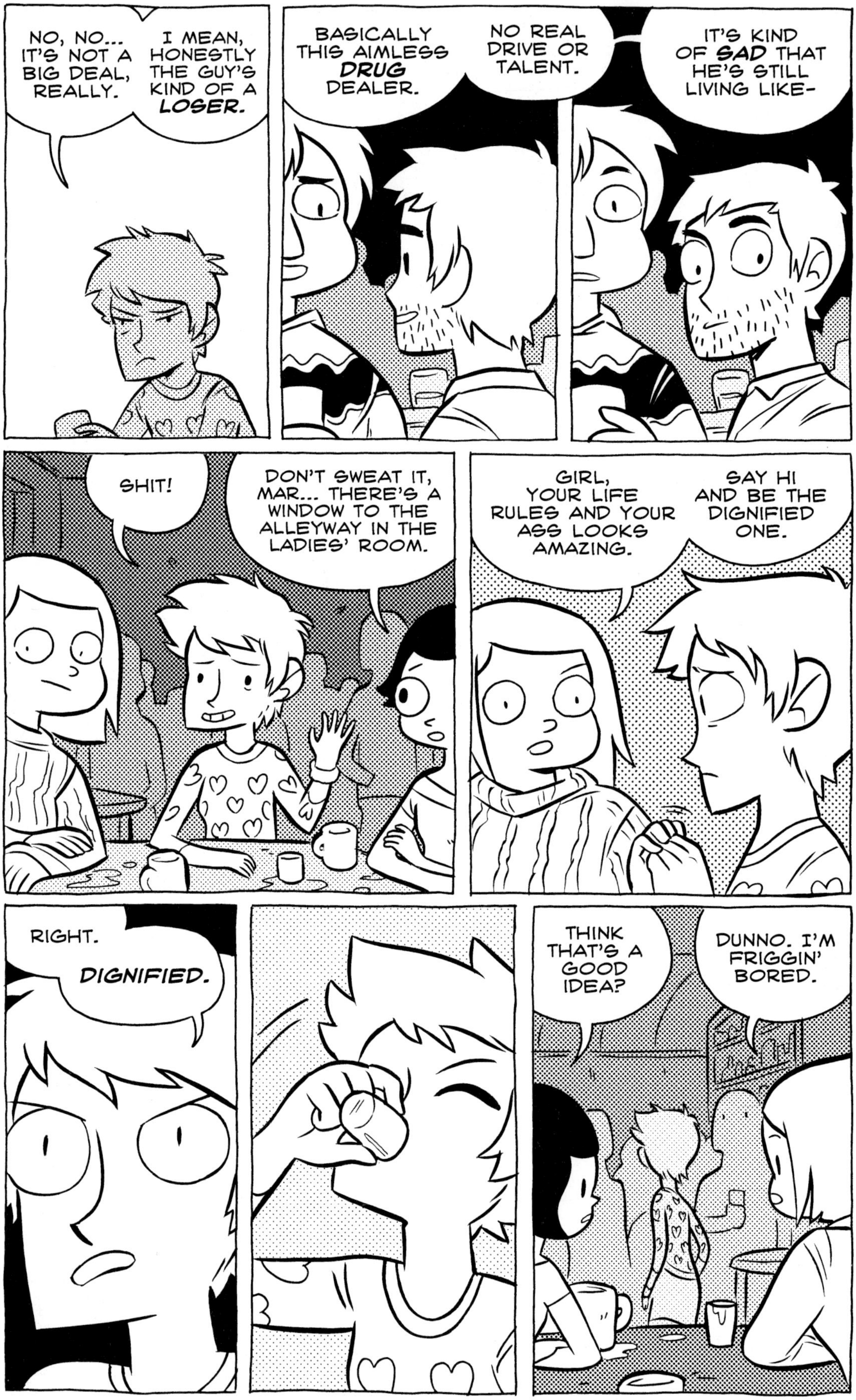
NO, NO... IT'S NOT A BIG DEAL, REALLY.
I MEAN, HONESTLY THE GUY'S KIND OF A LOSER.
BASICALLY THIS AIMLESS DRUG DEALER.
NO REAL DRIVE OR TALENT.
IT'S KIND OF SAD THAT HE'S STILL LIVING LIKE-
SHIT!
DON'T SWEAT IT, MAR... THERE'S A WINDOW TO THE ALLEYWAY IN THE LADIES' ROOM.
GIRL, YOUR LIFE RULES AND YOUR ASS LOOKS AMAZING.
SAY HI AND BE THE DIGNIFIED ONE.
RIGHT.
DIGNIFIED.
THINK THAT'S A GOOD IDEA?
DUNNO. I'M FRIGGIN' BORED.

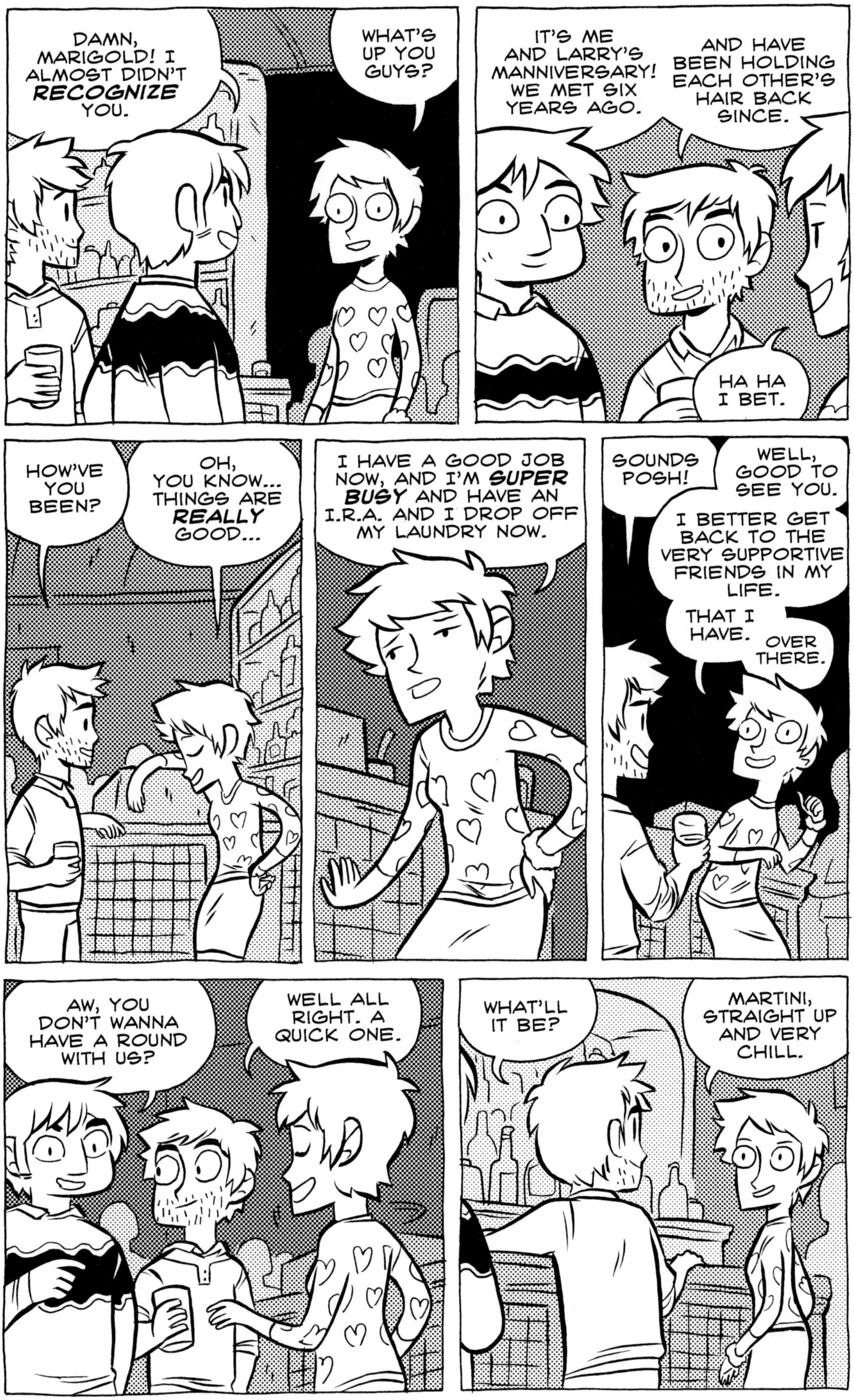
DAMN, MARIGOLD! I ALMOST DIDN'T RECOGNIZE YOU.
WHAT'S UP YOU GUYS?
IT'S ME AND LARRY'S MANNIVERSARY! WE MET SIX YEARS AGO.
AND HAVE BEEN HOLDING EACH OTHER'S HAIR BACK SINCE.
HA HA I BET.
HOW'VE YOU BEEN?
OH, YOU KNOW... THINGS ARE REALLY GOOD...
I HAVE A GOOD JOB NOW, AND I'M SUPER BUSY AND HAVE AN I.R.A. AND I DROP OFF MY LAUNDRY NOW.
SOUNDS POSH!
WELL, GOOD TO SEE YOU.
I BETTER GET BACK TO THE VERY SUPPORTIVE FRIENDS IN MY LIFE.
THAT I HAVE.
OVER THERE.
AW, YOU DON'T WANNA HAVE A ROUND WITH US?
WELL ALL RIGHT. A QUICK ONE.
WHAT'LL IT BE?
MARTINI, STRAIGHT UP AND VERY CHILL.

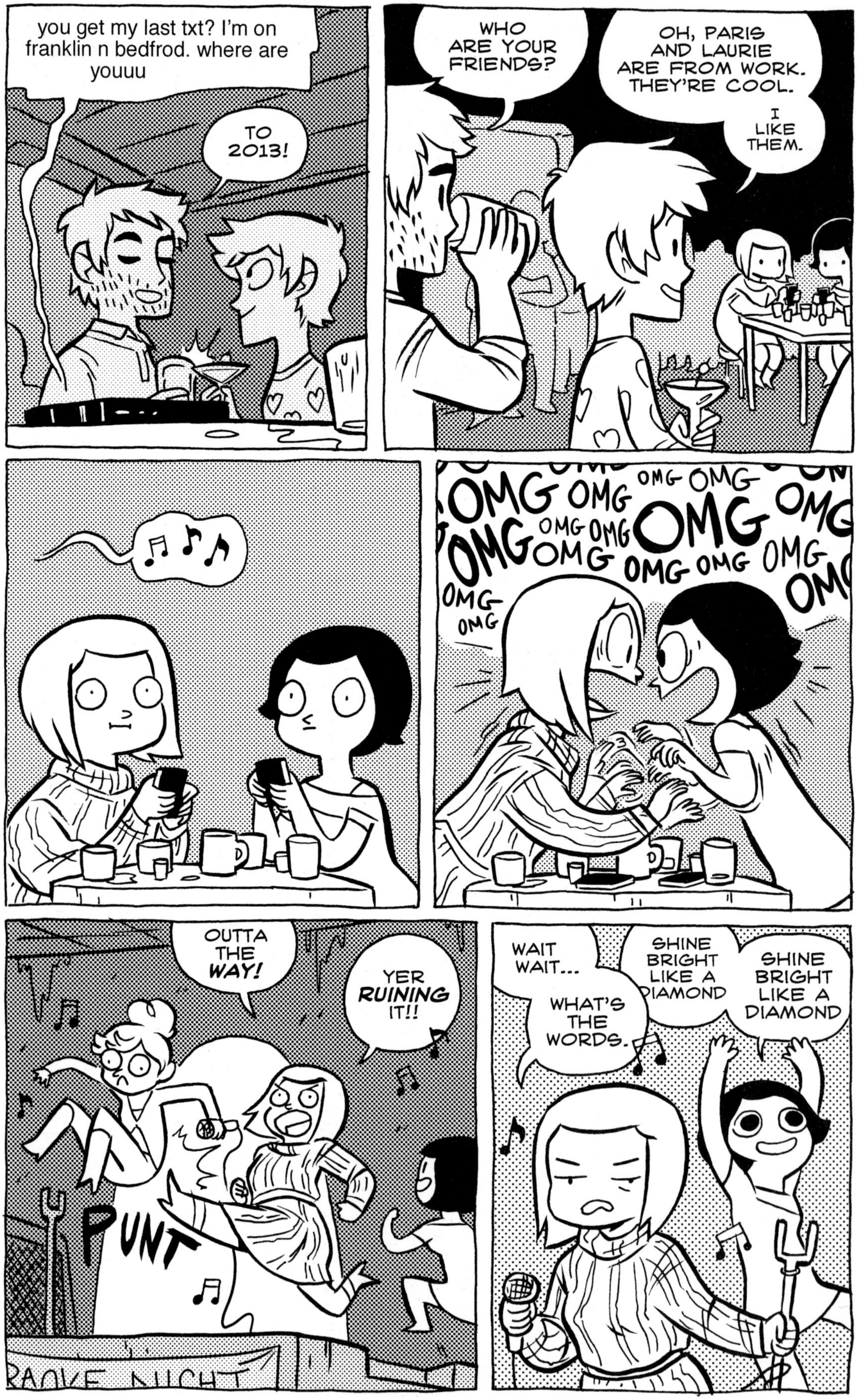
you get my last txt? I'm on franklin n bedfrod. where are youuu
TO 2013!
WHO ARE YOUR FRIENDS?
OH, PARIS AND LAURIE ARE FROM WORK. THEY'RE COOL.
I LIKE THEM.
OMG OMG OMG OMG OMG OMG OMG OMG OMG OMG OMG OMG OMG OMG OMG OMG
OUTTA THE ***WAY!***
YER ***RUINING*** IT!!
PUNT
WAIT WAIT...
WHAT'S THE WORDS.
SHINE BRIGHT LIKE A DIAMOND
SHINE BRIGHT LIKE A DIAMOND

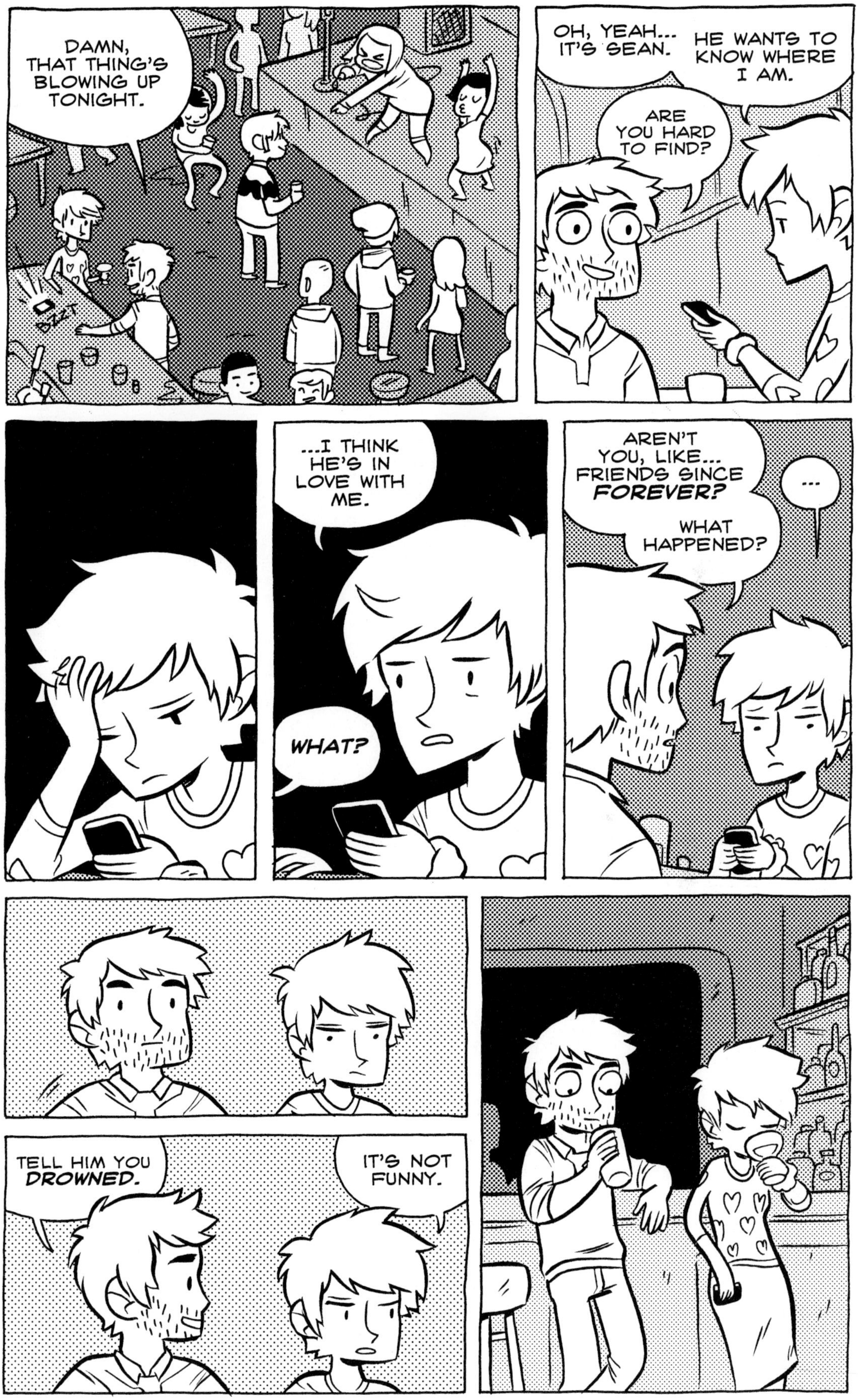
DAMN, THAT THING'S BLOWING UP TONIGHT.
OH, YEAH... IT'S SEAN.
HE WANTS TO KNOW WHERE I AM.
ARE YOU HARD TO FIND?
...I THINK HE'S IN LOVE WITH ME.
WHAT?
AREN'T YOU, LIKE... FRIENDS SINCE *FOREVER?*
WHAT HAPPENED?
...
TELL HIM YOU *DROWNED.*
IT'S NOT FUNNY.

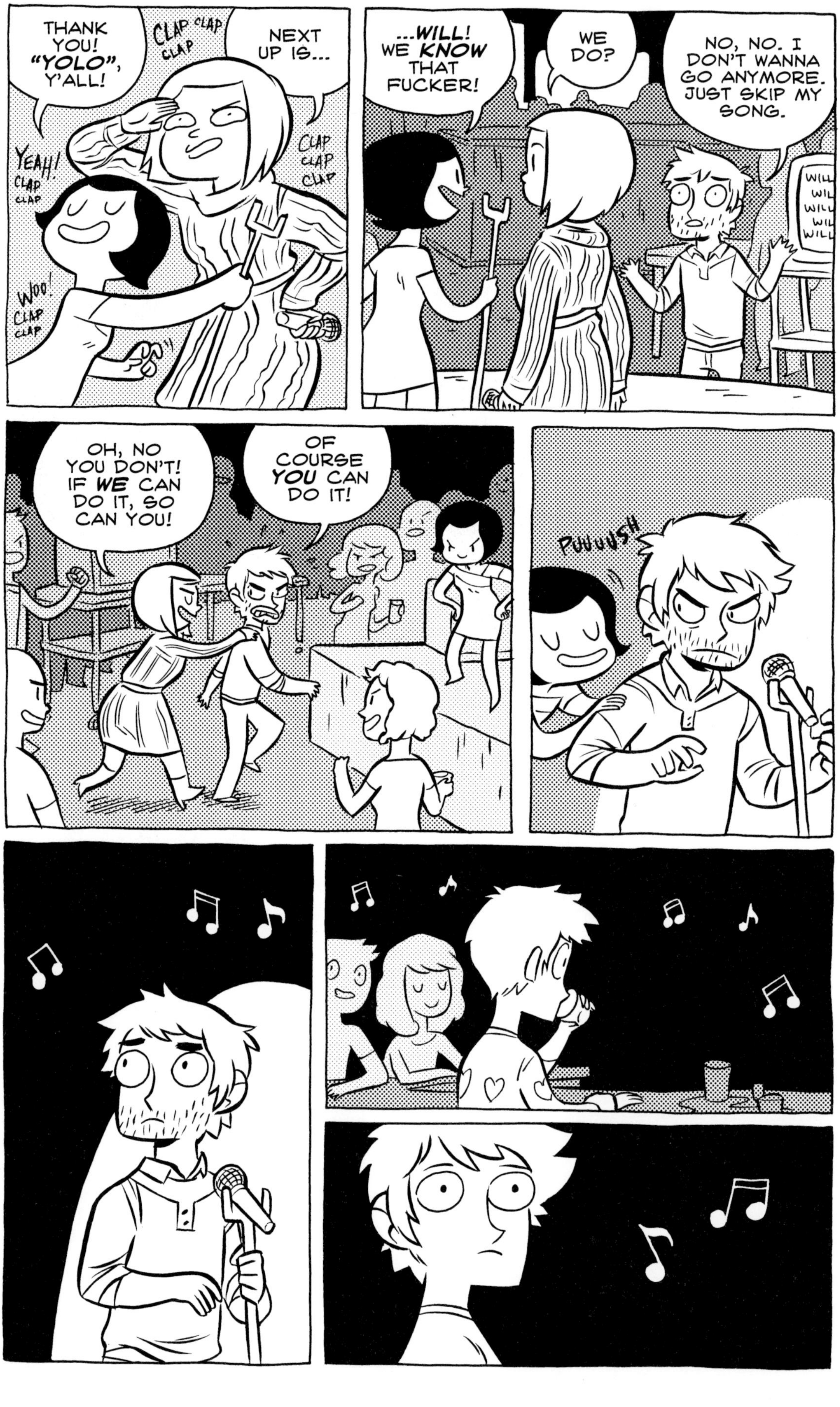
THANK YOU! "YOLO", Y'ALL!
CLAP CLAP CLAP
NEXT UP IS...
YEAH! CLAP CLAP
CLAP CLAP CLAP
WOO! CLAP CLAP
...WILL! WE KNOW THAT FUCKER!
WE DO?
NO, NO. I DON'T WANNA GO ANYMORE. JUST SKIP MY SONG.
OH, NO YOU DON'T! IF WE CAN DO IT, SO CAN YOU!
OF COURSE YOU CAN DO IT!
PUUUUSH

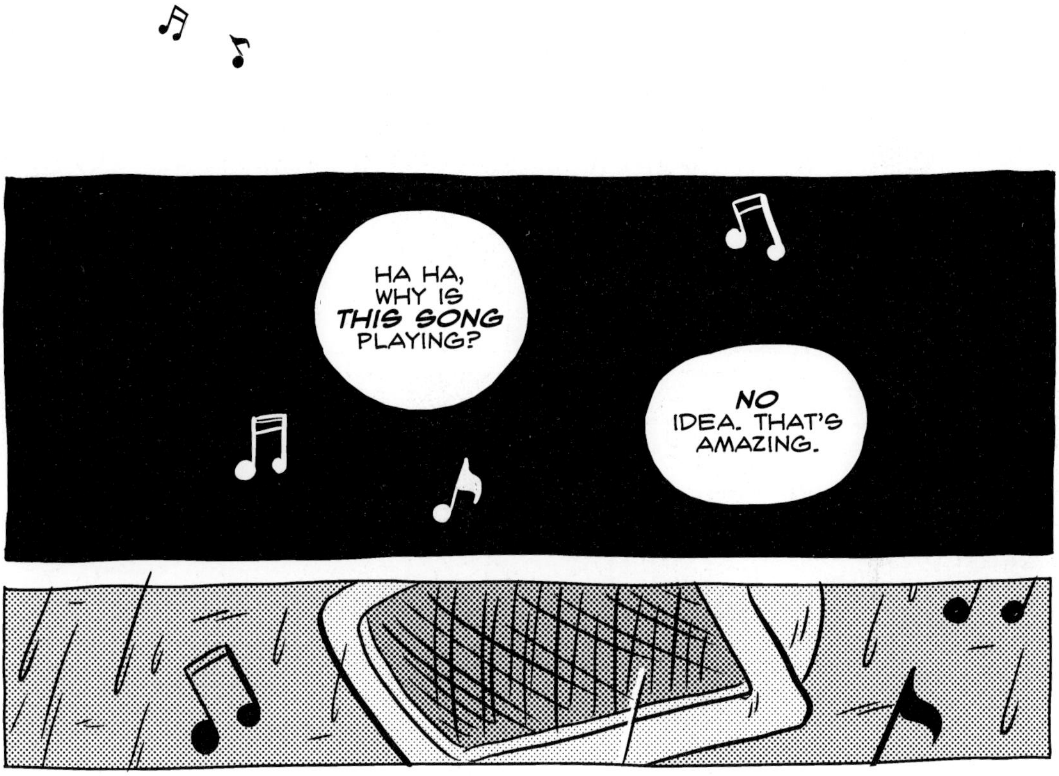
HA HA, WHY IS ***THIS SONG*** PLAYING?
NO IDEA. THAT'S AMAZING.

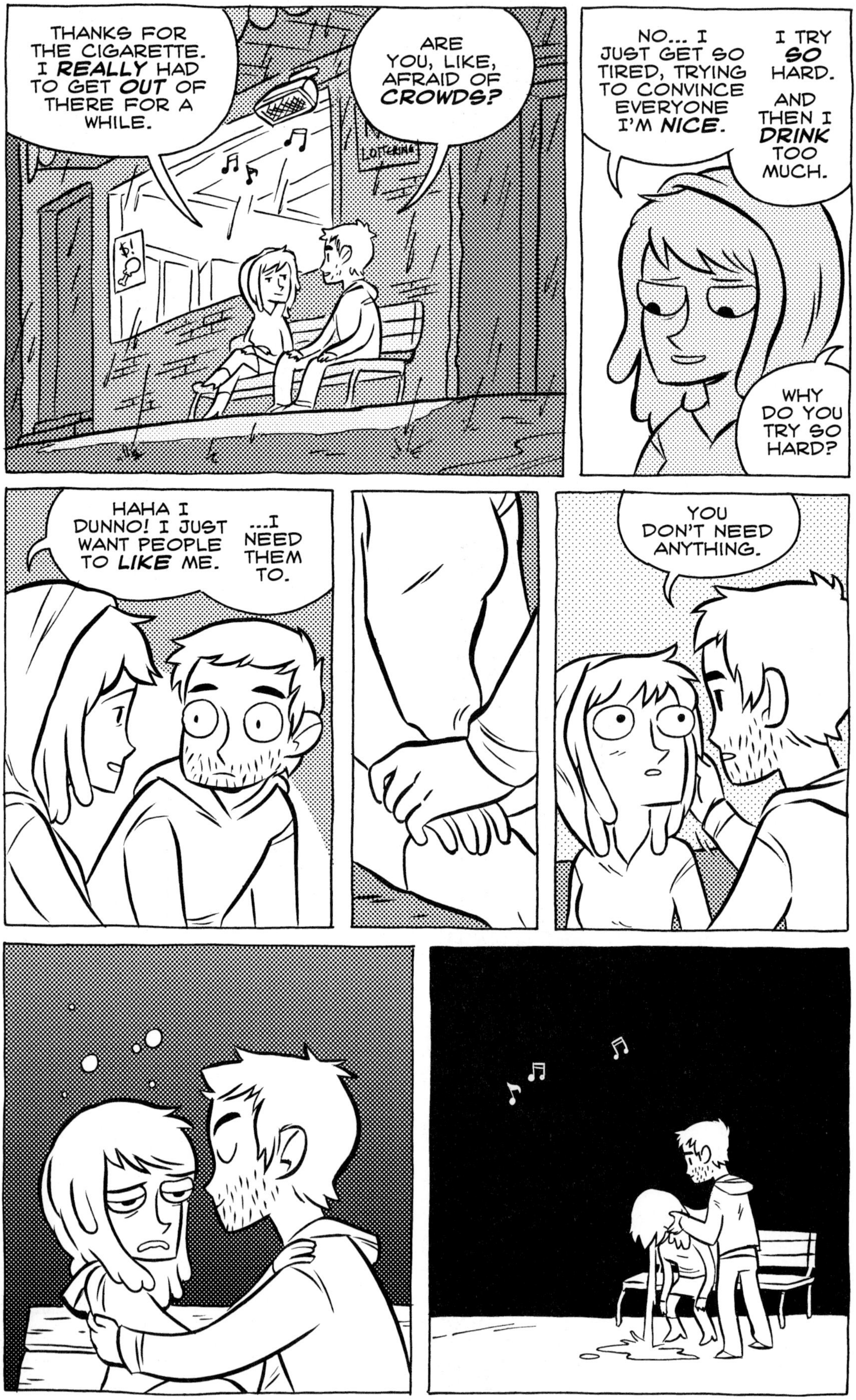
THANKS FOR THE CIGARETTE. I *REALLY* HAD TO GET *OUT* OF THERE FOR A WHILE.
ARE YOU, LIKE, AFRAID OF *CROWDS?*
NO... I JUST GET SO TIRED, TRYING TO CONVINCE EVERYONE I'M *NICE*.
I TRY *SO* HARD.
AND THEN I *DRINK* TOO MUCH.
WHY DO YOU TRY SO HARD?
HAHA I DUNNO! I JUST WANT PEOPLE TO *LIKE* ME.
...I NEED THEM TO.
YOU DON'T NEED ANYTHING.

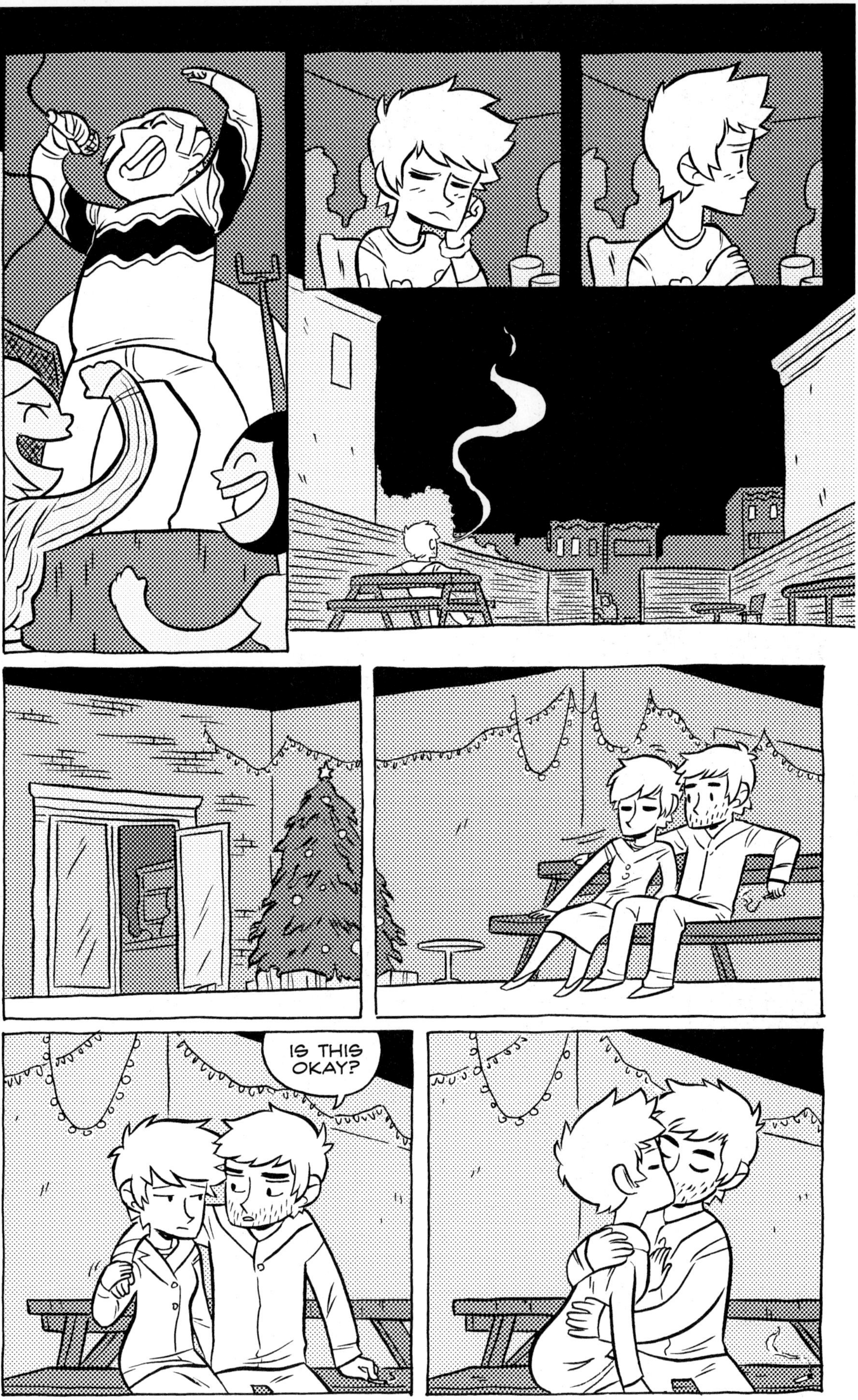
IS THIS
OKAY?

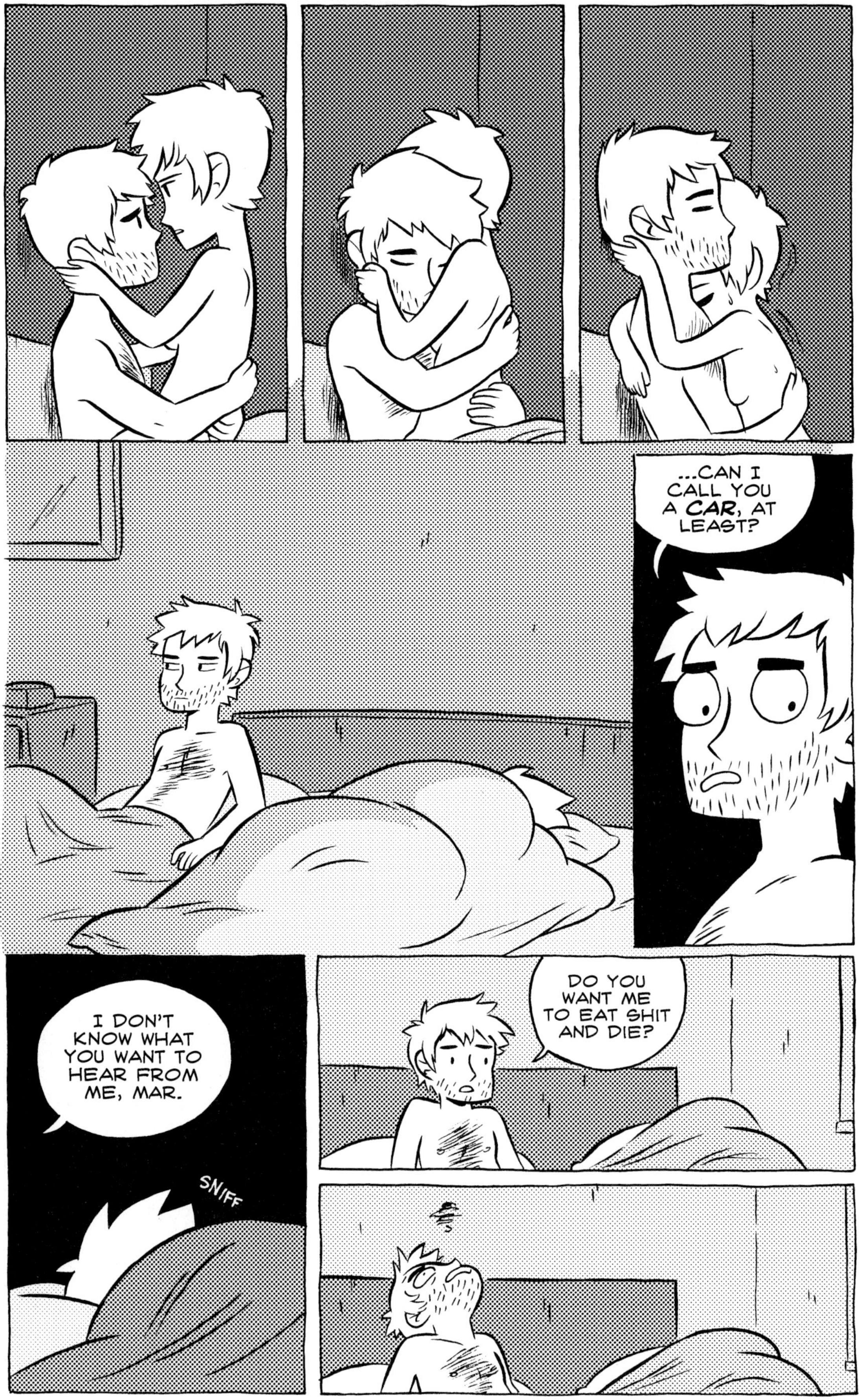
...CAN I CALL YOU A **CAR**, AT LEAST?
I DON'T KNOW WHAT YOU WANT TO HEAR FROM ME, MAR.
SNIFF
DO YOU WANT ME TO EAT SHIT AND DIE?

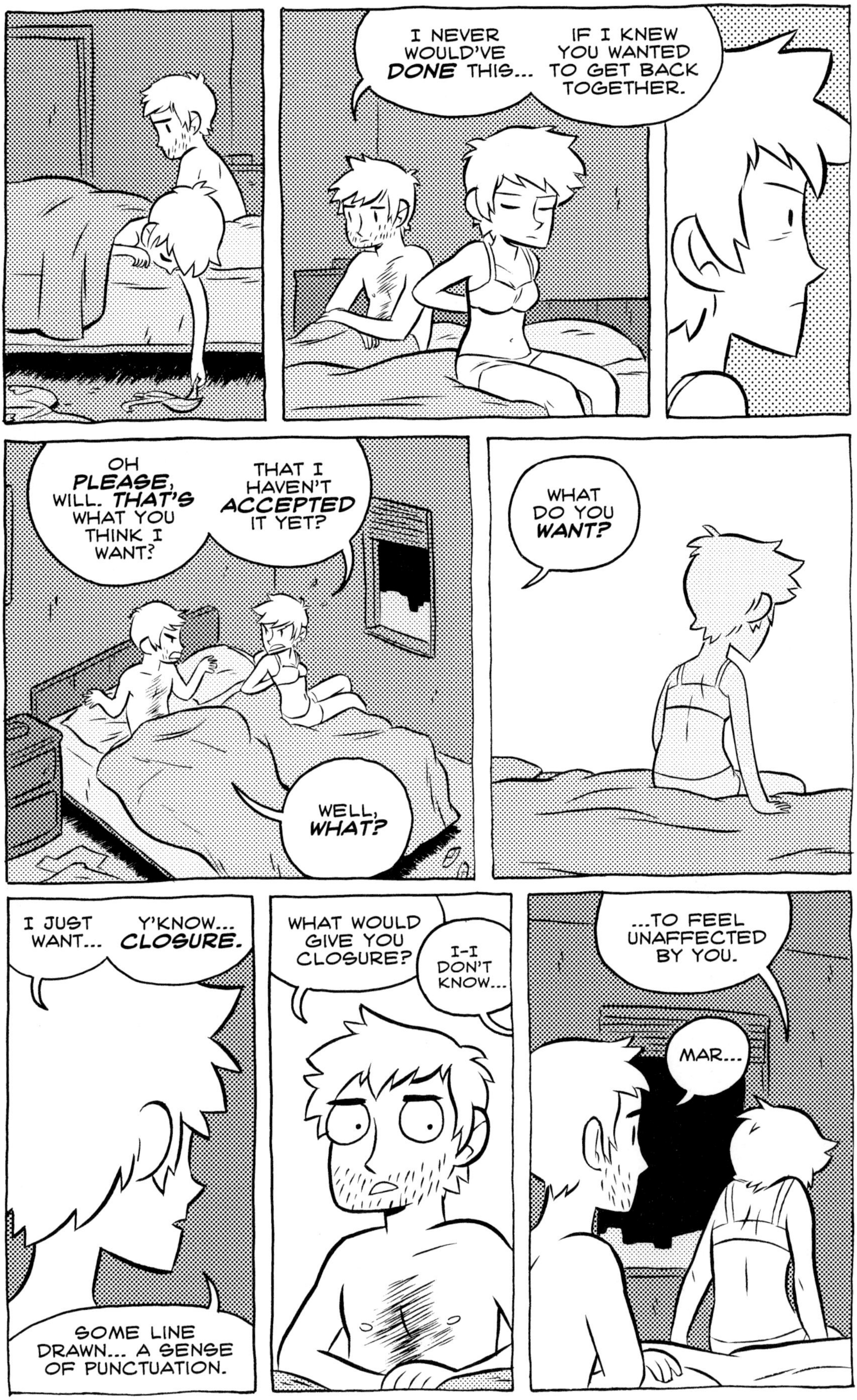
I NEVER WOULD'VE DONE THIS...
IF I KNEW YOU WANTED TO GET BACK TOGETHER.
OH PLEASE, WILL. THAT'S WHAT YOU THINK I WANT?
THAT I HAVEN'T ACCEPTED IT YET?
WELL, WHAT?
WHAT DO YOU WANT?
I JUST WANT...
Y'KNOW... CLOSURE.
SOME LINE DRAWN... A SENSE OF PUNCTUATION.
WHAT WOULD GIVE YOU CLOSURE?
I-I DON'T KNOW...
...TO FEEL UNAFFECTED BY YOU.
MAR...

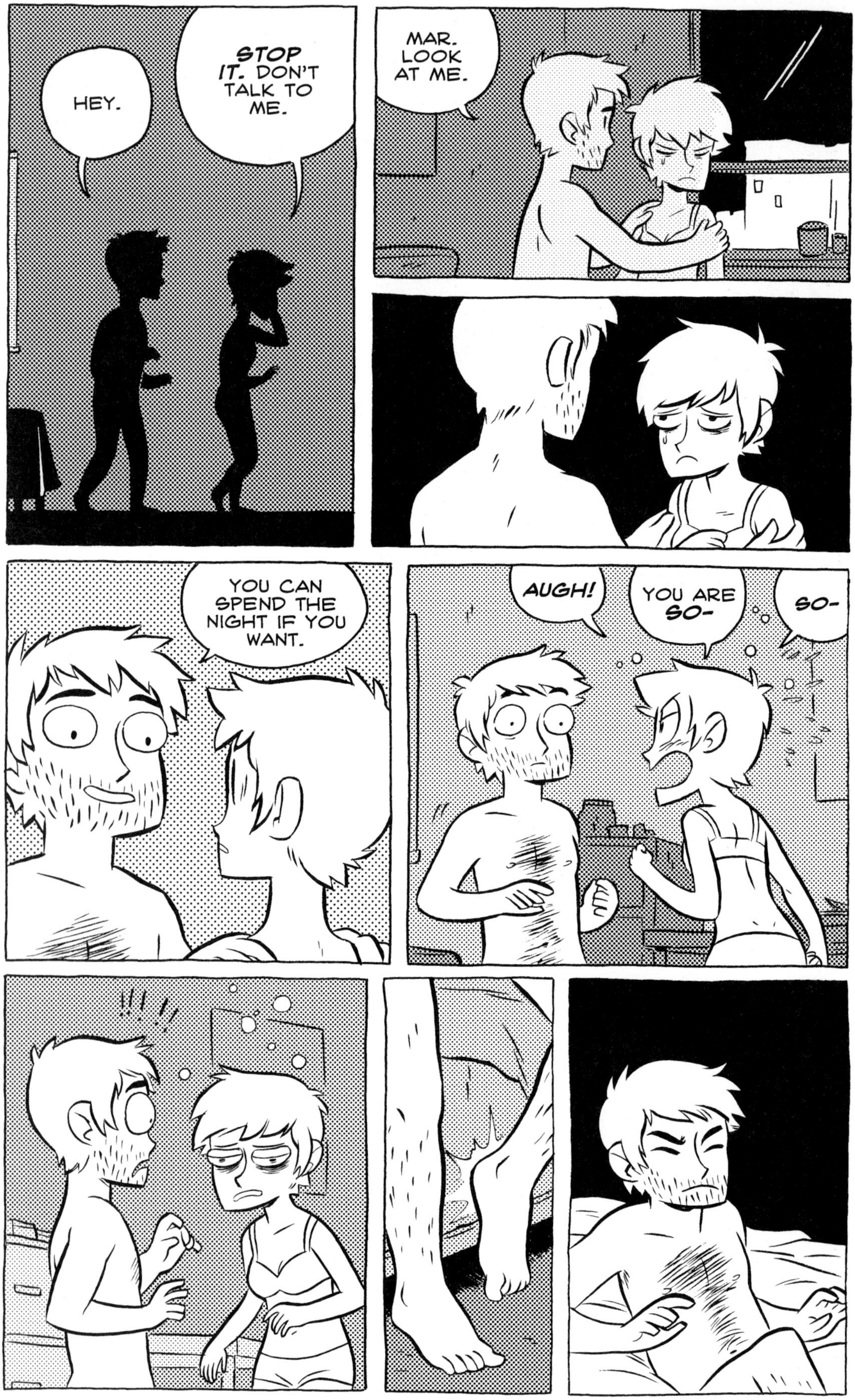
HEY.
STOP IT. DON'T TALK TO ME.
MAR. LOOK AT ME.
YOU CAN SPEND THE NIGHT IF YOU WANT.
AUGH!
YOU ARE SO-
SO-
!!!

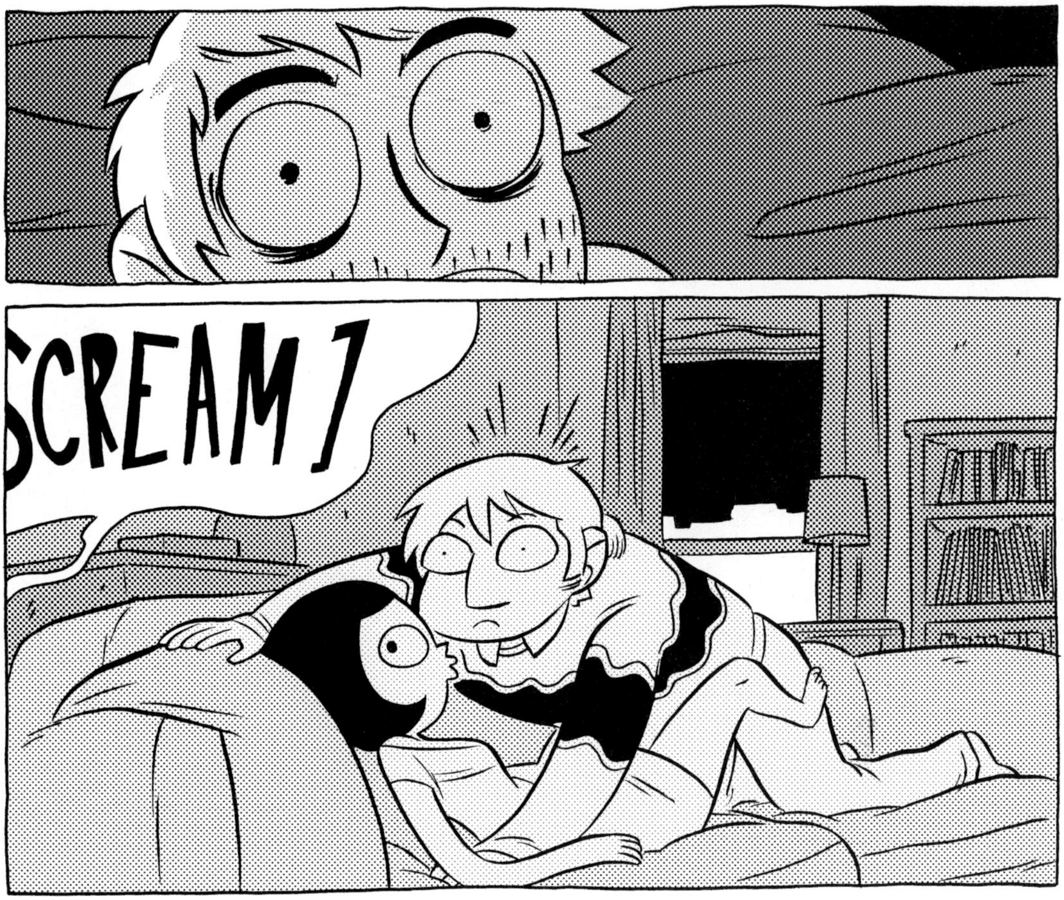
SCREAM]

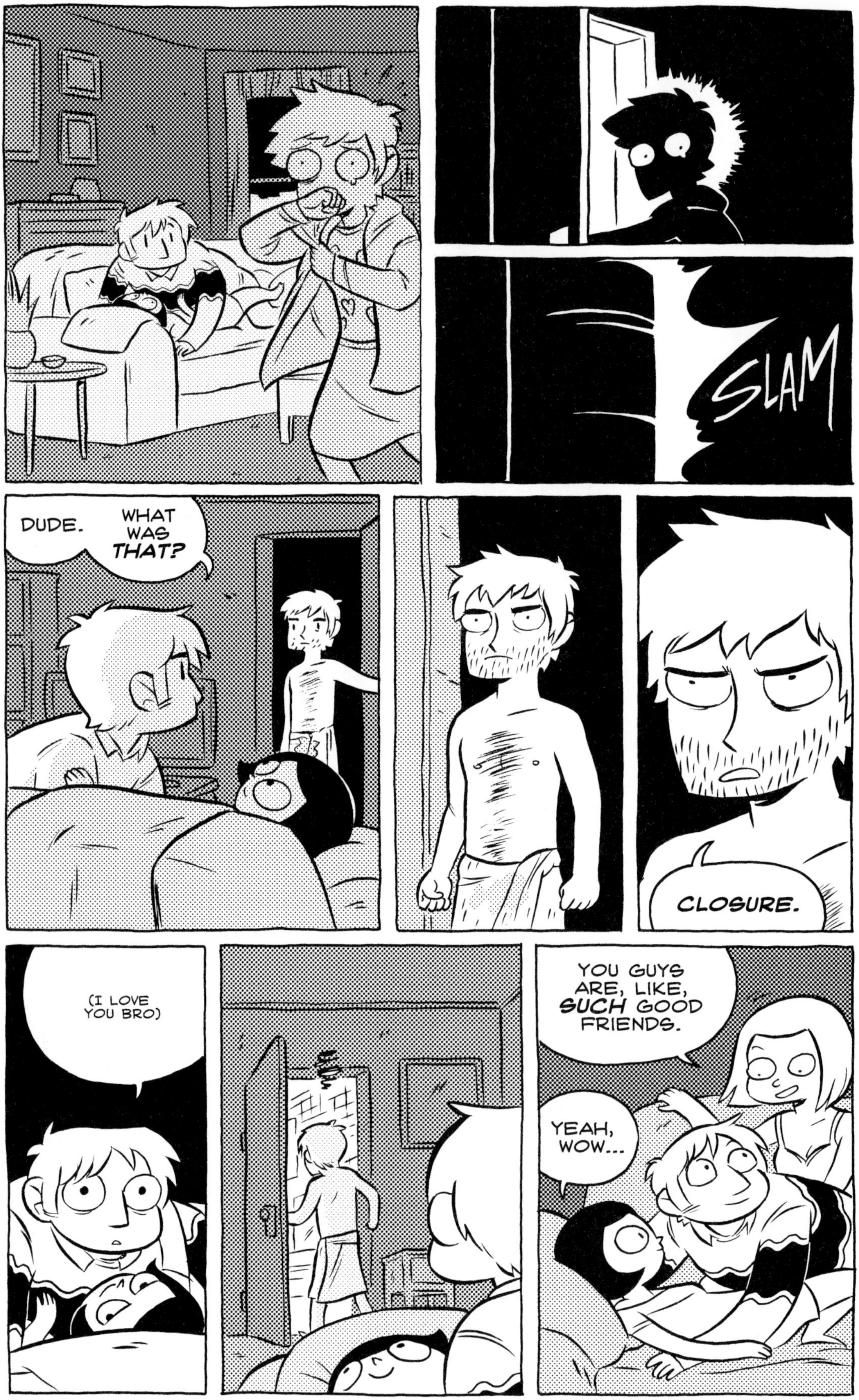
SLAM
DUDE.
WHAT WAS THAT?
CLOSURE.
(I LOVE YOU BRO)
YOU GUYS ARE, LIKE, SUCH GOOD FRIENDS.
YEAH, WOW...

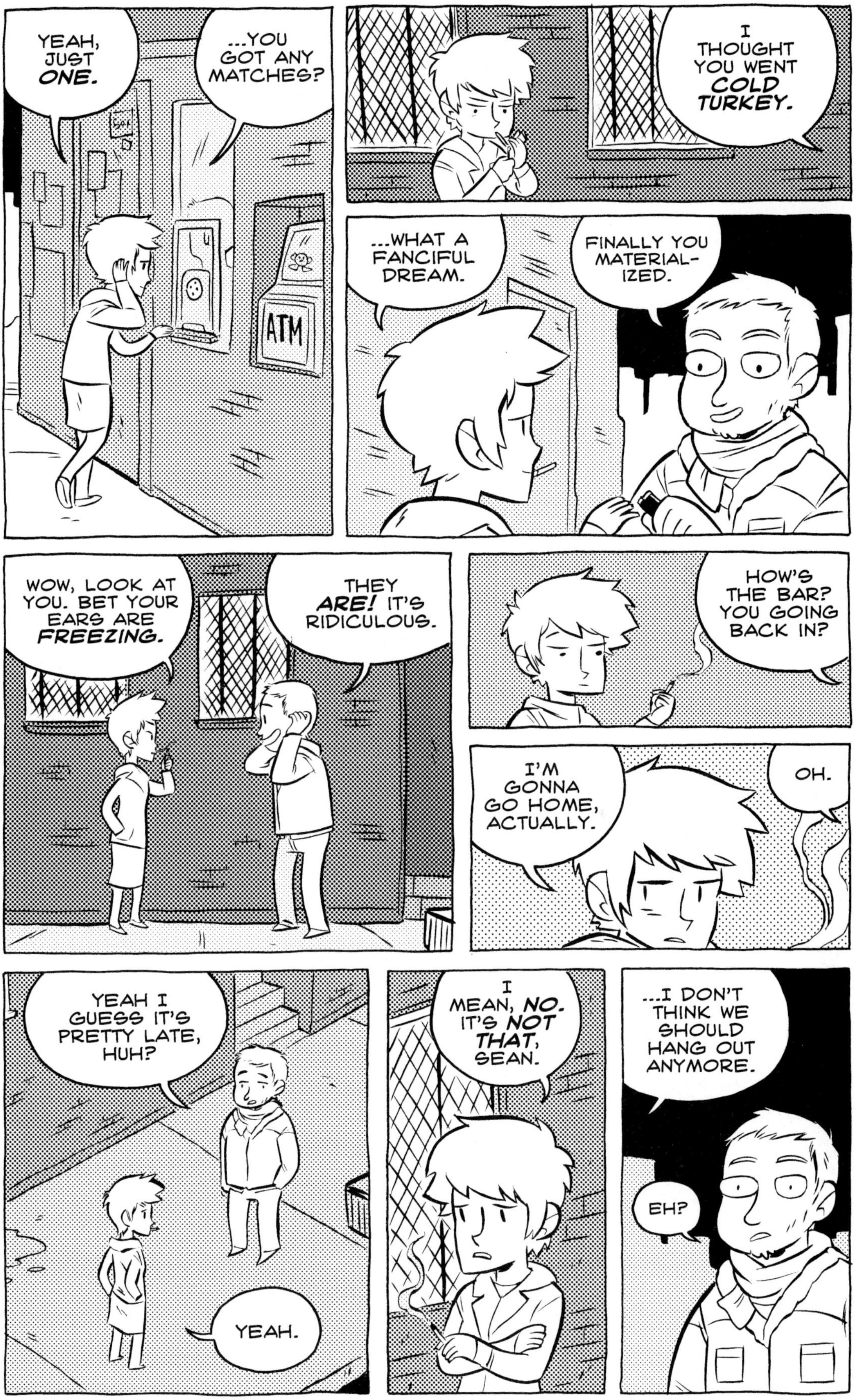
YEAH, JUST ONE.
...YOU GOT ANY MATCHES?
I THOUGHT YOU WENT COLD TURKEY.
...WHAT A FANCIFUL DREAM.
FINALLY YOU MATERIAL-IZED.
WOW, LOOK AT YOU. BET YOUR EARS ARE FREEZING.
THEY ARE! IT'S RIDICULOUS.
ATM
HOW'S THE BAR? YOU GOING BACK IN?
I'M GONNA GO HOME, ACTUALLY.
OH.
YEAH I GUESS IT'S PRETTY LATE, HUH?
YEAH.
I MEAN, NO. IT'S NOT THAT, SEAN.
...I DON'T THINK WE SHOULD HANG OUT ANYMORE.
EH?

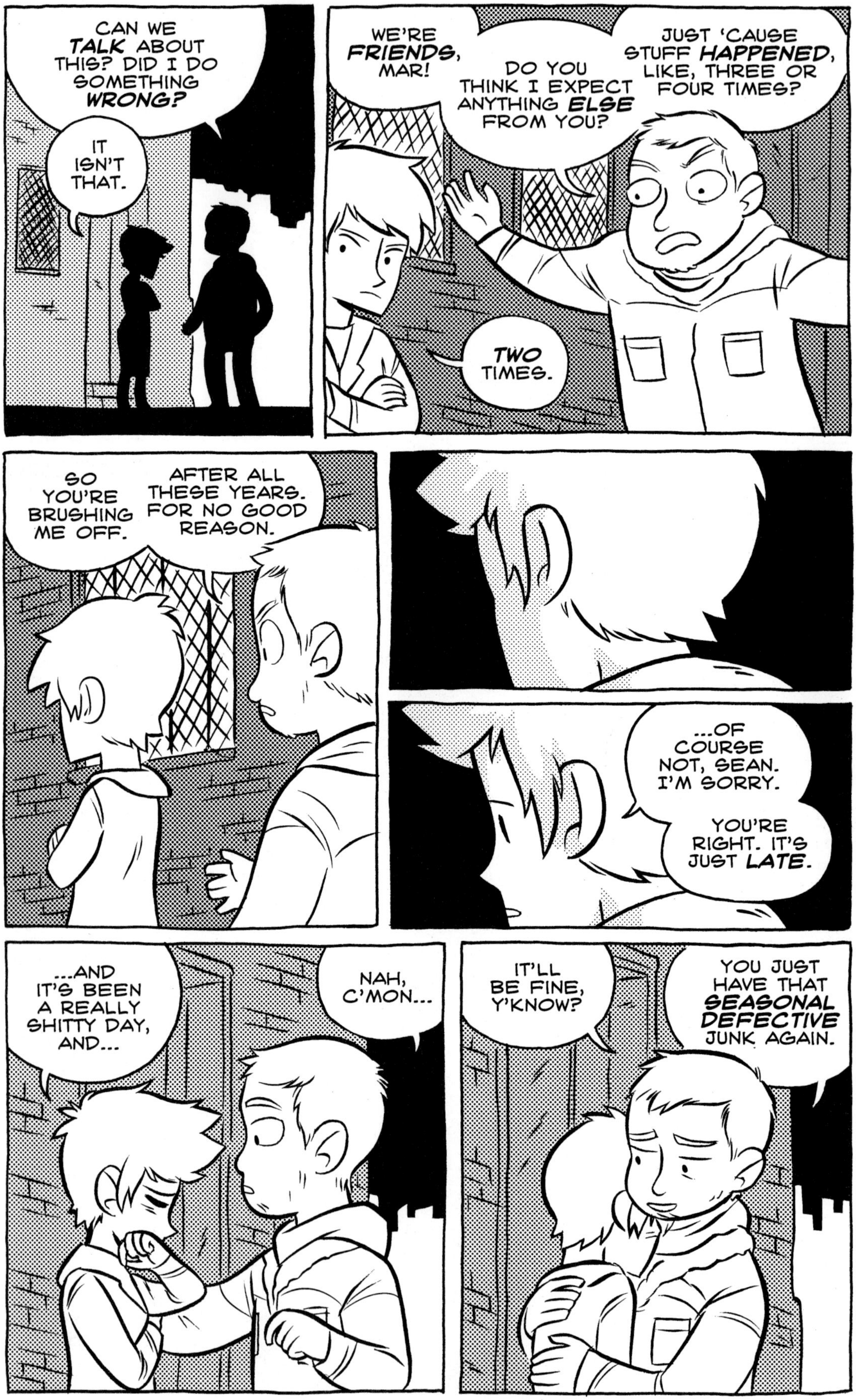
CAN WE TALK ABOUT THIS? DID I DO SOMETHING WRONG?
IT ISN'T THAT.
WE'RE FRIENDS, MAR!
DO YOU THINK I EXPECT ANYTHING ELSE FROM YOU?
JUST 'CAUSE STUFF HAPPENED, LIKE, THREE OR FOUR TIMES?
TWO TIMES.
SO YOU'RE BRUSHING ME OFF.
AFTER ALL THESE YEARS. FOR NO GOOD REASON.
...OF COURSE NOT, SEAN. I'M SORRY.
YOU'RE RIGHT. IT'S JUST LATE.
...AND IT'S BEEN A REALLY SHITTY DAY, AND...
NAH, C'MON...
IT'LL BE FINE, Y'KNOW?
YOU JUST HAVE THAT SEASONAL DEFECTIVE JUNK AGAIN.

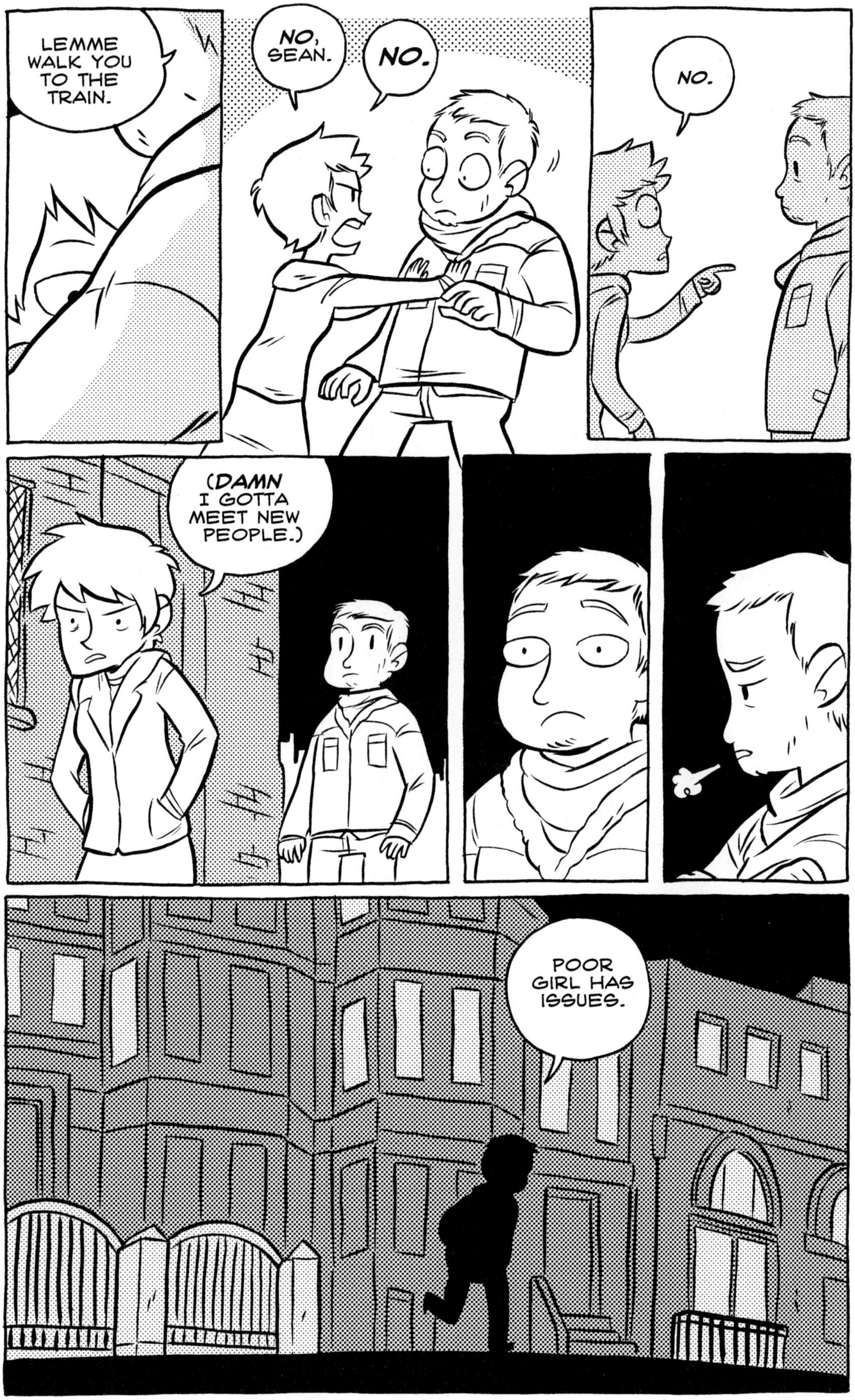
LEMME WALK YOU TO THE TRAIN.
NO, SEAN.
NO.
NO.
(DAMN I GOTTA MEET NEW PEOPLE.)
POOR GIRL HAS ISSUES.

41

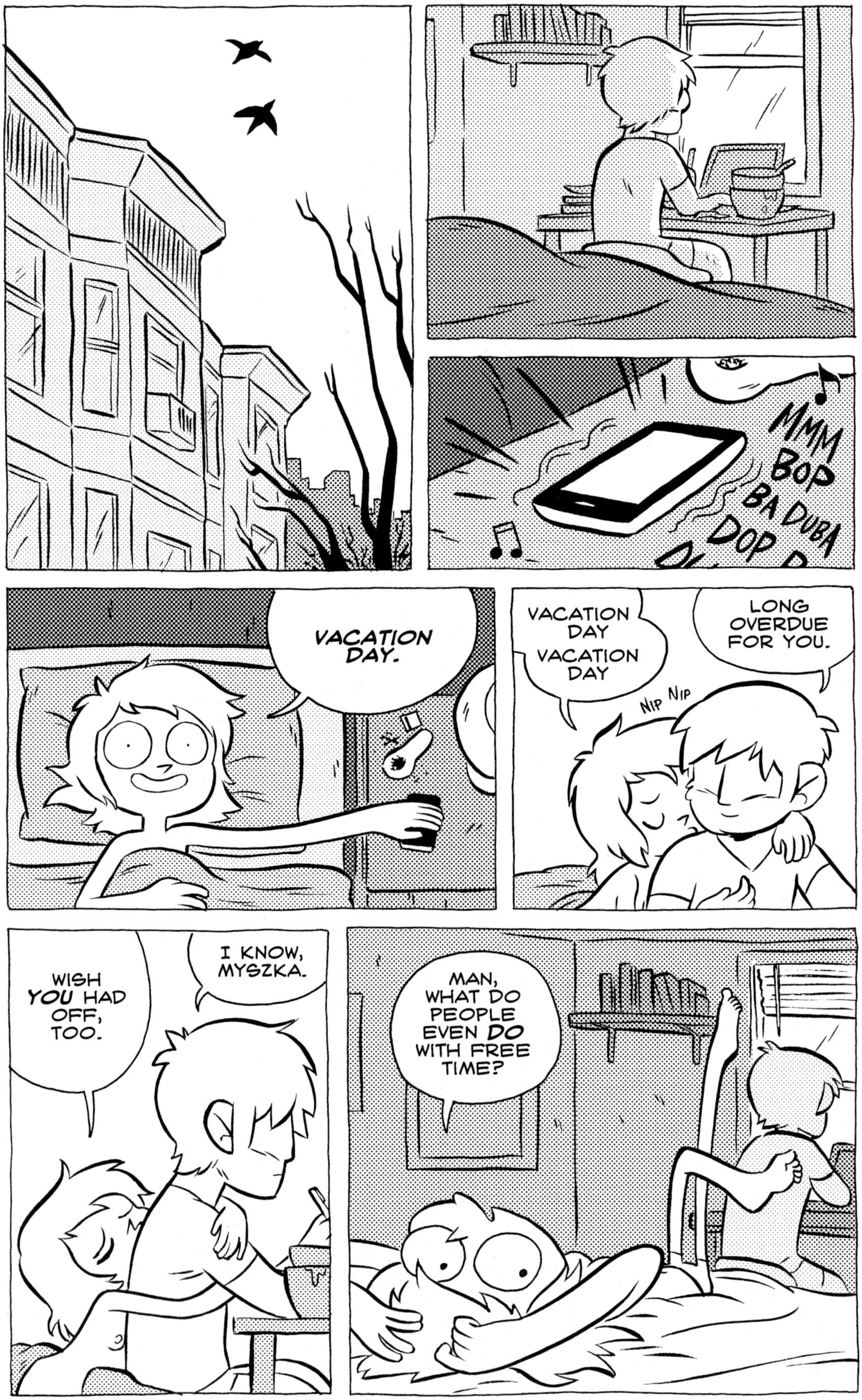
MMM BOP BA DUBA DOP
VACATION DAY.
VACATION DAY VACATION DAY
NIP NIP
LONG OVERDUE FOR YOU.
WISH YOU HAD OFF, TOO.
I KNOW, MYSZKA.
MAN, WHAT DO PEOPLE EVEN DO WITH FREE TIME?

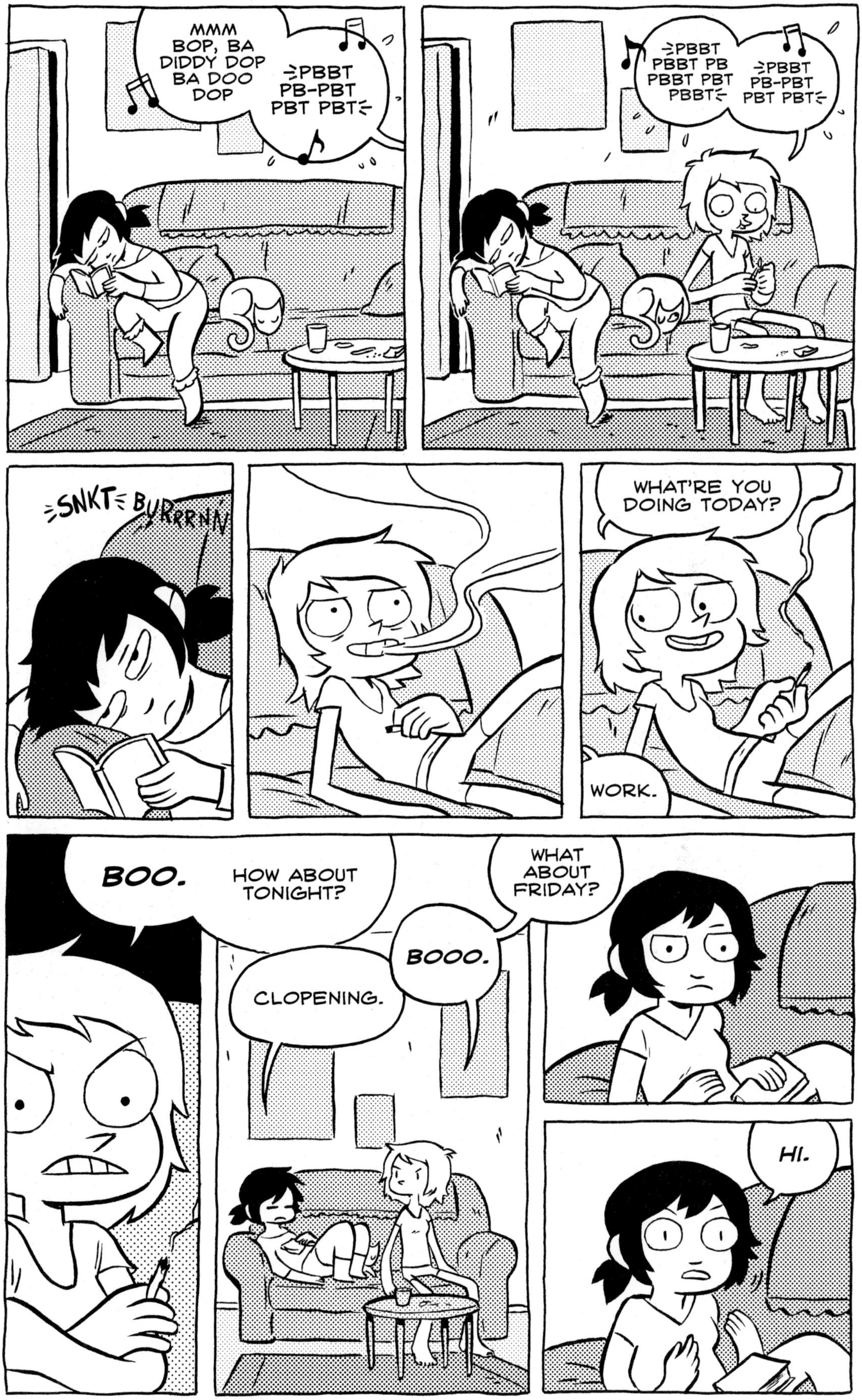
MMM BOP, BA DIDDY DOP BA DOO DOP
=PBBT PB-PBT PBT PBT=
=PBBT PBBT PB PBBT PBT PBBT=
=PBBT PB-PBT PBT PBT=
=SNKT= BURRRNN
WHAT'RE YOU DOING TODAY?
WORK.
BOO.
HOW ABOUT TONIGHT?
CLOPENING.
BOOO.
WHAT ABOUT FRIDAY?
HI.

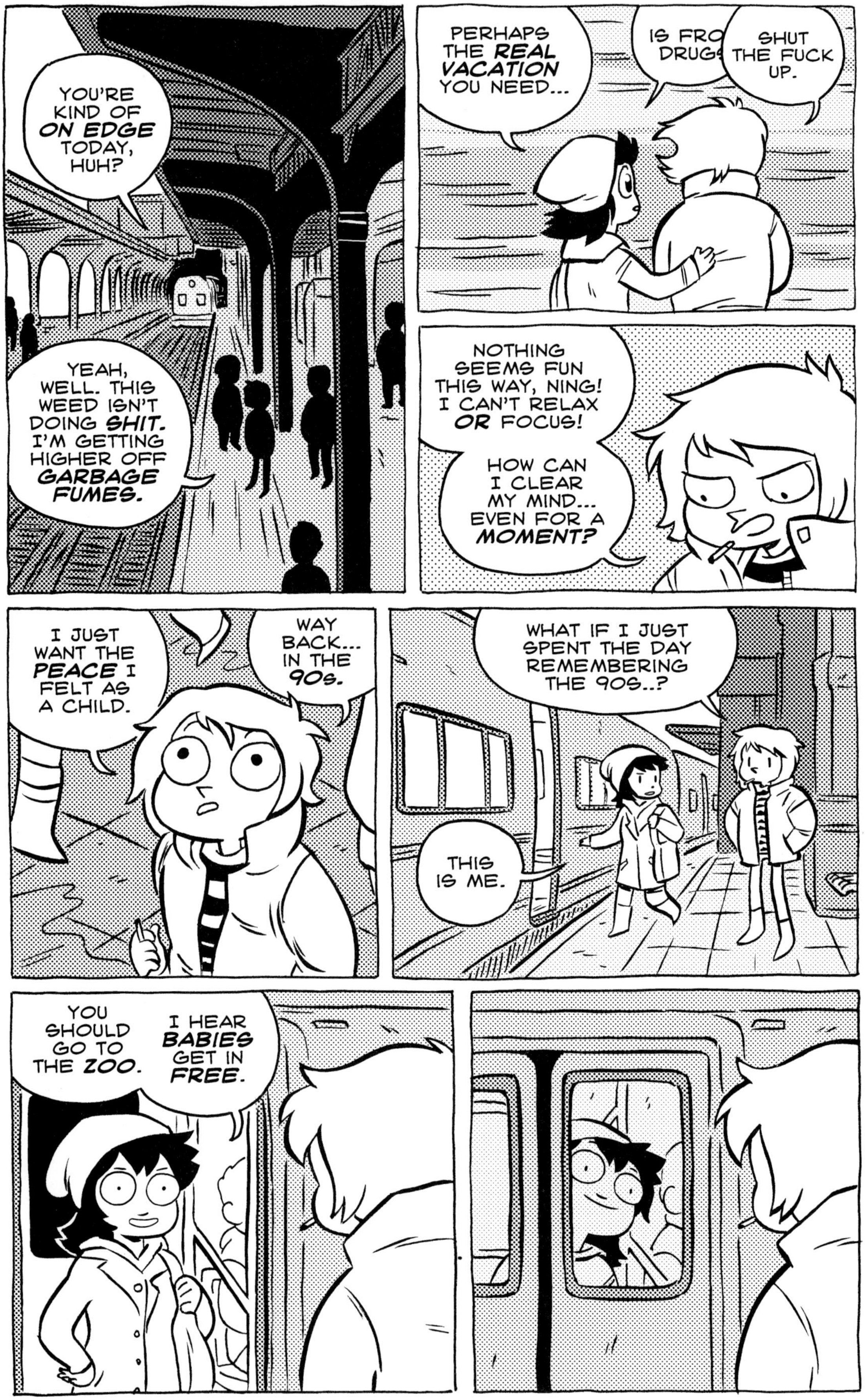

YOU'RE KIND OF ON EDGE TODAY, HUH?
YEAH, WELL. THIS WEED ISN'T DOING SHIT. I'M GETTING HIGHER OFF GARBAGE FUMES.
PERHAPS THE REAL VACATION YOU NEED...
IS FRO DRUGS
SHUT THE FUCK UP.
NOTHING SEEMS FUN THIS WAY, NING! I CAN'T RELAX OR FOCUS!
HOW CAN I CLEAR MY MIND... EVEN FOR A MOMENT?
I JUST WANT THE PEACE I FELT AS A CHILD.
WAY BACK... IN THE 90s.
WHAT IF I JUST SPENT THE DAY REMEMBERING THE 90S..?
THIS IS ME.
YOU SHOULD GO TO THE ZOO.
I HEAR BABIES GET IN FREE.

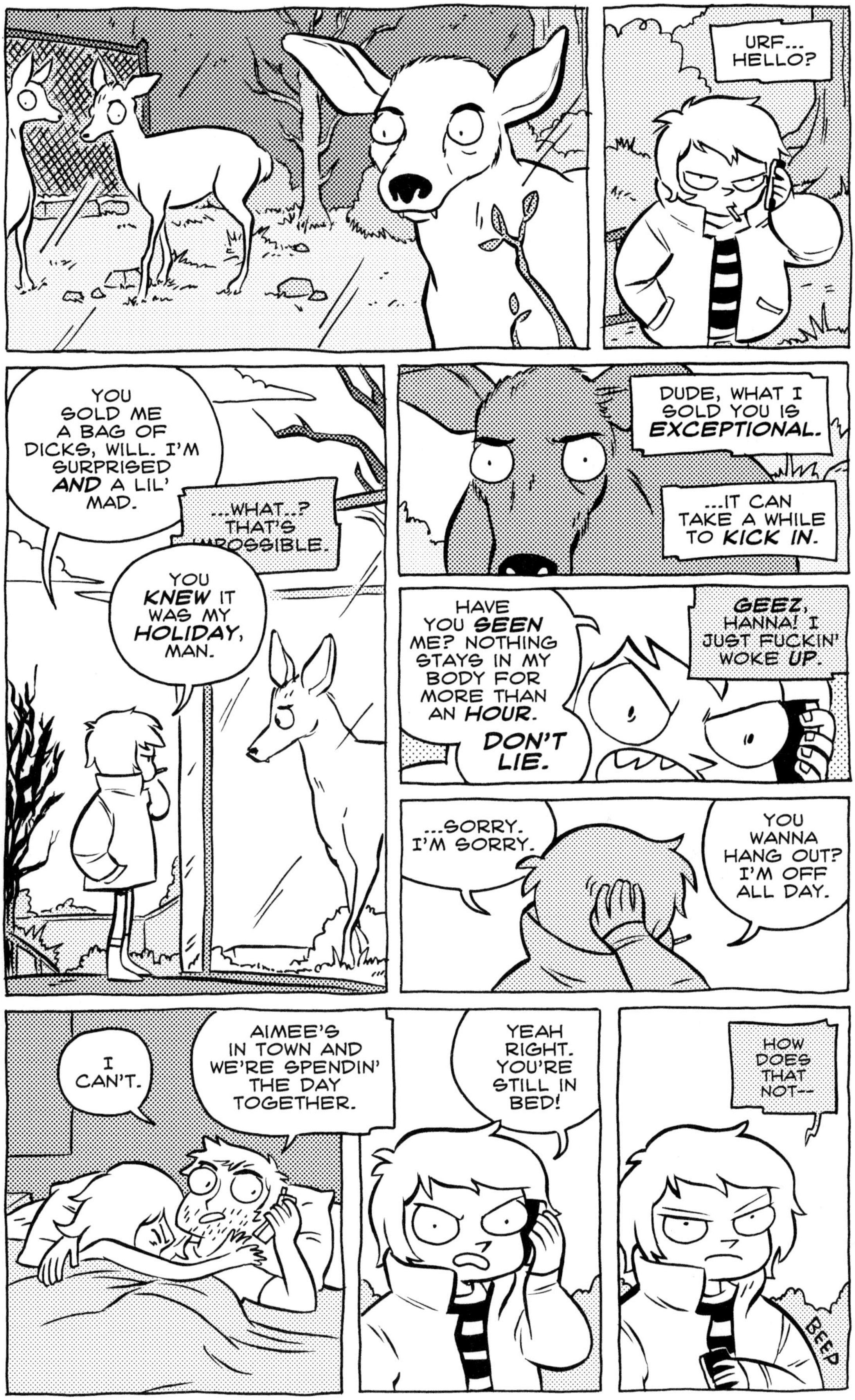
URF... HELLO?
YOU SOLD ME A BAG OF DICKS, WILL. I'M SURPRISED AND A LIL' MAD.
...WHAT..? THAT'S IMPOSSIBLE.
YOU KNEW IT WAS MY HOLIDAY, MAN.
DUDE, WHAT I SOLD YOU IS EXCEPTIONAL.
...IT CAN TAKE A WHILE TO KICK IN.
HAVE YOU SEEN ME? NOTHING STAYS IN MY BODY FOR MORE THAN AN HOUR.
DON'T LIE.
GEEZ, HANNA! I JUST FUCKIN' WOKE UP.
...SORRY. I'M SORRY.
YOU WANNA HANG OUT? I'M OFF ALL DAY.
I CAN'T.
AIMEE'S IN TOWN AND WE'RE SPENDIN' THE DAY TOGETHER.
YEAH RIGHT. YOU'RE STILL IN BED!
HOW DOES THAT NOT--
BEEP

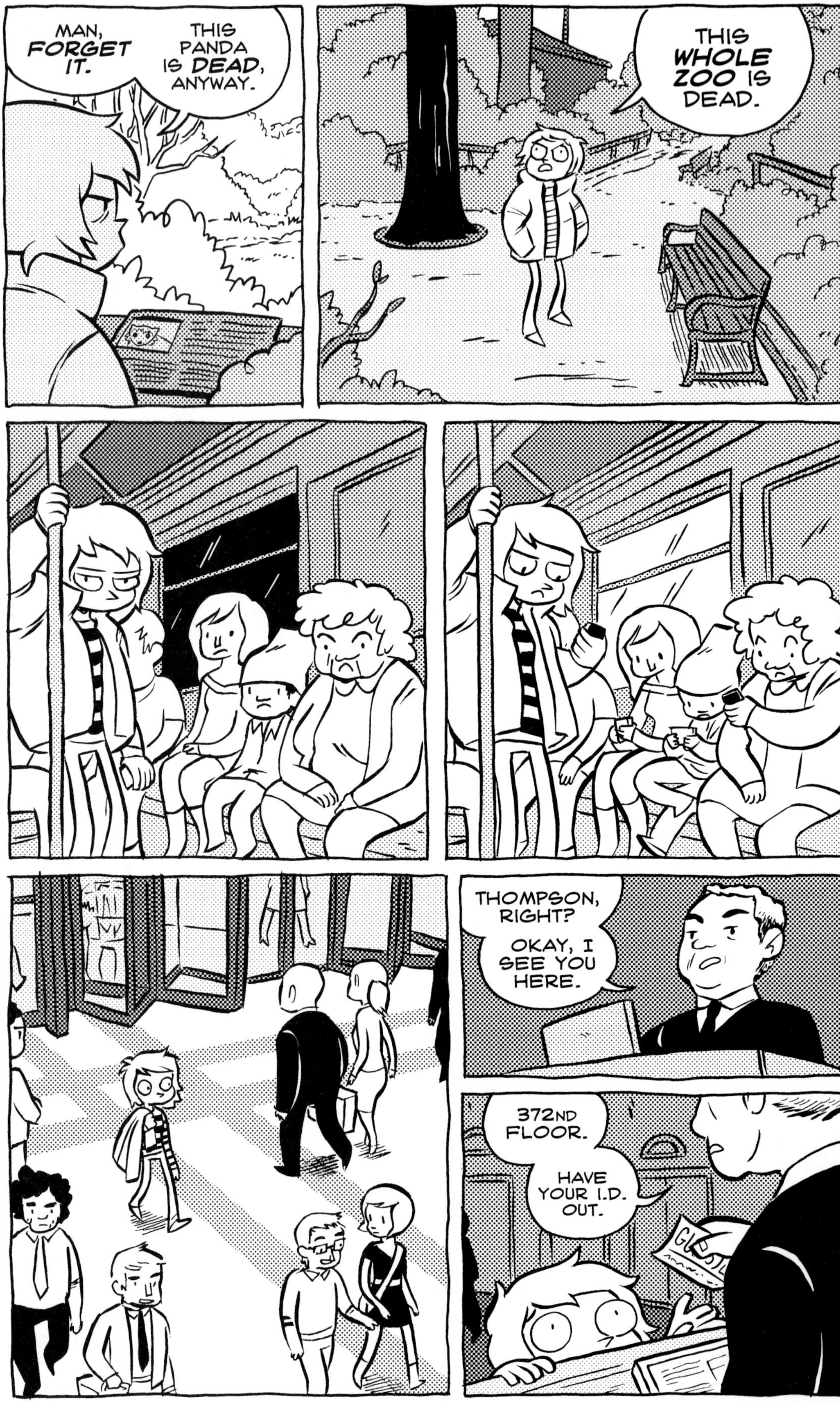
MAN, FORGET IT.
THIS PANDA IS DEAD, ANYWAY.
THIS WHOLE ZOO IS DEAD.
THOMPSON, RIGHT?
OKAY, I SEE YOU HERE.
372ND FLOOR.
HAVE YOUR I.D. OUT.

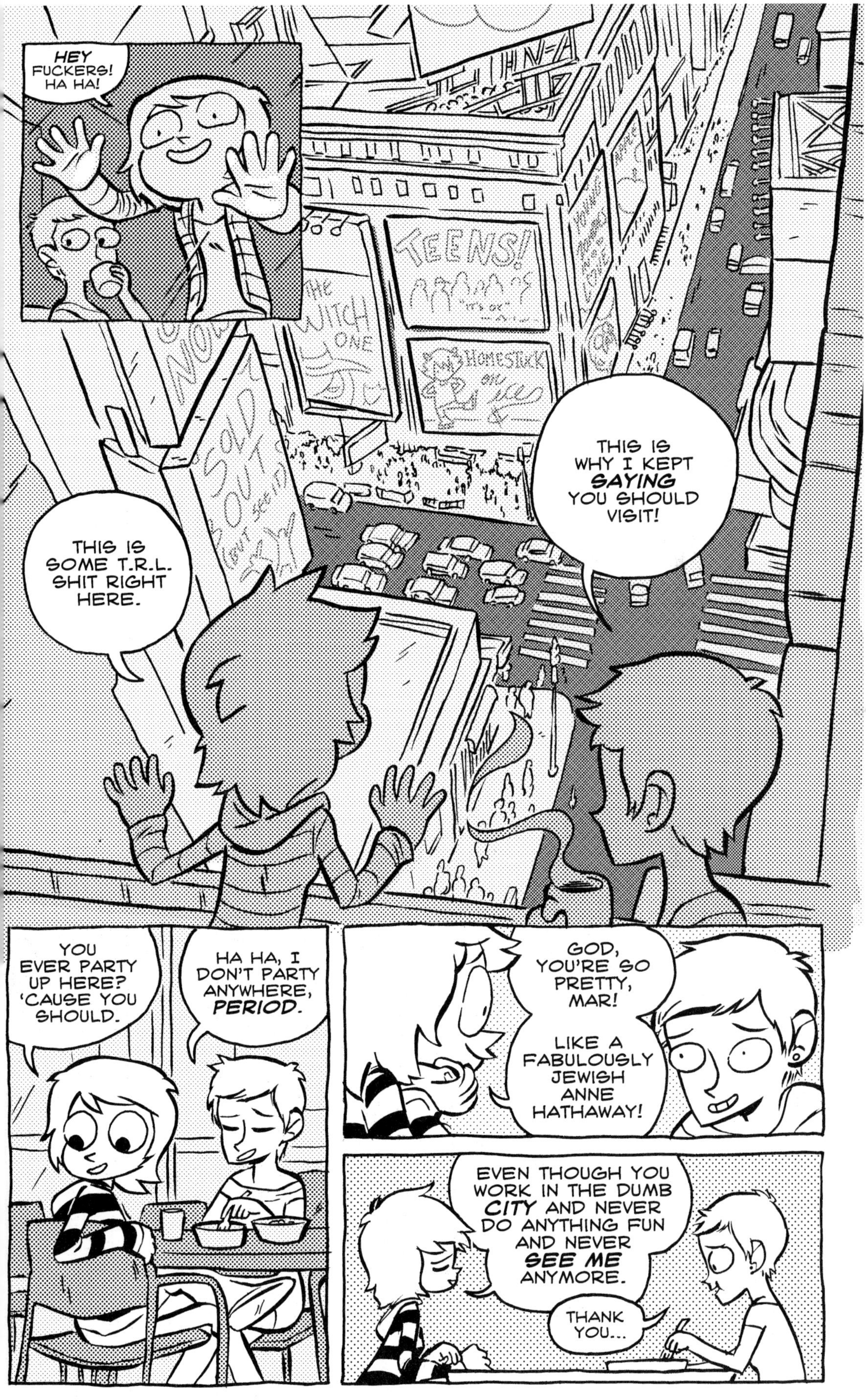
HEY FUCKERS! HA HA!
TEENS!
THE WITCH ONE
HOMESTUCK ON ICE
SOLD OUT
THIS IS SOME T.R.L. SHIT RIGHT HERE.
THIS IS WHY I KEPT SAYING YOU SHOULD VISIT!
YOU EVER PARTY UP HERE? 'CAUSE YOU SHOULD.
HA HA, I DON'T PARTY ANYWHERE, PERIOD.
GOD, YOU'RE SO PRETTY, MAR!
LIKE A FABULOUSLY JEWISH ANNE HATHAWAY!
EVEN THOUGH YOU WORK IN THE DUMB CITY AND NEVER DO ANYTHING FUN AND NEVER SEE ME ANYMORE.
THANK YOU...

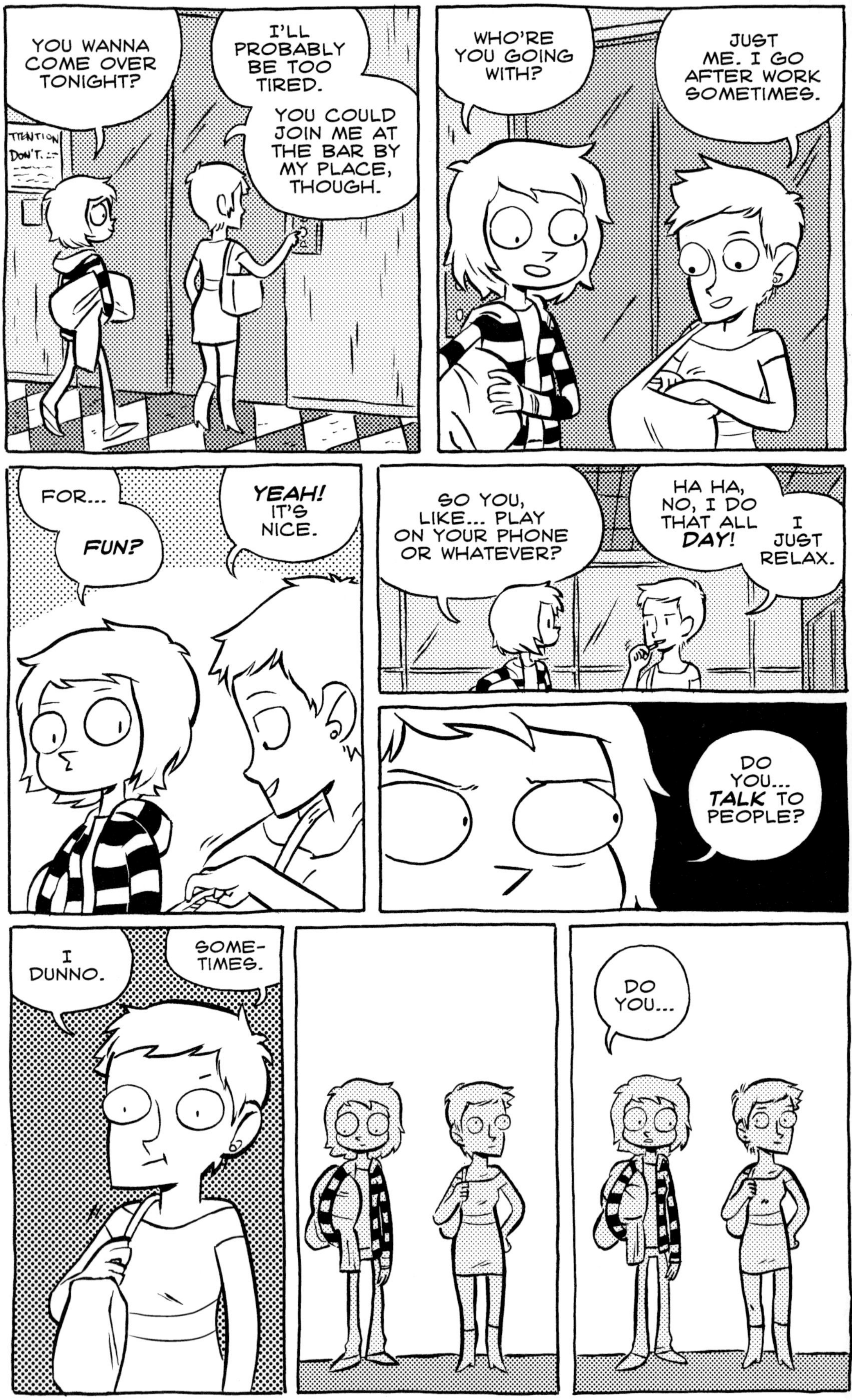

YOU WANNA COME OVER TONIGHT?
I'LL PROBABLY BE TOO TIRED.
YOU COULD JOIN ME AT THE BAR BY MY PLACE, THOUGH.
WHO'RE YOU GOING WITH?
JUST ME. I GO AFTER WORK SOMETIMES.
FOR...
FUN?
YEAH! IT'S NICE.
SO YOU, LIKE... PLAY ON YOUR PHONE OR WHATEVER?
HA HA, NO, I DO THAT ALL DAY!
I JUST RELAX.
DO YOU... TALK TO PEOPLE?
I DUNNO.
SOME-TIMES.
DO YOU...

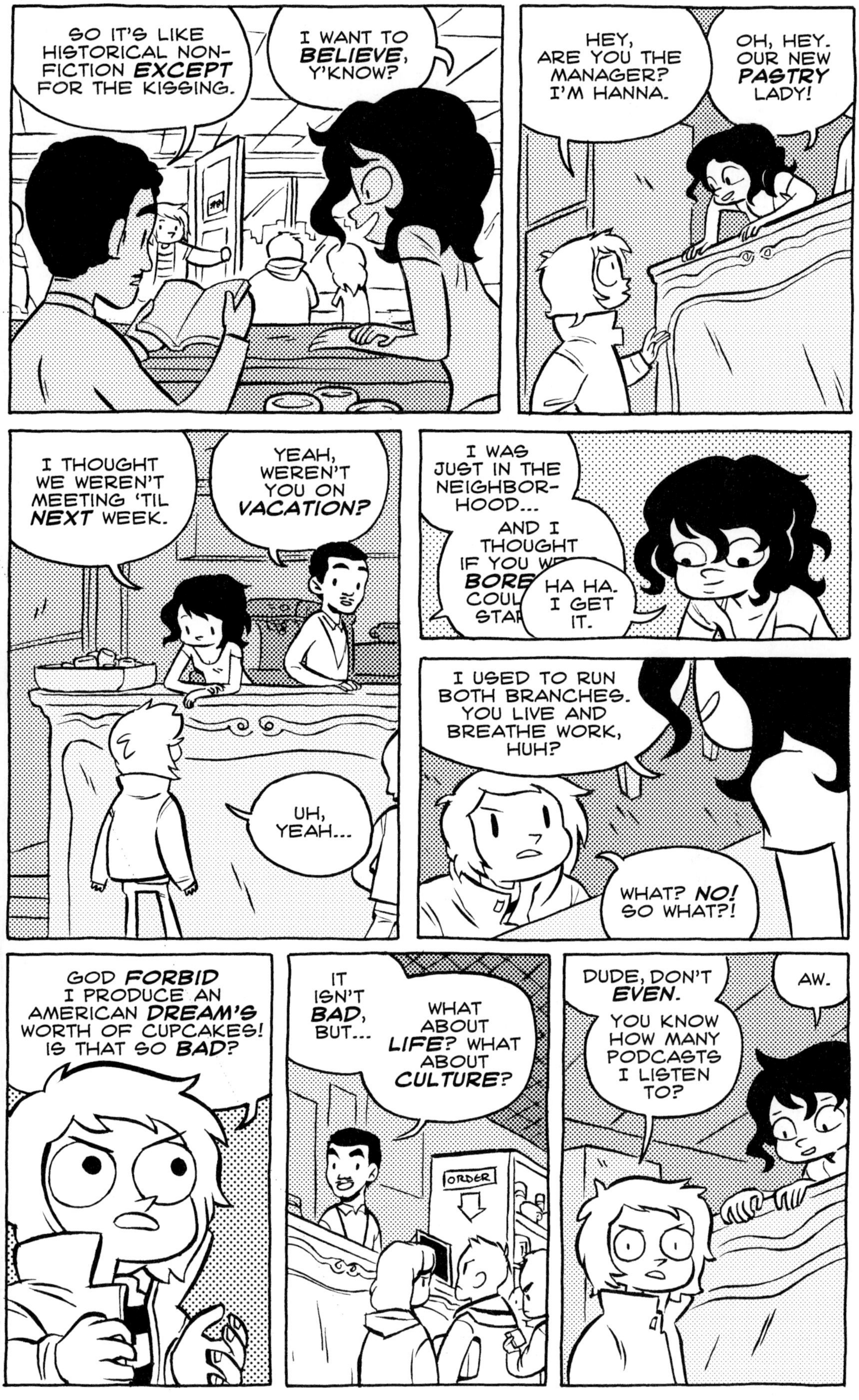
SO IT'S LIKE HISTORICAL NON-FICTION EXCEPT FOR THE KISSING.
I WANT TO BELIEVE, Y'KNOW?
HEY, ARE YOU THE MANAGER? I'M HANNA.
OH, HEY. OUR NEW PASTRY LADY!
I THOUGHT WE WEREN'T MEETING 'TIL NEXT WEEK.
YEAH, WEREN'T YOU ON VACATION?
UH, YEAH...
I WAS JUST IN THE NEIGHBOR-HOOD...
HA HA. I GET IT.
I USED TO RUN BOTH BRANCHES. YOU LIVE AND BREATHE WORK, HUH?
WHAT? NO! SO WHAT?!
GOD FORBID I PRODUCE AN AMERICAN DREAM'S WORTH OF CUPCAKES! IS THAT SO BAD?
IT ISN'T BAD, BUT...
WHAT ABOUT LIFE? WHAT ABOUT CULTURE?
ORDER
DUDE, DON'T EVEN.
YOU KNOW HOW MANY PODCASTS I LISTEN TO?
AW.

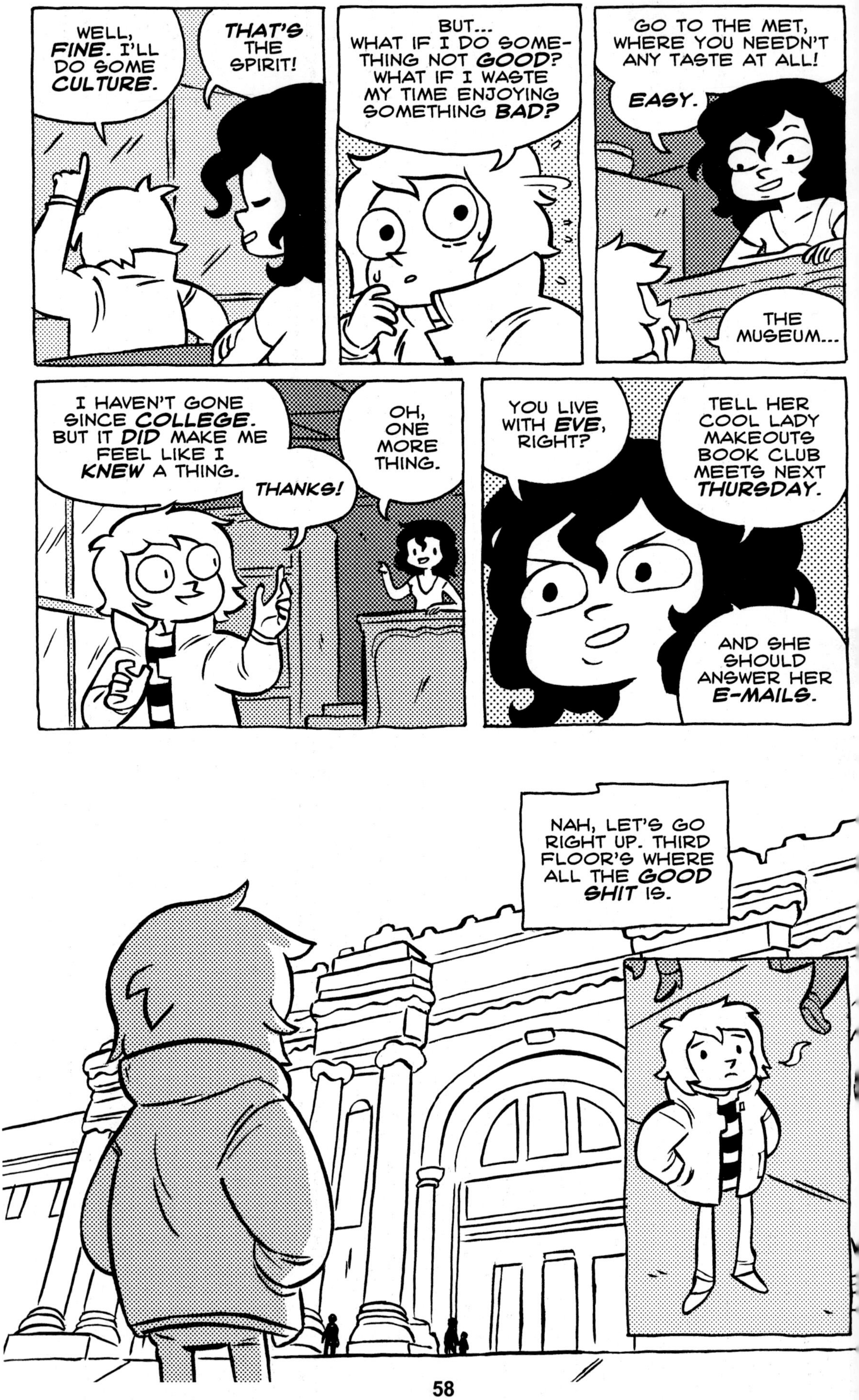

WELL, FINE. I'LL DO SOME CULTURE.
THAT'S THE SPIRIT!
BUT... WHAT IF I DO SOME-THING NOT GOOD? WHAT IF I WASTE MY TIME ENJOYING SOMETHING BAD?
GO TO THE MET, WHERE YOU NEEDN'T ANY TASTE AT ALL!
EASY.
THE MUSEUM...
I HAVEN'T GONE SINCE COLLEGE. BUT IT DID MAKE ME FEEL LIKE I KNEW A THING.
THANKS!
OH, ONE MORE THING.
YOU LIVE WITH EVE, RIGHT?
TELL HER COOL LADY MAKEOUTS BOOK CLUB MEETS NEXT THURSDAY.
AND SHE SHOULD ANSWER HER E-MAILS.
NAH, LET'S GO RIGHT UP. THIRD FLOOR'S WHERE ALL THE GOOD SHIT IS.

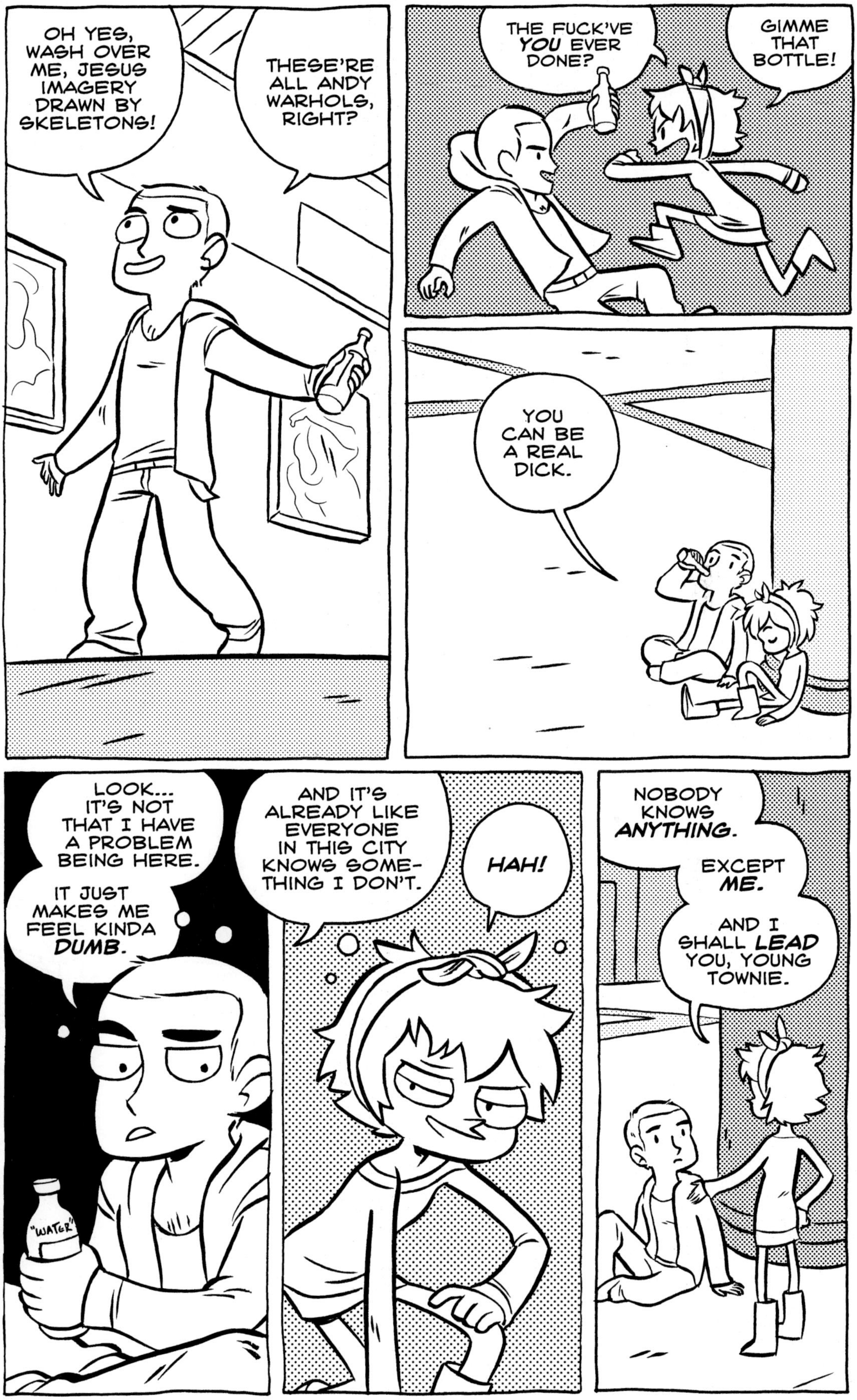
OH YES, WASH OVER ME, JESUS IMAGERY DRAWN BY SKELETONS!
THESE'RE ALL ANDY WARHOLS, RIGHT?
THE FUCK'VE *YOU* EVER DONE?
GIMME THAT BOTTLE!
YOU CAN BE A REAL DICK.
LOOK... IT'S NOT THAT I HAVE A PROBLEM BEING HERE.
IT JUST MAKES ME FEEL KINDA *DUMB*.
"WATER"
AND IT'S ALREADY LIKE EVERYONE IN THIS CITY KNOWS SOME-THING I DON'T.
HAH!
NOBODY KNOWS *ANYTHING*.
EXCEPT *ME*.
AND I SHALL *LEAD* YOU, YOUNG TOWNIE.

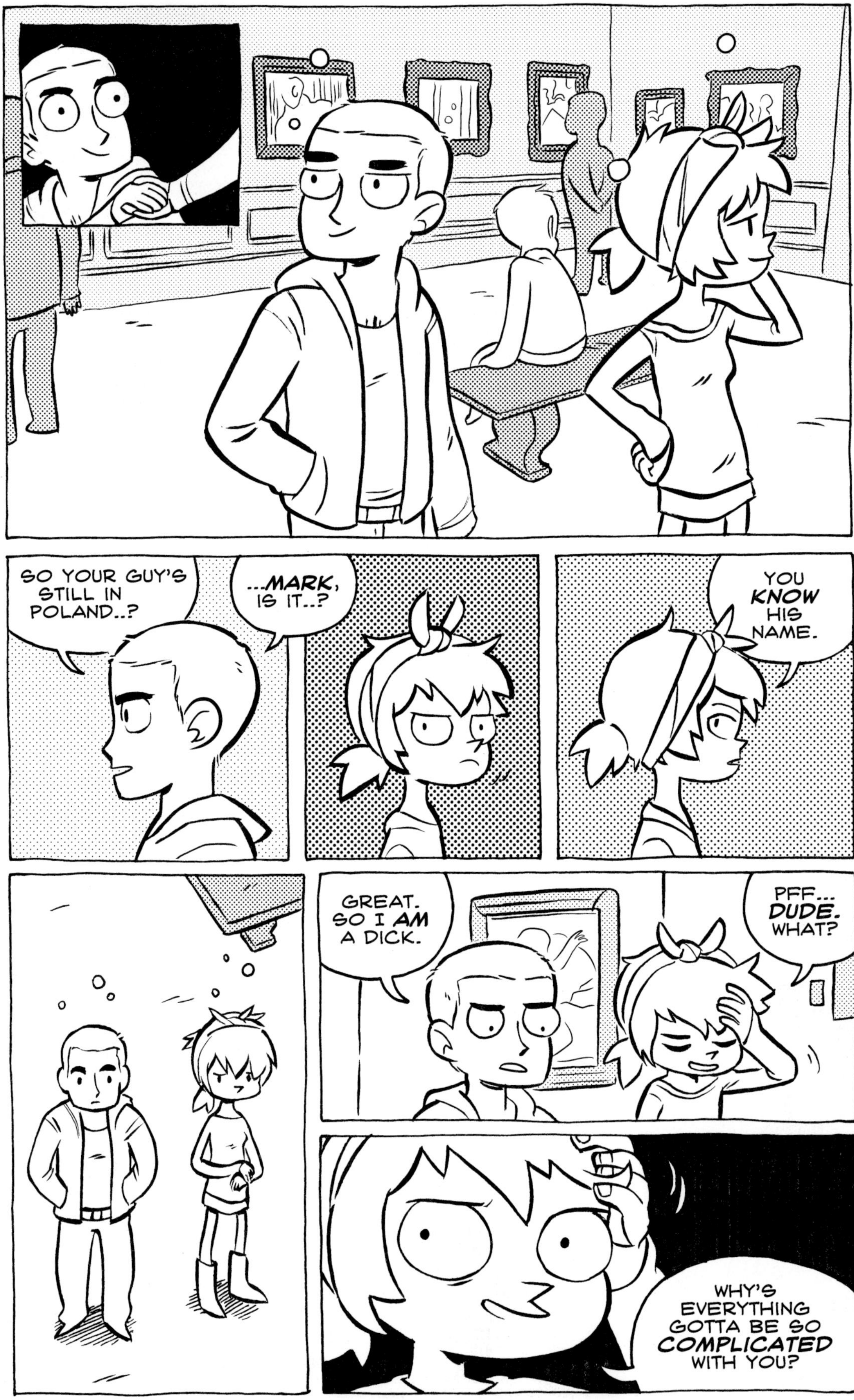
SO YOUR GUY'S STILL IN POLAND..?
...MARK, IS IT..?
YOU KNOW HIS NAME.
GREAT. SO I AM A DICK.
PFF... DUDE. WHAT?
WHY'S EVERYTHING GOTTA BE SO COMPLICATED WITH YOU?

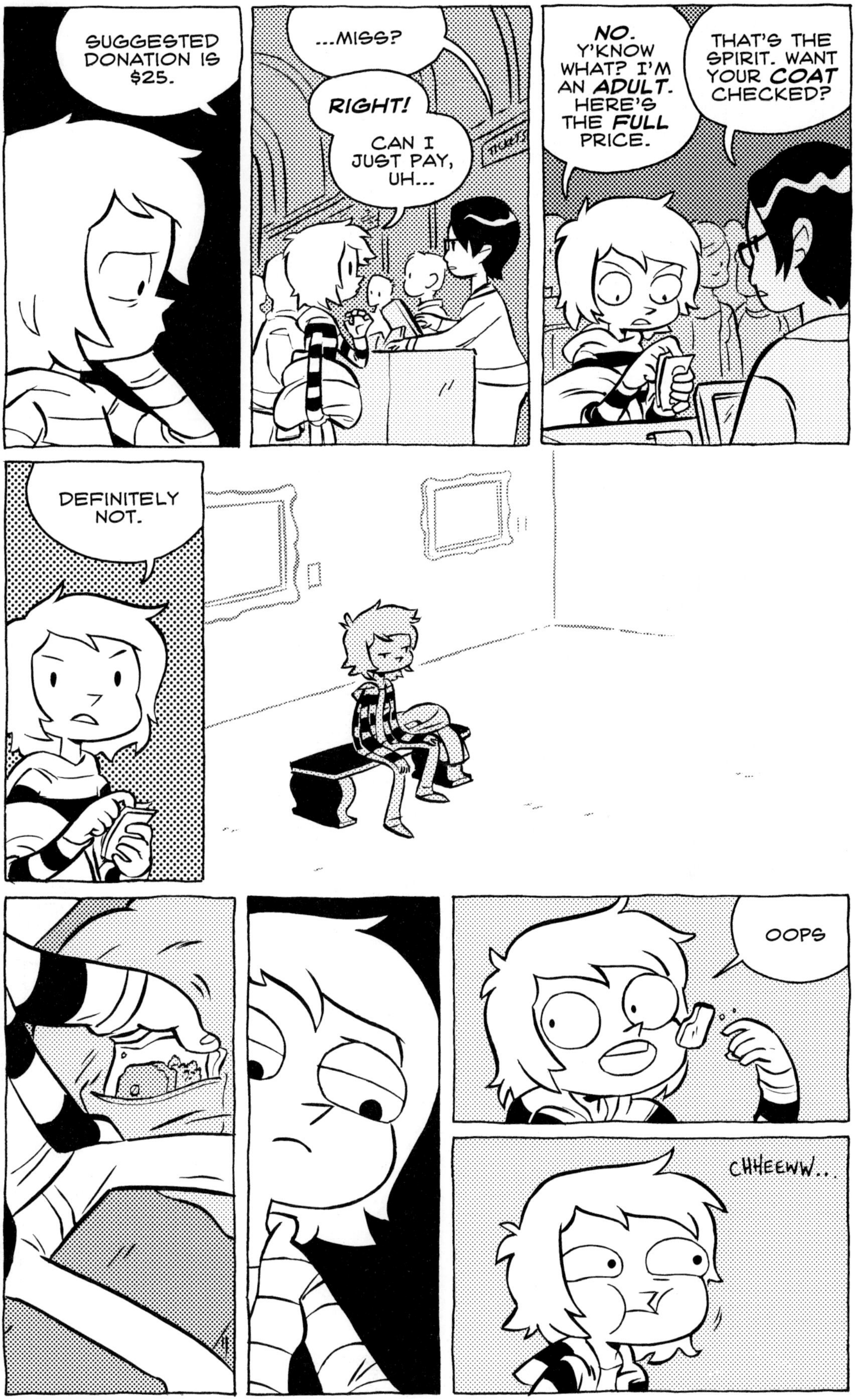
SUGGESTED DONATION IS $25.
...MISS?
RIGHT!
CAN I JUST PAY, UH...
TICKETS
NO. Y'KNOW WHAT? I'M AN ADULT. HERE'S THE FULL PRICE.
THAT'S THE SPIRIT. WANT YOUR COAT CHECKED?
DEFINITELY NOT.
OOPS
CHHEEWW..

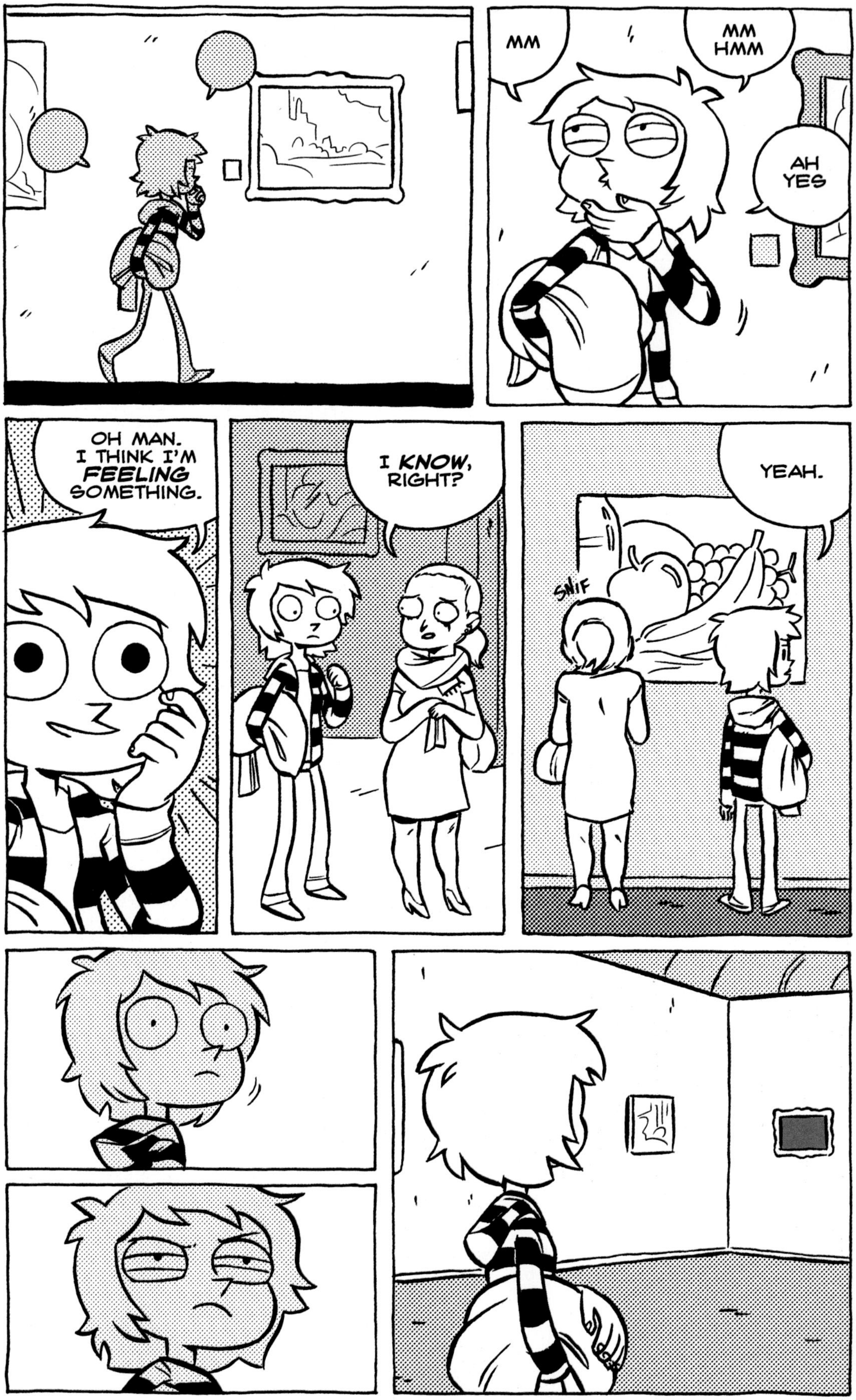
MM
MM HMM
AH YES
OH MAN. I THINK I'M *FEELING* SOMETHING.
I *KNOW*, RIGHT?
YEAH.
SNIF

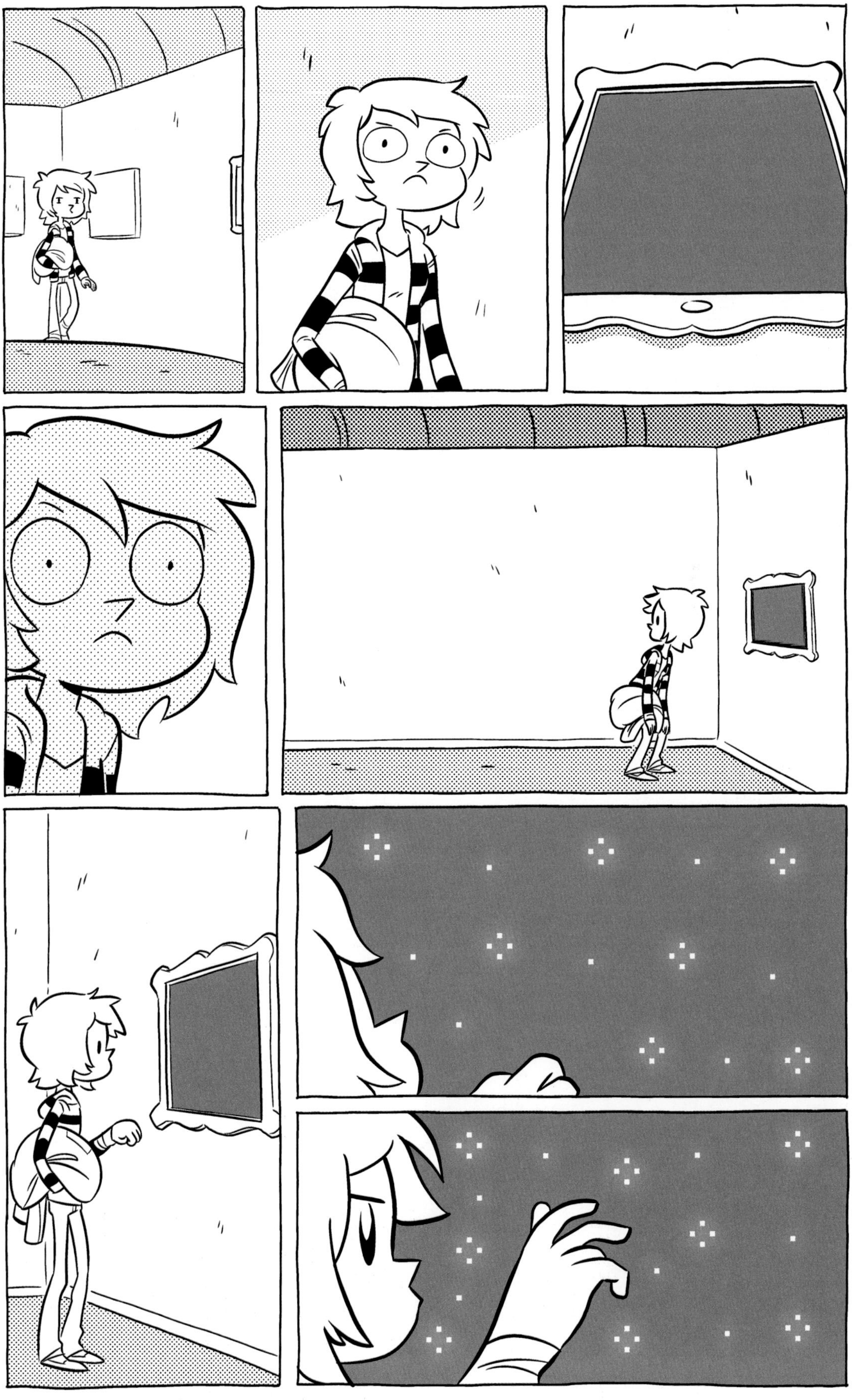

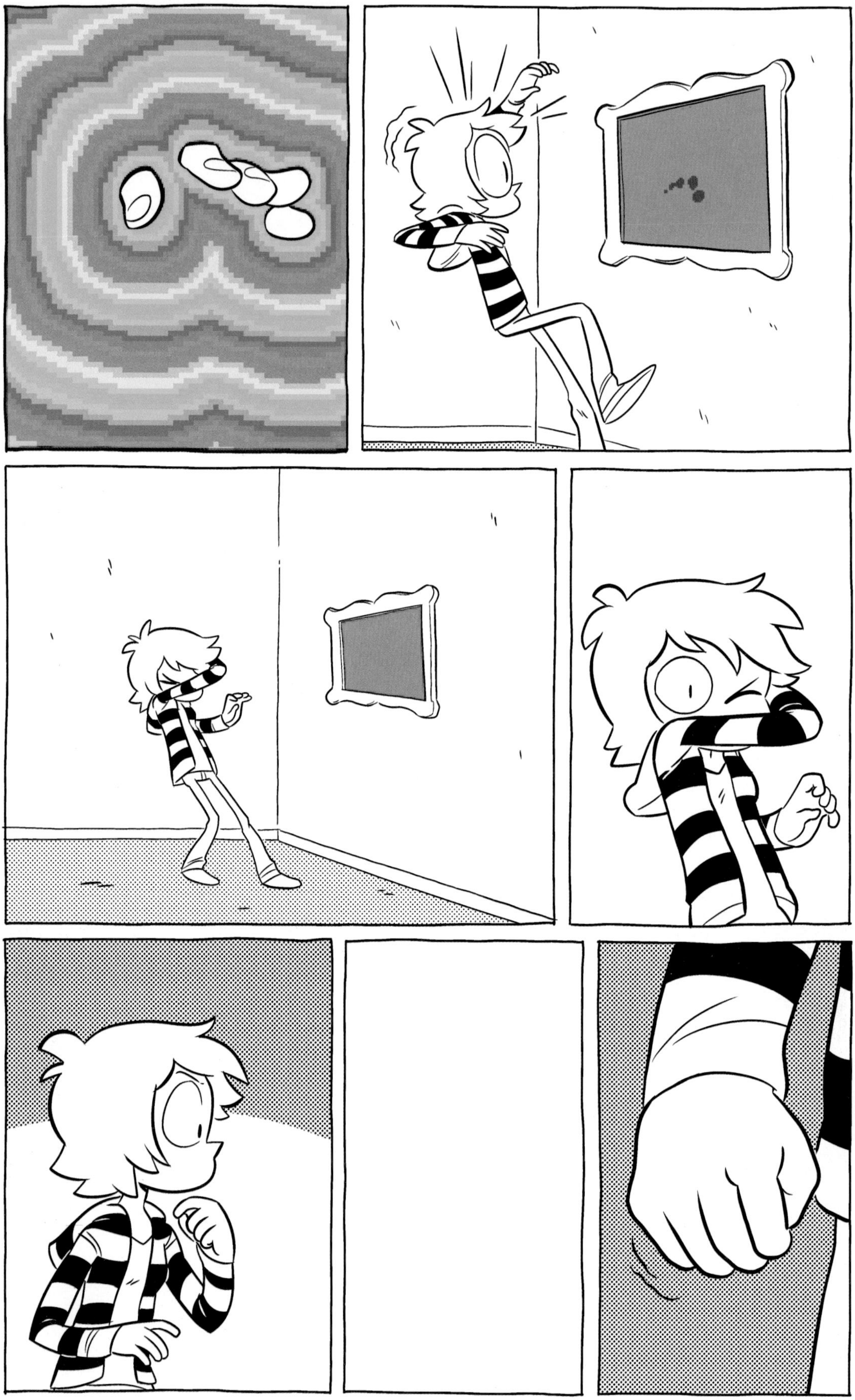

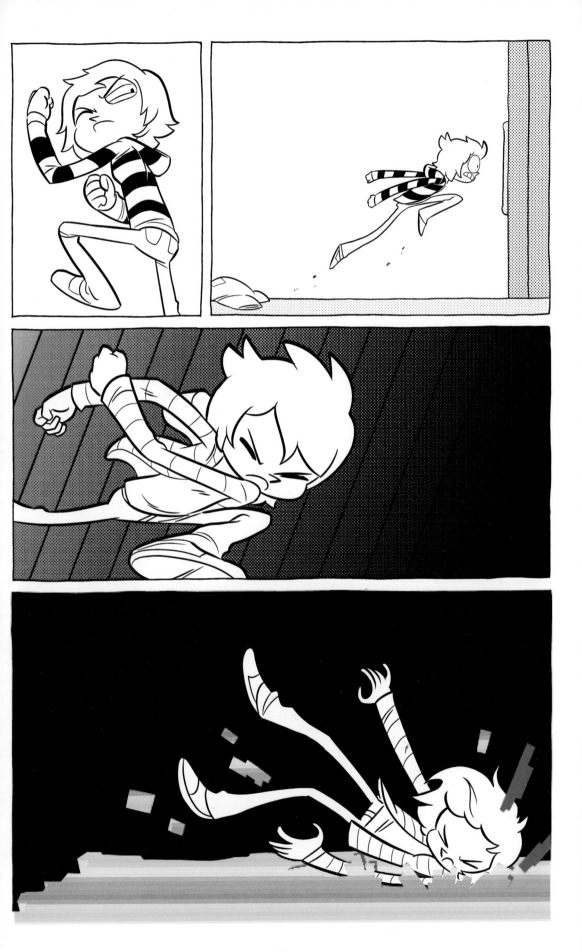

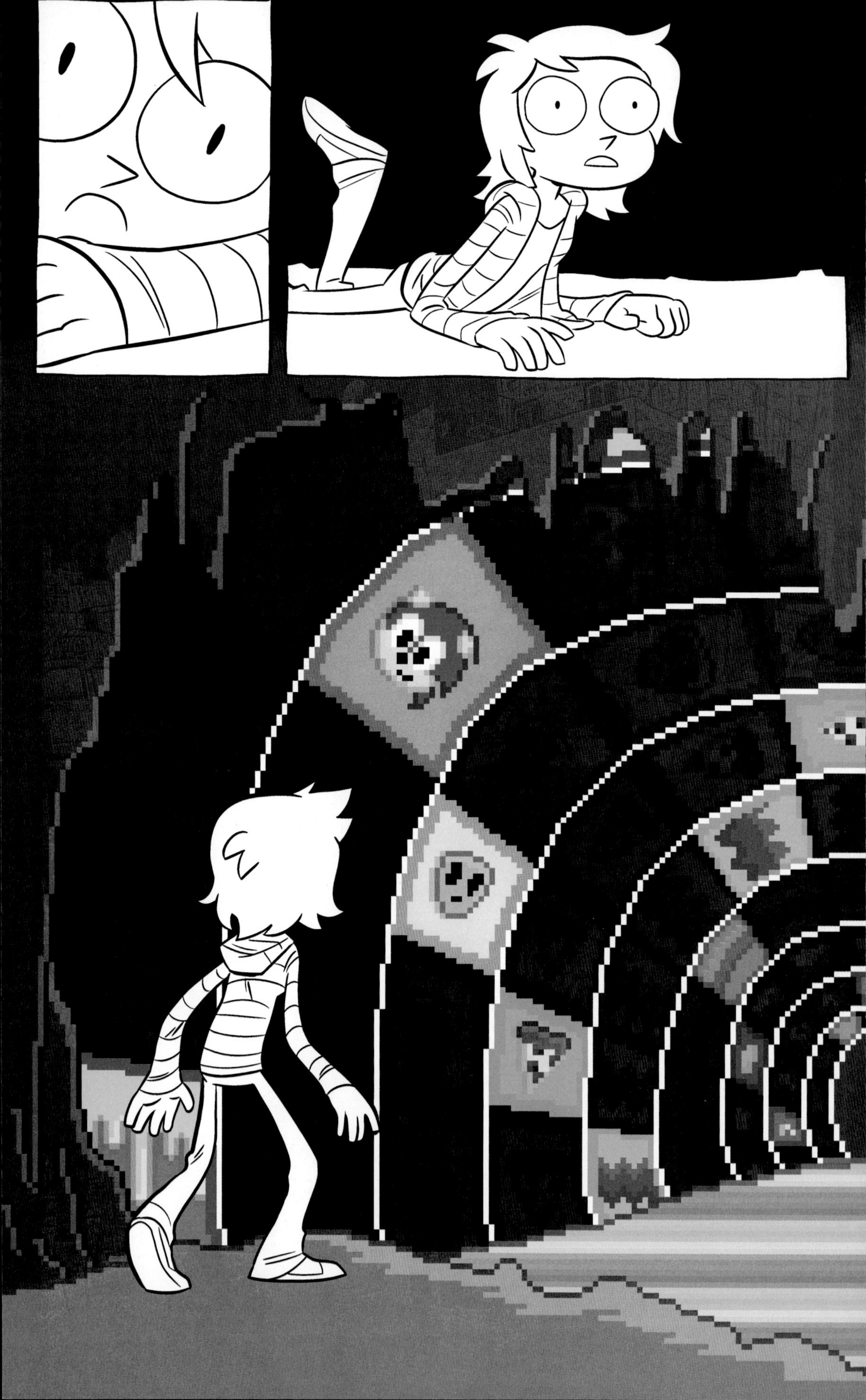

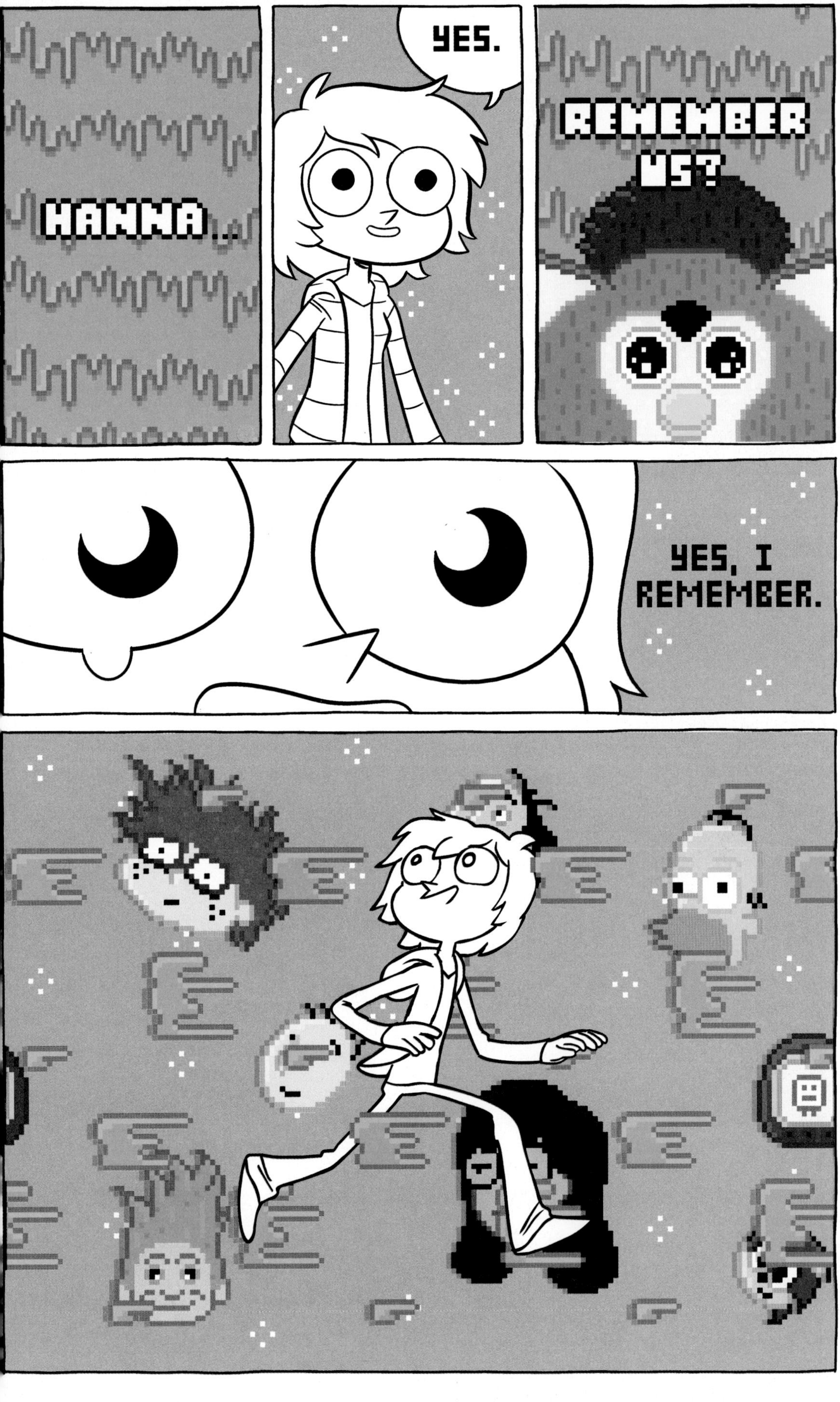
HANNA...
YES.
REMEMBER US?
YES, I REMEMBER.

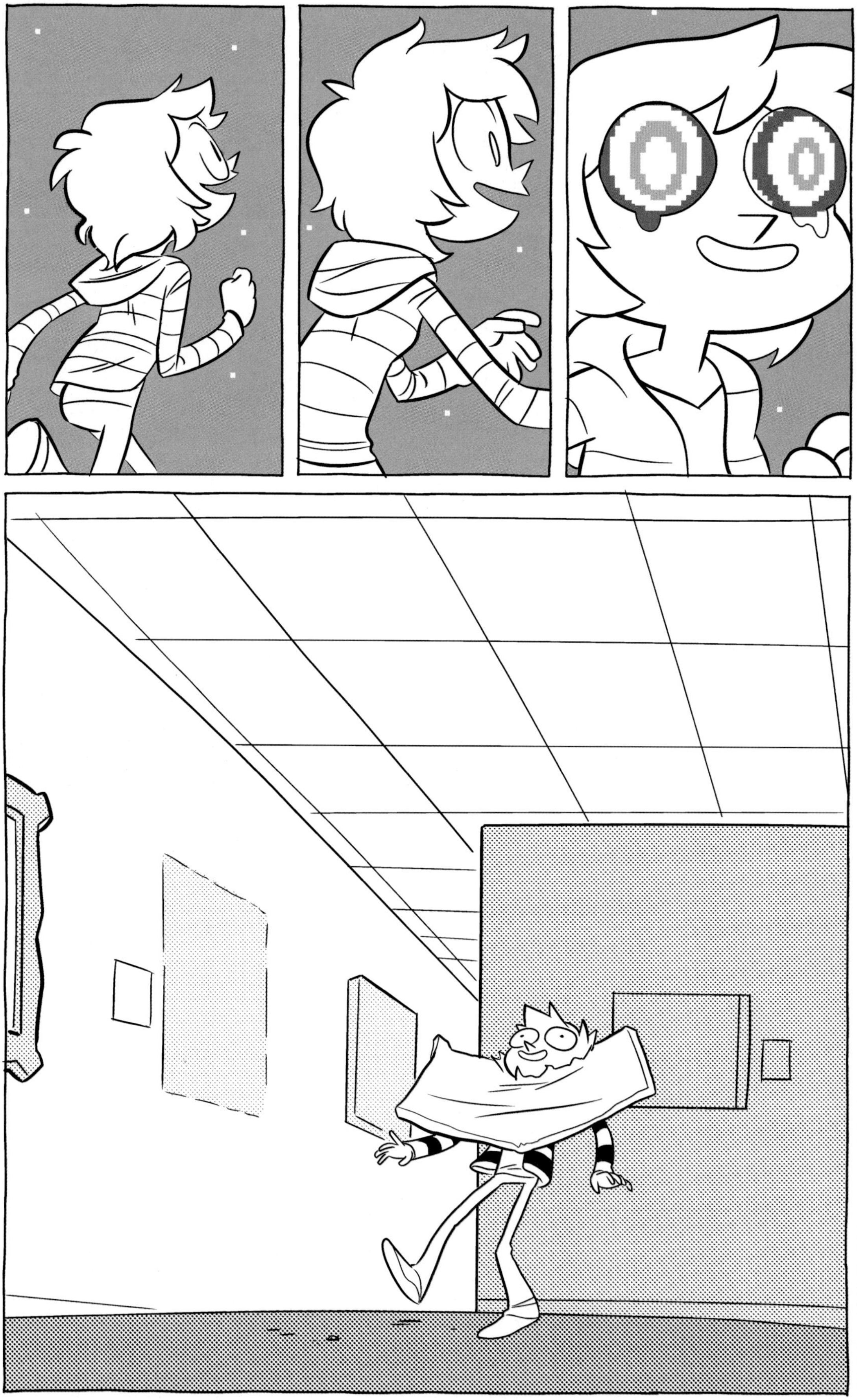

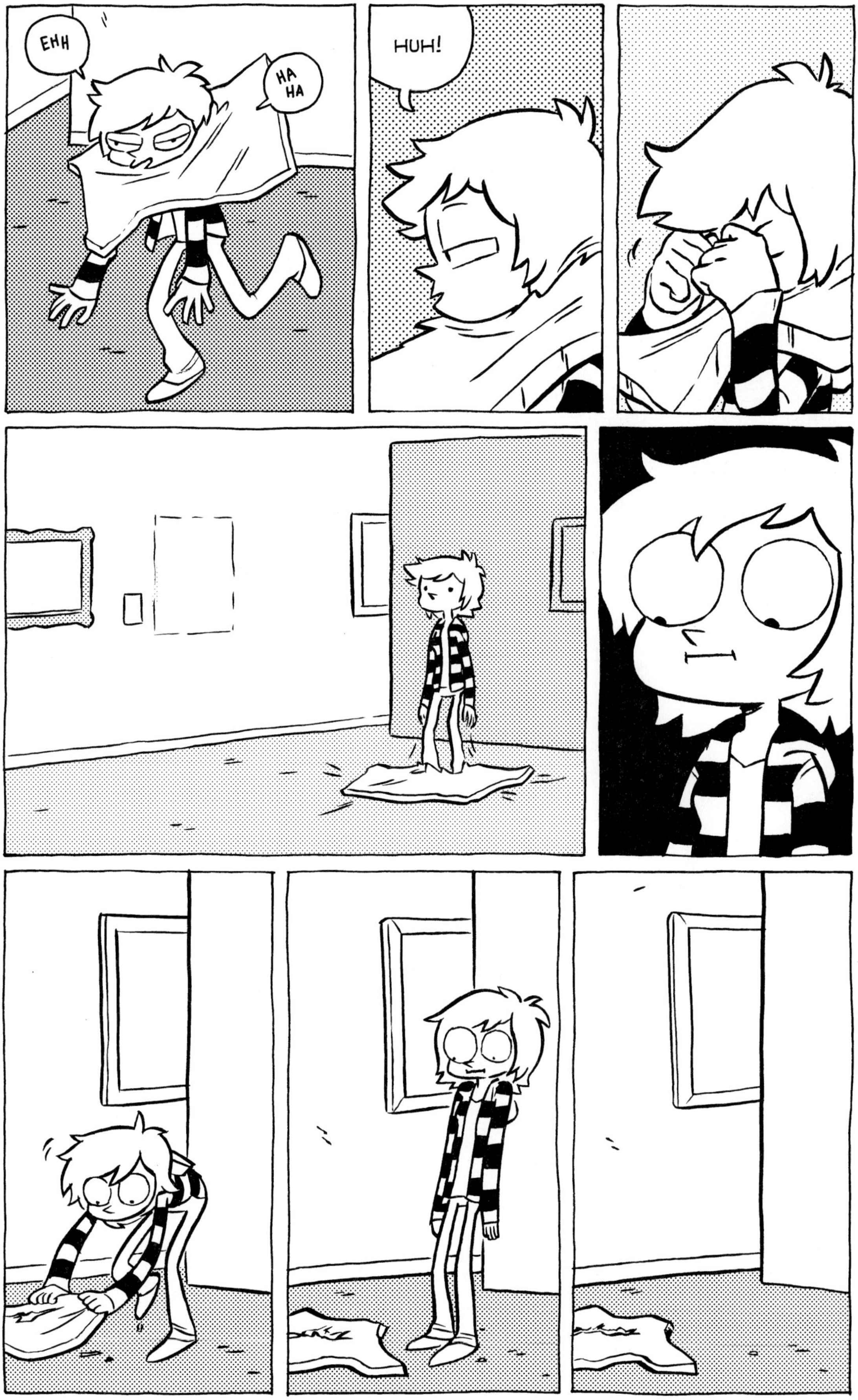
EHH
HA HA
HUH!

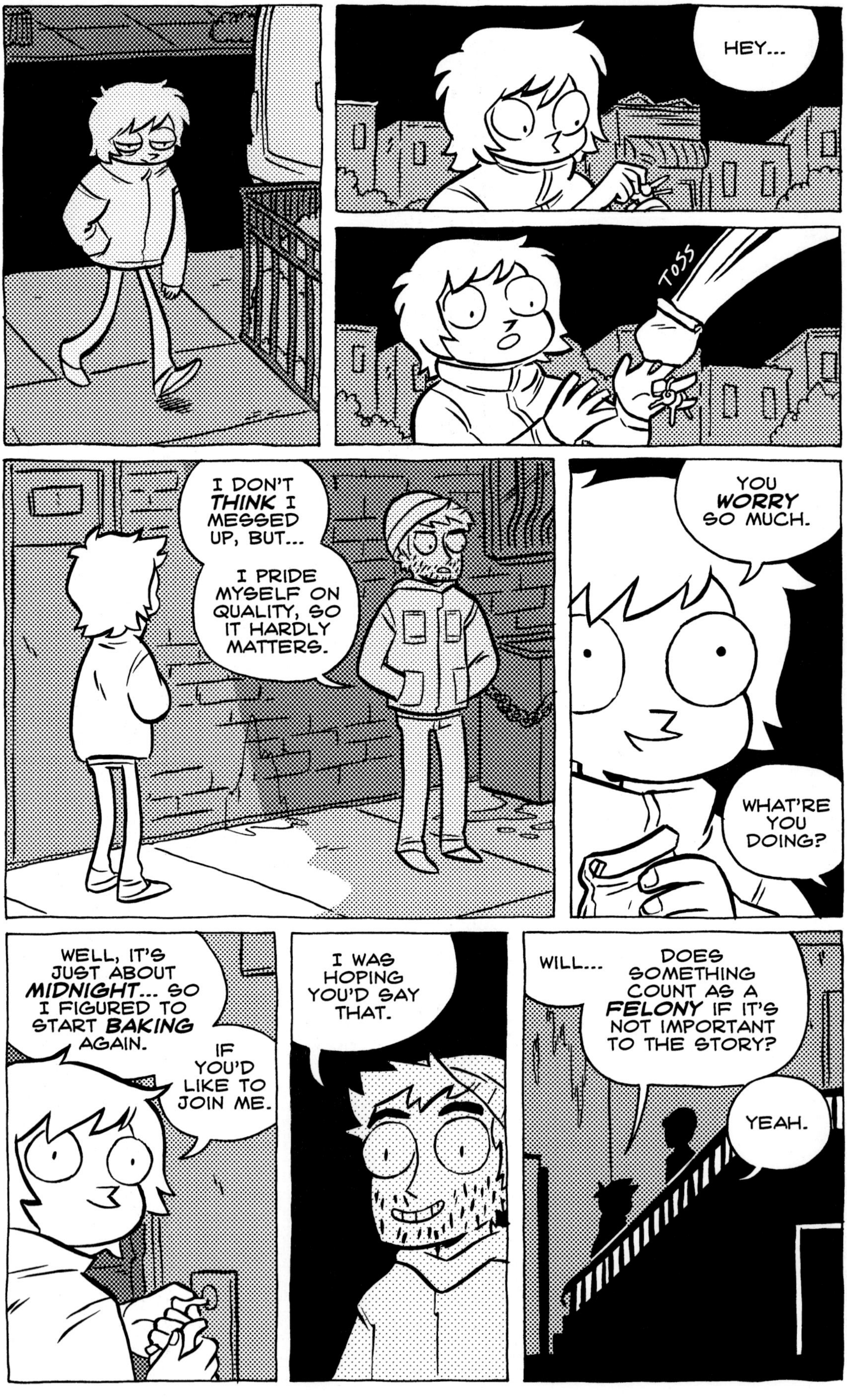
HEY...
TOSS
I DON'T THINK I MESSED UP, BUT...
I PRIDE MYSELF ON QUALITY, SO IT HARDLY MATTERS.
YOU WORRY SO MUCH.
WHAT'RE YOU DOING?
WELL, IT'S JUST ABOUT MIDNIGHT... SO I FIGURED TO START BAKING AGAIN.
IF YOU'D LIKE TO JOIN ME.
I WAS HOPING YOU'D SAY THAT.
WILL...
DOES SOMETHING COUNT AS A FELONY IF IT'S NOT IMPORTANT TO THE STORY?
YEAH.

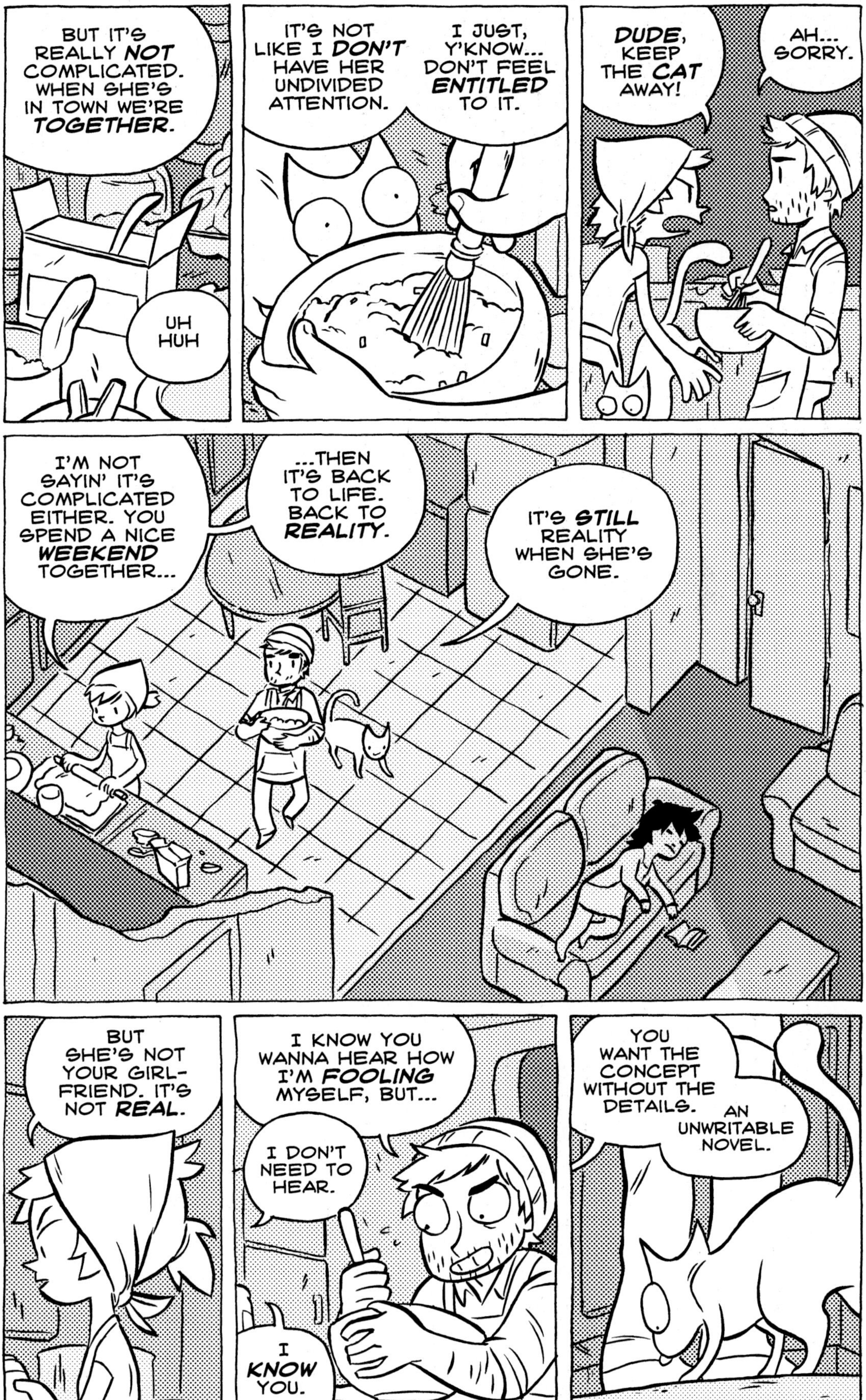

BUT IT'S REALLY NOT COMPLICATED. WHEN SHE'S IN TOWN WE'RE TOGETHER.
UH HUH
IT'S NOT LIKE I DON'T HAVE HER UNDIVIDED ATTENTION.
I JUST, Y'KNOW... DON'T FEEL ENTITLED TO IT.
DUDE, KEEP THE CAT AWAY!
AH... SORRY.
I'M NOT SAYIN' IT'S COMPLICATED EITHER. YOU SPEND A NICE WEEKEND TOGETHER...
...THEN IT'S BACK TO LIFE. BACK TO REALITY.
IT'S STILL REALITY WHEN SHE'S GONE.
BUT SHE'S NOT YOUR GIRL-FRIEND. IT'S NOT REAL.
I KNOW YOU WANNA HEAR HOW I'M FOOLING MYSELF, BUT...
I DON'T NEED TO HEAR.
I KNOW YOU.
YOU WANT THE CONCEPT WITHOUT THE DETAILS.
AN UNWRITABLE NOVEL.

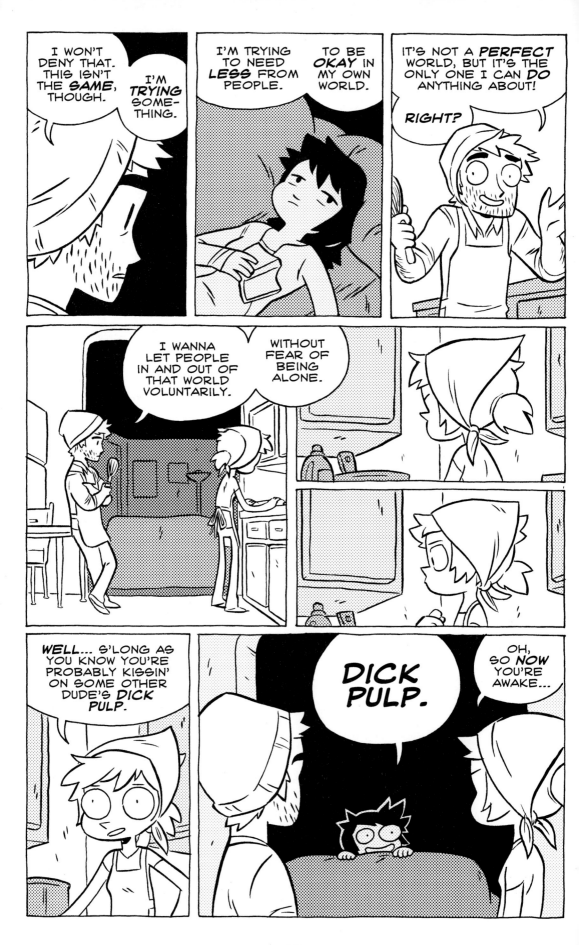

I WON'T DENY THAT. THIS ISN'T THE **SAME**, THOUGH.

I'M **TRYING** SOMETHING.

I'M TRYING TO NEED **LESS** FROM PEOPLE.

TO BE **OKAY** IN MY OWN WORLD.

IT'S NOT A **PERFECT** WORLD, BUT IT'S THE ONLY ONE I CAN **DO** ANYTHING ABOUT!

RIGHT?

I WANNA LET PEOPLE IN AND OUT OF THAT WORLD VOLUNTARILY.

WITHOUT FEAR OF BEING ALONE.

WELL... S'LONG AS YOU KNOW YOU'RE PROBABLY KISSIN' ON SOME OTHER DUDE'S **DICK PULP.**

DICK PULP.

OH, SO **NOW** YOU'RE AWAKE...

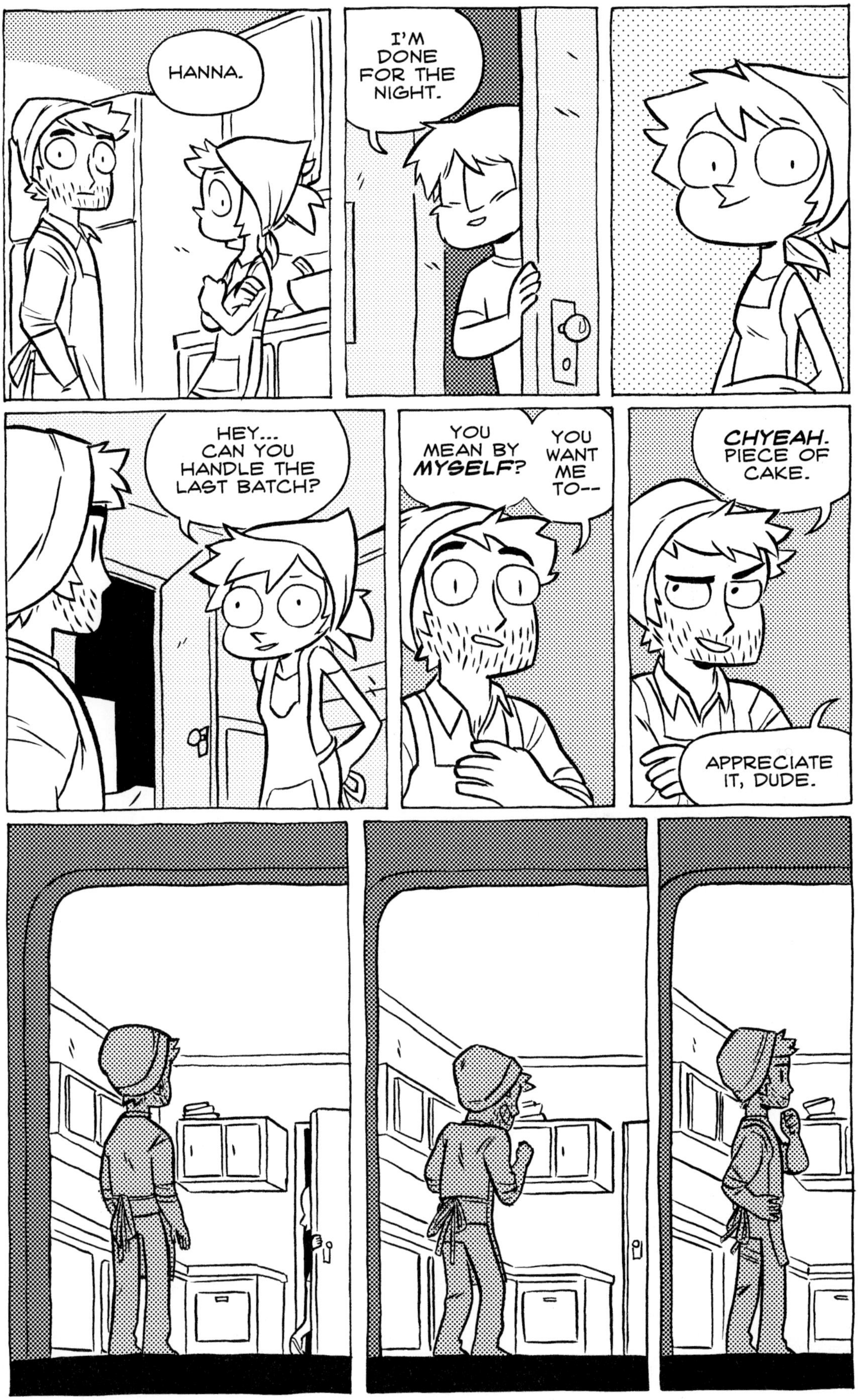
HANNA.
I'M DONE FOR THE NIGHT.
HEY... CAN YOU HANDLE THE LAST BATCH?
YOU MEAN BY *MYSELF*?
YOU WANT ME TO--
CHYEAH. PIECE OF CAKE.
APPRECIATE IT, DUDE.

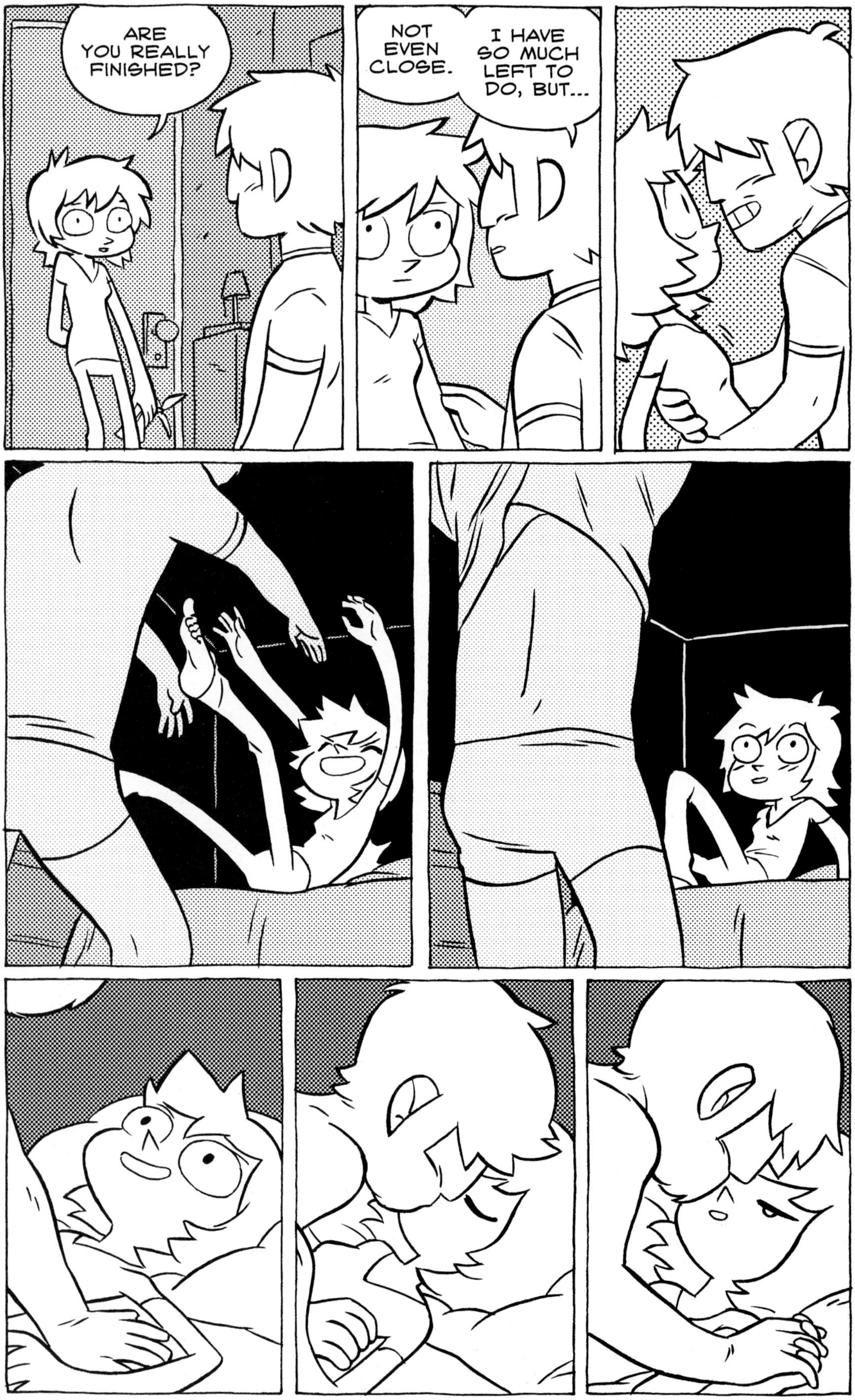
ARE YOU REALLY FINISHED?
NOT EVEN CLOSE.
I HAVE SO MUCH LEFT TO DO, BUT...

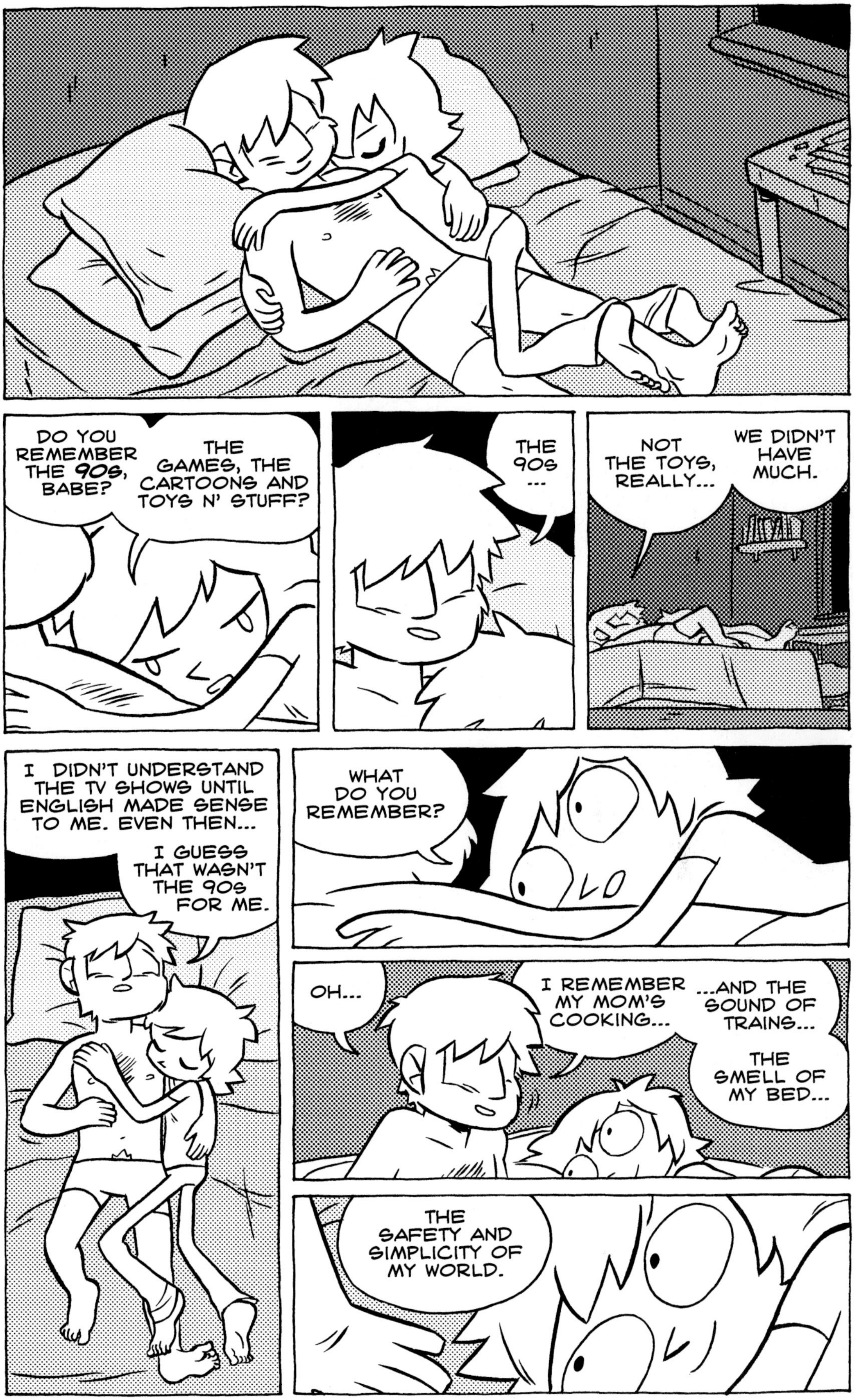
DO YOU REMEMBER THE 90s, BABE?
THE GAMES, THE CARTOONS AND TOYS N' STUFF?
THE 90s ...
NOT THE TOYS, REALLY...
WE DIDN'T HAVE MUCH.
I DIDN'T UNDERSTAND THE TV SHOWS UNTIL ENGLISH MADE SENSE TO ME. EVEN THEN...
I GUESS THAT WASN'T THE 90s FOR ME.
WHAT DO YOU REMEMBER?
OH...
I REMEMBER MY MOM'S COOKING...
...AND THE SOUND OF TRAINS...
THE SMELL OF MY BED...
THE SAFETY AND SIMPLICITY OF MY WORLD.

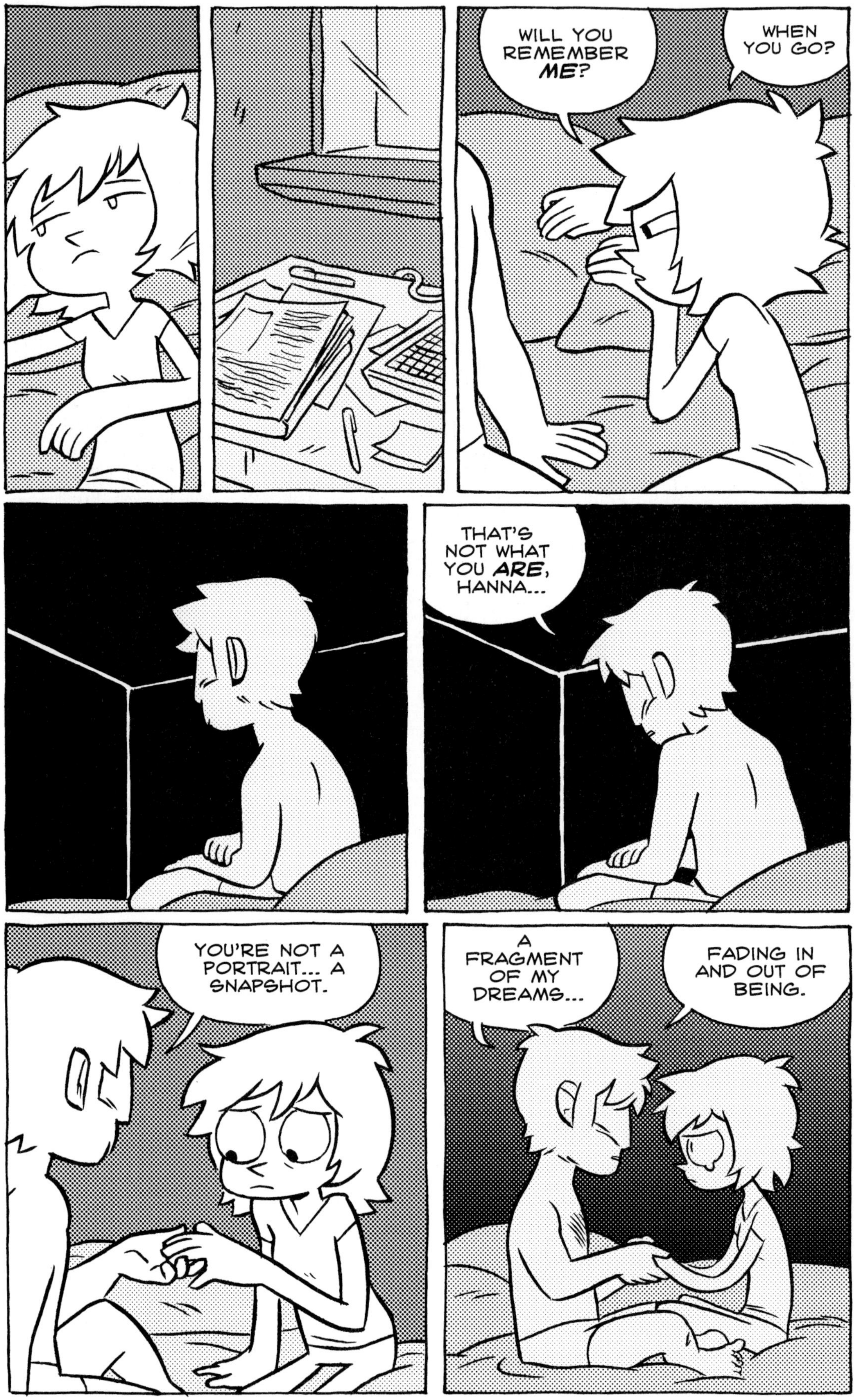
WILL YOU REMEMBER ME?
WHEN YOU GO?
THAT'S NOT WHAT YOU ARE, HANNA...
YOU'RE NOT A PORTRAIT... A SNAPSHOT.
A FRAGMENT OF MY DREAMS...
FADING IN AND OUT OF BEING.

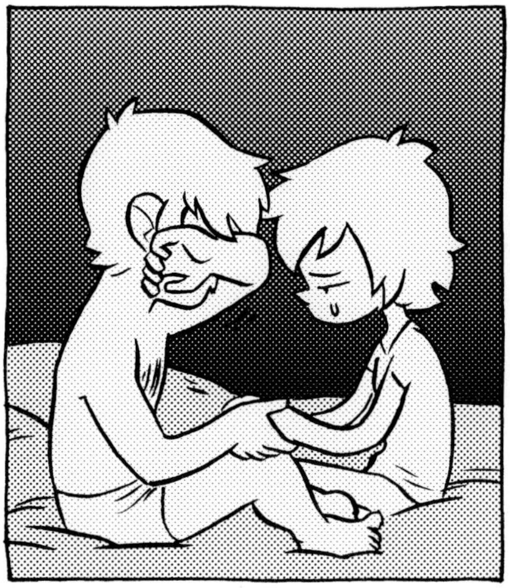

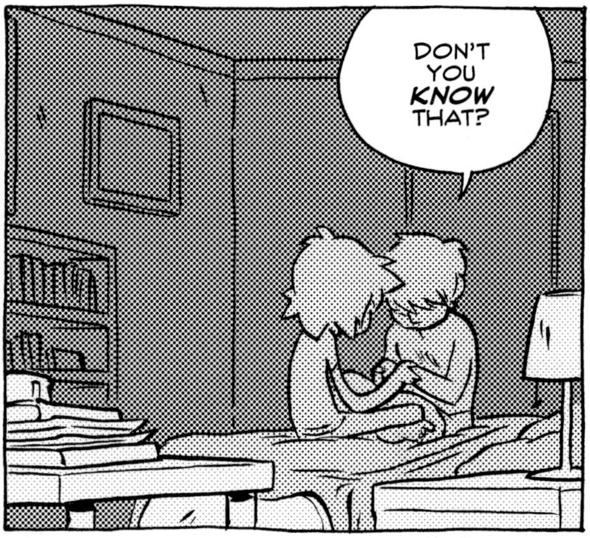
DON'T YOU KNOW THAT?

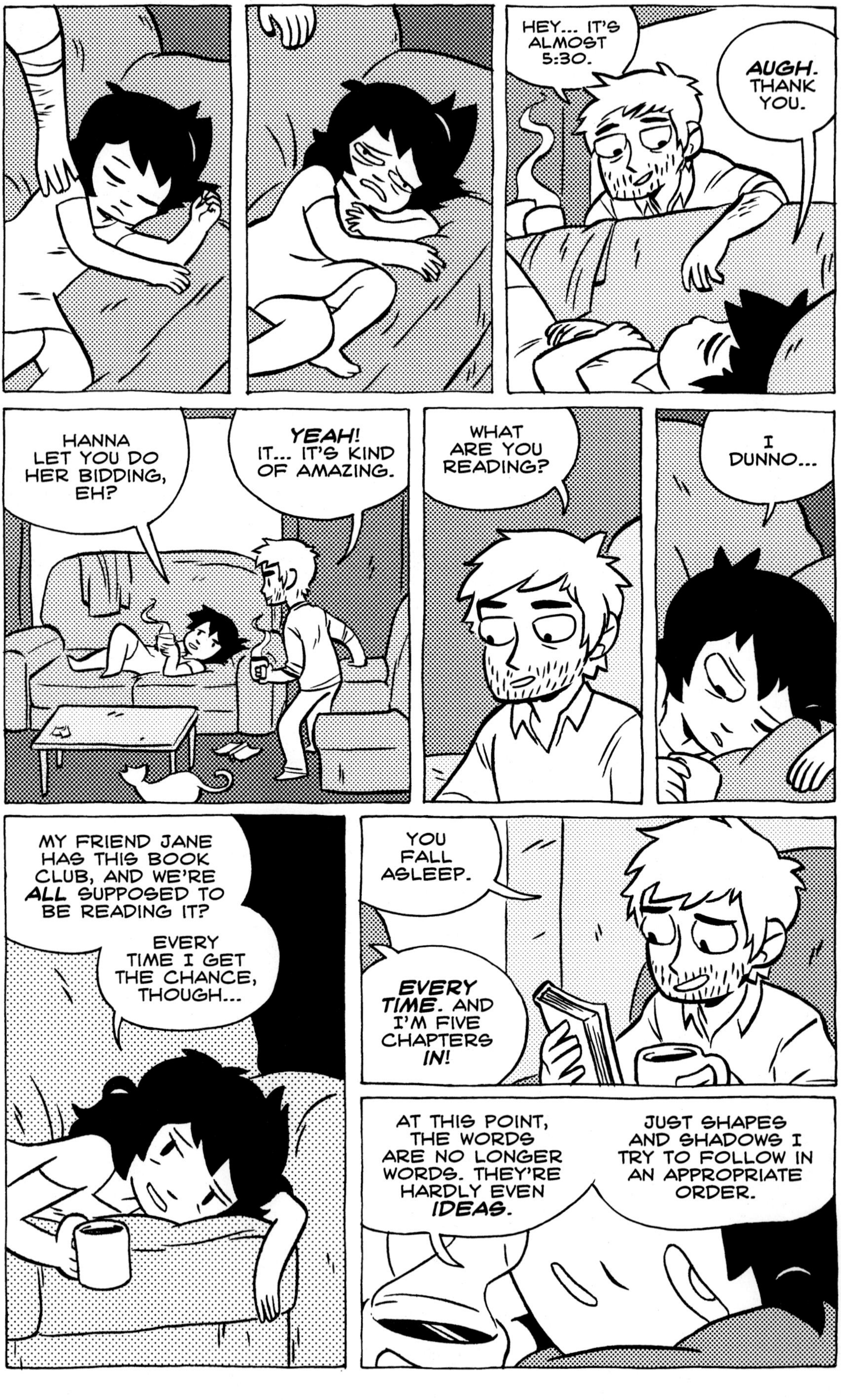
HEY... IT'S ALMOST 5:30.
AUGH. THANK YOU.
HANNA LET YOU DO HER BIDDING, EH?
YEAH! IT... IT'S KIND OF AMAZING.
WHAT ARE YOU READING?
I DUNNO...
MY FRIEND JANE HAS THIS BOOK CLUB, AND WE'RE ALL SUPPOSED TO BE READING IT?
EVERY TIME I GET THE CHANCE, THOUGH...
YOU FALL ASLEEP.
EVERY TIME. AND I'M FIVE CHAPTERS IN!
AT THIS POINT, THE WORDS ARE NO LONGER WORDS. THEY'RE HARDLY EVEN IDEAS.
JUST SHAPES AND SHADOWS I TRY TO FOLLOW IN AN APPROPRIATE ORDER.

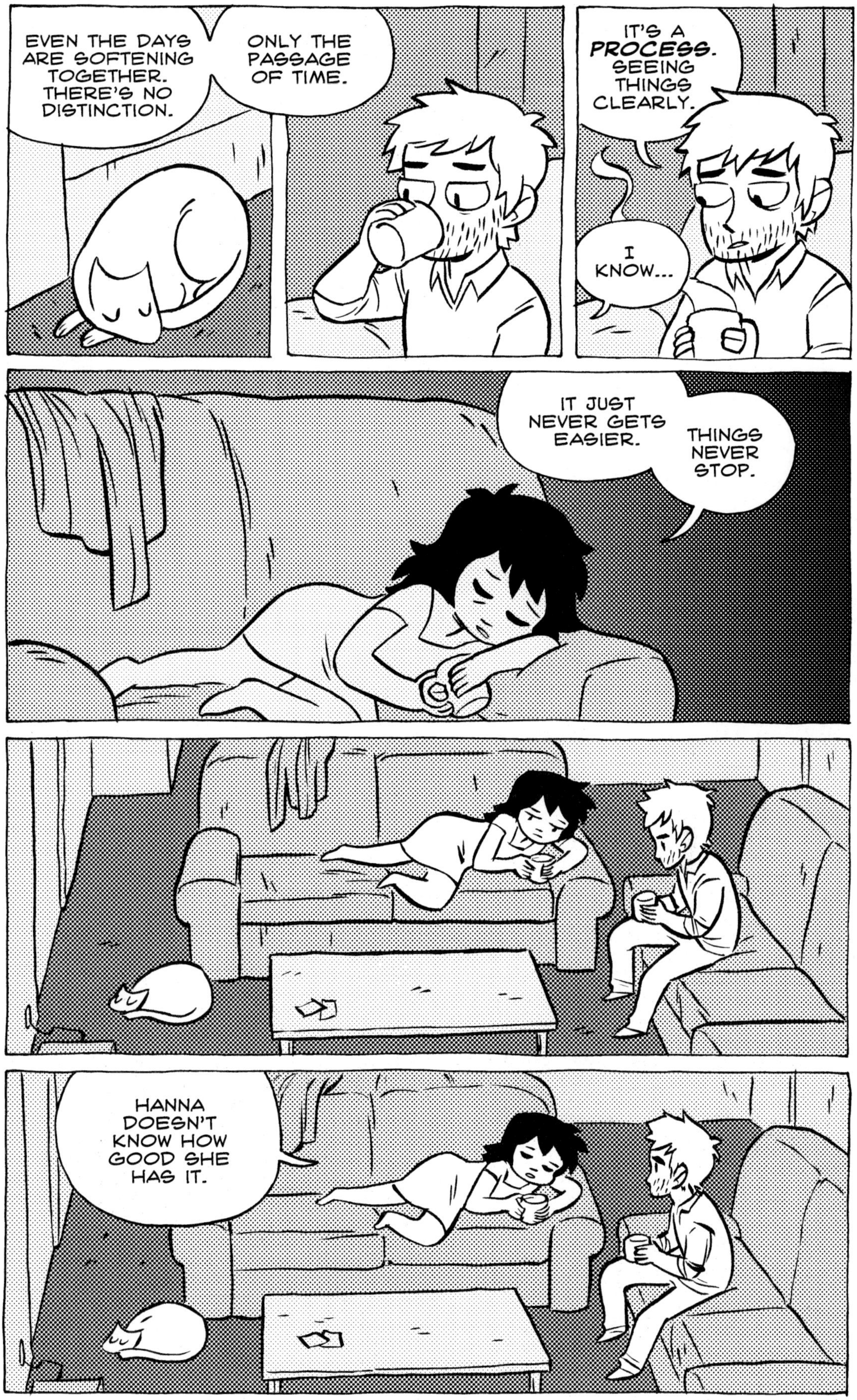
EVEN THE DAYS ARE SOFTENING TOGETHER. THERE'S NO DISTINCTION.
ONLY THE PASSAGE OF TIME.
IT'S A PROCESS. SEEING THINGS CLEARLY.
I KNOW...
IT JUST NEVER GETS EASIER.
THINGS NEVER STOP.
HANNA DOESN'T KNOW HOW GOOD SHE HAS IT.

42

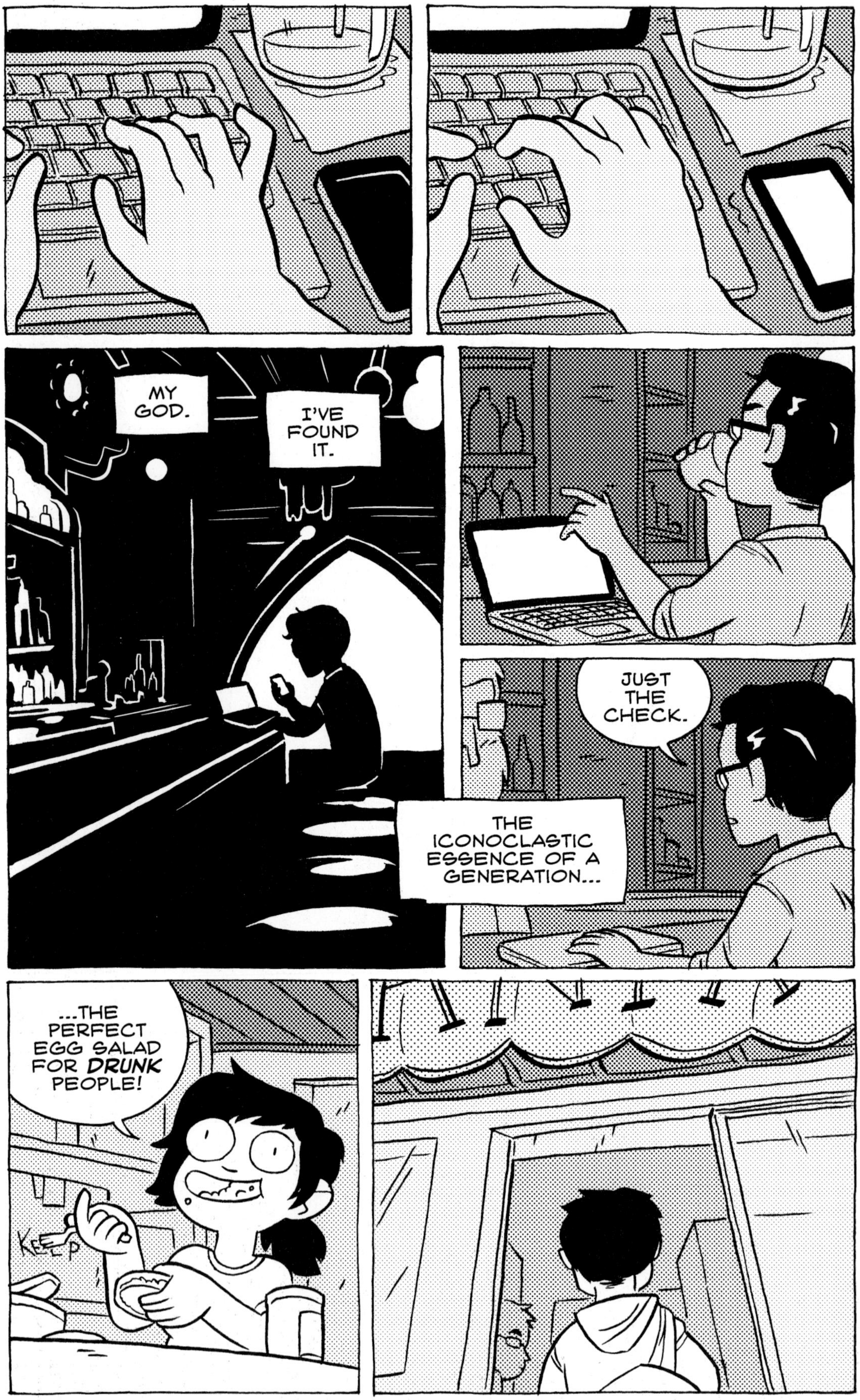

MY GOD.
I'VE FOUND IT.
JUST THE CHECK.
THE ICONOCLASTIC ESSENCE OF A GENERATION...
...THE PERFECT EGG SALAD FOR DRUNK PEOPLE!

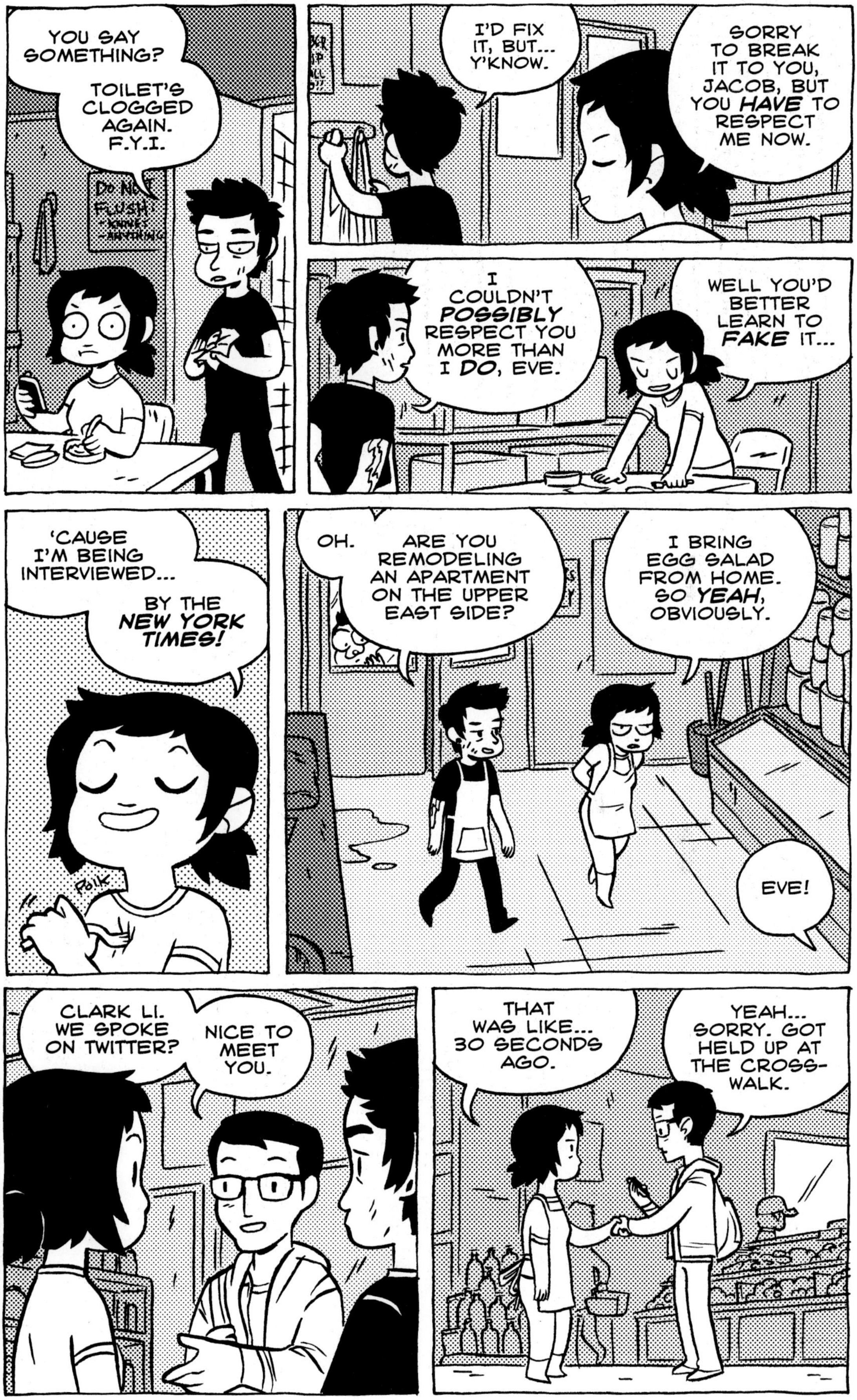
YOU SAY SOMETHING?
TOILET'S CLOGGED AGAIN. F.Y.I.
DO NOT FLUSH
I'D FIX IT, BUT... Y'KNOW.
SORRY TO BREAK IT TO YOU, JACOB, BUT YOU HAVE TO RESPECT ME NOW.
I COULDN'T POSSIBLY RESPECT YOU MORE THAN I DO, EVE.
WELL YOU'D BETTER LEARN TO FAKE IT...
'CAUSE I'M BEING INTERVIEWED...
BY THE NEW YORK TIMES!
POIK
OH.
ARE YOU REMODELING AN APARTMENT ON THE UPPER EAST SIDE?
I BRING EGG SALAD FROM HOME. SO YEAH, OBVIOUSLY.
EVE!
CLARK LI. WE SPOKE ON TWITTER?
NICE TO MEET YOU.
THAT WAS LIKE... 30 SECONDS AGO.
YEAH... SORRY. GOT HELD UP AT THE CROSS-WALK.

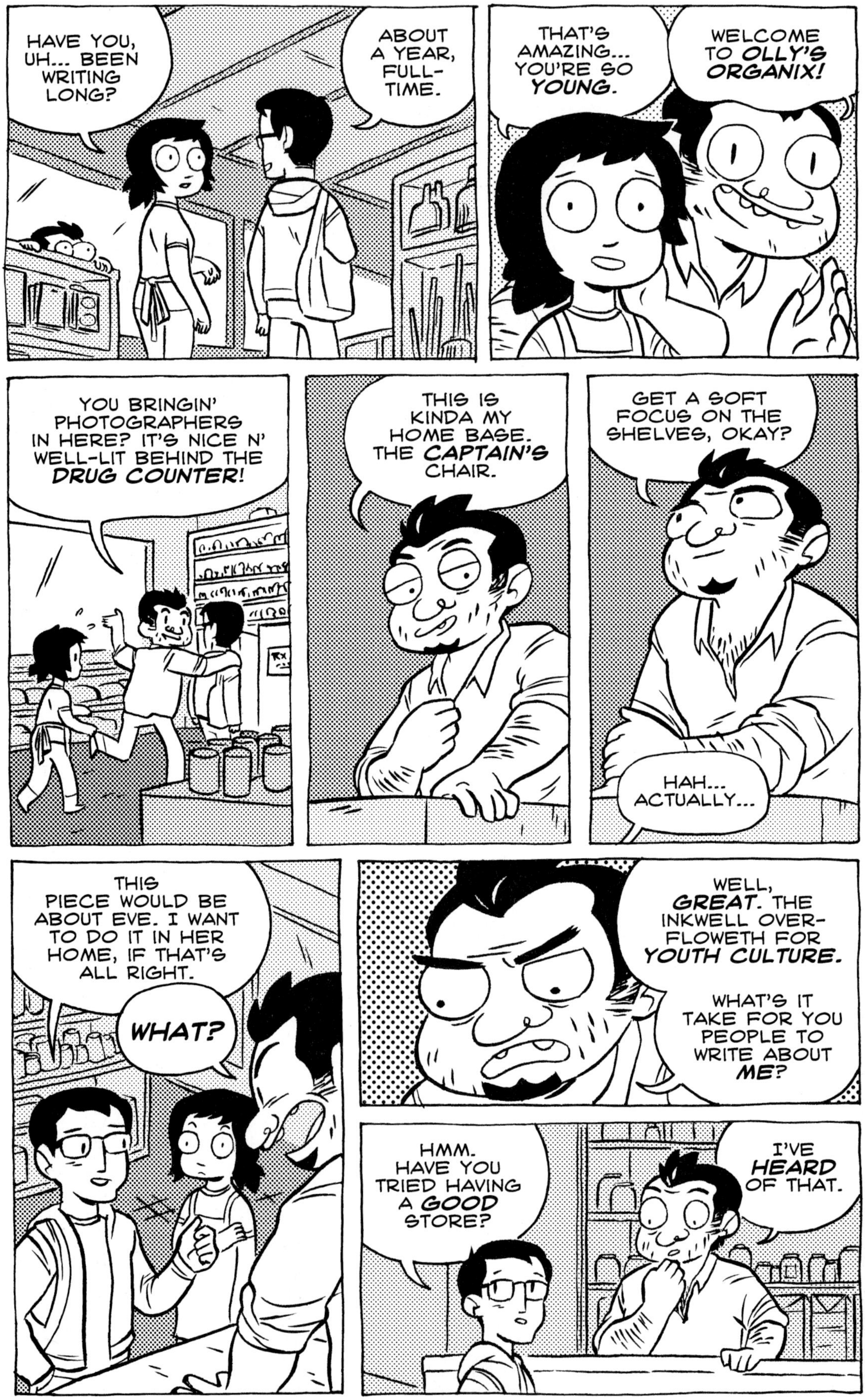
HAVE YOU, UH... BEEN WRITING LONG?
ABOUT A YEAR, FULL-TIME.
THAT'S AMAZING... YOU'RE SO YOUNG.
WELCOME TO OLLY'S ORGANIX!
YOU BRINGIN' PHOTOGRAPHERS IN HERE? IT'S NICE N' WELL-LIT BEHIND THE DRUG COUNTER!
THIS IS KINDA MY HOME BASE. THE CAPTAIN'S CHAIR.
GET A SOFT FOCUS ON THE SHELVES, OKAY?
HAH... ACTUALLY...
THIS PIECE WOULD BE ABOUT EVE. I WANT TO DO IT IN HER HOME, IF THAT'S ALL RIGHT.
WHAT?
WELL, GREAT. THE INKWELL OVER-FLOWETH FOR YOUTH CULTURE.
WHAT'S IT TAKE FOR YOU PEOPLE TO WRITE ABOUT ME?
HMM. HAVE YOU TRIED HAVING A GOOD STORE?
I'VE HEARD OF THAT.

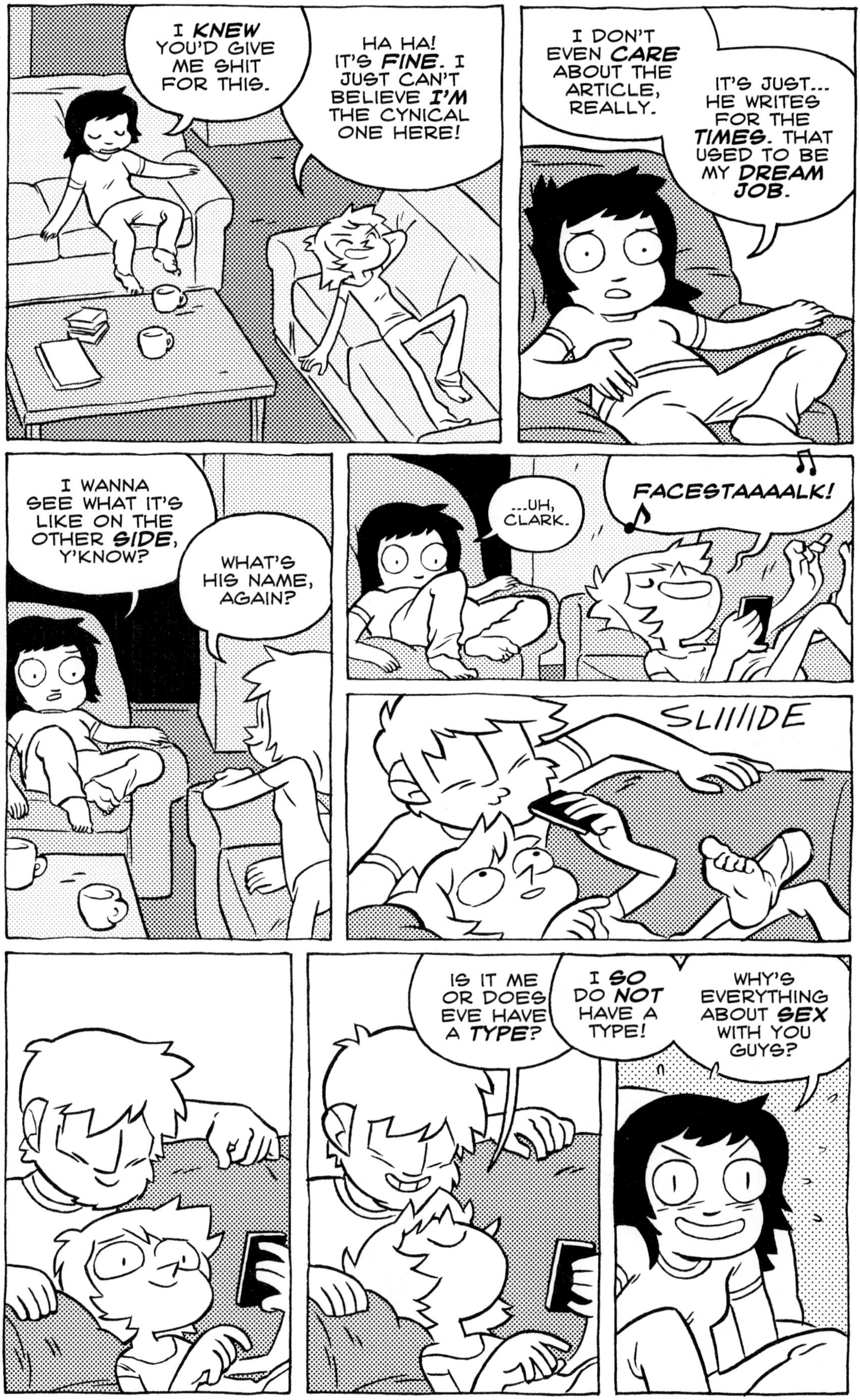
I KNEW YOU'D GIVE ME SHIT FOR THIS.
HA HA! IT'S FINE. I JUST CAN'T BELIEVE I'M THE CYNICAL ONE HERE!
I DON'T EVEN CARE ABOUT THE ARTICLE, REALLY.
IT'S JUST... HE WRITES FOR THE TIMES. THAT USED TO BE MY DREAM JOB.
I WANNA SEE WHAT IT'S LIKE ON THE OTHER SIDE, Y'KNOW?
WHAT'S HIS NAME, AGAIN?
...UH, CLARK.
FACESTAAAALK!
SLIIIIDE
IS IT ME OR DOES EVE HAVE A TYPE?
I SO DO NOT HAVE A TYPE!
WHY'S EVERYTHING ABOUT SEX WITH YOU GUYS?

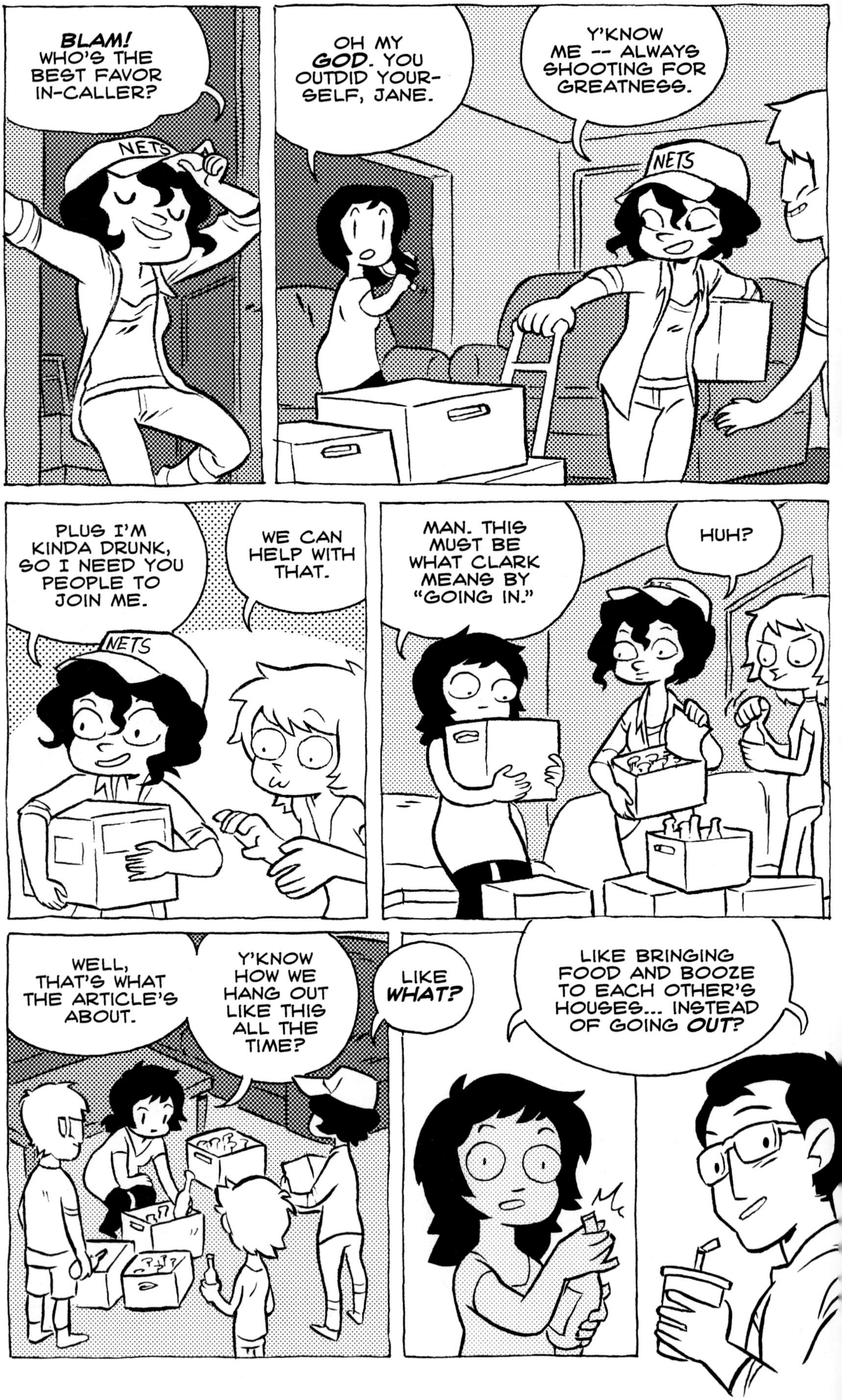
BLAM! WHO'S THE BEST FAVOR IN-CALLER?
OH MY GOD. YOU OUTDID YOUR-SELF, JANE.
Y'KNOW ME -- ALWAYS SHOOTING FOR GREATNESS.
NETS
PLUS I'M KINDA DRUNK, SO I NEED YOU PEOPLE TO JOIN ME.
WE CAN HELP WITH THAT.
MAN. THIS MUST BE WHAT CLARK MEANS BY "GOING IN."
HUH?
WELL, THAT'S WHAT THE ARTICLE'S ABOUT.
Y'KNOW HOW WE HANG OUT LIKE THIS ALL THE TIME?
LIKE WHAT?
LIKE BRINGING FOOD AND BOOZE TO EACH OTHER'S HOUSES... INSTEAD OF GOING OUT?

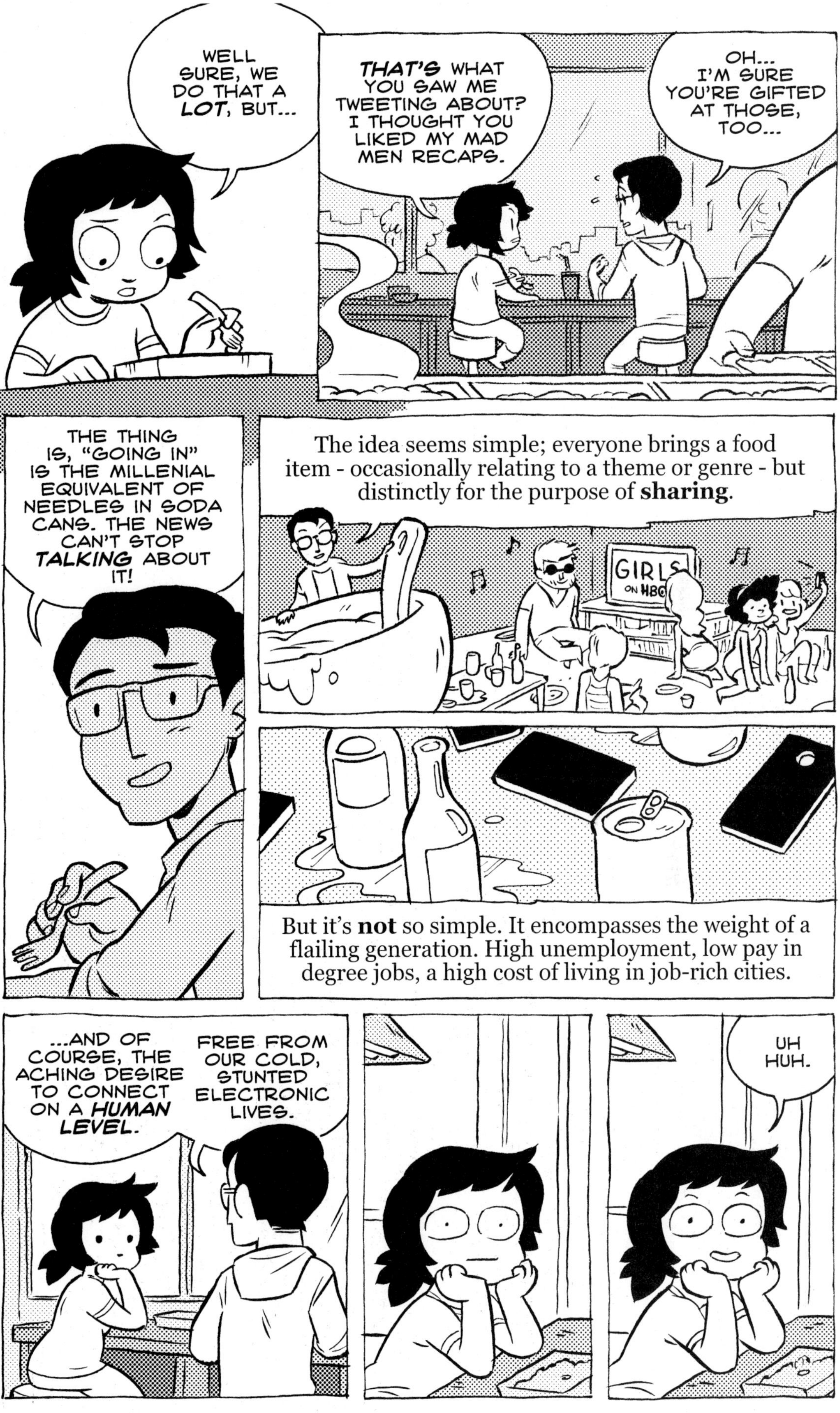
WELL SURE, WE DO THAT A *LOT*, BUT...
THAT'S WHAT YOU SAW ME TWEETING ABOUT? I THOUGHT YOU LIKED MY MAD MEN RECAPS.
OH... I'M SURE YOU'RE GIFTED AT THOSE, TOO...
THE THING IS, "GOING IN" IS THE MILLENIAL EQUIVALENT OF NEEDLES IN SODA CANS. THE NEWS CAN'T STOP *TALKING* ABOUT IT!
The idea seems simple; everyone brings a food item - occasionally relating to a theme or genre - but distinctly for the purpose of **sharing**.
GIRLS ON HBO
But it's **not** so simple. It encompasses the weight of a flailing generation. High unemployment, low pay in degree jobs, a high cost of living in job-rich cities.
...AND OF COURSE, THE ACHING DESIRE TO CONNECT ON A *HUMAN LEVEL*.
FREE FROM OUR COLD, STUNTED ELECTRONIC LIVES.
UH HUH.

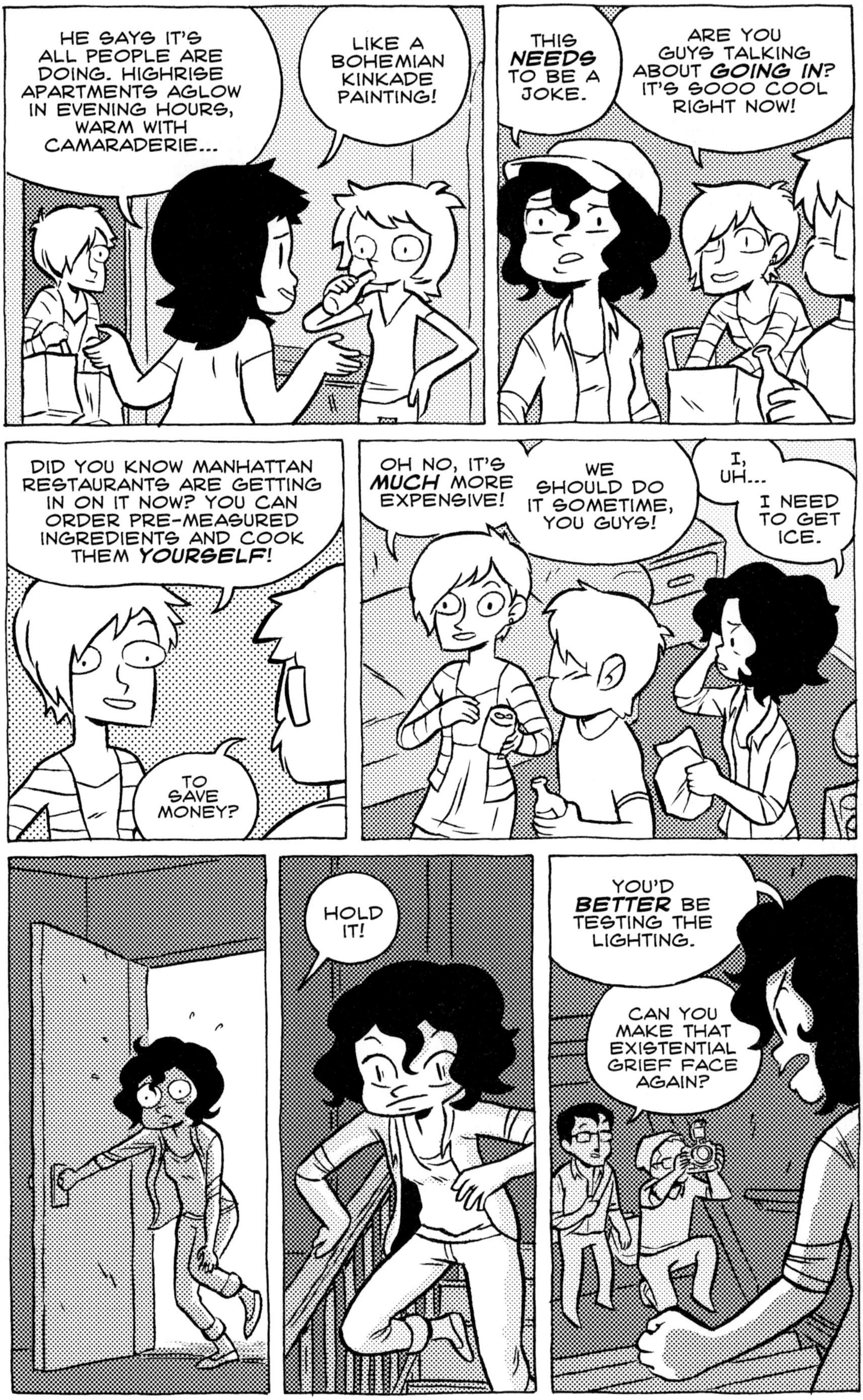
HE SAYS IT'S ALL PEOPLE ARE DOING. HIGHRISE APARTMENTS AGLOW IN EVENING HOURS, WARM WITH CAMARADERIE...
LIKE A BOHEMIAN KINKADE PAINTING!
THIS NEEDS TO BE A JOKE.
ARE YOU GUYS TALKING ABOUT GOING IN? IT'S SOOO COOL RIGHT NOW!
DID YOU KNOW MANHATTAN RESTAURANTS ARE GETTING IN ON IT NOW? YOU CAN ORDER PRE-MEASURED INGREDIENTS AND COOK THEM YOURSELF!
TO SAVE MONEY?
OH NO, IT'S MUCH MORE EXPENSIVE!
WE SHOULD DO IT SOMETIME, YOU GUYS!
I, UH...
I NEED TO GET ICE.
HOLD IT!
YOU'D BETTER BE TESTING THE LIGHTING.
CAN YOU MAKE THAT EXISTENTIAL GRIEF FACE AGAIN?

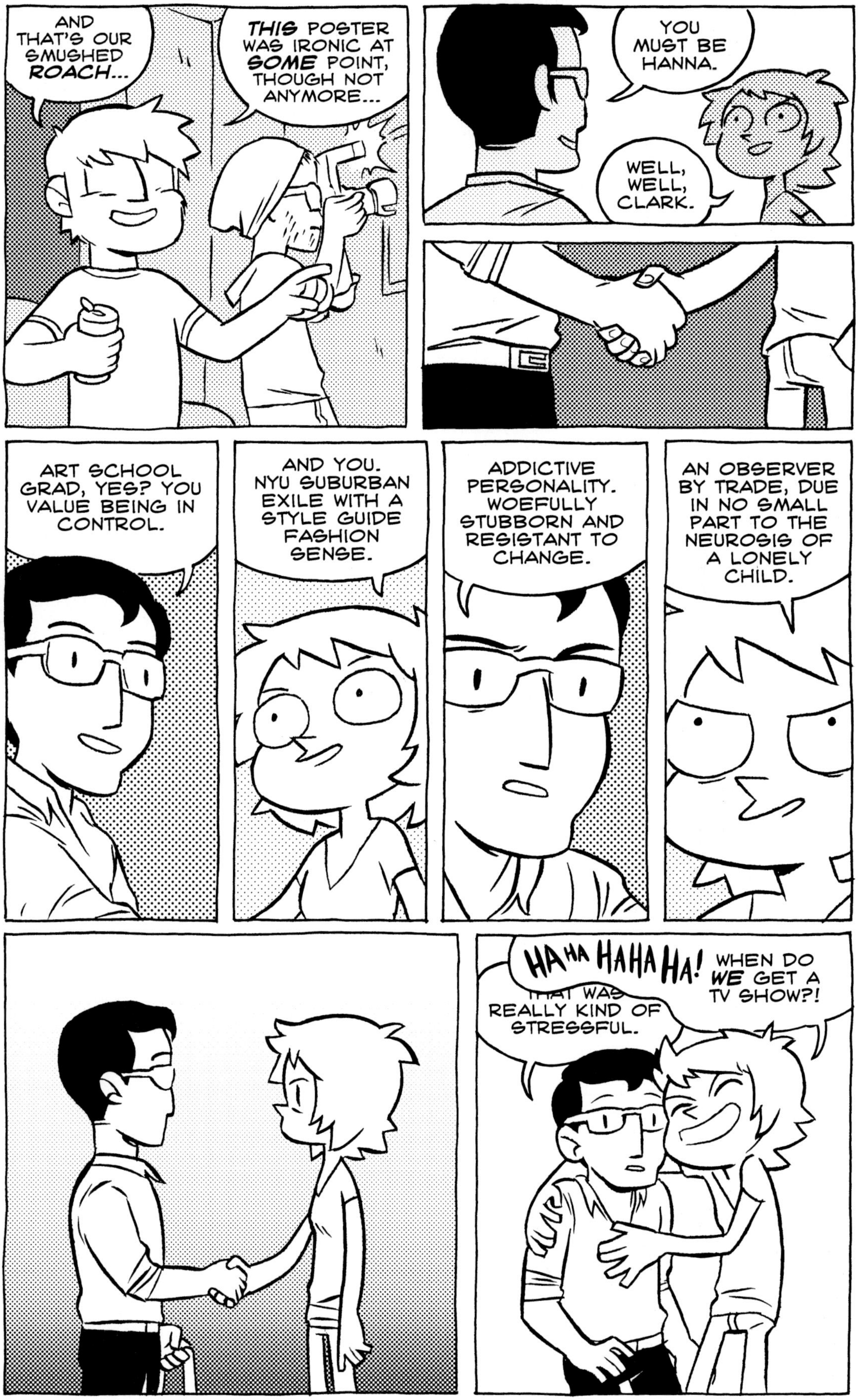
AND THAT'S OUR SMUSHED ROACH...
THIS POSTER WAS IRONIC AT SOME POINT, THOUGH NOT ANYMORE...
YOU MUST BE HANNA.
WELL, WELL, CLARK.
ART SCHOOL GRAD, YES? YOU VALUE BEING IN CONTROL.
AND YOU. NYU SUBURBAN EXILE WITH A STYLE GUIDE FASHION SENSE.
ADDICTIVE PERSONALITY. WOEFULLY STUBBORN AND RESISTANT TO CHANGE.
AN OBSERVER BY TRADE, DUE IN NO SMALL PART TO THE NEUROSIS OF A LONELY CHILD.
HAHA HAHAHA! WHEN DO WE GET A TV SHOW?!
THAT WAS REALLY KIND OF STRESSFUL.

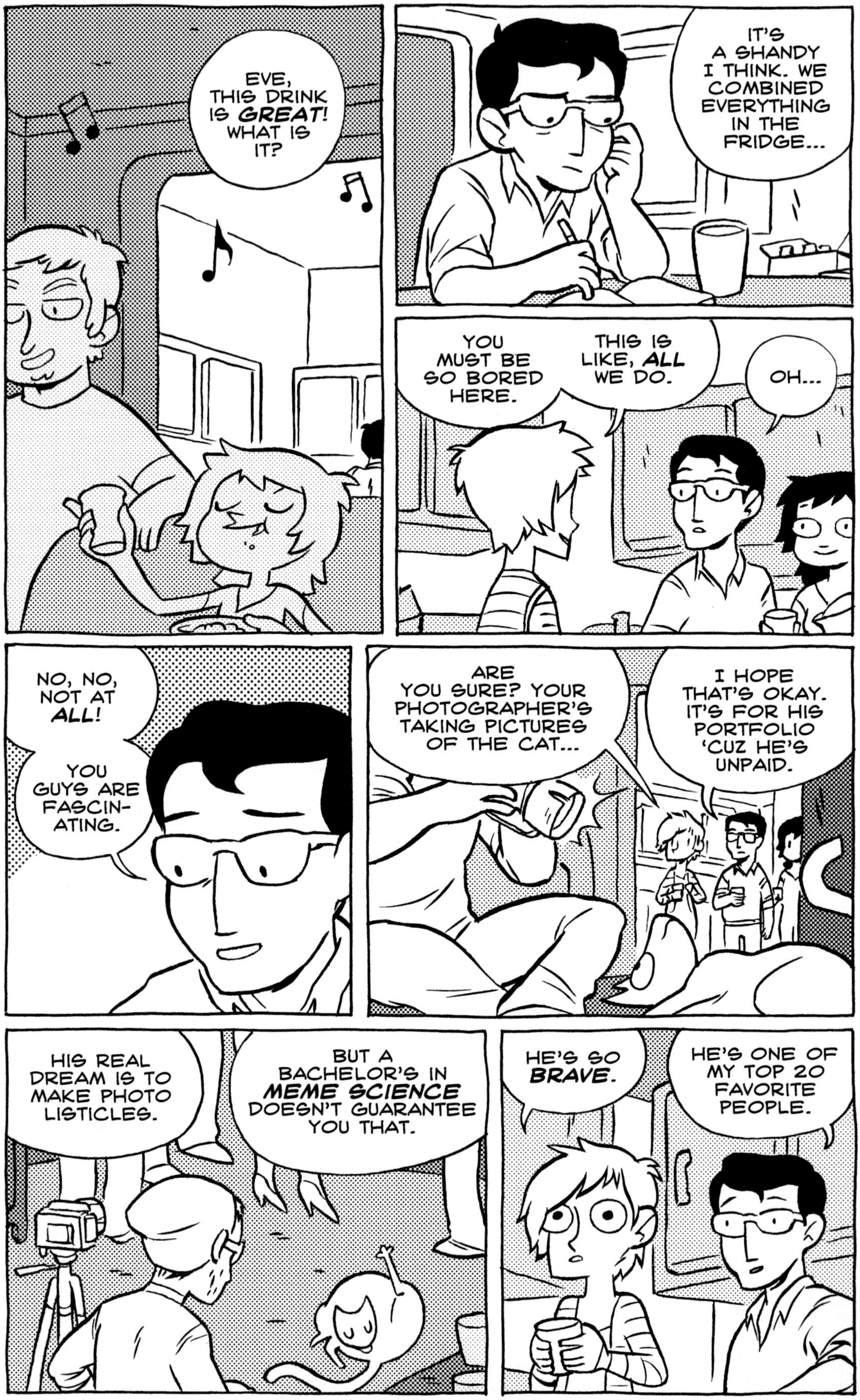
EVE, THIS DRINK IS ***GREAT***! WHAT IS IT?
IT'S A SHANDY I THINK. WE COMBINED EVERYTHING IN THE FRIDGE...
YOU MUST BE SO BORED HERE.
THIS IS LIKE, ***ALL*** WE DO.
OH...
NO, NO, NOT AT ***ALL***!
YOU GUYS ARE FASCIN-ATING.
ARE YOU SURE? YOUR PHOTOGRAPHER'S TAKING PICTURES OF THE CAT...
I HOPE THAT'S OKAY. IT'S FOR HIS PORTFOLIO 'CUZ HE'S UNPAID.
HIS REAL DREAM IS TO MAKE PHOTO LISTICLES.
BUT A BACHELOR'S IN ***MEME SCIENCE*** DOESN'T GUARANTEE YOU THAT.
HE'S SO ***BRAVE***.
HE'S ONE OF MY TOP 20 FAVORITE PEOPLE.

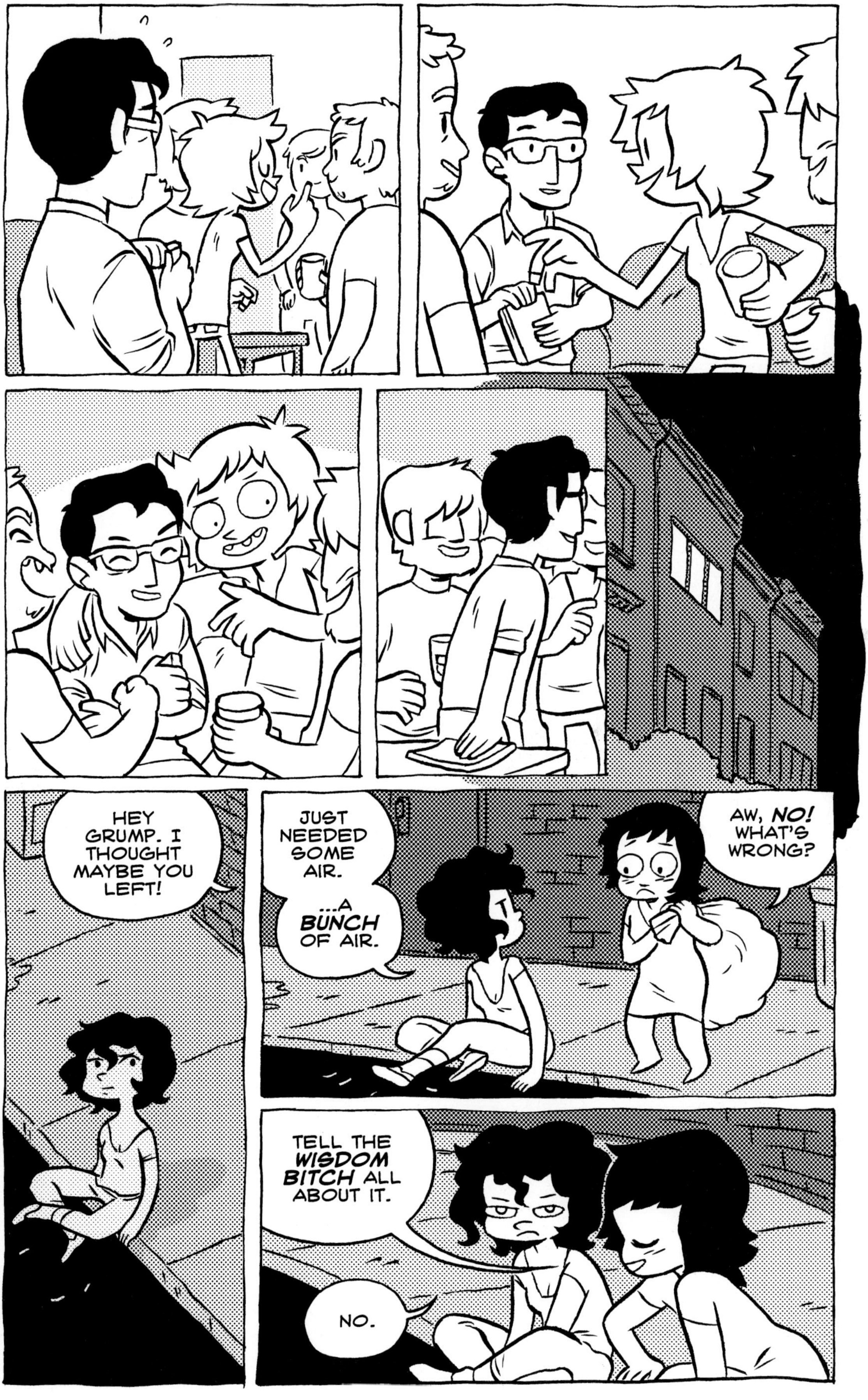
HEY GRUMP. I THOUGHT MAYBE YOU LEFT!
JUST NEEDED SOME AIR.
...A BUNCH OF AIR.
AW, NO! WHAT'S WRONG?
TELL THE WISDOM BITCH ALL ABOUT IT.
NO.

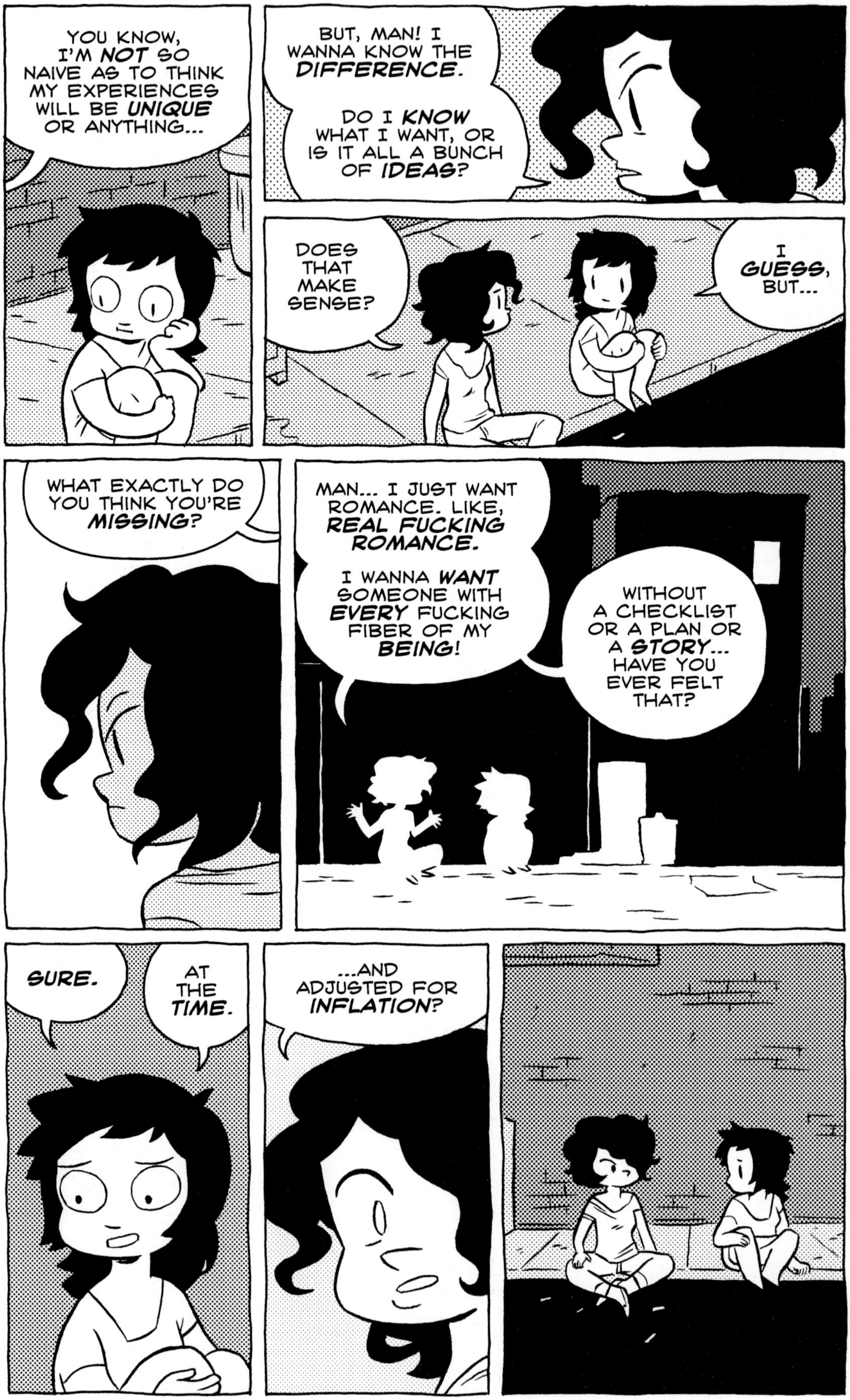
YOU KNOW, I'M NOT SO NAIVE AS TO THINK MY EXPERIENCES WILL BE UNIQUE OR ANYTHING...
BUT, MAN! I WANNA KNOW THE DIFFERENCE.
DO I KNOW WHAT I WANT, OR IS IT ALL A BUNCH OF IDEAS?
DOES THAT MAKE SENSE?
I GUESS, BUT...
WHAT EXACTLY DO YOU THINK YOU'RE MISSING?
MAN... I JUST WANT ROMANCE. LIKE, REAL FUCKING ROMANCE.
I WANNA WANT SOMEONE WITH EVERY FUCKING FIBER OF MY BEING!
WITHOUT A CHECKLIST OR A PLAN OR A STORY... HAVE YOU EVER FELT THAT?
SURE.
AT THE TIME.
...AND ADJUSTED FOR INFLATION?

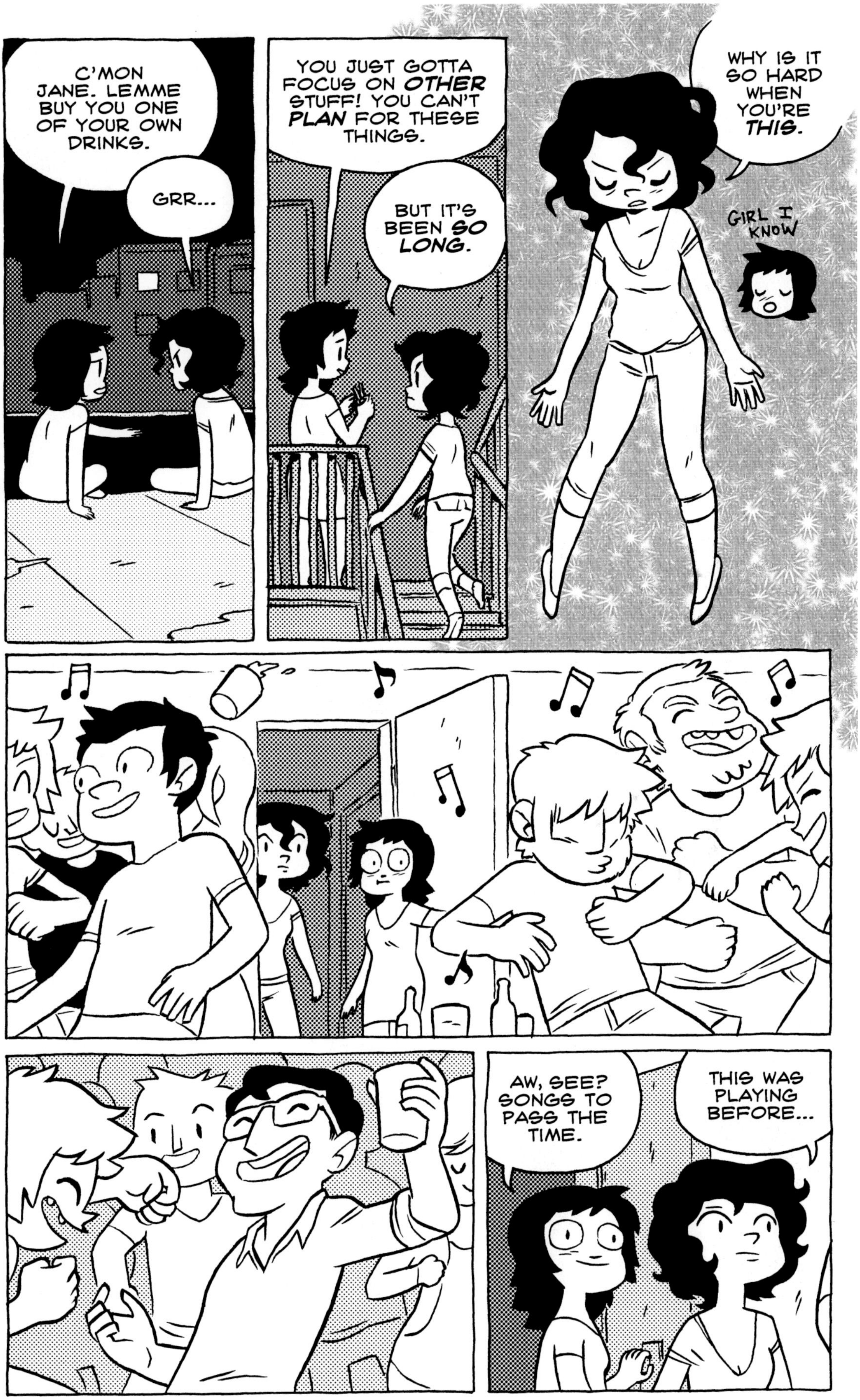
C'MON JANE. LEMME BUY YOU ONE OF YOUR OWN DRINKS.
GRR...
YOU JUST GOTTA FOCUS ON OTHER STUFF! YOU CAN'T PLAN FOR THESE THINGS.
BUT IT'S BEEN SO LONG.
WHY IS IT SO HARD WHEN YOU'RE THIS.
GIRL I KNOW
AW, SEE? SONGS TO PASS THE TIME.
THIS WAS PLAYING BEFORE...

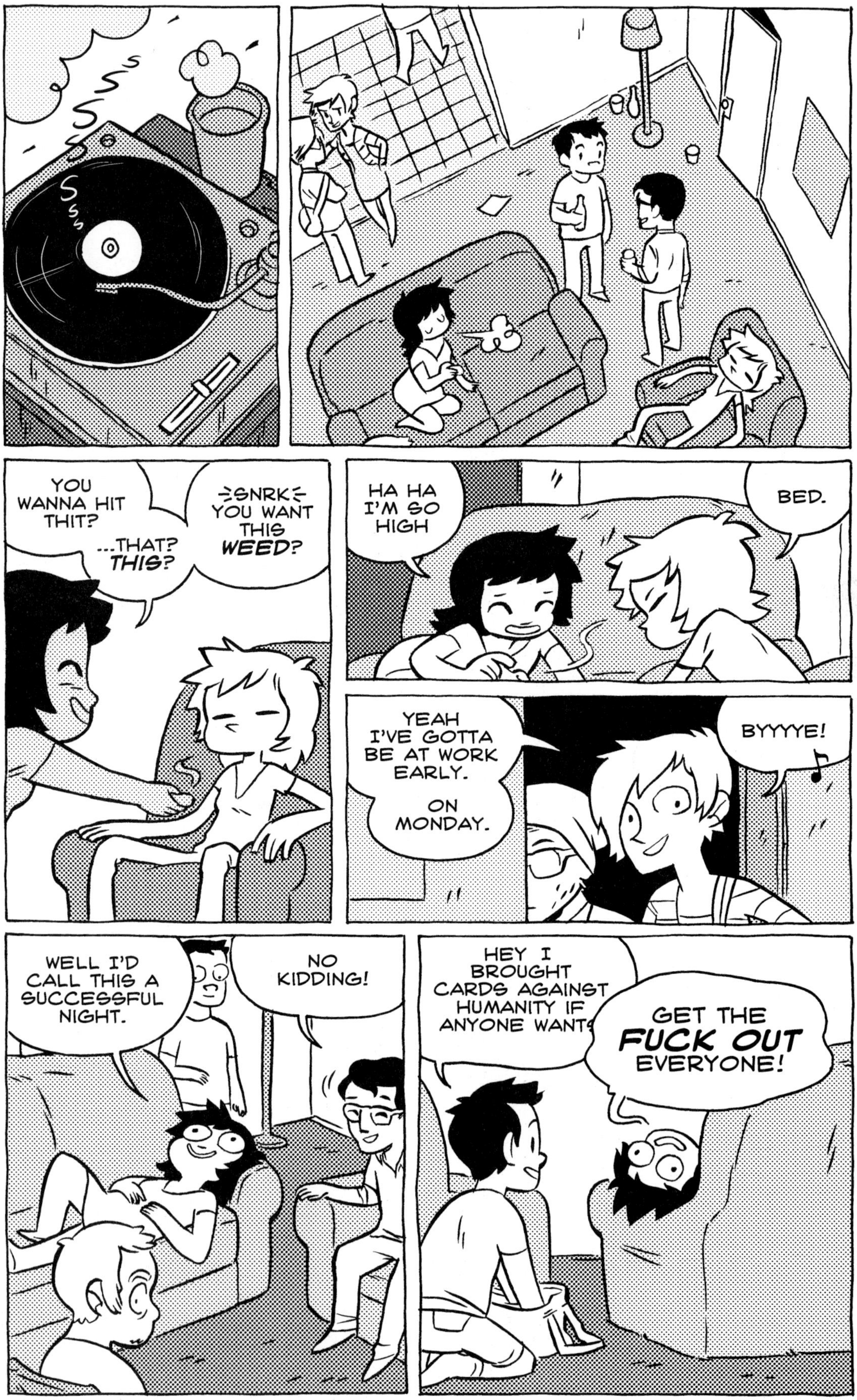

YOU WANNA HIT THIT?
...THAT? THIS?
SNRK YOU WANT THIS WEED?
HA HA I'M SO HIGH
BED.
YEAH I'VE GOTTA BE AT WORK EARLY.
ON MONDAY.
BYYYYE!
WELL I'D CALL THIS A SUCCESSFUL NIGHT.
NO KIDDING!
HEY I BROUGHT CARDS AGAINST HUMANITY IF ANYONE WANTS
GET THE FUCK OUT EVERYONE!

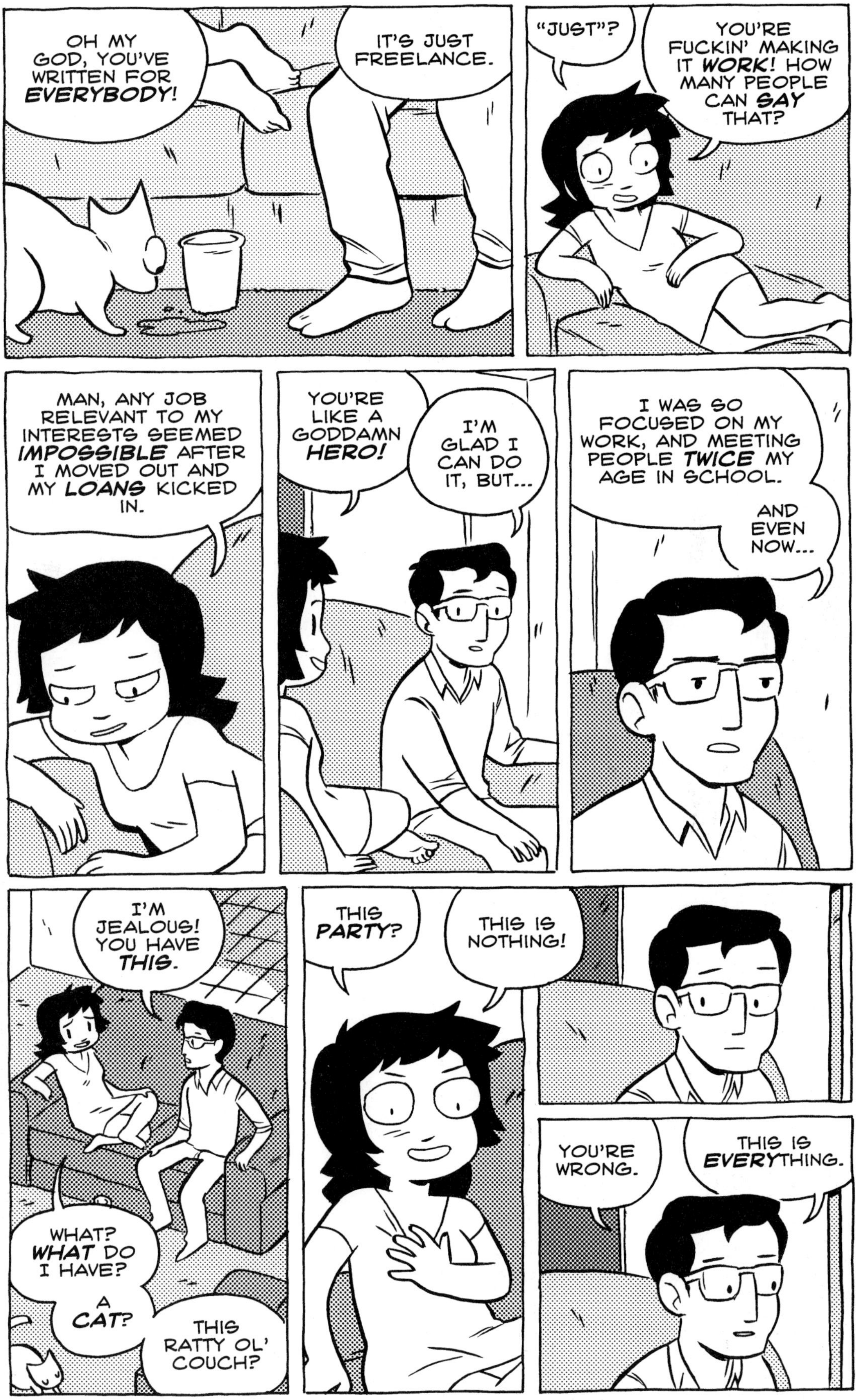
OH MY GOD, YOU'VE WRITTEN FOR EVERYBODY!
IT'S JUST FREELANCE.
"JUST"?
YOU'RE FUCKIN' MAKING IT WORK! HOW MANY PEOPLE CAN SAY THAT?
MAN, ANY JOB RELEVANT TO MY INTERESTS SEEMED IMPOSSIBLE AFTER I MOVED OUT AND MY LOANS KICKED IN.
YOU'RE LIKE A GODDAMN HERO!
I'M GLAD I CAN DO IT, BUT...
I WAS SO FOCUSED ON MY WORK, AND MEETING PEOPLE TWICE MY AGE IN SCHOOL.
AND EVEN NOW...
I'M JEALOUS! YOU HAVE THIS.
WHAT? WHAT DO I HAVE?
A CAT?
THIS RATTY OL' COUCH?
THIS PARTY?
THIS IS NOTHING!
YOU'RE WRONG.
THIS IS EVERYTHING.

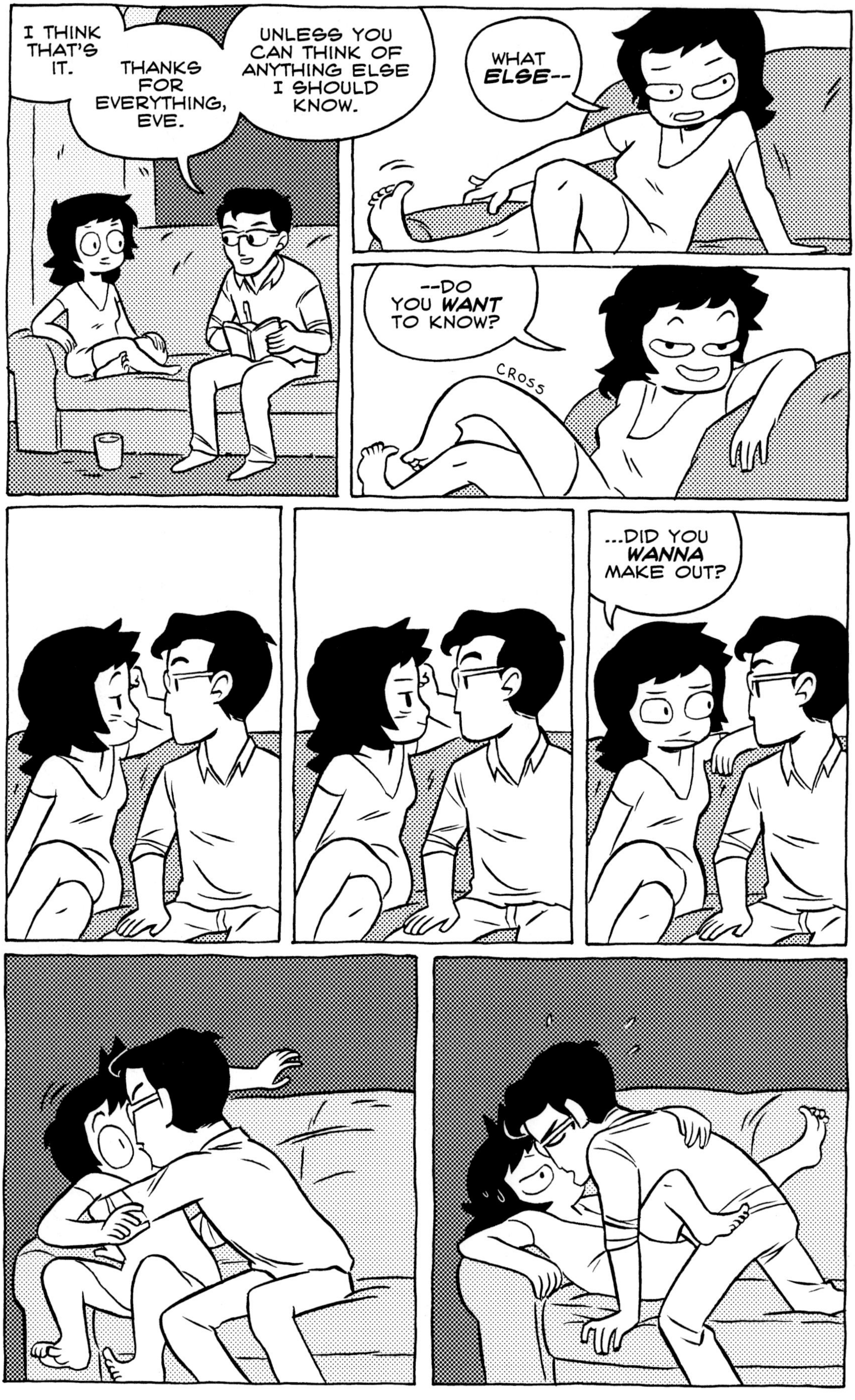
I THINK THAT'S IT.
THANKS FOR EVERYTHING, EVE.
UNLESS YOU CAN THINK OF ANYTHING ELSE I SHOULD KNOW.
WHAT *ELSE*--
--DO YOU *WANT* TO KNOW?
CROSS
...DID YOU *WANNA* MAKE OUT?

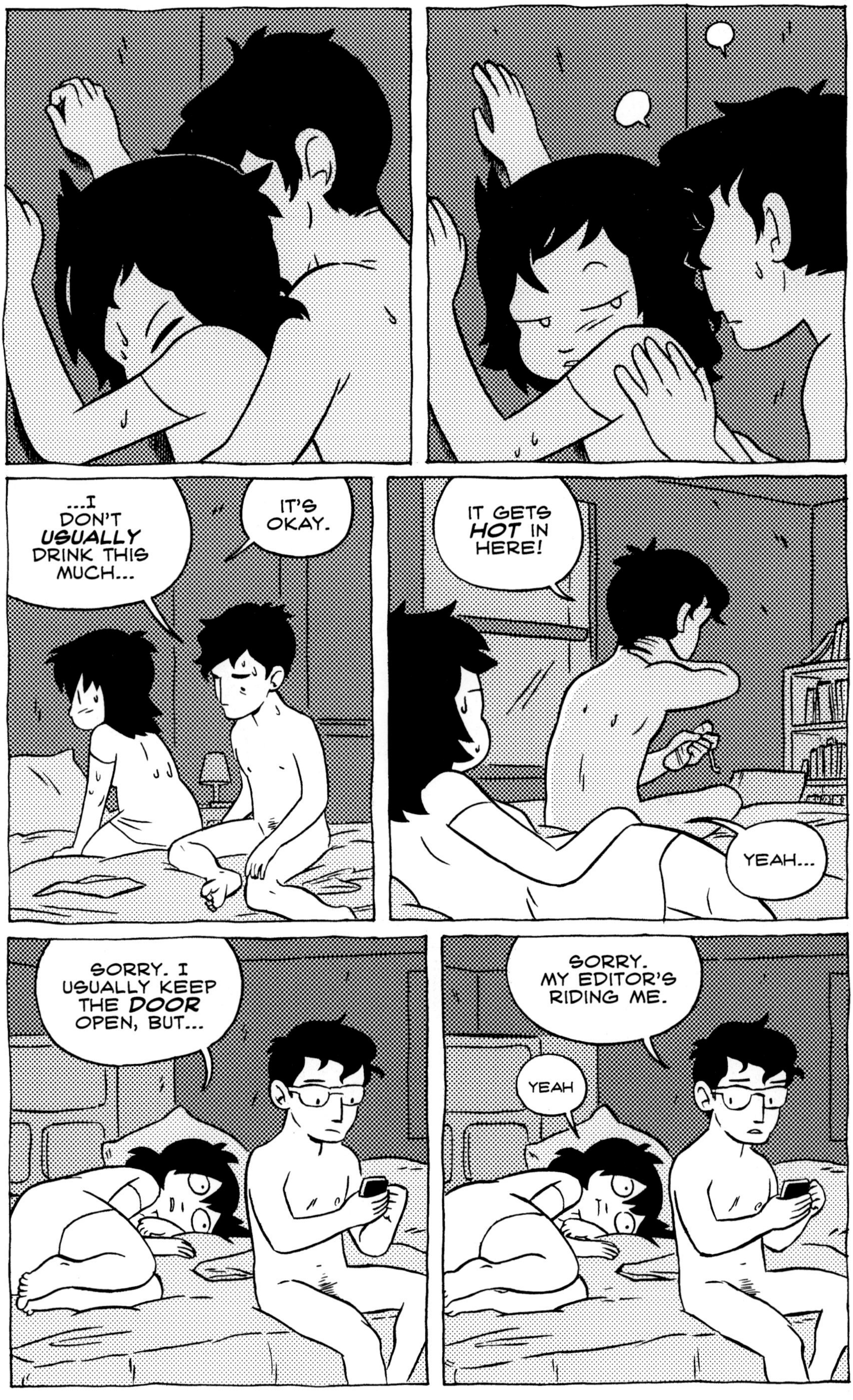
...I DON'T USUALLY DRINK THIS MUCH...
IT'S OKAY.
IT GETS HOT IN HERE!
YEAH...
SORRY. I USUALLY KEEP THE DOOR OPEN, BUT...
SORRY. MY EDITOR'S RIDING ME.
YEAH

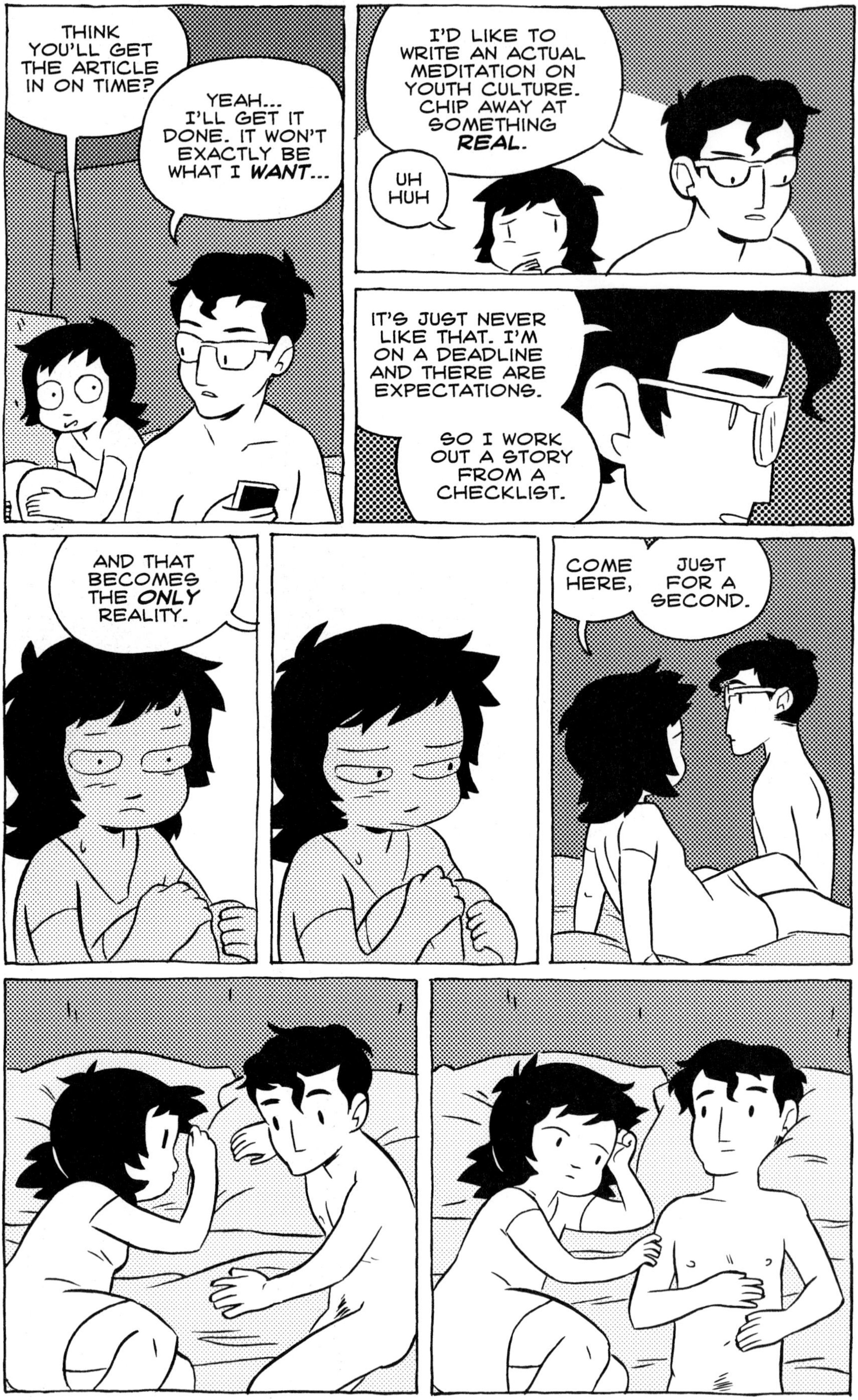
THINK YOU'LL GET THE ARTICLE IN ON TIME?
YEAH... I'LL GET IT DONE. IT WON'T EXACTLY BE WHAT I *WANT*...
I'D LIKE TO WRITE AN ACTUAL MEDITATION ON YOUTH CULTURE. CHIP AWAY AT SOMETHING *REAL*.
UH HUH
IT'S JUST NEVER LIKE THAT. I'M ON A DEADLINE AND THERE ARE EXPECTATIONS.
SO I WORK OUT A STORY FROM A CHECKLIST.
AND THAT BECOMES THE *ONLY* REALITY.
COME HERE,
JUST FOR A SECOND.

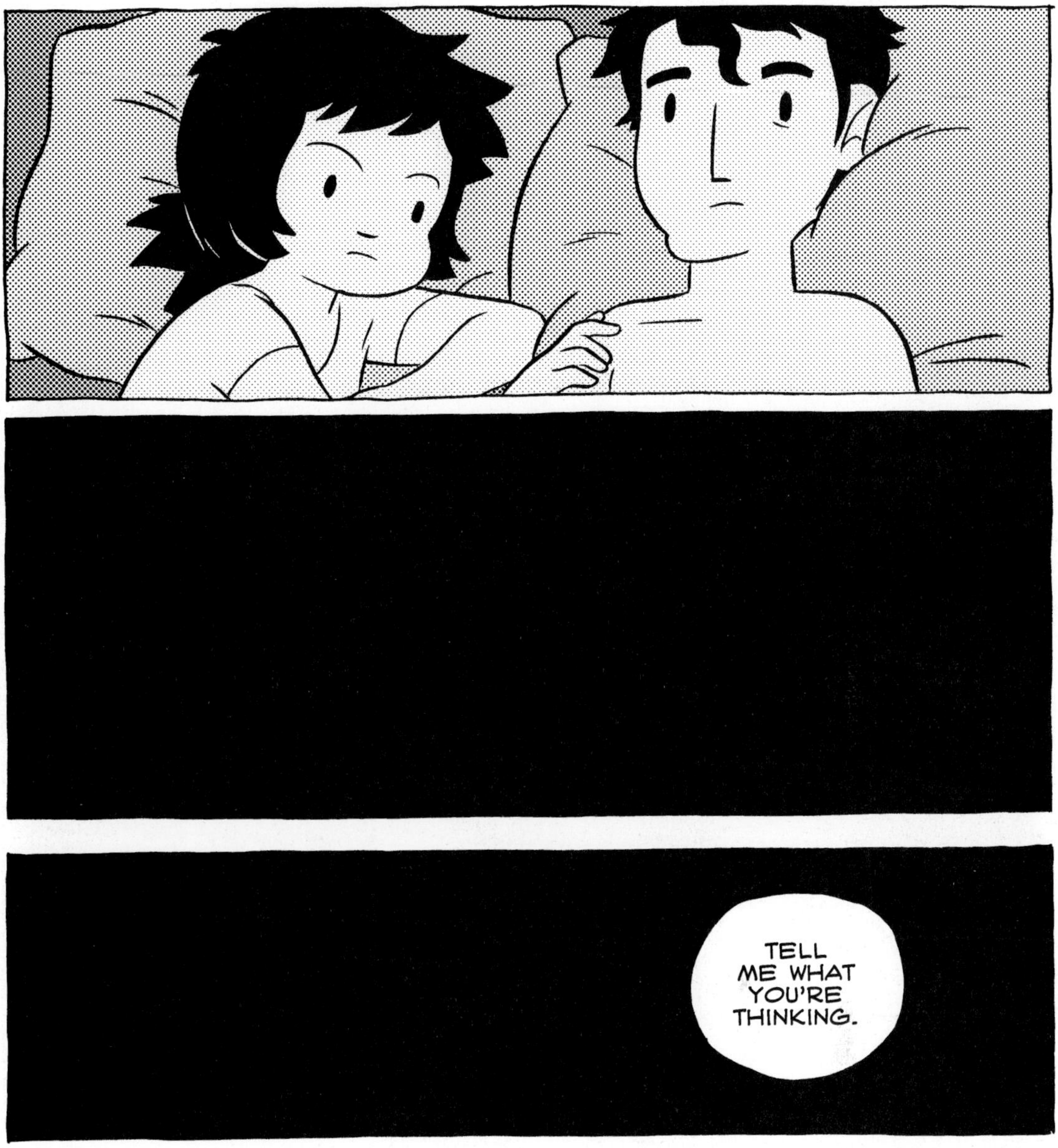
TELL ME WHAT YOU'RE THINKING.

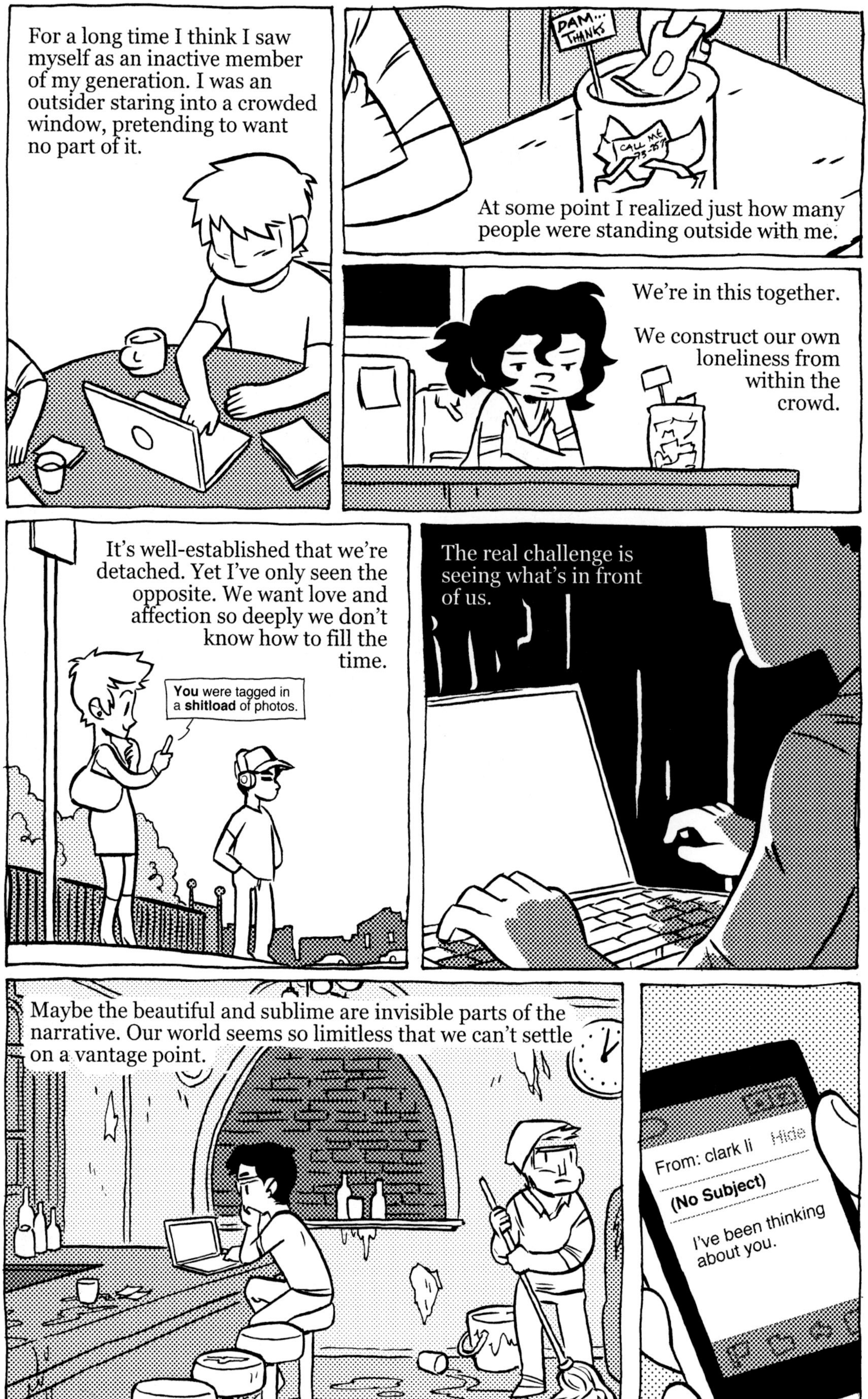
For a long time I think I saw myself as an inactive member of my generation. I was an outsider staring into a crowded window, pretending to want no part of it.
DAM... THANKS
At some point I realized just how many people were standing outside with me.
We're in this together.
We construct our own loneliness from within the crowd.
It's well-established that we're detached. Yet I've only seen the opposite. We want love and affection so deeply we don't know how to fill the time.
You were tagged in a shitload of photos.
The real challenge is seeing what's in front of us.
Maybe the beautiful and sublime are invisible parts of the narrative. Our world seems so limitless that we can't settle on a vantage point.
From: clark li
Hide
(No Subject)
I've been thinking about you.

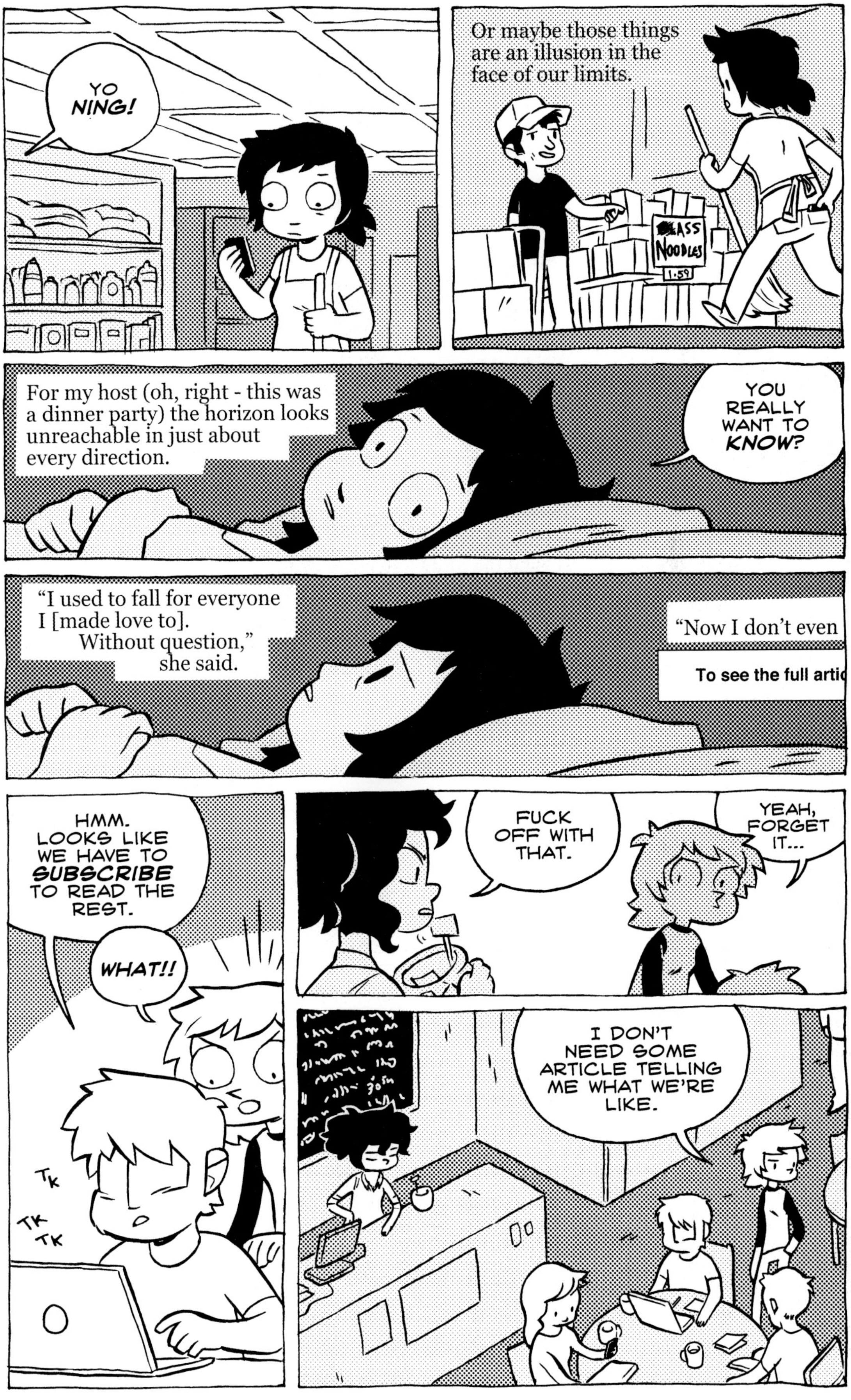
YO NING!
Or maybe those things are an illusion in the face of our limits.
NOODLES
1.59
For my host (oh, right - this was a dinner party) the horizon looks unreachable in just about every direction.
YOU REALLY WANT TO KNOW?
“I used to fall for everyone I [made love to]. Without question,” she said.
“Now I don’t even
To see the full artic
HMM. LOOKS LIKE WE HAVE TO SUBSCRIBE TO READ THE REST.
WHAT!!
TK
TK TK
FUCK OFF WITH THAT.
YEAH, FORGET IT...
I DON’T NEED SOME ARTICLE TELLING ME WHAT WE’RE LIKE.

43

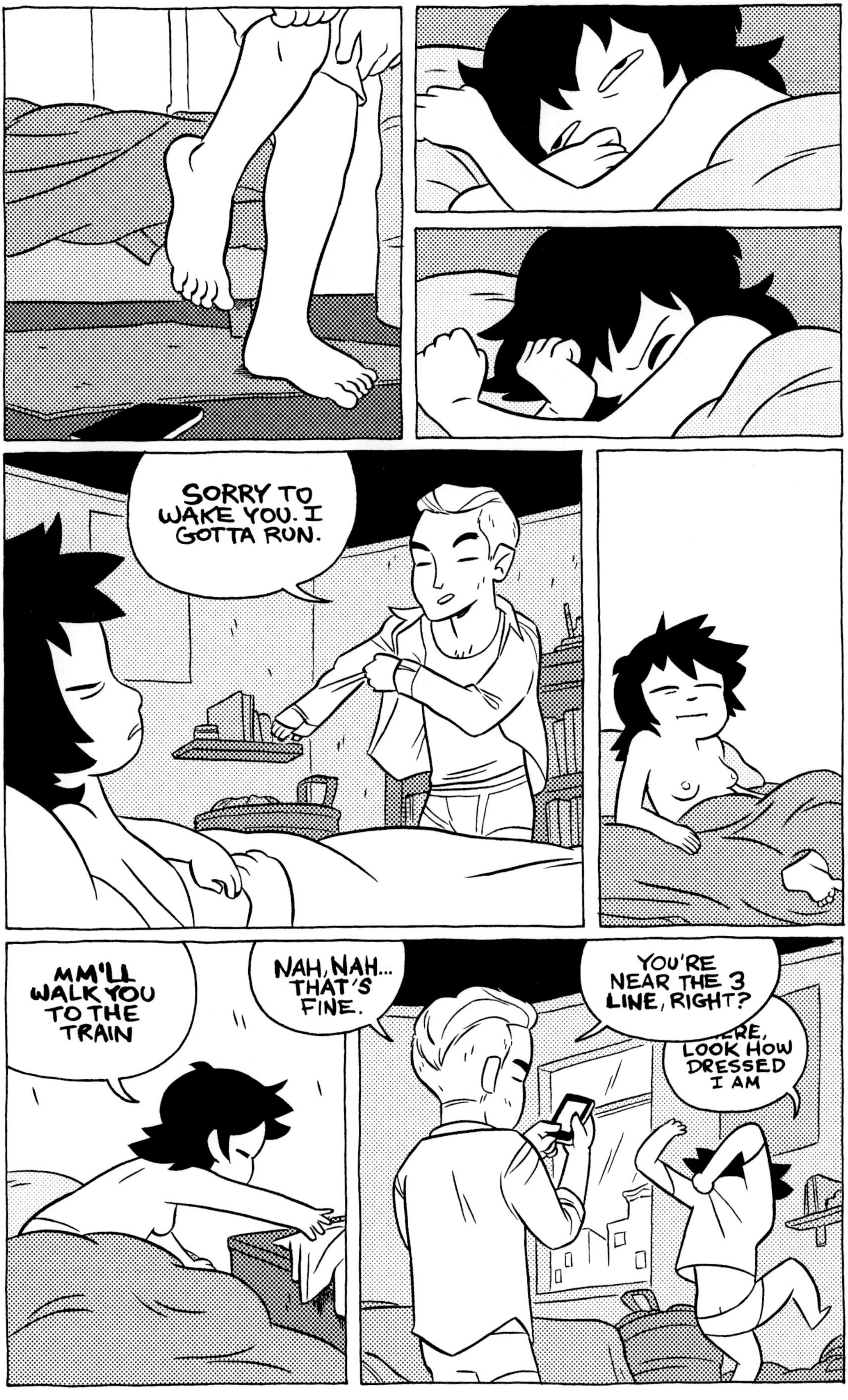

SORRY TO WAKE YOU. I GOTTA RUN.
MM'LL WALK YOU TO THE TRAIN
NAH, NAH... THAT'S FINE.
YOU'RE NEAR THE 3 LINE, RIGHT?
LOOK HOW DRESSED I AM

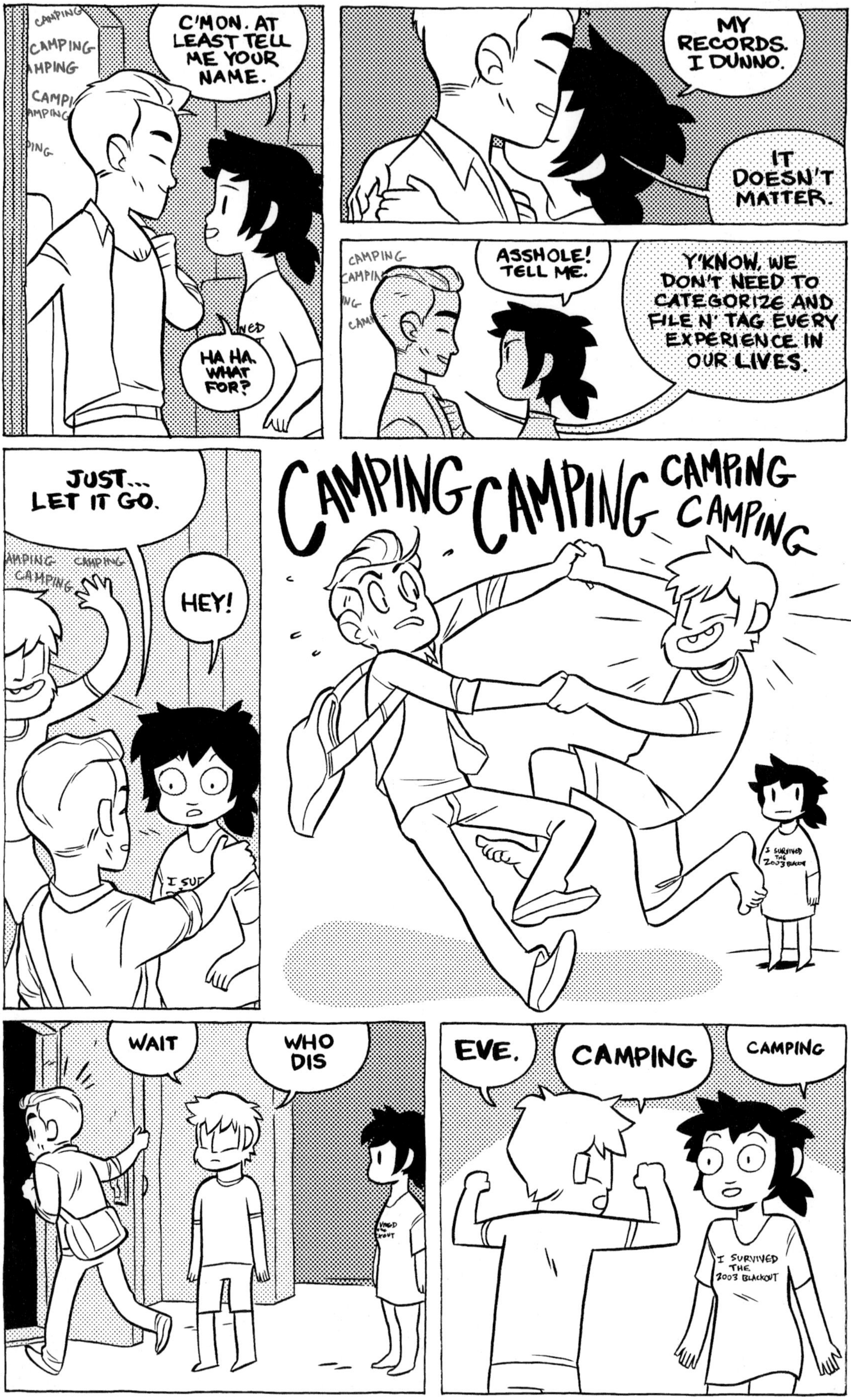
CAMPING
CAMPING
C'MON. AT LEAST TELL ME YOUR NAME.
HA HA. WHAT FOR?
MY RECORDS. I DUNNO.
IT DOESN'T MATTER.
CAMPING
ASSHOLE! TELL ME.
Y'KNOW, WE DON'T NEED TO CATEGORIZE AND FILE N' TAG EVERY EXPERIENCE IN OUR LIVES.
JUST... LET IT GO.
HEY!
CAMPING CAMPING CAMPING CAMPING
I SURVIVED THE 2003 BLACKOUT
WAIT
WHO DIS
EVE.
CAMPING
CAMPING
I SURVIVED THE 2003 BLACKOUT

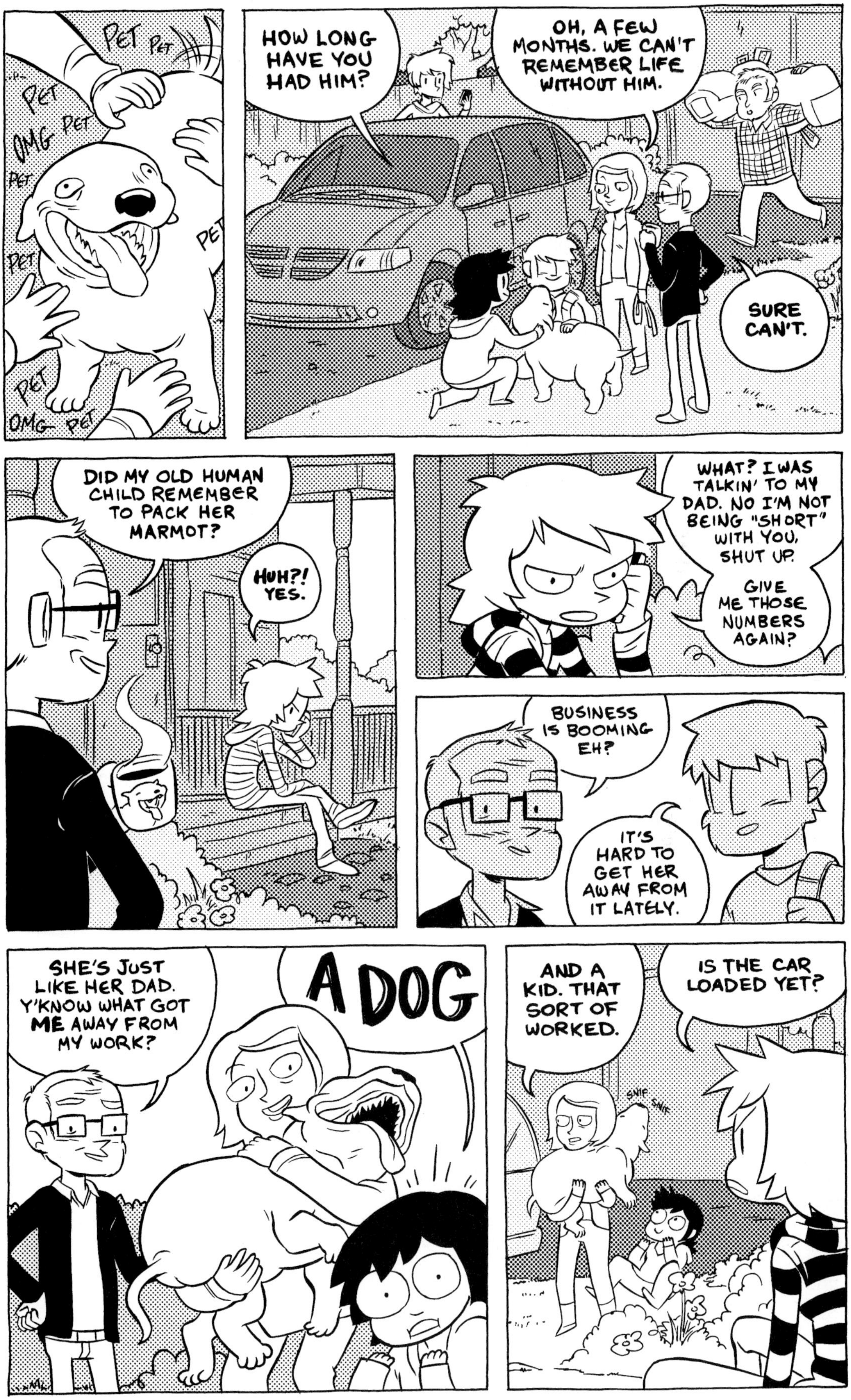
PET PET
PET
OMG PET
PET
PET
PET
PET
OMG PET
HOW LONG HAVE YOU HAD HIM?
OH, A FEW MONTHS. WE CAN'T REMEMBER LIFE WITHOUT HIM.
SURE CAN'T.
DID MY OLD HUMAN CHILD REMEMBER TO PACK HER MARMOT?
HUH?! YES.
WHAT? I WAS TALKIN' TO MY DAD. NO I'M NOT BEING "SHORT" WITH YOU, SHUT UP.
GIVE ME THOSE NUMBERS AGAIN?
BUSINESS IS BOOMING EH?
IT'S HARD TO GET HER AWAY FROM IT LATELY.
SHE'S JUST LIKE HER DAD. Y'KNOW WHAT GOT ME AWAY FROM MY WORK?
A DOG
AND A KID. THAT SORT OF WORKED.
IS THE CAR LOADED YET?

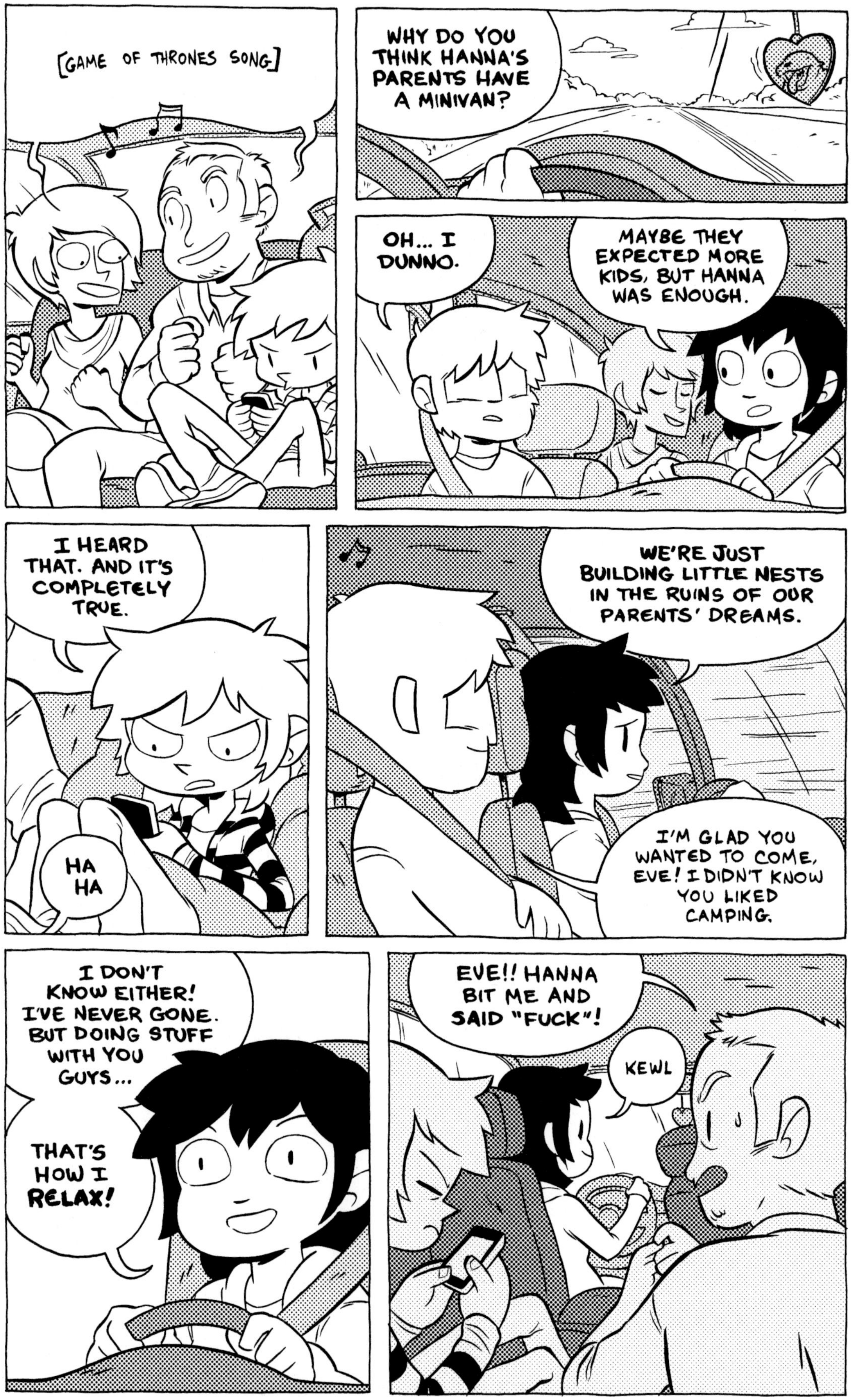
[GAME OF THRONES SONG]
WHY DO YOU THINK HANNA'S PARENTS HAVE A MINIVAN?
OH... I DUNNO.
MAYBE THEY EXPECTED MORE KIDS, BUT HANNA WAS ENOUGH.
I HEARD THAT. AND IT'S COMPLETELY TRUE.
HA HA
WE'RE JUST BUILDING LITTLE NESTS IN THE RUINS OF OUR PARENTS' DREAMS.
I'M GLAD YOU WANTED TO COME, EVE! I DIDN'T KNOW YOU LIKED CAMPING.
I DON'T KNOW EITHER! I'VE NEVER GONE. BUT DOING STUFF WITH YOU GUYS...
THAT'S HOW I RELAX!
EVE!! HANNA BIT ME AND SAID "FUCK"!
KEWL

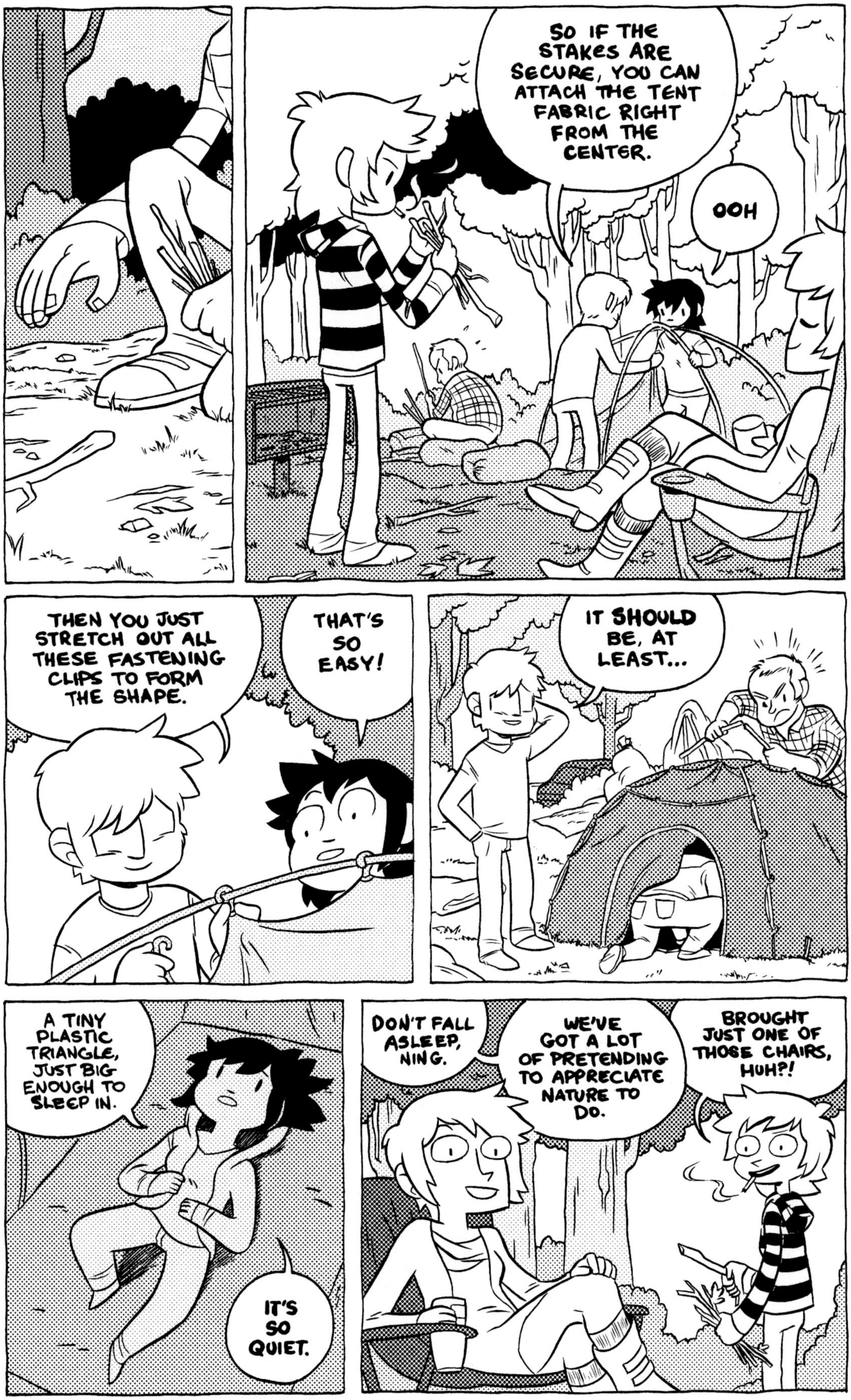
SO IF THE STAKES ARE SECURE, YOU CAN ATTACH THE TENT FABRIC RIGHT FROM THE CENTER.
OOH
THEN YOU JUST STRETCH OUT ALL THESE FASTENING CLIPS TO FORM THE SHAPE.
THAT'S SO EASY!
IT SHOULD BE, AT LEAST...
A TINY PLASTIC TRIANGLE, JUST BIG ENOUGH TO SLEEP IN.
IT'S SO QUIET.
DON'T FALL ASLEEP, NING.
WE'VE GOT A LOT OF PRETENDING TO APPRECIATE NATURE TO DO.
BROUGHT JUST ONE OF THOSE CHAIRS, HUH?!

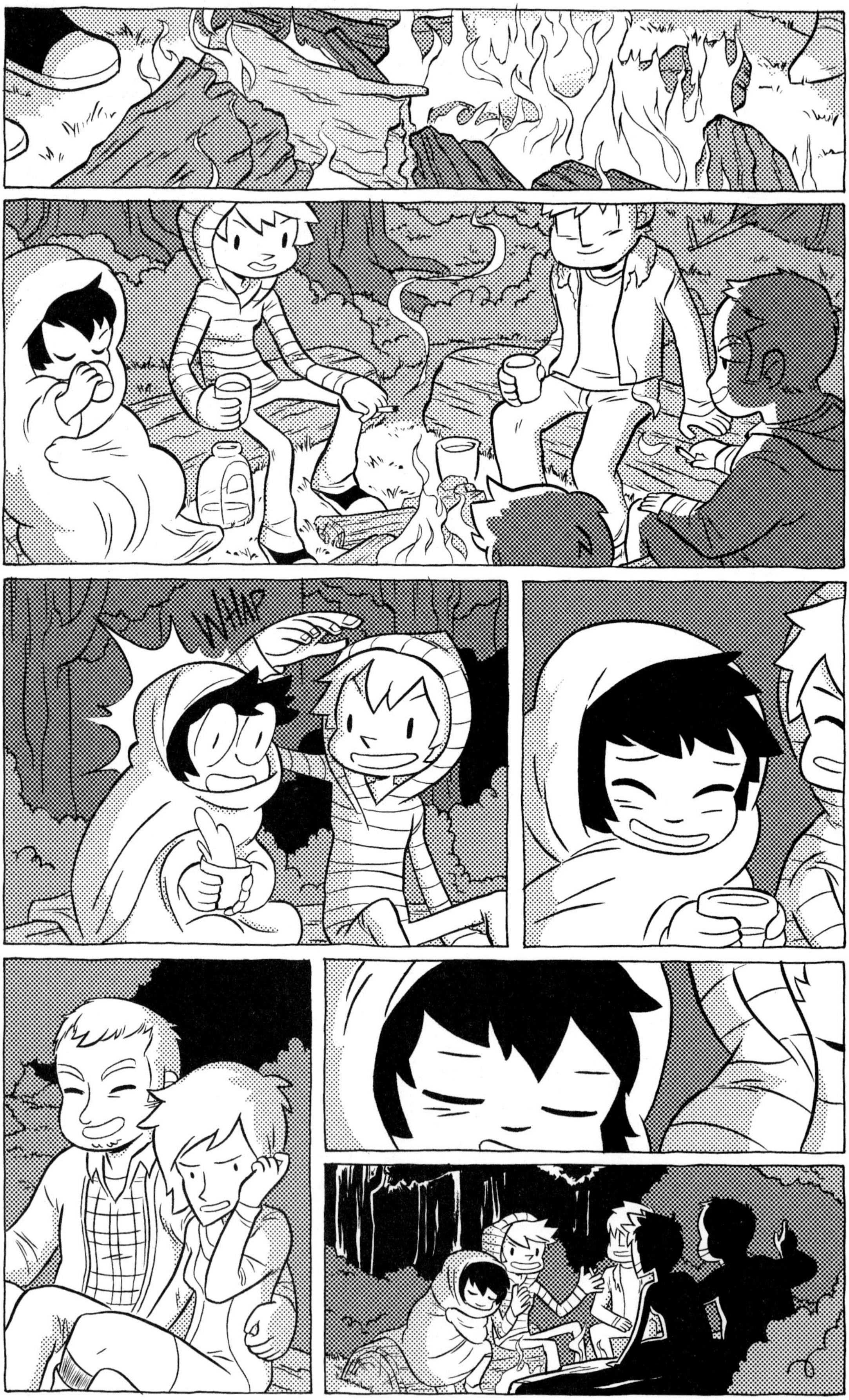
WHAP

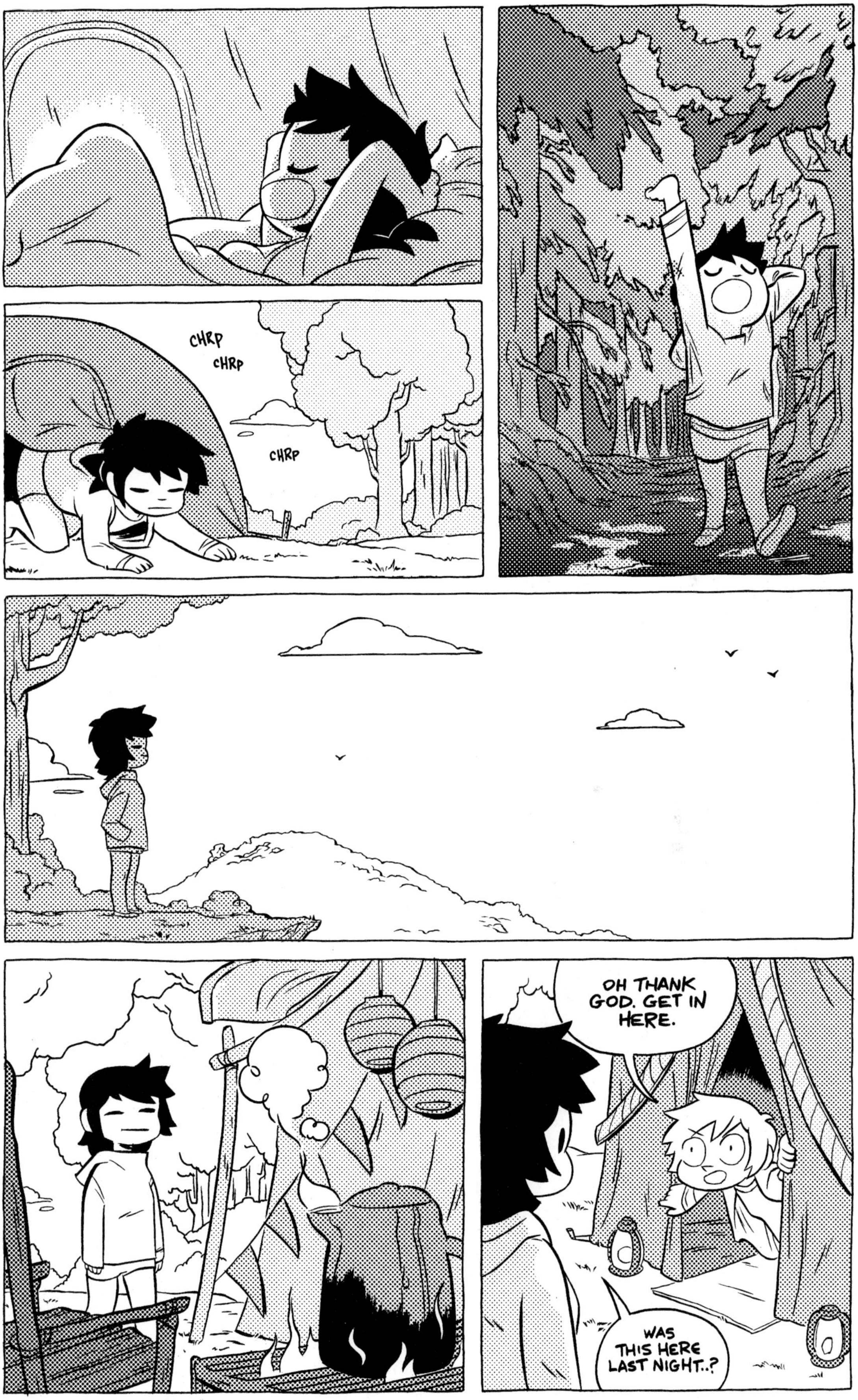
CHRP
CHRP
CHRP
OH THANK GOD. GET IN HERE.
WAS THIS HERE LAST NIGHT..?

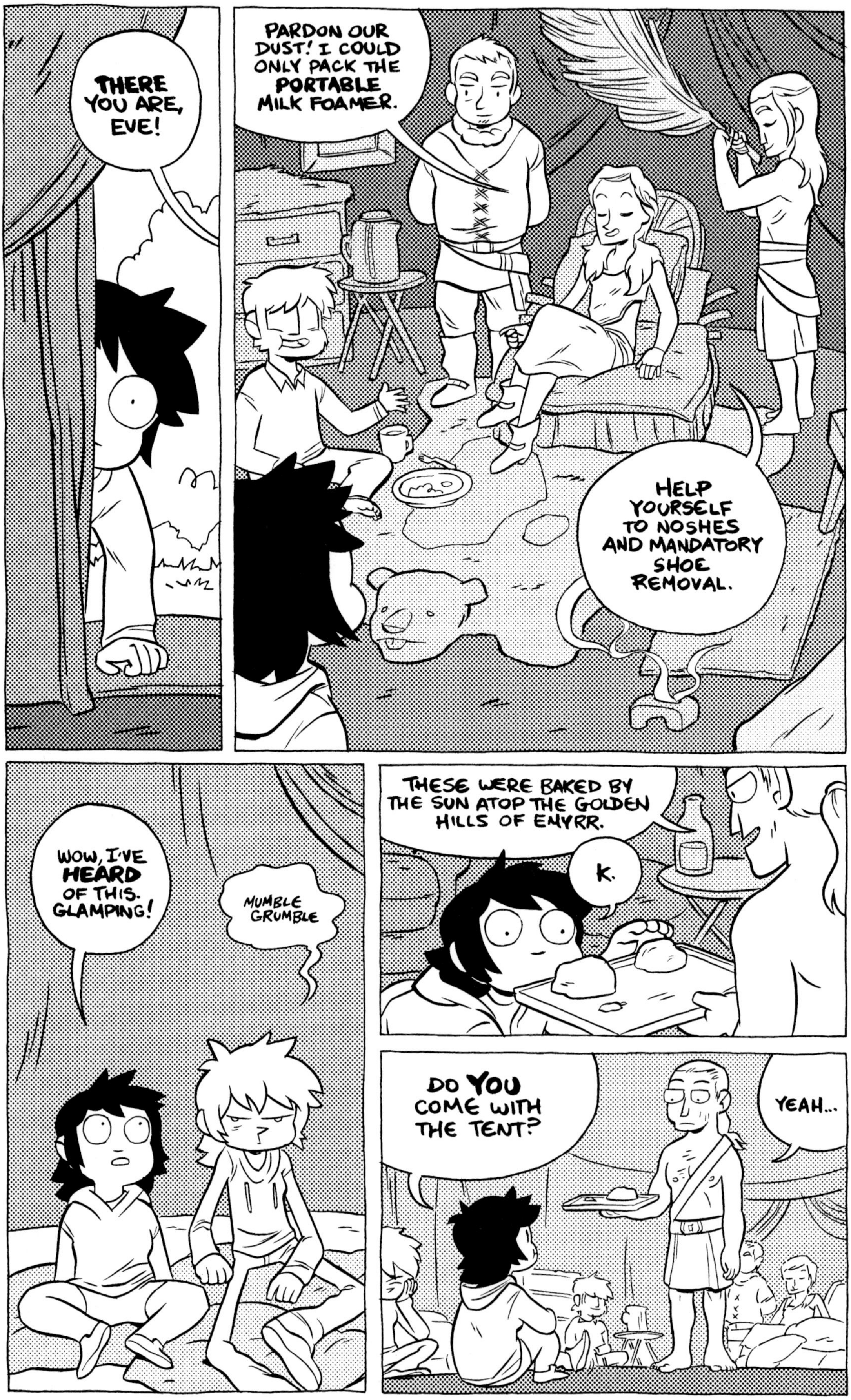
THERE YOU ARE, EVE!
PARDON OUR DUST! I COULD ONLY PACK THE PORTABLE MILK FOAMER.
HELP YOURSELF TO NOSHES AND MANDATORY SHOE REMOVAL.
WOW, I'VE HEARD OF THIS. GLAMPING!
MUMBLE GRUMBLE
THESE WERE BAKED BY THE SUN ATOP THE GOLDEN HILLS OF ENYRR.
K.
DO YOU COME WITH THE TENT?
YEAH...

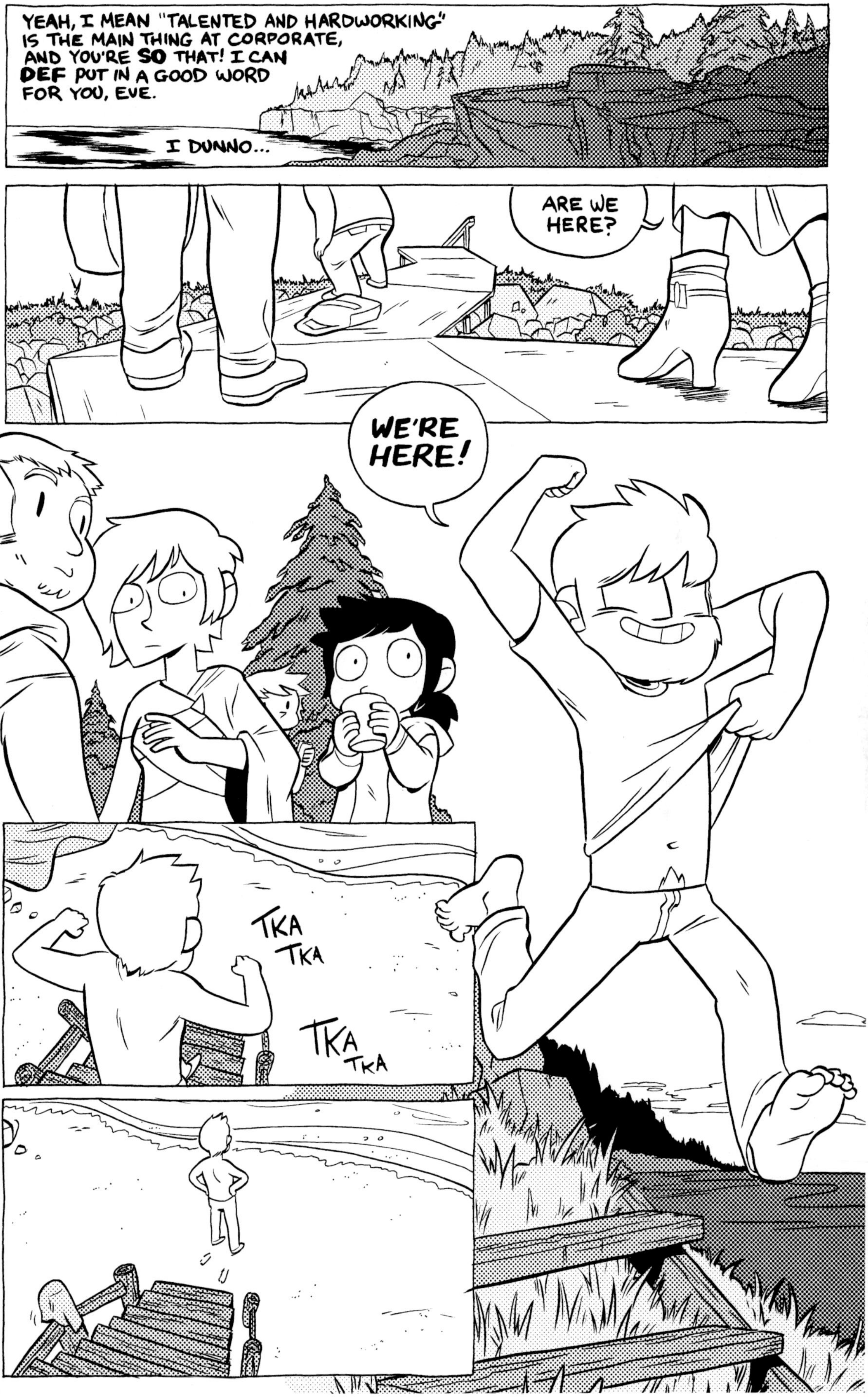
YEAH, I MEAN "TALENTED AND HARDWORKING" IS THE MAIN THING AT CORPORATE, AND YOU'RE **SO** THAT! I CAN **DEF** PUT IN A GOOD WORD FOR YOU, EVE.
I DUNNO...
ARE WE HERE?
WE'RE HERE!
TKA TKA
TKA TKA

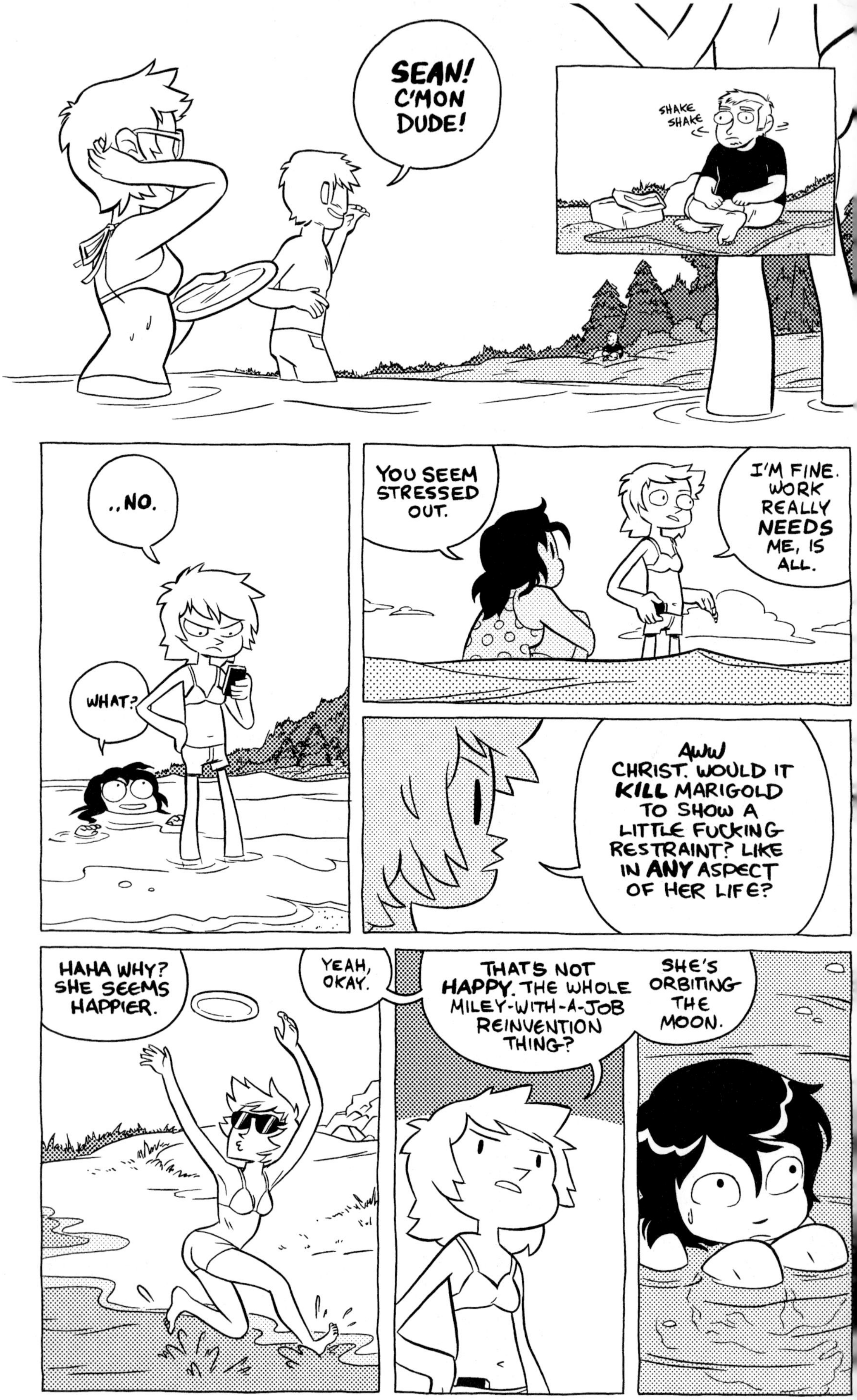
SEAN! C'MON DUDE!
SHAKE SHAKE
..NO.
WHAT?
YOU SEEM STRESSED OUT.
I'M FINE. WORK REALLY NEEDS ME, IS ALL.
AWW CHRIST. WOULD IT KILL MARIGOLD TO SHOW A LITTLE FUCKING RESTRAINT? LIKE IN ANY ASPECT OF HER LIFE?
HAHA WHY? SHE SEEMS HAPPIER.
YEAH, OKAY.
THAT'S NOT HAPPY. THE WHOLE MILEY-WITH-A-JOB REINVENTION THING?
SHE'S ORBITING THE MOON.

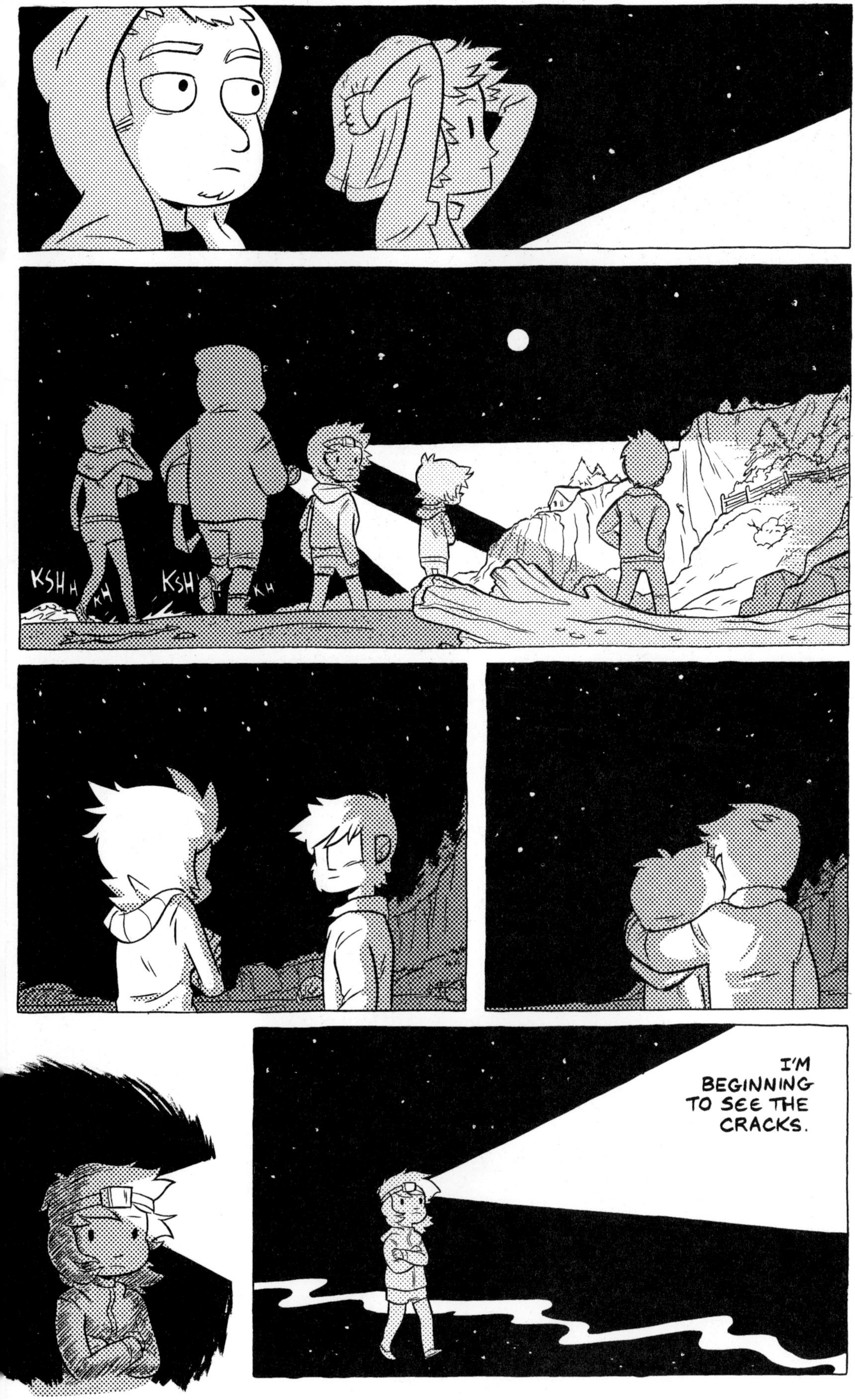
KSHH KH
KSHH KH
I'M BEGINNING TO SEE THE CRACKS.

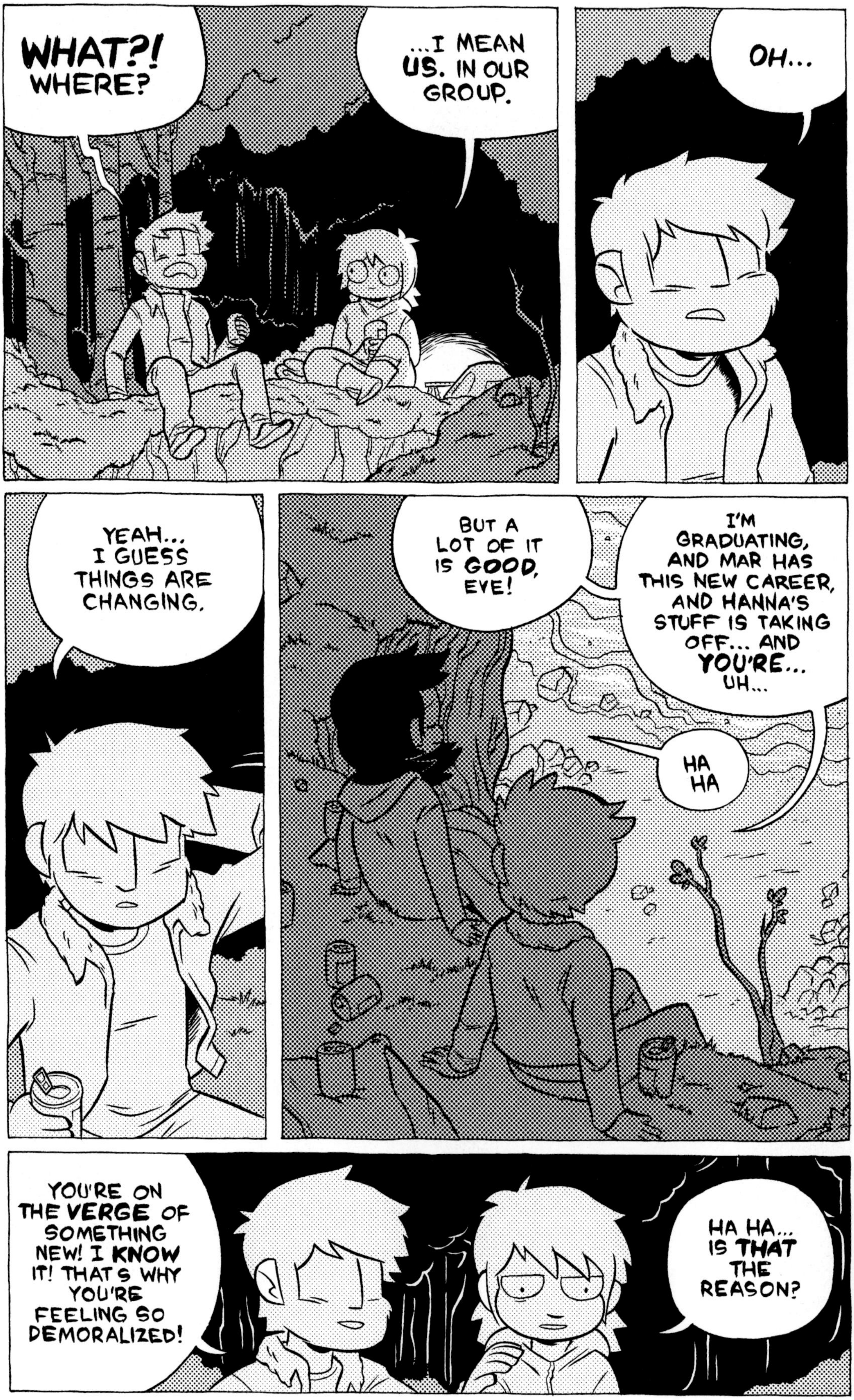
WHAT?! WHERE?
...I MEAN US. IN OUR GROUP.
OH...
YEAH... I GUESS THINGS ARE CHANGING.
BUT A LOT OF IT IS GOOD, EVE!
I'M GRADUATING, AND MAR HAS THIS NEW CAREER, AND HANNA'S STUFF IS TAKING OFF... AND YOU'RE... UH...
HA HA
YOU'RE ON THE VERGE OF SOMETHING NEW! I KNOW IT! THAT'S WHY YOU'RE FEELING SO DEMORALIZED!
HA HA... IS THAT THE REASON?

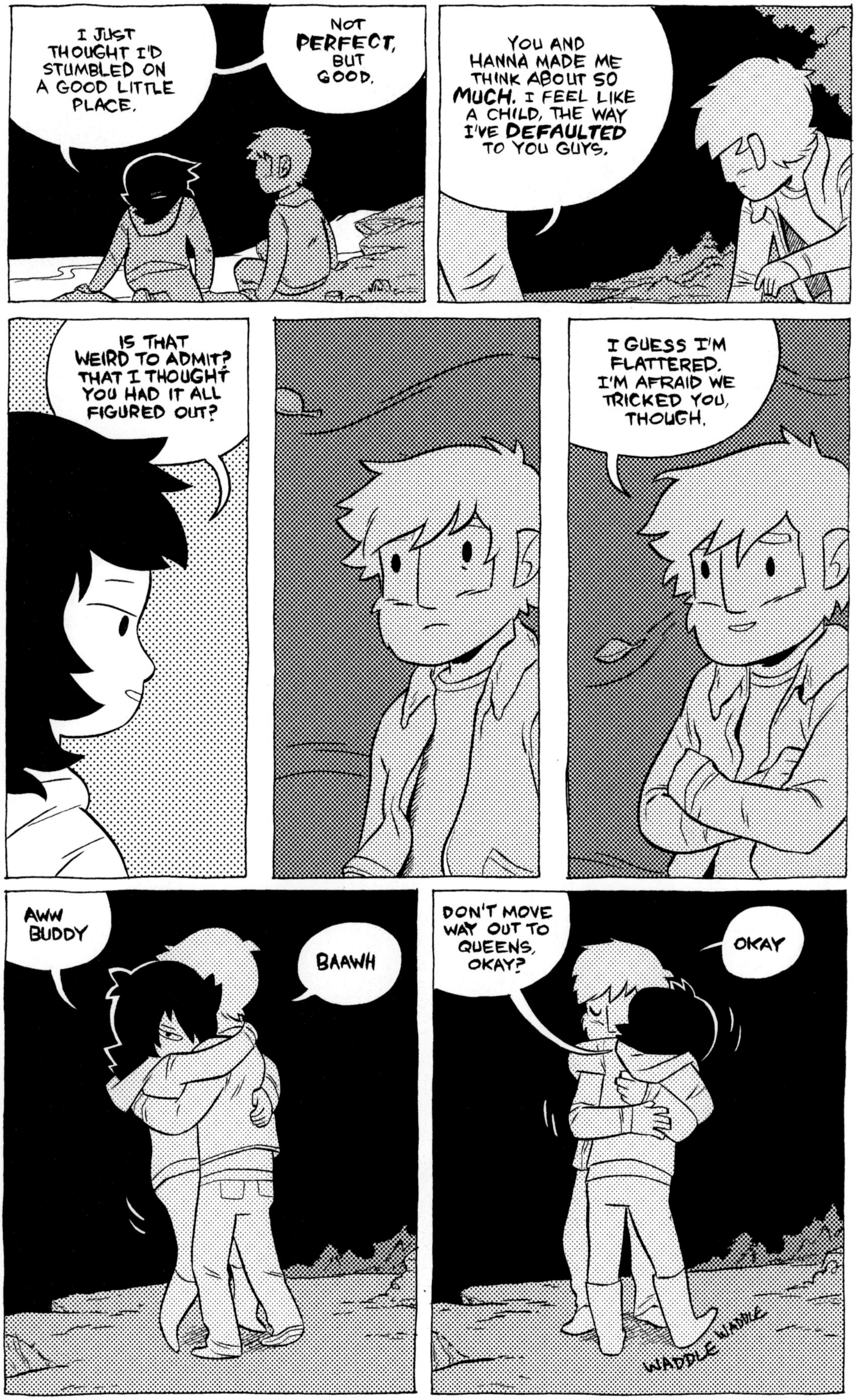
I JUST THOUGHT I'D STUMBLED ON A GOOD LITTLE PLACE.
NOT PERFECT, BUT GOOD.
YOU AND HANNA MADE ME THINK ABOUT SO MUCH. I FEEL LIKE A CHILD, THE WAY I'VE DEFAULTED TO YOU GUYS.
IS THAT WEIRD TO ADMIT? THAT I THOUGHT YOU HAD IT ALL FIGURED OUT?
I GUESS I'M FLATTERED. I'M AFRAID WE TRICKED YOU, THOUGH.
AWW BUDDY
BAAWH
DON'T MOVE WAY OUT TO QUEENS, OKAY?
OKAY
WADDLE WADDLE

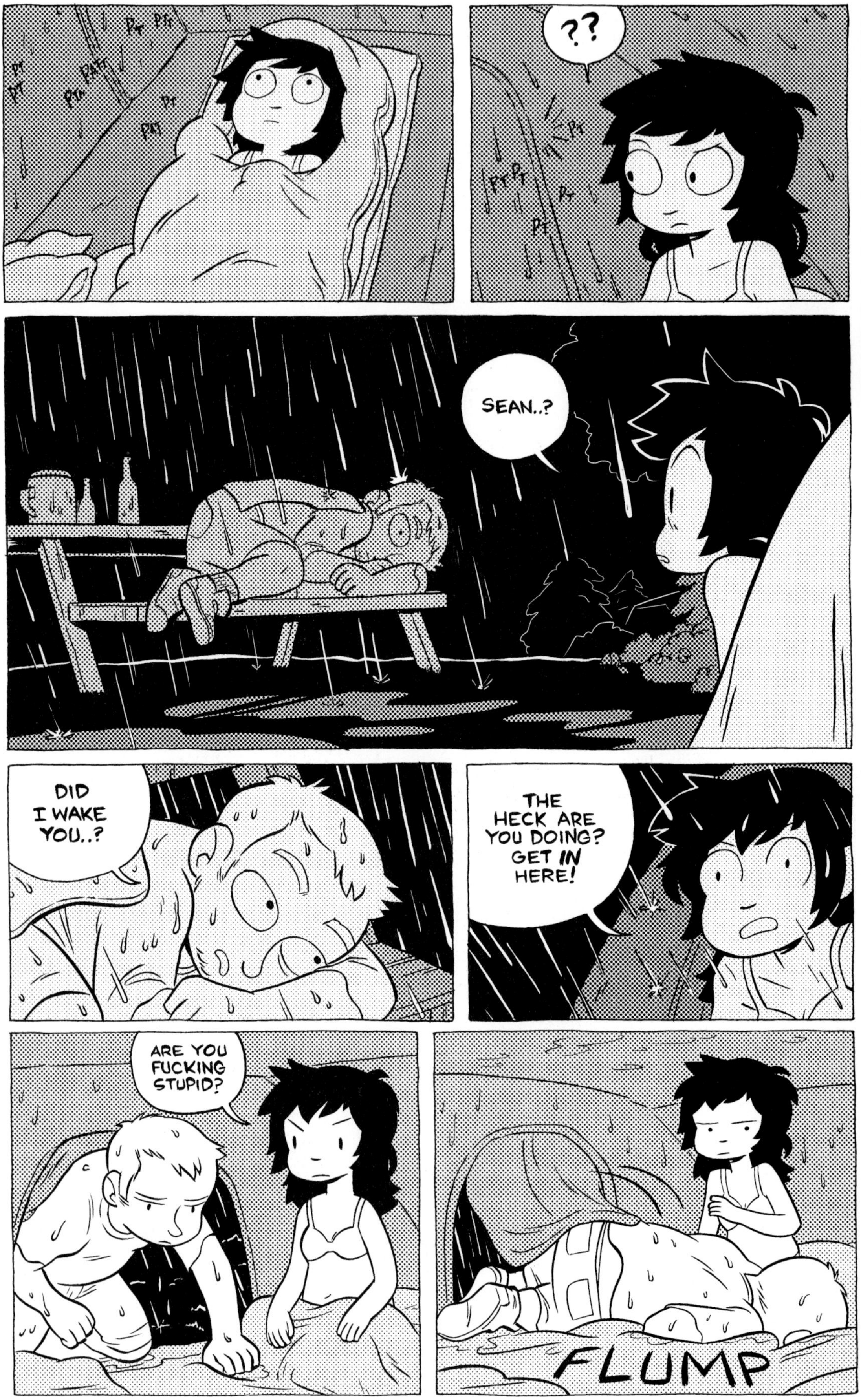
PT PT
PT
PT
PTT
PTT
PT
PTT
??
PT PT
PT PT
PT
PT
SEAN..?
DID I WAKE YOU..?
THE HECK ARE YOU DOING? GET IN HERE!
ARE YOU FUCKING STUPID?
FLUMP

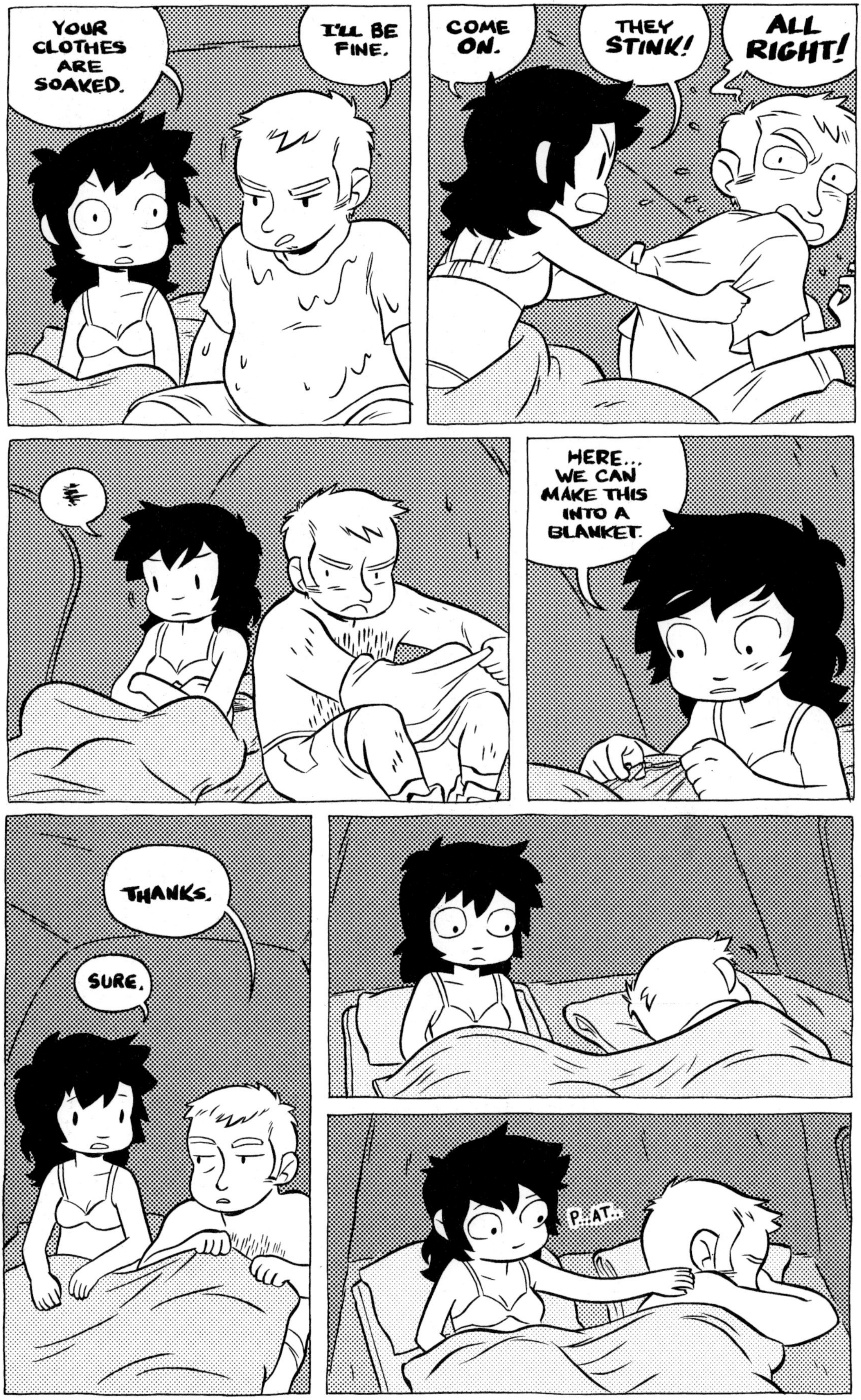
YOUR CLOTHES ARE SOAKED.
I'LL BE FINE.
COME ON.
THEY STINK!
ALL RIGHT!
HERE... WE CAN MAKE THIS INTO A BLANKET.
THANKS.
SURE.
P...AT..

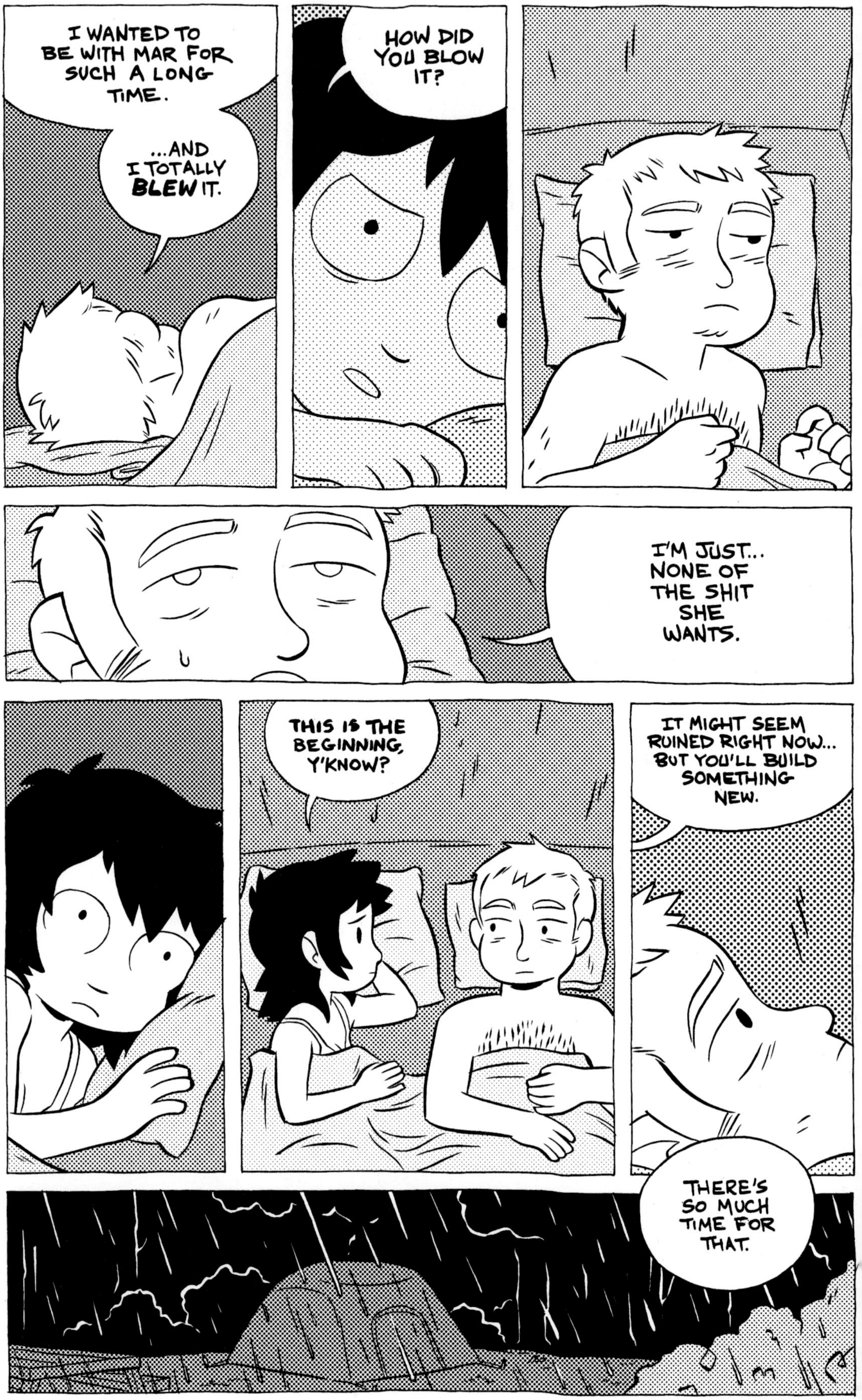
I WANTED TO BE WITH MAR FOR SUCH A LONG TIME.
...AND I TOTALLY BLEW IT.
HOW DID YOU BLOW IT?
I'M JUST... NONE OF THE SHIT SHE WANTS.
THIS IS THE BEGINNING, Y'KNOW?
IT MIGHT SEEM RUINED RIGHT NOW... BUT YOU'LL BUILD SOMETHING NEW.
THERE'S SO MUCH TIME FOR THAT.

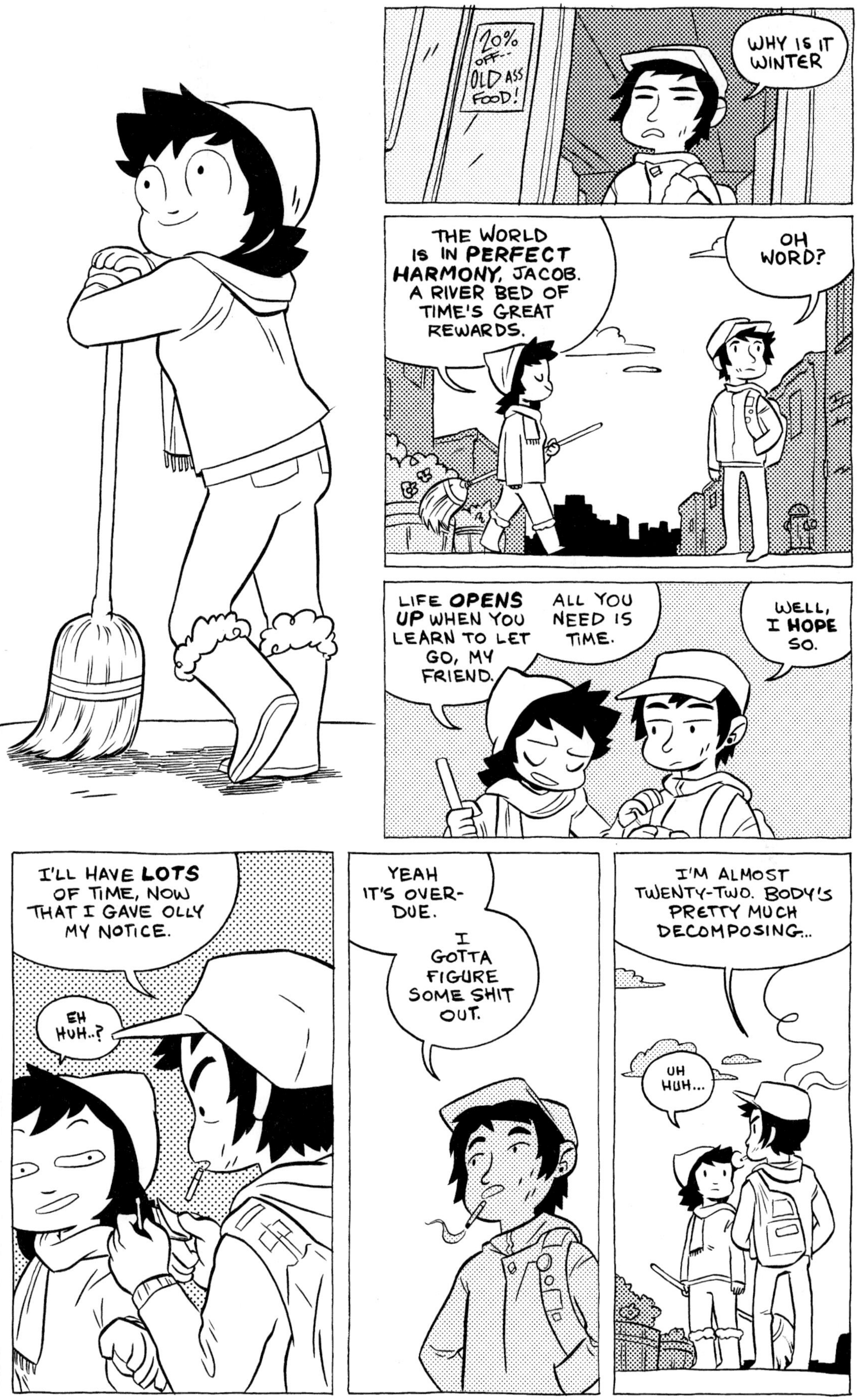
20% OFF-- OLD ASS FOOD!
WHY IS IT WINTER
THE WORLD IS IN PERFECT HARMONY, JACOB. A RIVER BED OF TIME'S GREAT REWARDS.
OH WORD?
LIFE OPENS UP WHEN YOU LEARN TO LET GO, MY FRIEND.
ALL YOU NEED IS TIME.
WELL, I HOPE SO.
I'LL HAVE LOTS OF TIME, NOW THAT I GAVE OLLY MY NOTICE.
EH HUH..?
YEAH IT'S OVER-DUE.
I GOTTA FIGURE SOME SHIT OUT.
I'M ALMOST TWENTY-TWO. BODY'S PRETTY MUCH DECOMPOSING..
UH HUH...

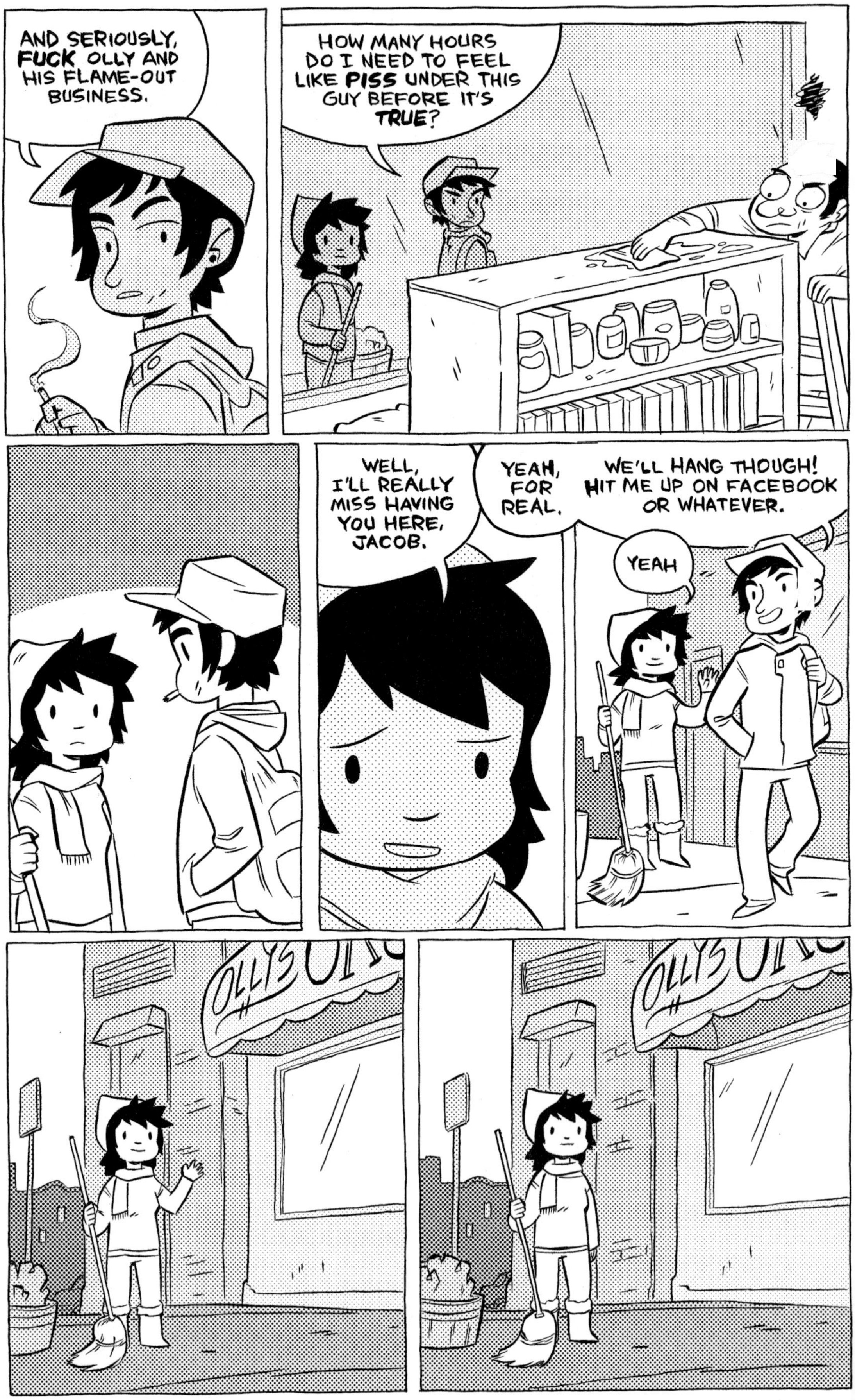
AND SERIOUSLY, FUCK OLLY AND HIS FLAME-OUT BUSINESS.
HOW MANY HOURS DO I NEED TO FEEL LIKE PISS UNDER THIS GUY BEFORE IT'S TRUE?
WELL, I'LL REALLY MISS HAVING YOU HERE, JACOB.
YEAH, FOR REAL.
WE'LL HANG THOUGH! HIT ME UP ON FACEBOOK OR WHATEVER.
YEAH
OLLY'S

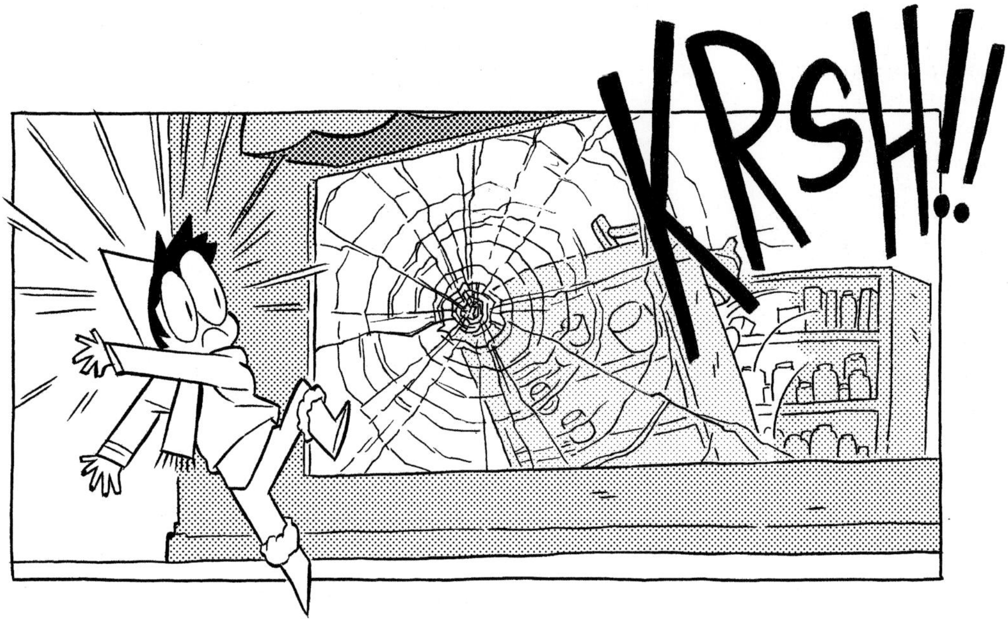
KRSH!!

44

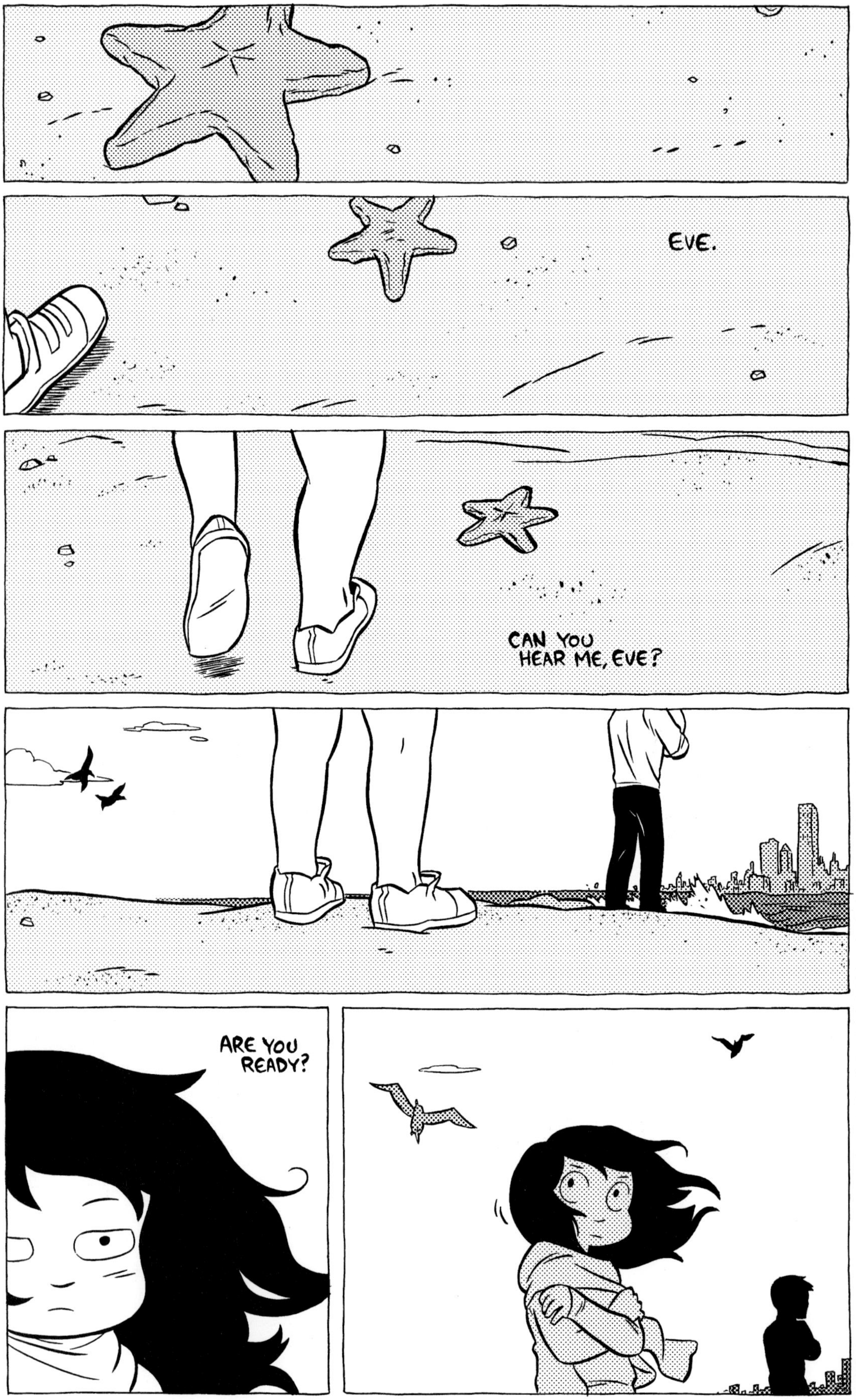
EVE.
CAN YOU HEAR ME, EVE?
ARE YOU READY?

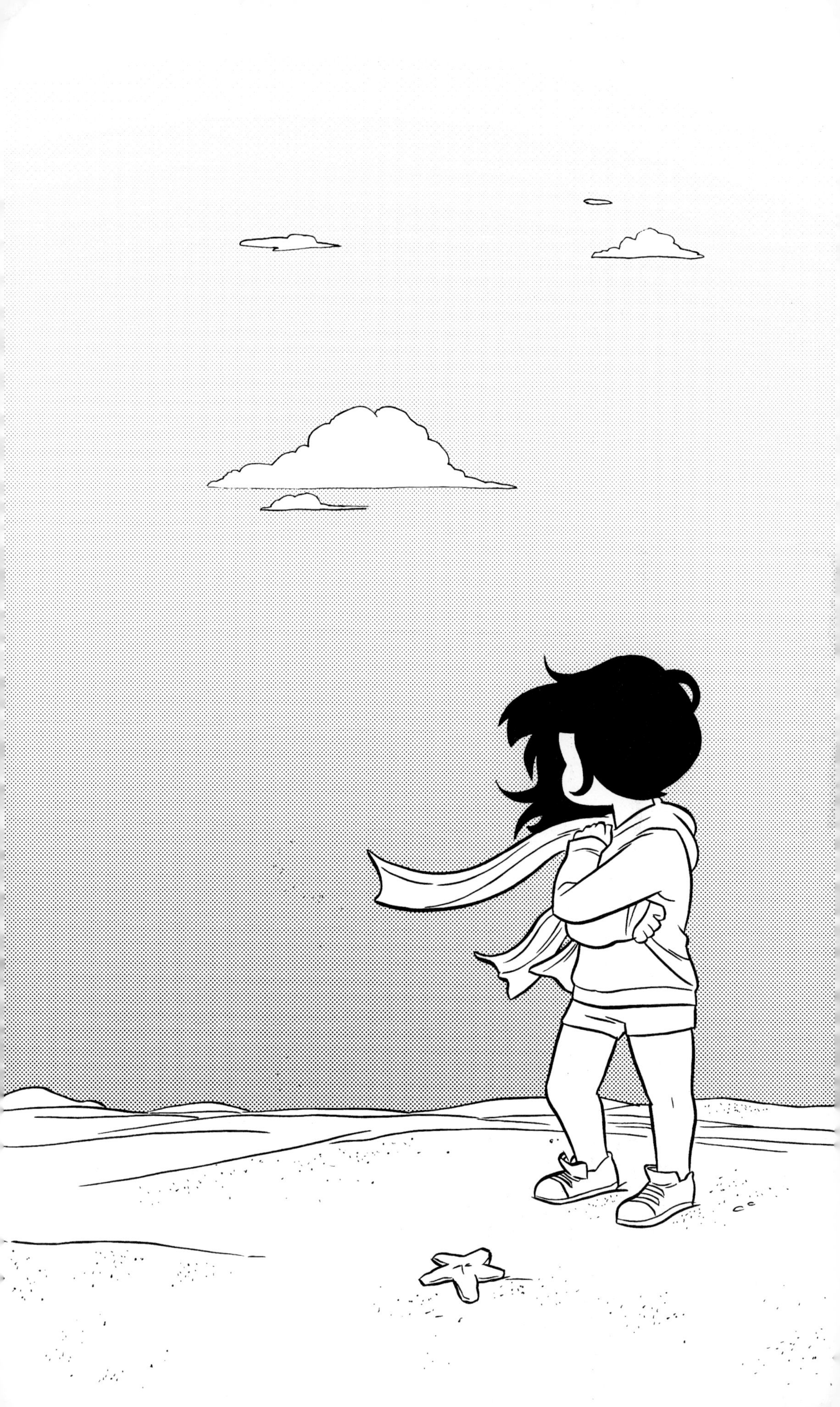

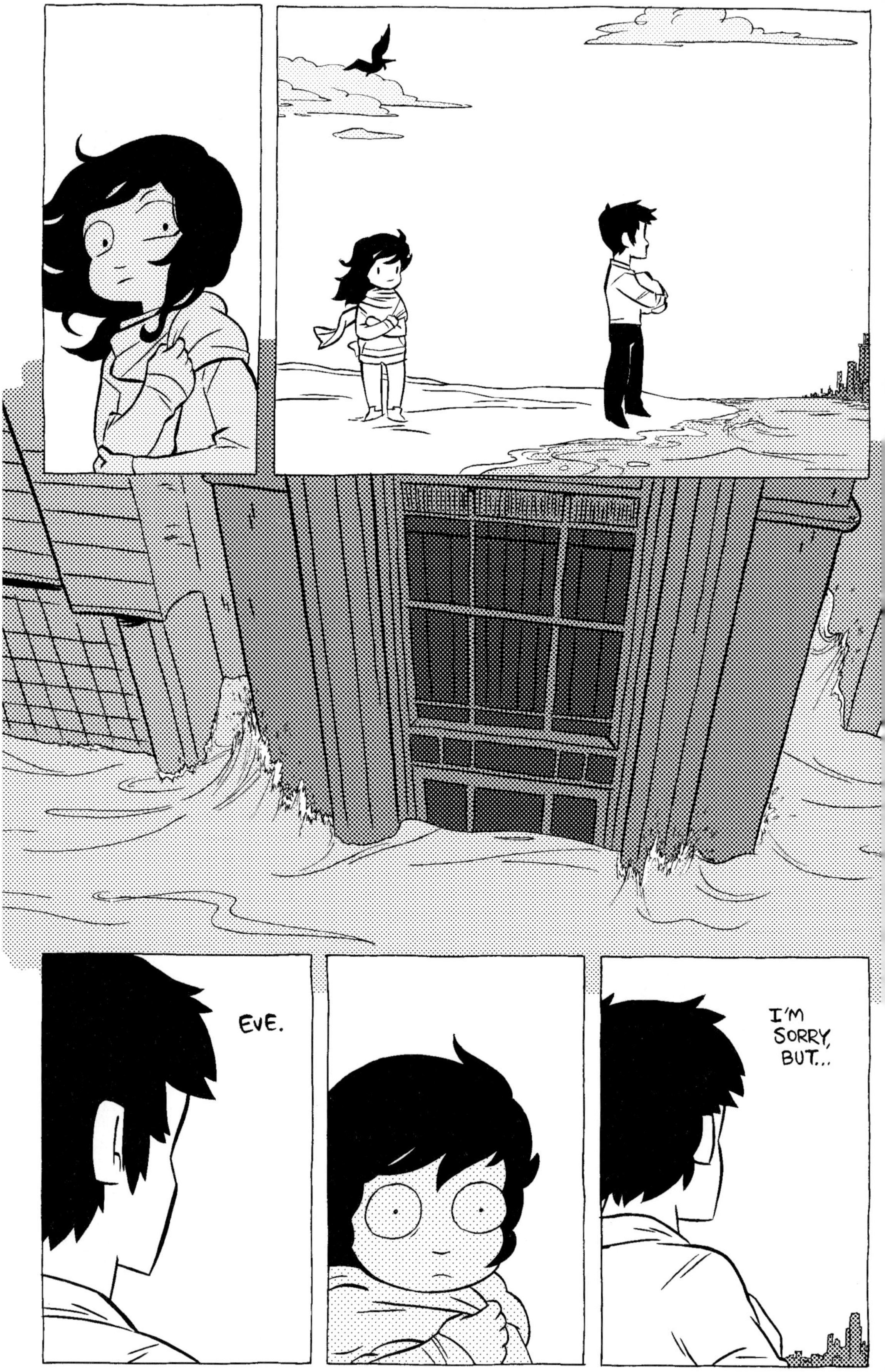
EVE.
I'M SORRY, BUT...

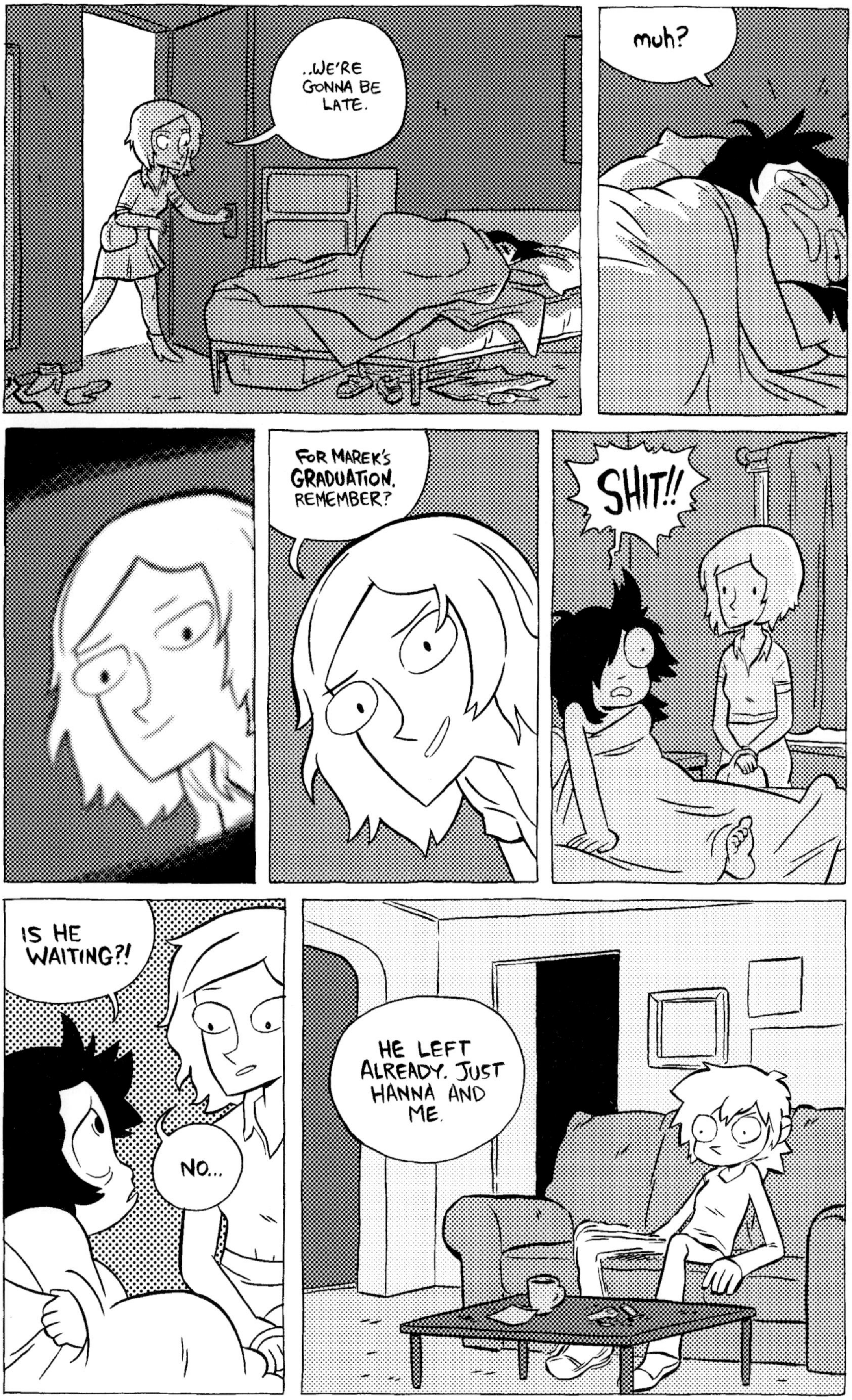
..WE'RE GONNA BE LATE.
muh?
FOR MAREK'S GRADUATION. REMEMBER?
SHIT!!
IS HE WAITING?!
NO...
HE LEFT ALREADY. JUST HANNA AND ME.

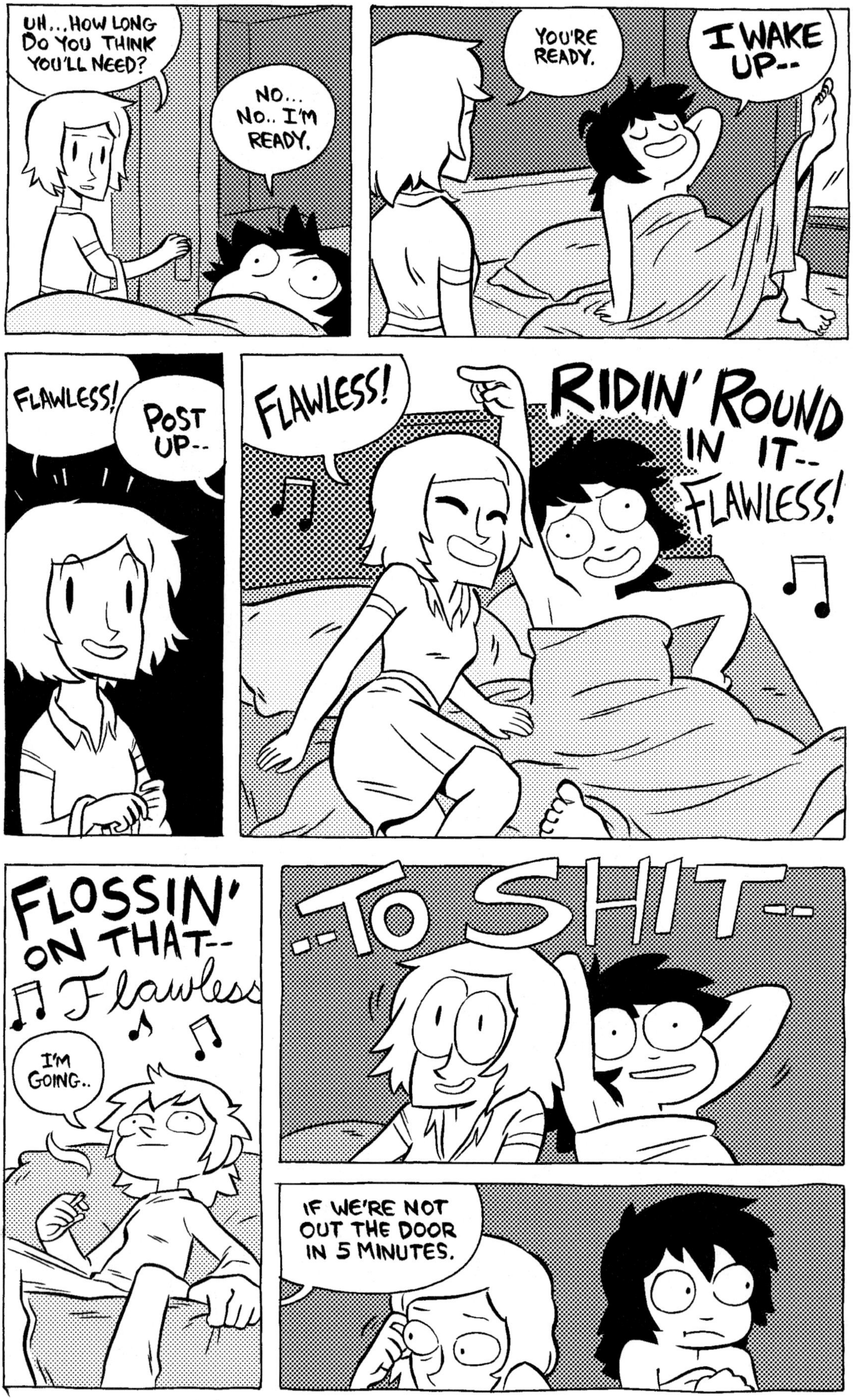

UH... HOW LONG DO YOU THINK YOU'LL NEED?
NO... NO.. I'M READY.
YOU'RE READY.
I WAKE UP--
FLAWLESS!
POST UP--
FLAWLESS!
RIDIN' ROUND IN IT-- FLAWLESS!
FLOSSIN' ON THAT-- Flawless
I'M GOING..
--TO SHIT--
IF WE'RE NOT OUT THE DOOR IN 5 MINUTES.

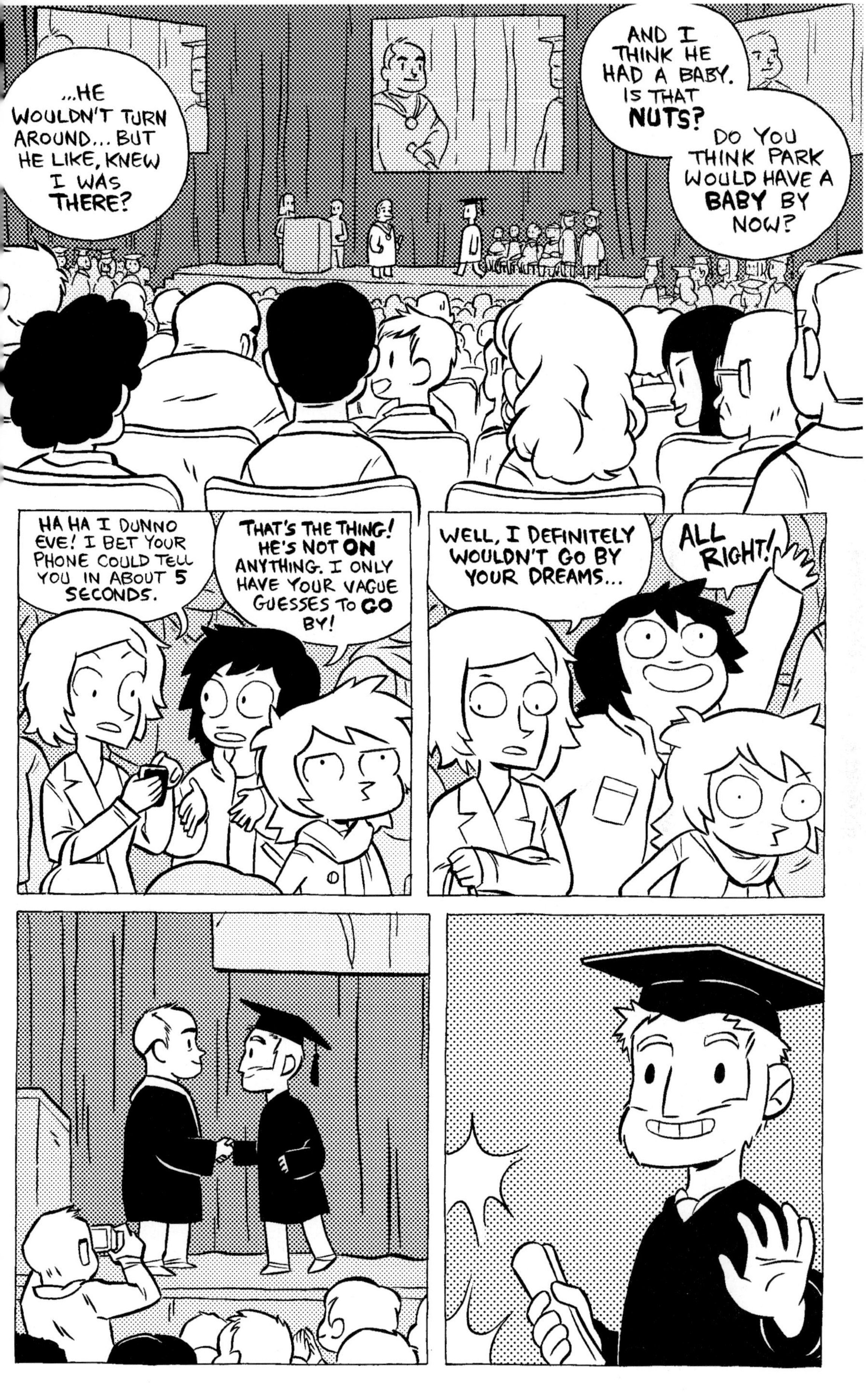
...HE WOULDN'T TURN AROUND... BUT HE LIKE, KNEW I WAS THERE?
AND I THINK HE HAD A BABY. IS THAT NUTS?
DO YOU THINK PARK WOULD HAVE A BABY BY NOW?
HA HA I DUNNO EVE! I BET YOUR PHONE COULD TELL YOU IN ABOUT 5 SECONDS.
THAT'S THE THING! HE'S NOT ON ANYTHING. I ONLY HAVE YOUR VAGUE GUESSES TO GO BY!
WELL, I DEFINITELY WOULDN'T GO BY YOUR DREAMS...
ALL RIGHT!

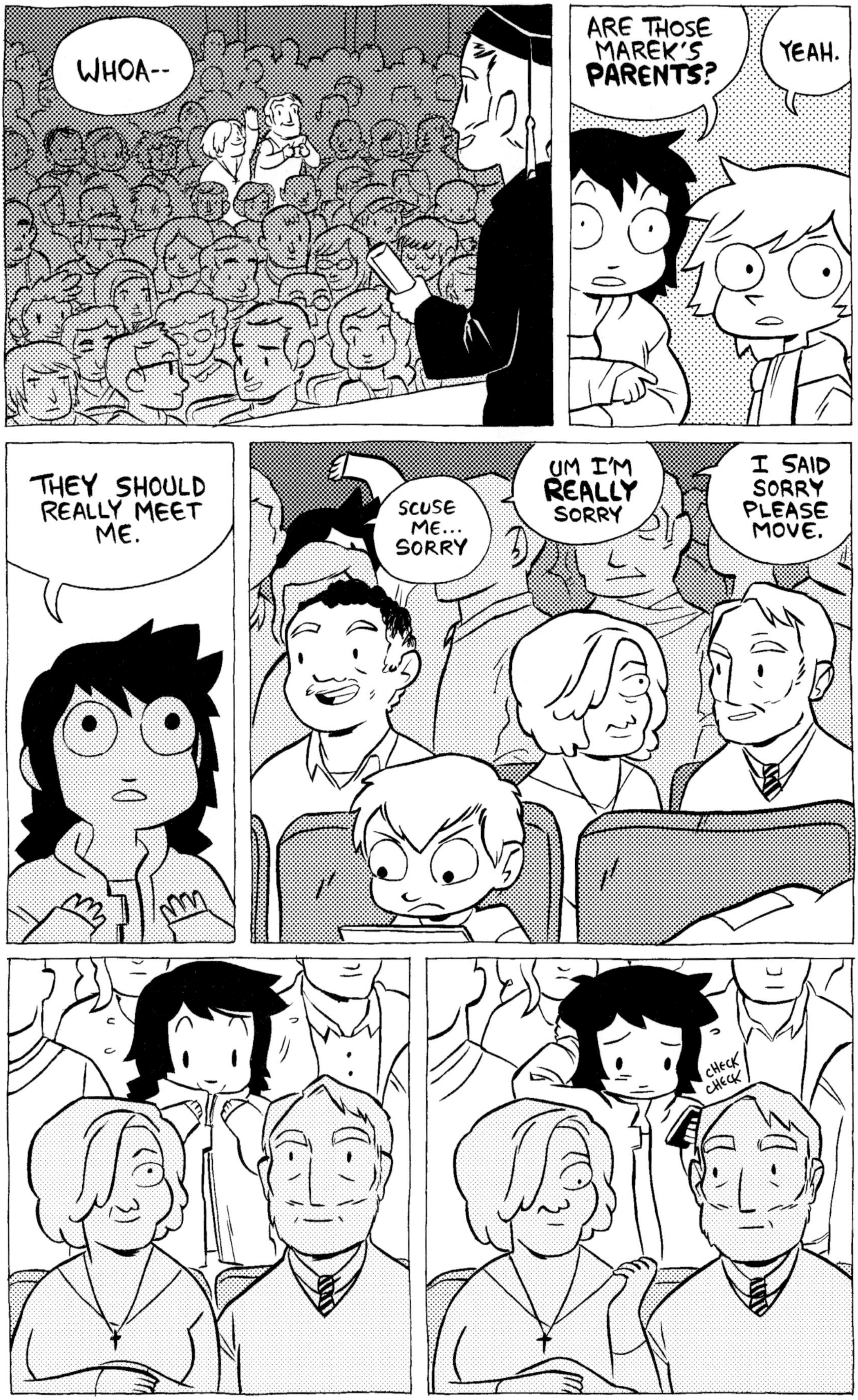
WHOA--
ARE THOSE MAREK'S **PARENTS?**
YEAH.
THEY SHOULD REALLY MEET ME.
SCUSE ME... SORRY
UM I'M **REALLY** SORRY
I SAID SORRY PLEASE MOVE.
CHECK CHECK

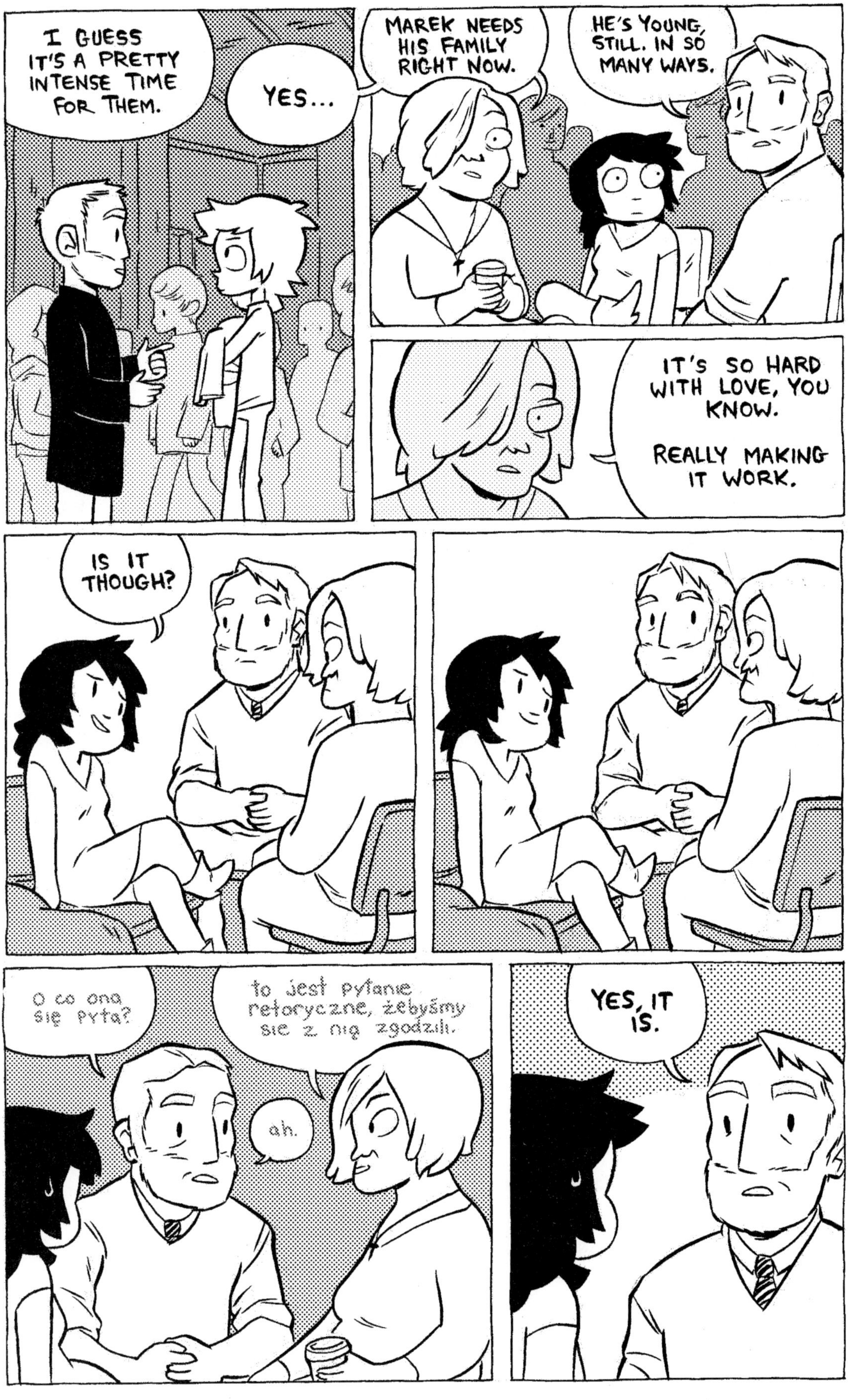

I GUESS IT'S A PRETTY INTENSE TIME FOR THEM.
YES...
MAREK NEEDS HIS FAMILY RIGHT NOW.
HE'S YOUNG, STILL. IN SO MANY WAYS.
IT'S SO HARD WITH LOVE, YOU KNOW.
REALLY MAKING IT WORK.
IS IT THOUGH?
o co ona się pyta?
to jest pytanie retoryczne, żebyśmy sie z nią zgodzili.
ah.
YES, IT IS.

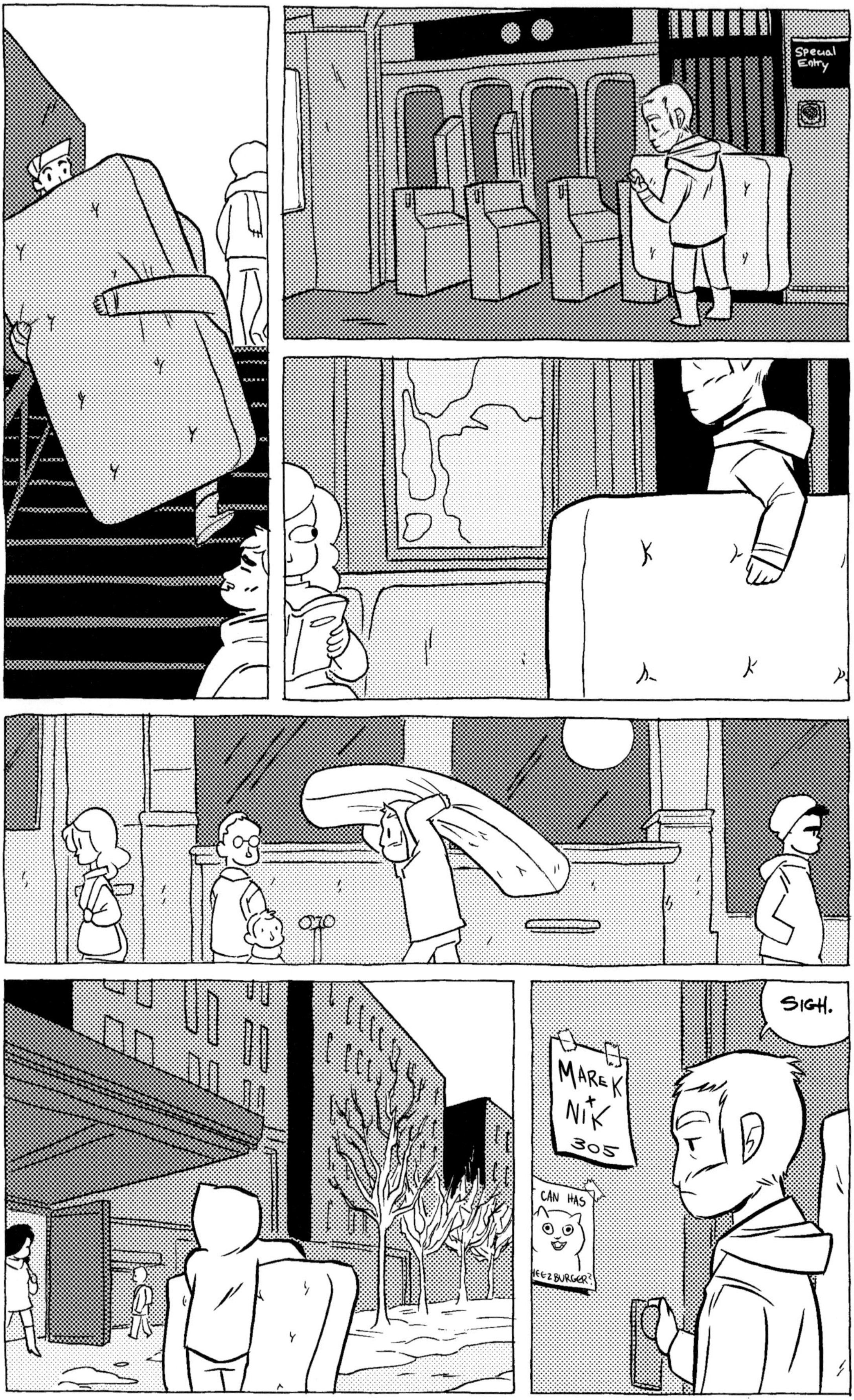
Special Entry
MAREK + NIK 305
CAN HAS
HEEZBURGER?
SIGH.

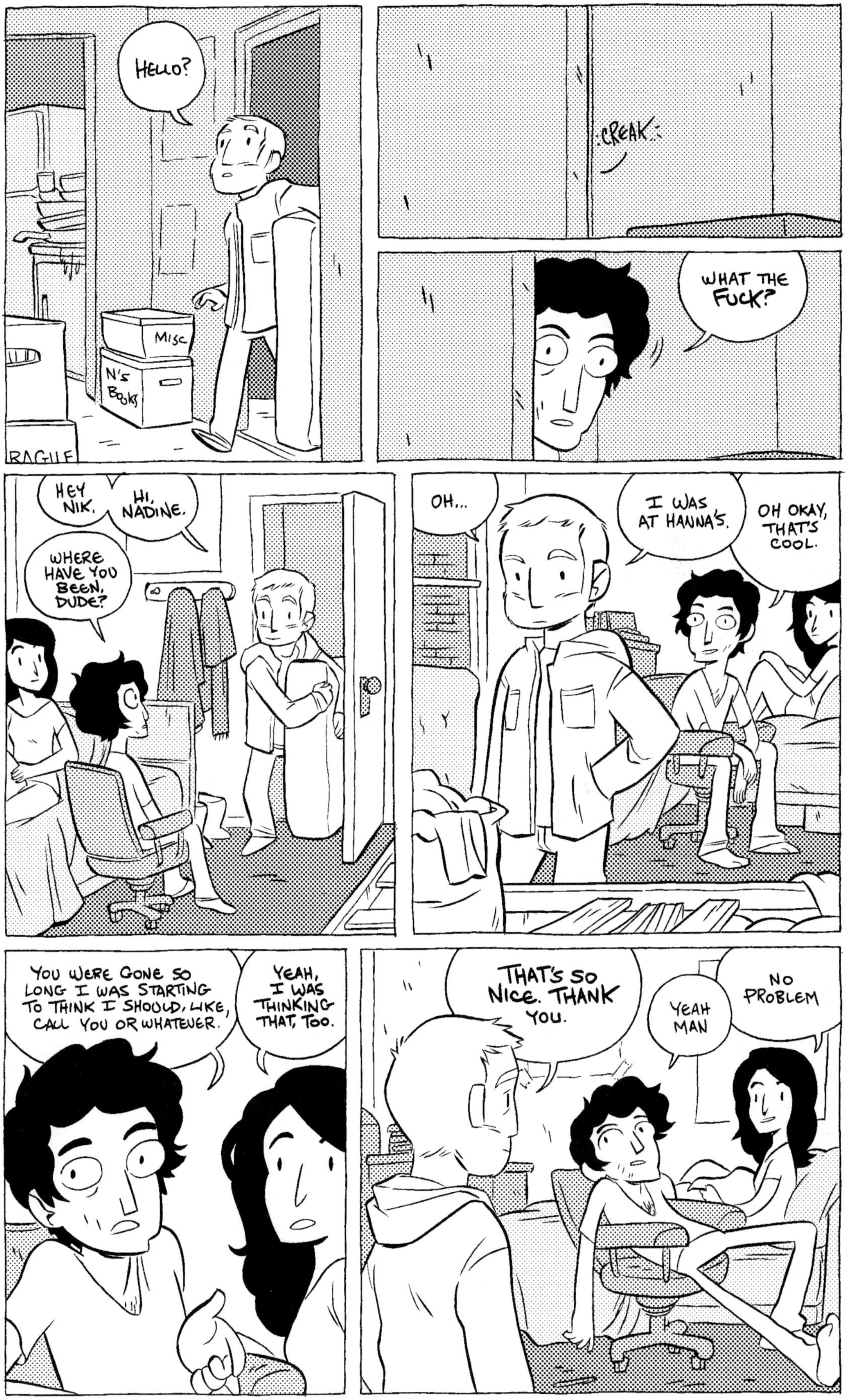

HELLO?
MISC
N'S BOOKS
CREAK
WHAT THE FUCK?
HEY NIK.
HI, NADINE.
WHERE HAVE YOU BEEN, DUDE?
OH...
I WAS AT HANNA'S.
OH OKAY, THAT'S COOL.
YOU WERE GONE SO LONG I WAS STARTING TO THINK I SHOULD, LIKE, CALL YOU OR WHATEVER.
YEAH, I WAS THINKING THAT, TOO.
THAT'S SO NICE. THANK YOU.
YEAH MAN
NO PROBLEM

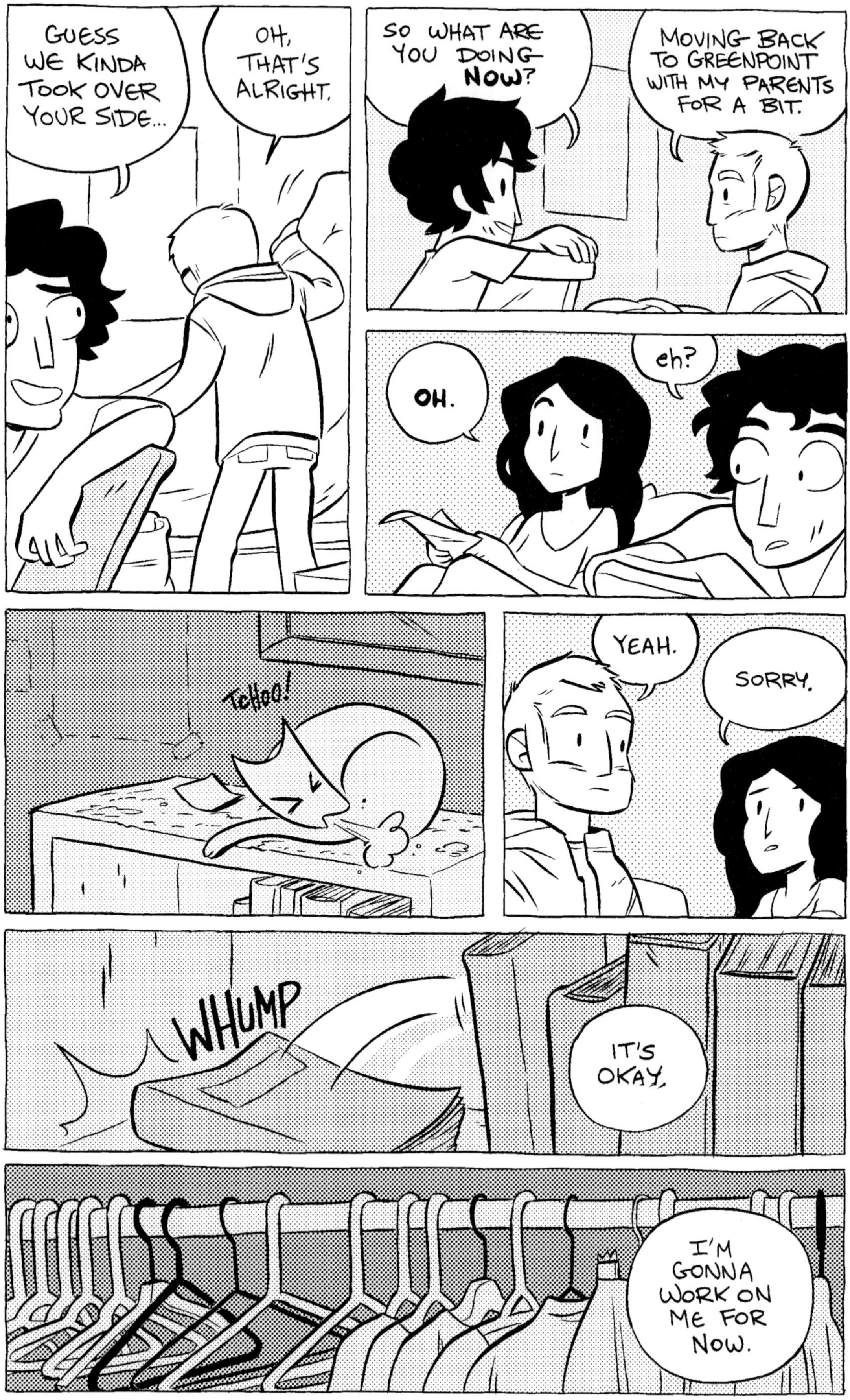
GUESS WE KINDA TOOK OVER YOUR SIDE...
OH, THAT'S ALRIGHT.
SO WHAT ARE YOU DOING NOW?
MOVING BACK TO GREENPOINT WITH MY PARENTS FOR A BIT.
OH.
eh?
TCHOO!
YEAH.
SORRY.
WHUMP
IT'S OKAY.
I'M GONNA WORK ON ME FOR NOW.

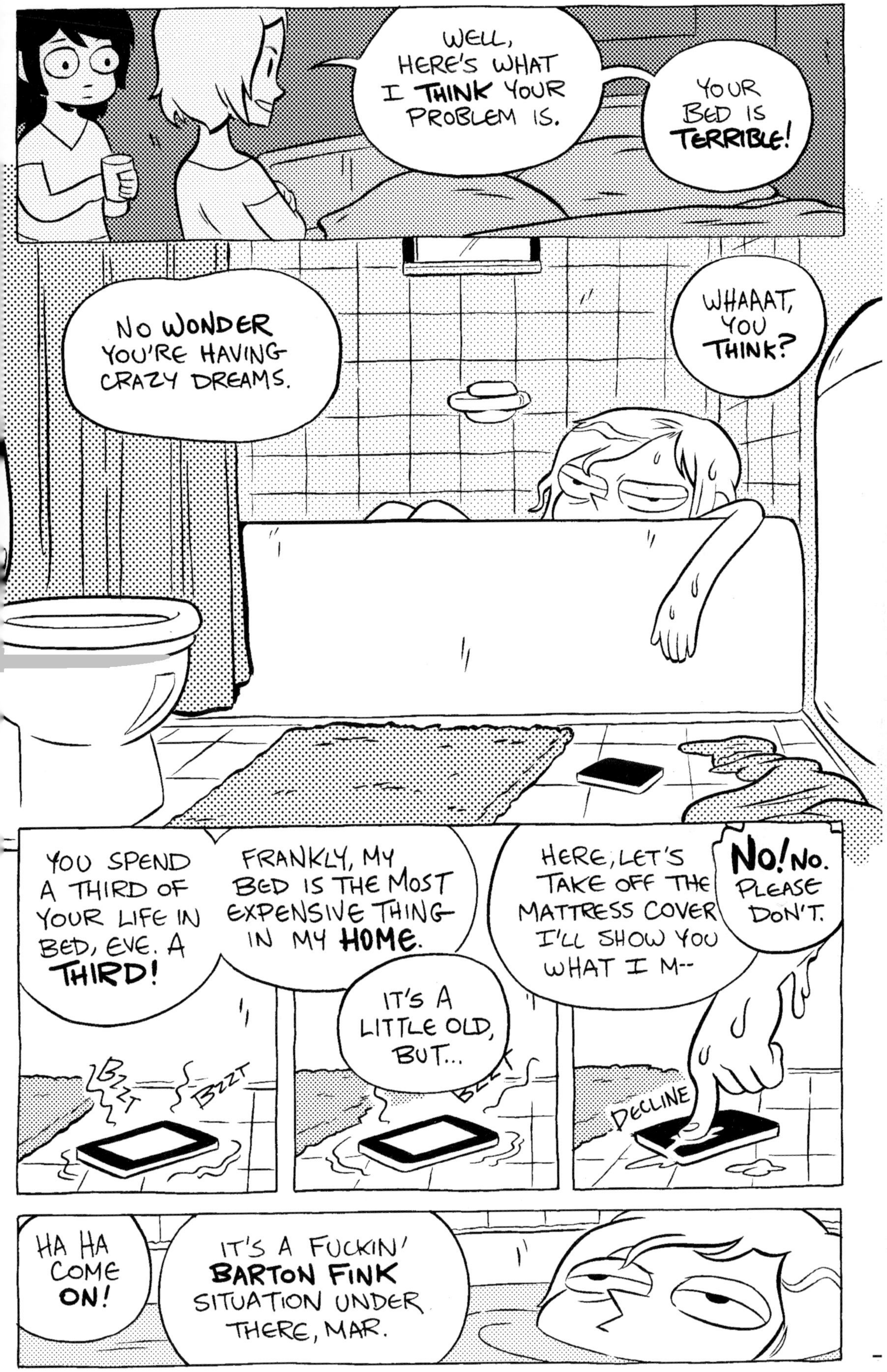

WELL, HERE'S WHAT I THINK YOUR PROBLEM IS.
YOUR BED IS TERRIBLE!
NO WONDER YOU'RE HAVING CRAZY DREAMS.
WHAAAT, YOU THINK?
YOU SPEND A THIRD OF YOUR LIFE IN BED, EVE. A THIRD!
FRANKLY, MY BED IS THE MOST EXPENSIVE THING IN MY HOME.
IT'S A LITTLE OLD, BUT...
BZZT
BZZT
HERE, LET'S TAKE OFF THE MATTRESS COVER I'LL SHOW YOU WHAT I M--
NO! NO. PLEASE DON'T.
DECLINE
HA HA COME ON!
IT'S A FUCKIN' BARTON FINK SITUATION UNDER THERE, MAR.

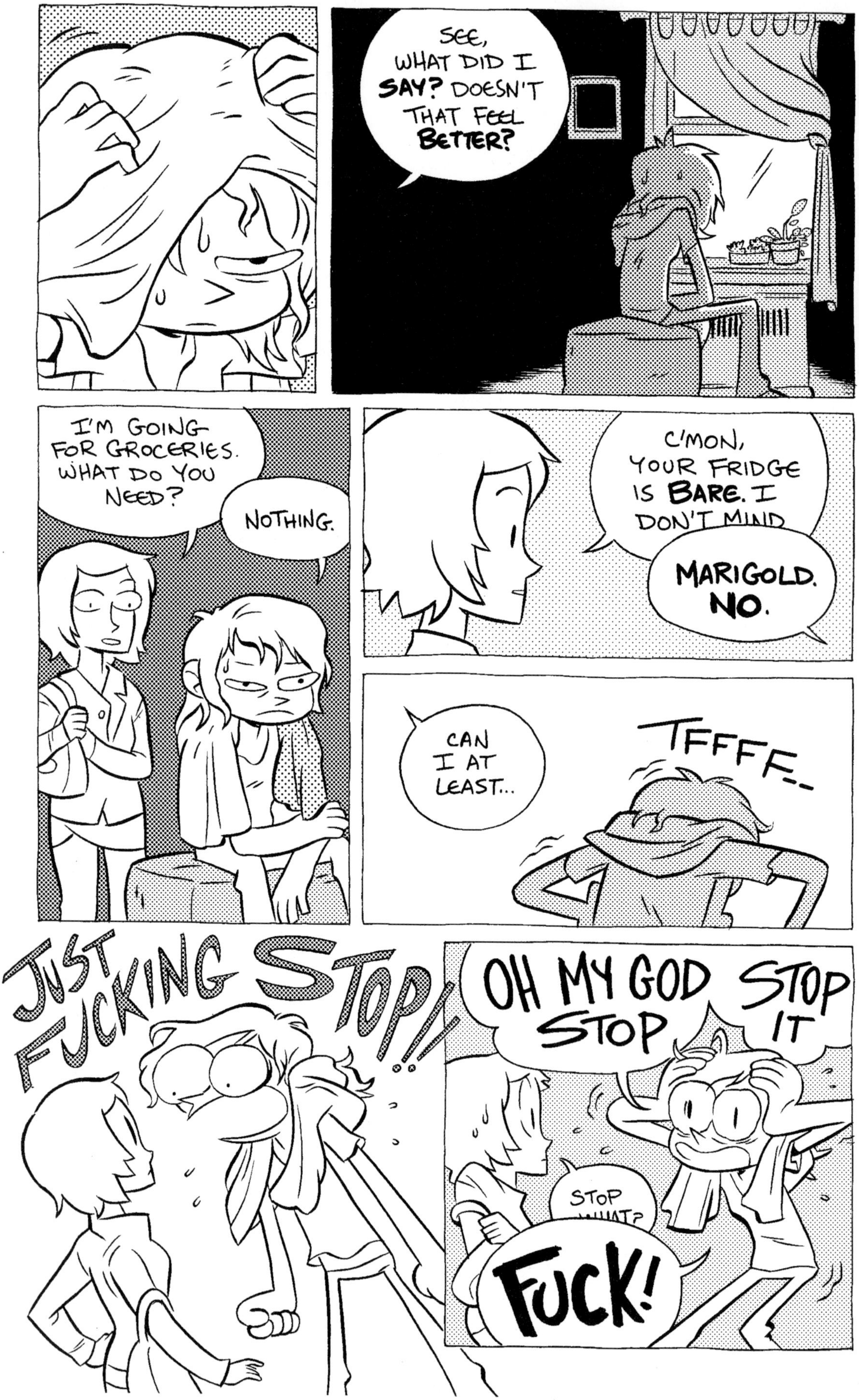
SEE, WHAT DID I SAY? DOESN'T THAT FEEL BETTER?
I'M GOING FOR GROCERIES. WHAT DO YOU NEED?
NOTHING.
C'MON, YOUR FRIDGE IS BARE. I DON'T MIND
MARIGOLD. NO.
CAN I AT LEAST...
TFFFF--
JUST FUCKING STOP!!
OH MY GOD STOP
STOP IT
STOP
FUCK!

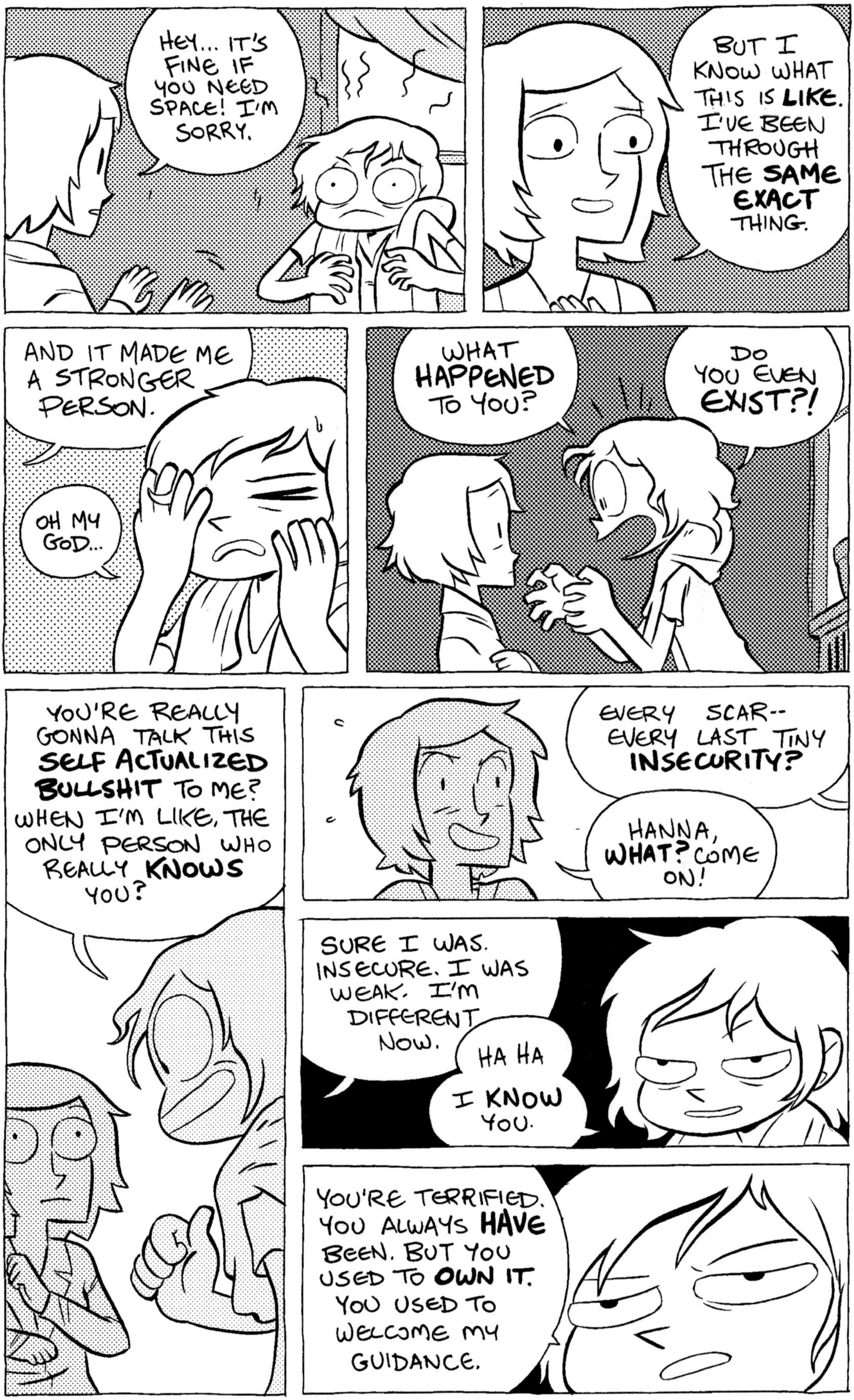
HEY... IT'S FINE IF YOU NEED SPACE! I'M SORRY.
BUT I KNOW WHAT THIS IS **LIKE**. I'VE BEEN THROUGH THE **SAME EXACT** THING.
AND IT MADE ME A STRONGER PERSON.
OH MY GOD...
WHAT **HAPPENED** TO YOU?
DO YOU EVEN **EXIST?!**
YOU'RE REALLY GONNA TALK THIS **SELF ACTUALIZED BULLSHIT** TO ME? WHEN I'M LIKE, THE ONLY PERSON WHO REALLY **KNOWS** YOU?
EVERY SCAR-- EVERY LAST TINY **INSECURITY?**
HANNA, **WHAT?** COME ON!
SURE I WAS. INSECURE. I WAS WEAK. I'M DIFFERENT NOW.
HA HA
I **KNOW** YOU.
YOU'RE TERRIFIED. YOU ALWAYS **HAVE** BEEN. BUT YOU USED TO **OWN IT**. YOU USED TO WELCOME MY GUIDANCE.

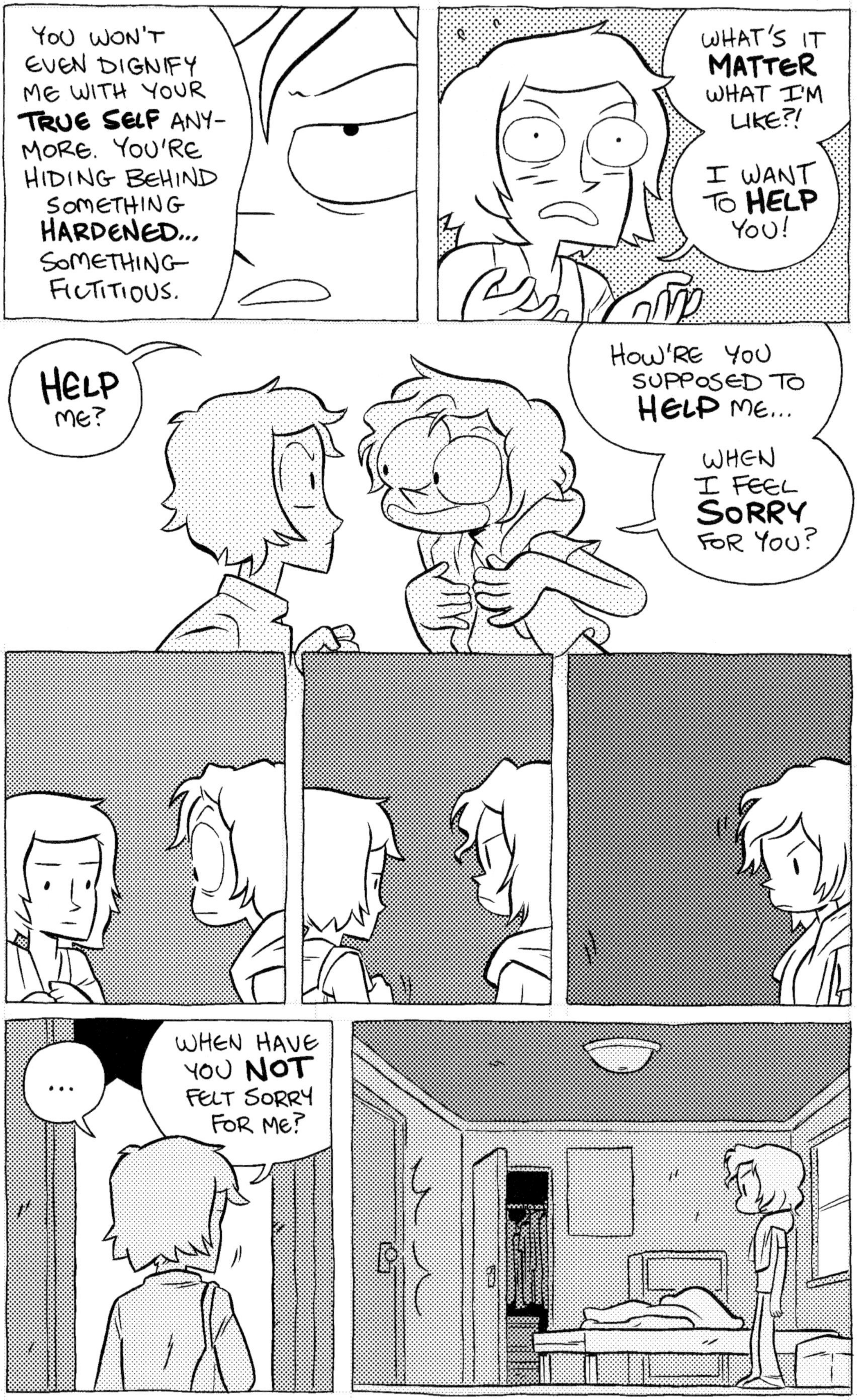
YOU WON'T EVEN DIGNIFY ME WITH YOUR TRUE SELF ANYMORE. YOU'RE HIDING BEHIND SOMETHING HARDENED... SOMETHING FICTITIOUS.
WHAT'S IT MATTER WHAT I'M LIKE?!
I WANT TO HELP YOU!
HELP ME?
HOW'RE YOU SUPPOSED TO HELP ME...
WHEN I FEEL SORRY FOR YOU?
...
WHEN HAVE YOU NOT FELT SORRY FOR ME?

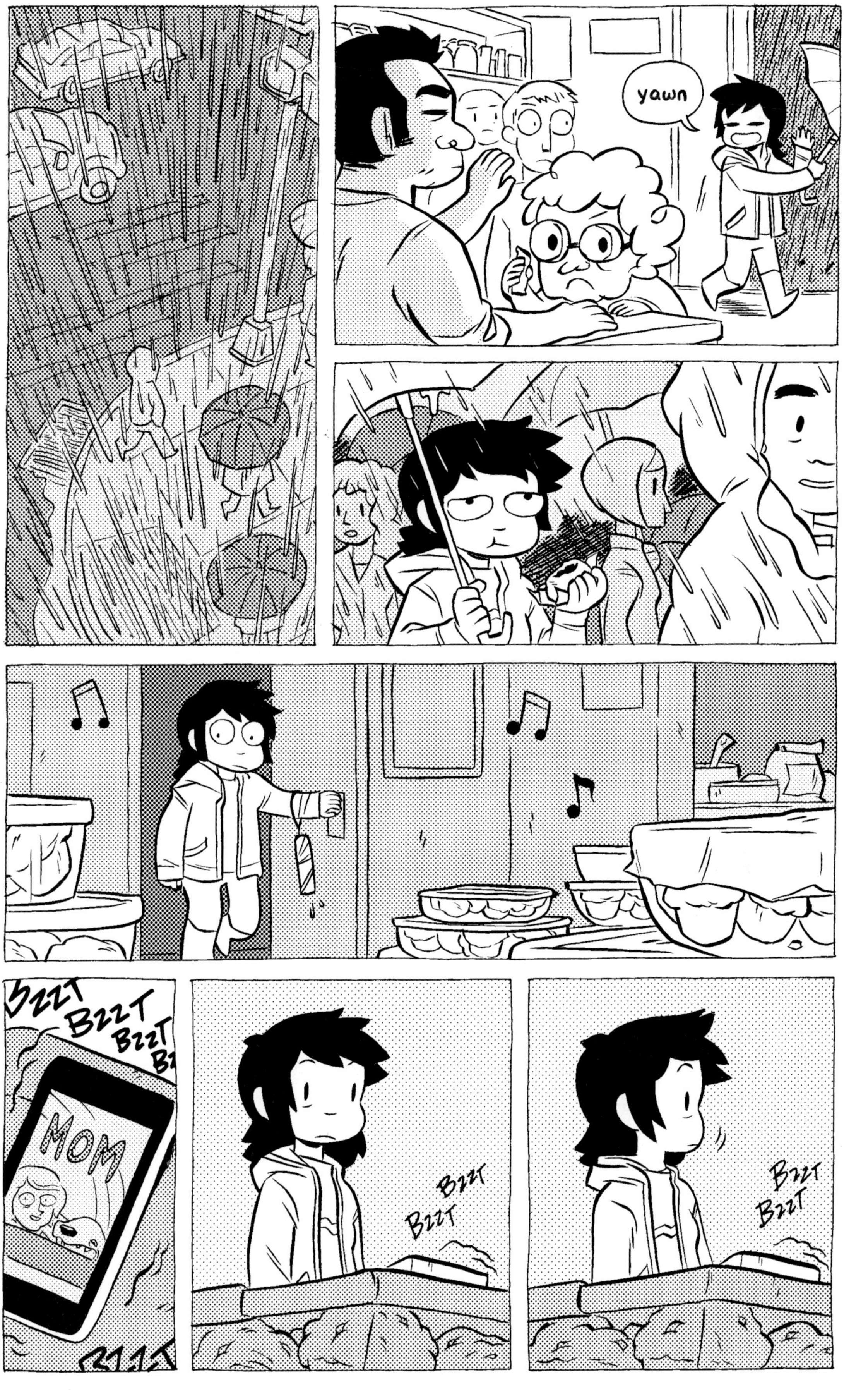

yawn
BZZT
BZZT
BZZT
MOM
BZZT
BZZT
BZZT
BZZT

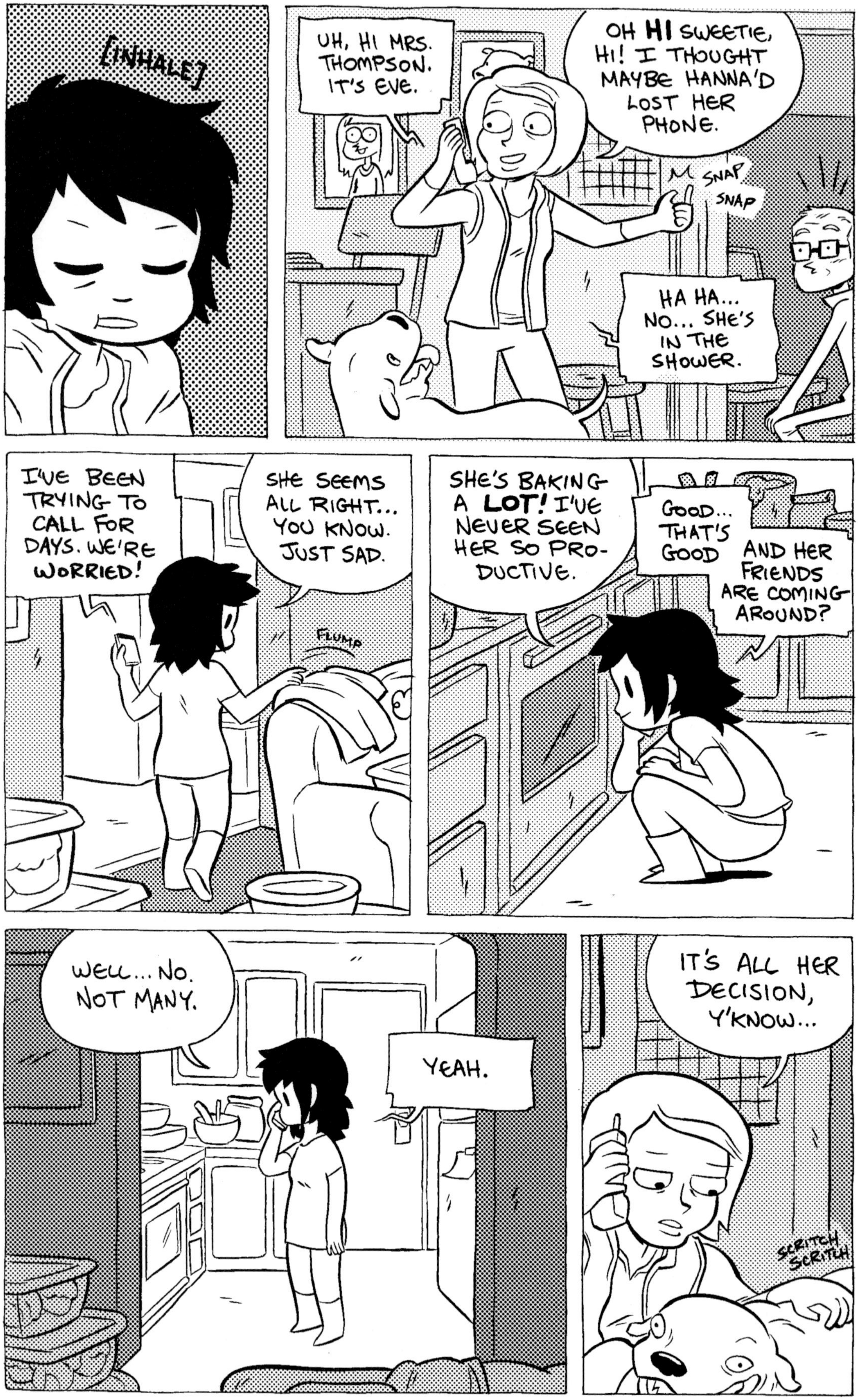
[INHALE]
UH, HI MRS. THOMPSON. IT'S EVE.
OH HI SWEETIE, HI! I THOUGHT MAYBE HANNA'D LOST HER PHONE.
SNAP
SNAP
HA HA... NO... SHE'S IN THE SHOWER.
I'VE BEEN TRYING TO CALL FOR DAYS. WE'RE WORRIED!
SHE SEEMS ALL RIGHT... YOU KNOW. JUST SAD.
FLUMP
SHE'S BAKING A LOT! I'VE NEVER SEEN HER SO PRO-DUCTIVE.
GOOD... THAT'S GOOD
AND HER FRIENDS ARE COMING AROUND?
WELL... NO. NOT MANY.
YEAH.
IT'S ALL HER DECISION, Y'KNOW...
SCRITCH
SCRITCH

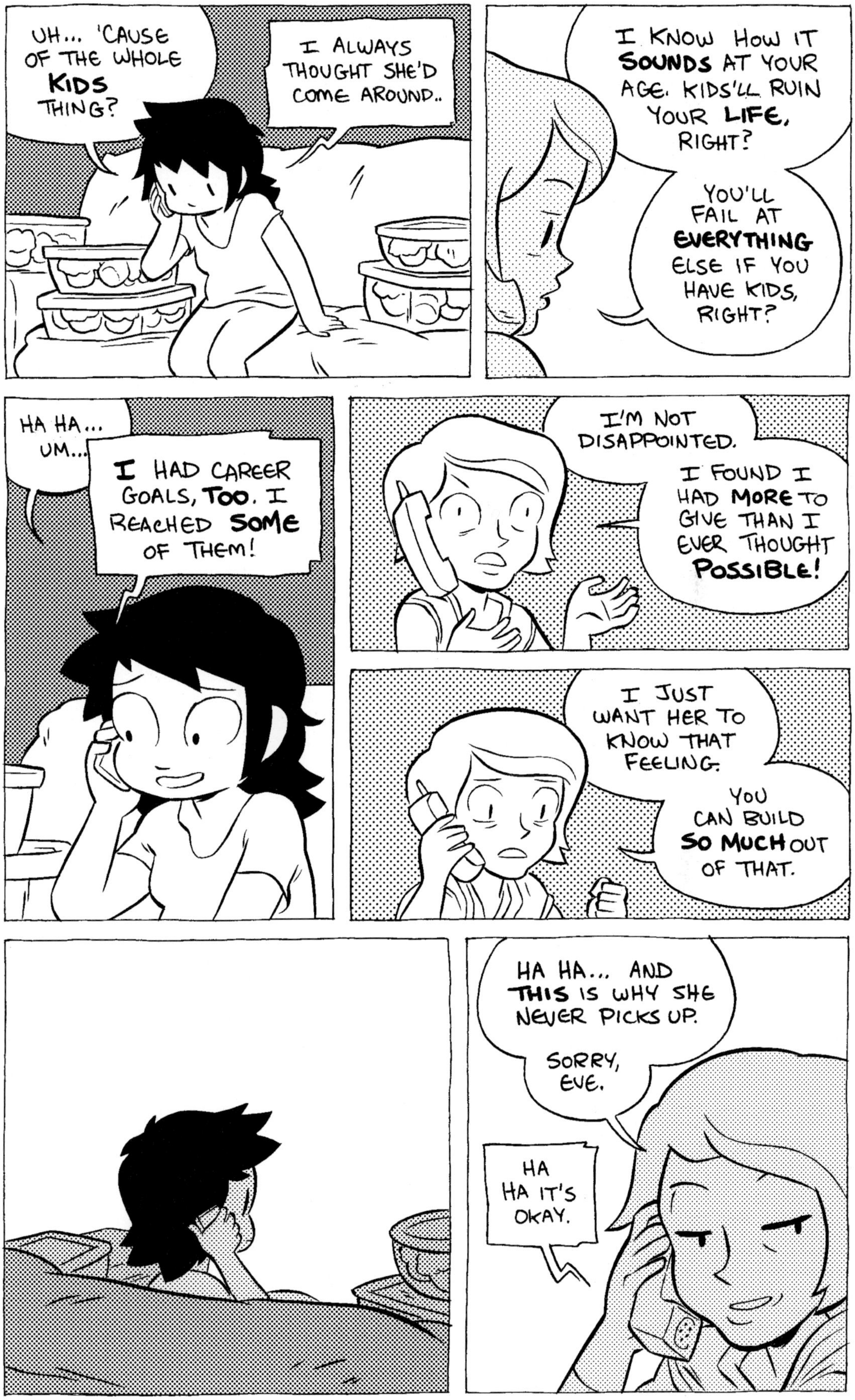
UH... 'CAUSE OF THE WHOLE KIDS THING?
I ALWAYS THOUGHT SHE'D COME AROUND..
I KNOW HOW IT SOUNDS AT YOUR AGE. KIDS'LL RUIN YOUR LIFE, RIGHT?
YOU'LL FAIL AT EVERYTHING ELSE IF YOU HAVE KIDS, RIGHT?
HA HA... UM...
I HAD CAREER GOALS, TOO. I REACHED SOME OF THEM!
I'M NOT DISAPPOINTED.
I FOUND I HAD MORE TO GIVE THAN I EVER THOUGHT POSSIBLE!
I JUST WANT HER TO KNOW THAT FEELING.
YOU CAN BUILD SO MUCH OUT OF THAT.
HA HA... AND THIS IS WHY SHE NEVER PICKS UP.
SORRY, EVE.
HA HA IT'S OKAY.

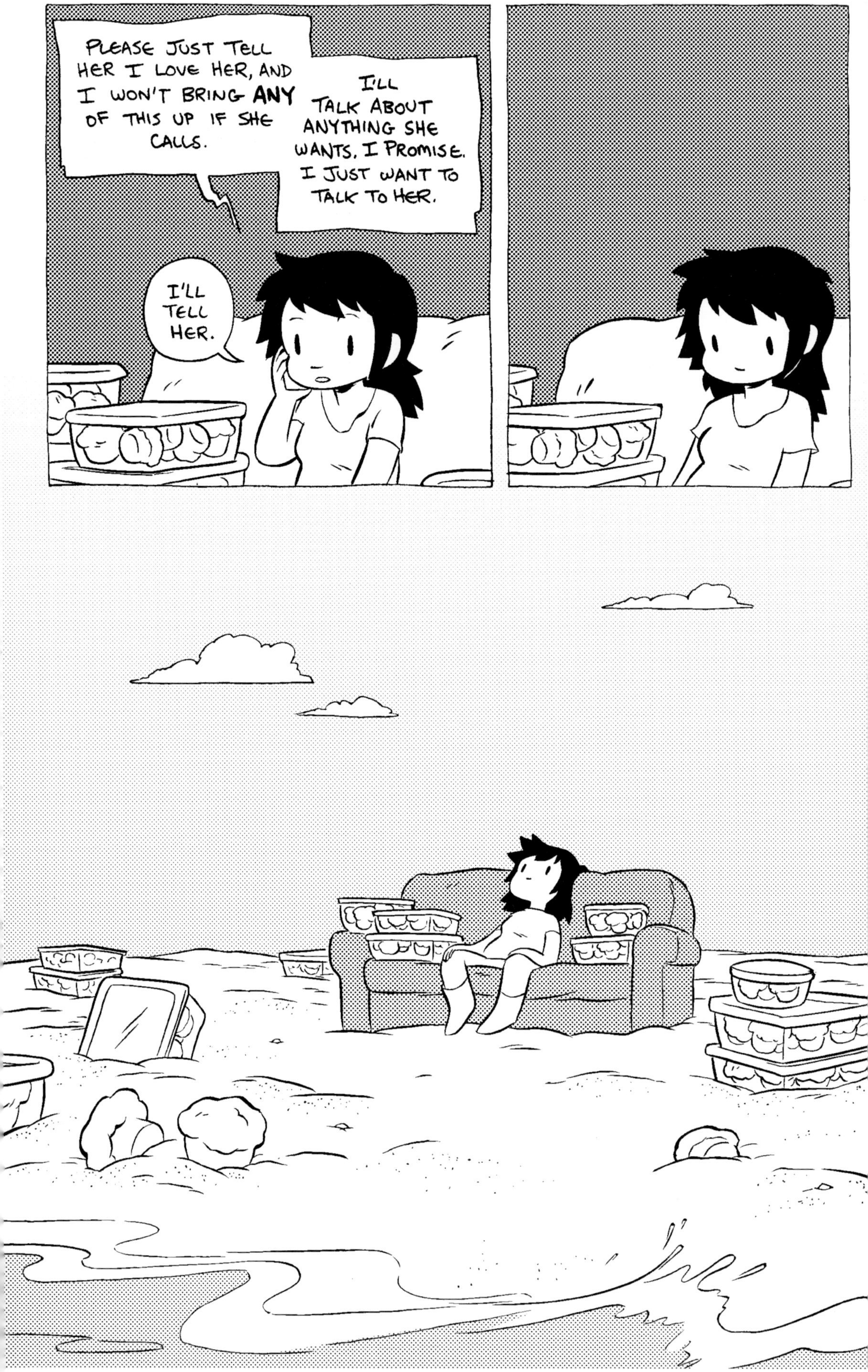
PLEASE JUST TELL HER I LOVE HER, AND I WON'T BRING ANY OF THIS UP IF SHE CALLS.
I'LL TALK ABOUT ANYTHING SHE WANTS. I PROMISE. I JUST WANT TO TALK TO HER.
I'LL TELL HER.

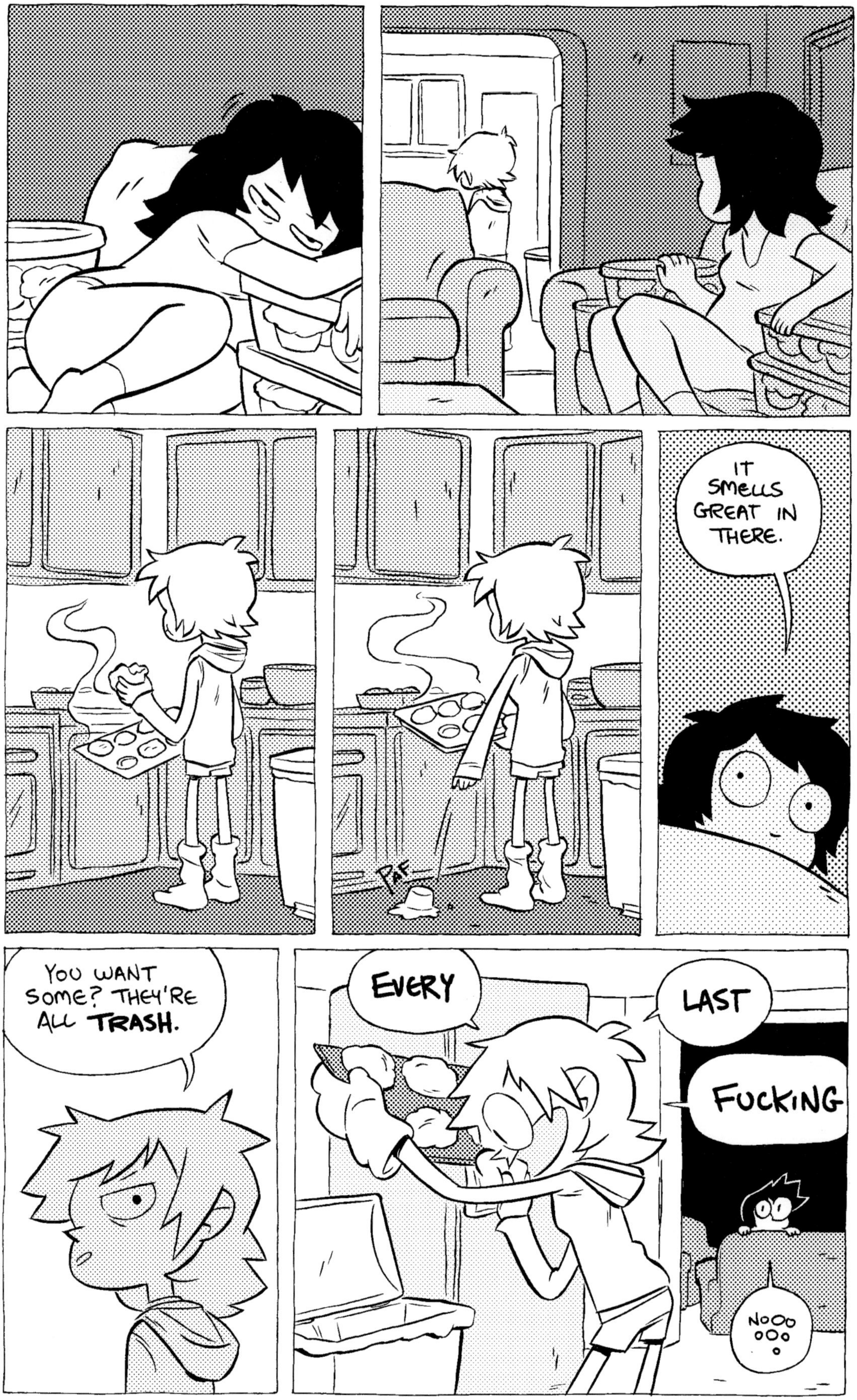
PAF
IT SMELLS GREAT IN THERE.
YOU WANT SOME? THEY'RE ALL TRASH.
EVERY
LAST
FUCKING
NOOOOOOO

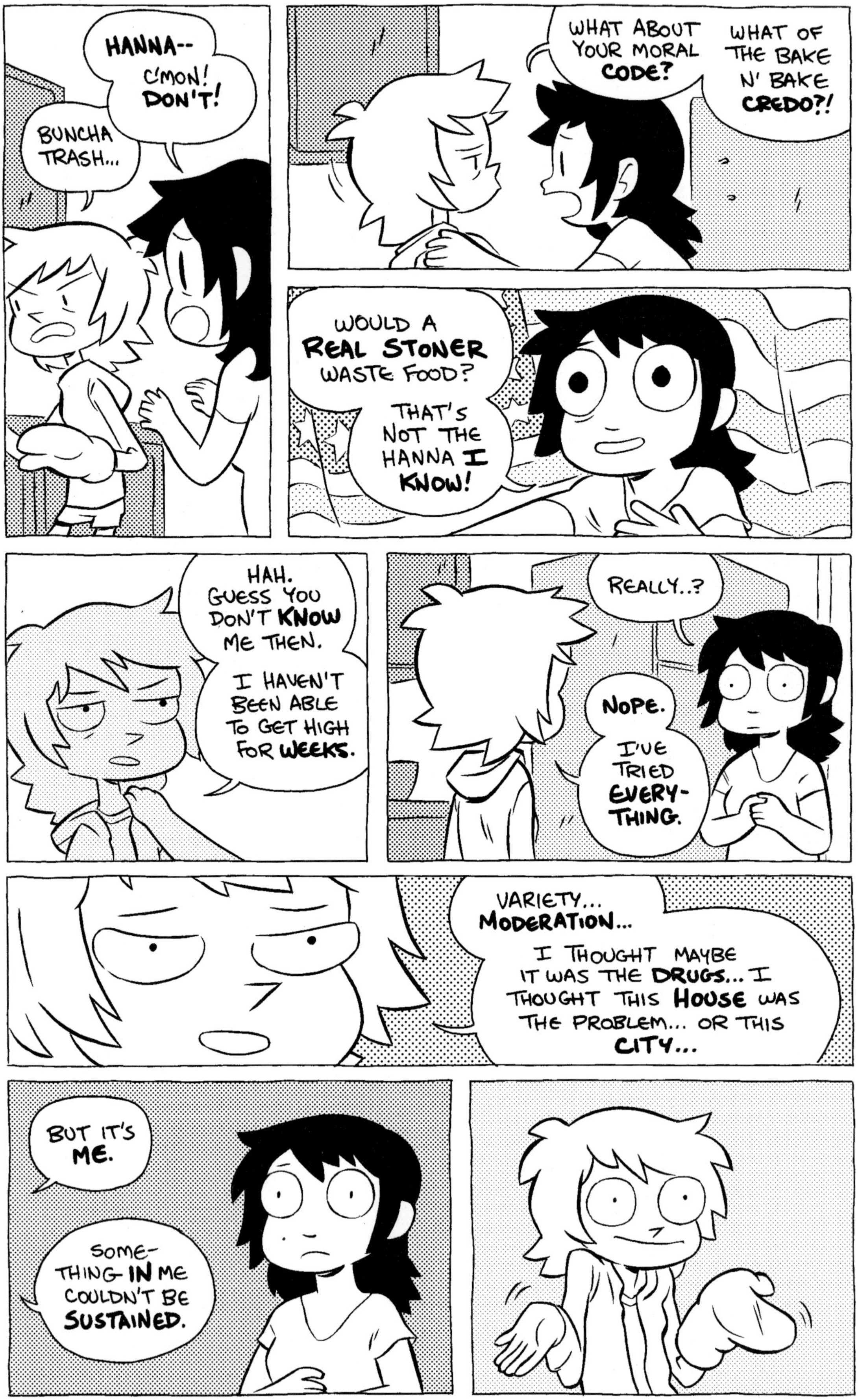
HANNA--
C'MON! DON'T!
BUNCHA TRASH...
WHAT ABOUT YOUR MORAL CODE?
WHAT OF THE BAKE N' BAKE CREDO?!
WOULD A REAL STONER WASTE FOOD?
THAT'S NOT THE HANNA I KNOW!
HAH. GUESS YOU DON'T KNOW ME THEN.
I HAVEN'T BEEN ABLE TO GET HIGH FOR WEEKS.
REALLY..?
NOPE.
I'VE TRIED EVERY-THING.
VARIETY... MODERATION...
I THOUGHT MAYBE IT WAS THE DRUGS... I THOUGHT THIS HOUSE WAS THE PROBLEM... OR THIS CITY...
BUT IT'S ME.
SOME-THING IN ME COULDN'T BE SUSTAINED.

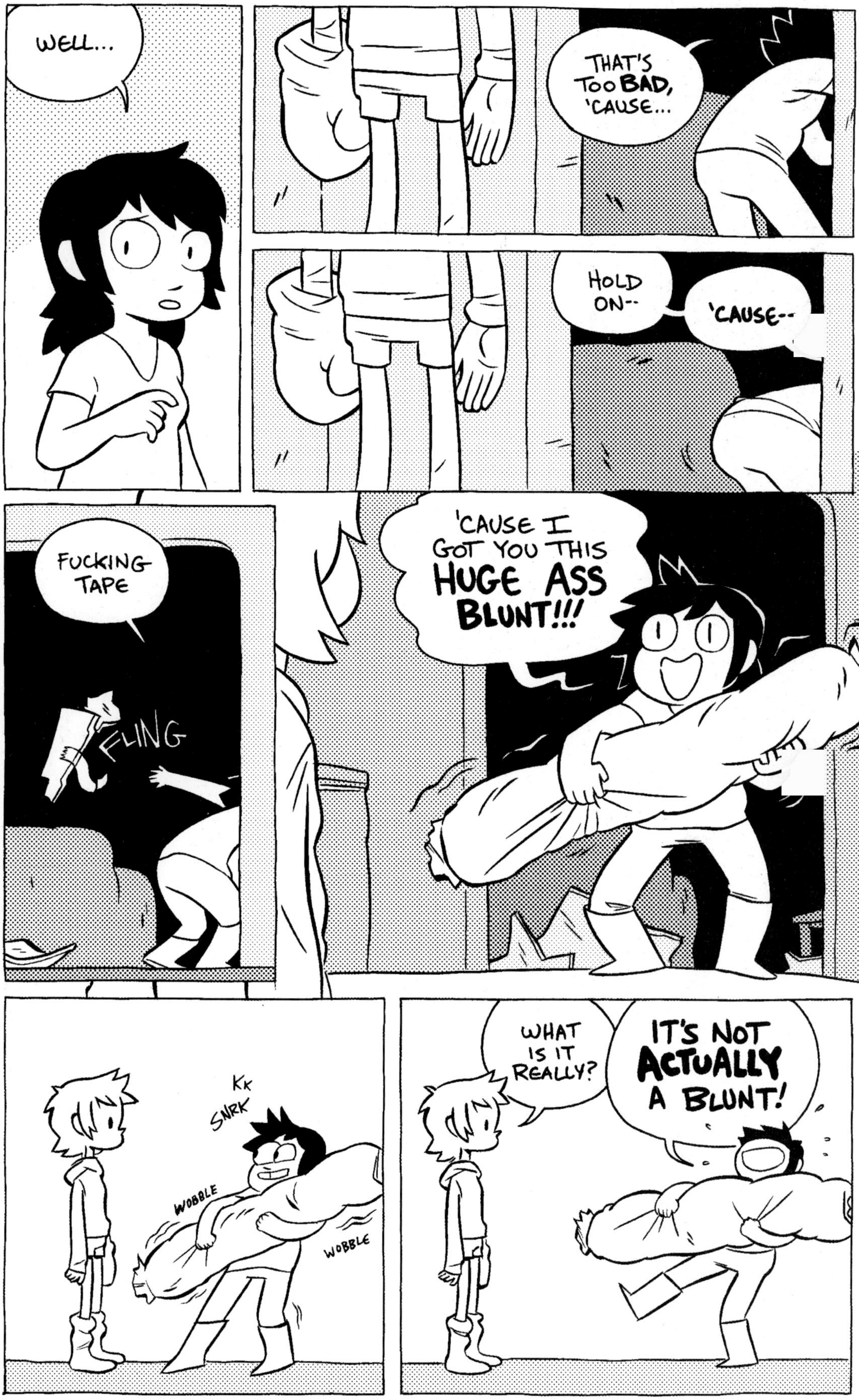
WELL...
THAT'S TOO BAD, 'CAUSE...
HOLD ON--
'CAUSE--
FUCKING TAPE
FLING
'CAUSE I GOT YOU THIS HUGE ASS BLUNT!!!
KK SNRK
WOBBLE
WOBBLE
WHAT IS IT REALLY?
IT'S NOT ACTUALLY A BLUNT!

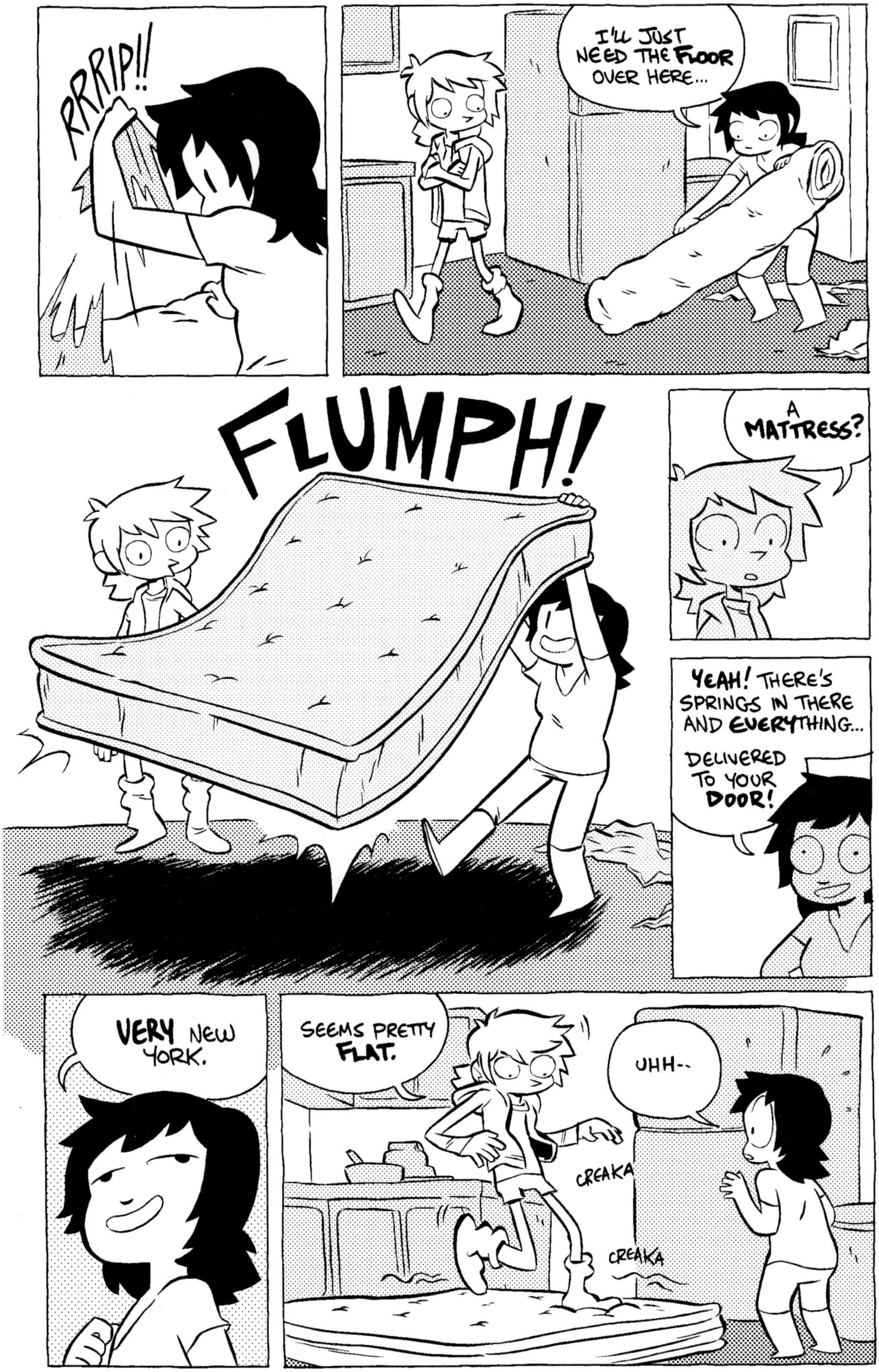
RRRIP!!
I'LL JUST NEED THE FLOOR OVER HERE...
FLUMPH!
A MATTRESS?
YEAH! THERE'S SPRINGS IN THERE AND EVERYTHING...
DELIVERED TO YOUR DOOR!
VERY NEW YORK.
SEEMS PRETTY FLAT.
UHH--
CREAKA
CREAKA

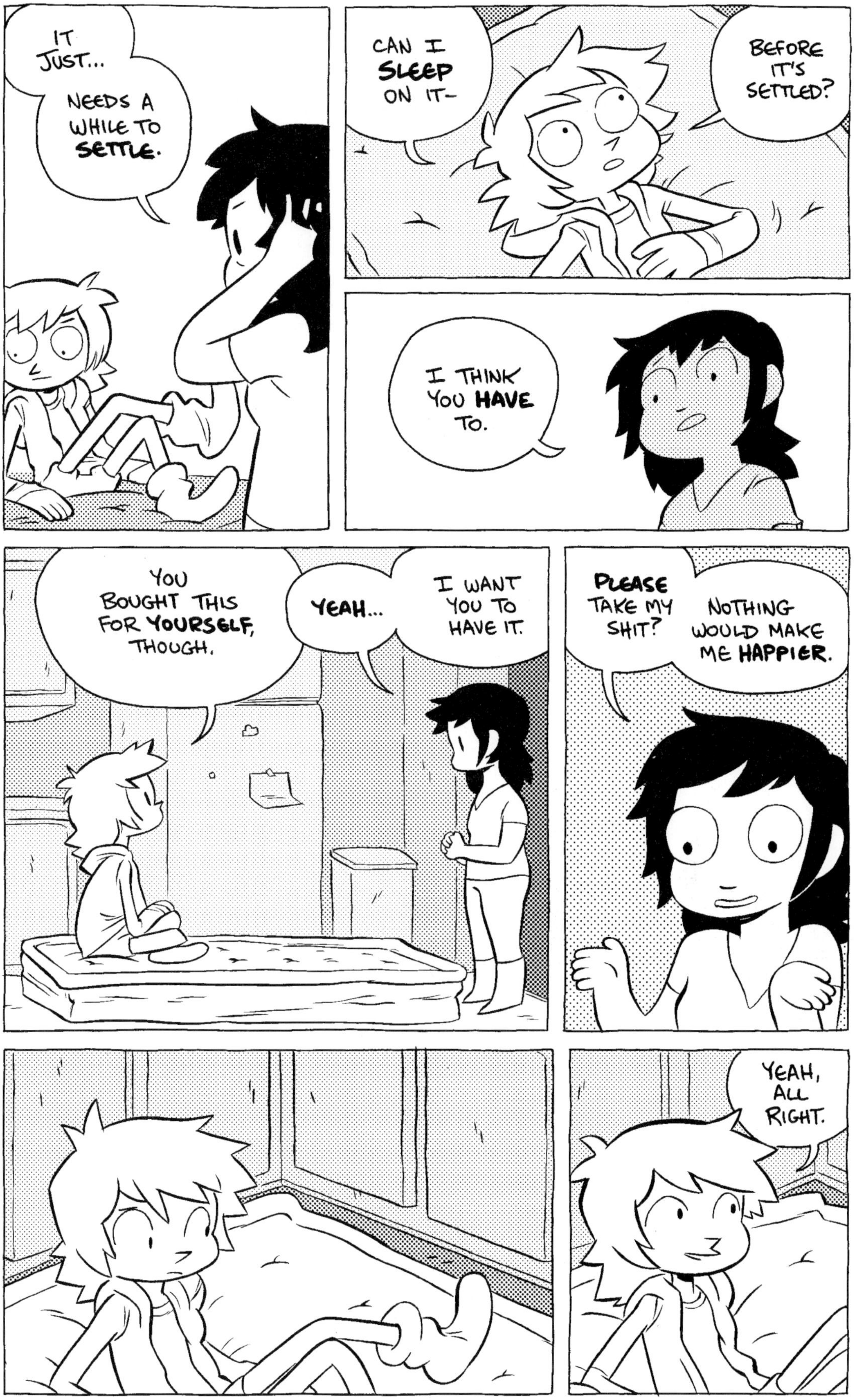

IT JUST...
NEEDS A WHILE TO SETTLE.
CAN I SLEEP ON IT-
BEFORE IT'S SETTLED?
I THINK YOU HAVE TO.
YOU BOUGHT THIS FOR YOURSELF, THOUGH.
YEAH...
I WANT YOU TO HAVE IT.
PLEASE TAKE MY SHIT?
NOTHING WOULD MAKE ME HAPPIER.
YEAH, ALL RIGHT.

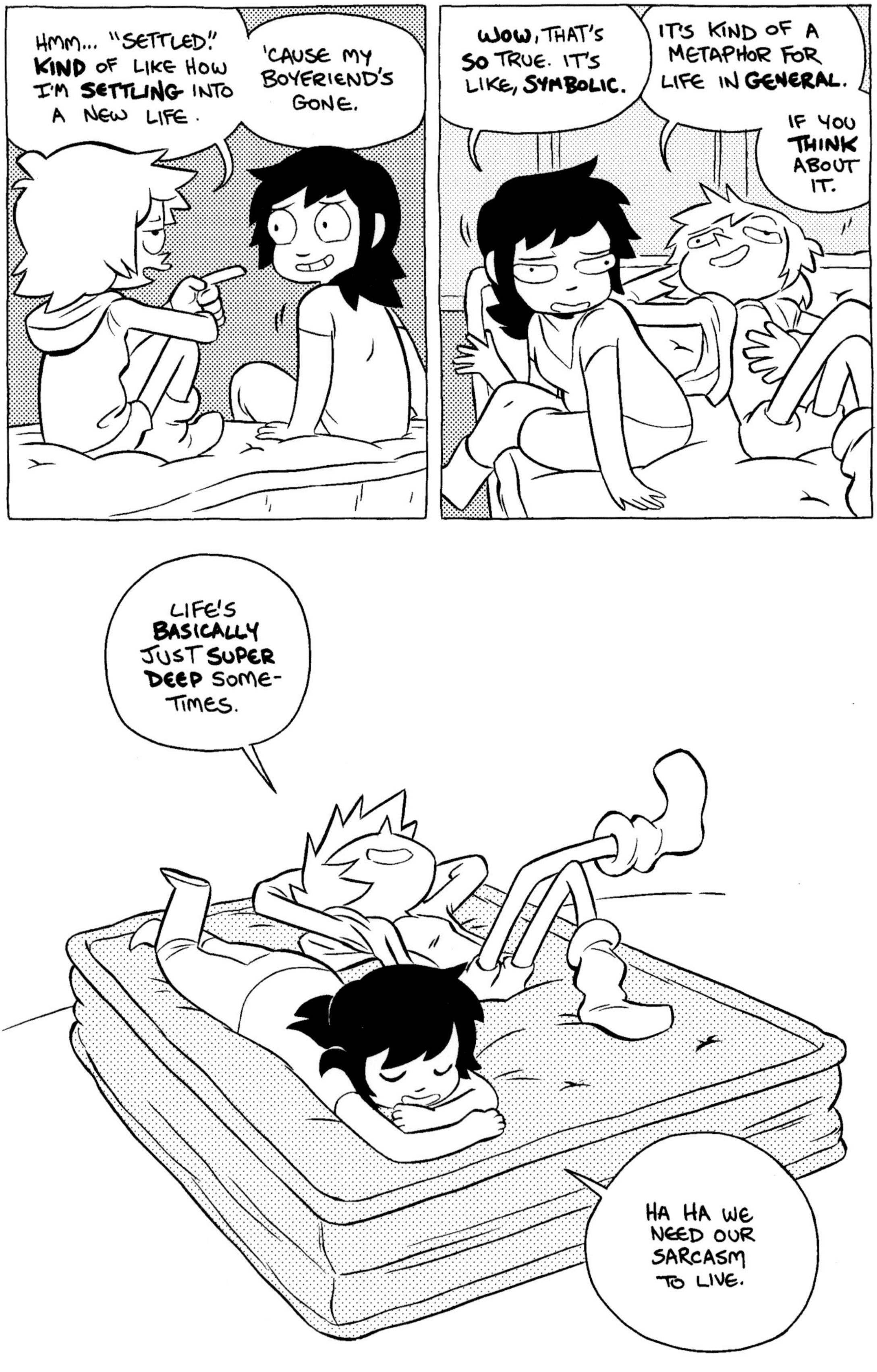

HMM... "SETTLED." KIND OF LIKE HOW I'M SETTLING INTO A NEW LIFE.
'CAUSE MY BOYFRIEND'S GONE.
WOW, THAT'S SO TRUE. IT'S LIKE, SYMBOLIC.
IT'S KIND OF A METAPHOR FOR LIFE IN GENERAL.
IF YOU THINK ABOUT IT.
LIFE'S BASICALLY JUST SUPER DEEP SOME-TIMES.
HA HA WE NEED OUR SARCASM TO LIVE.

45

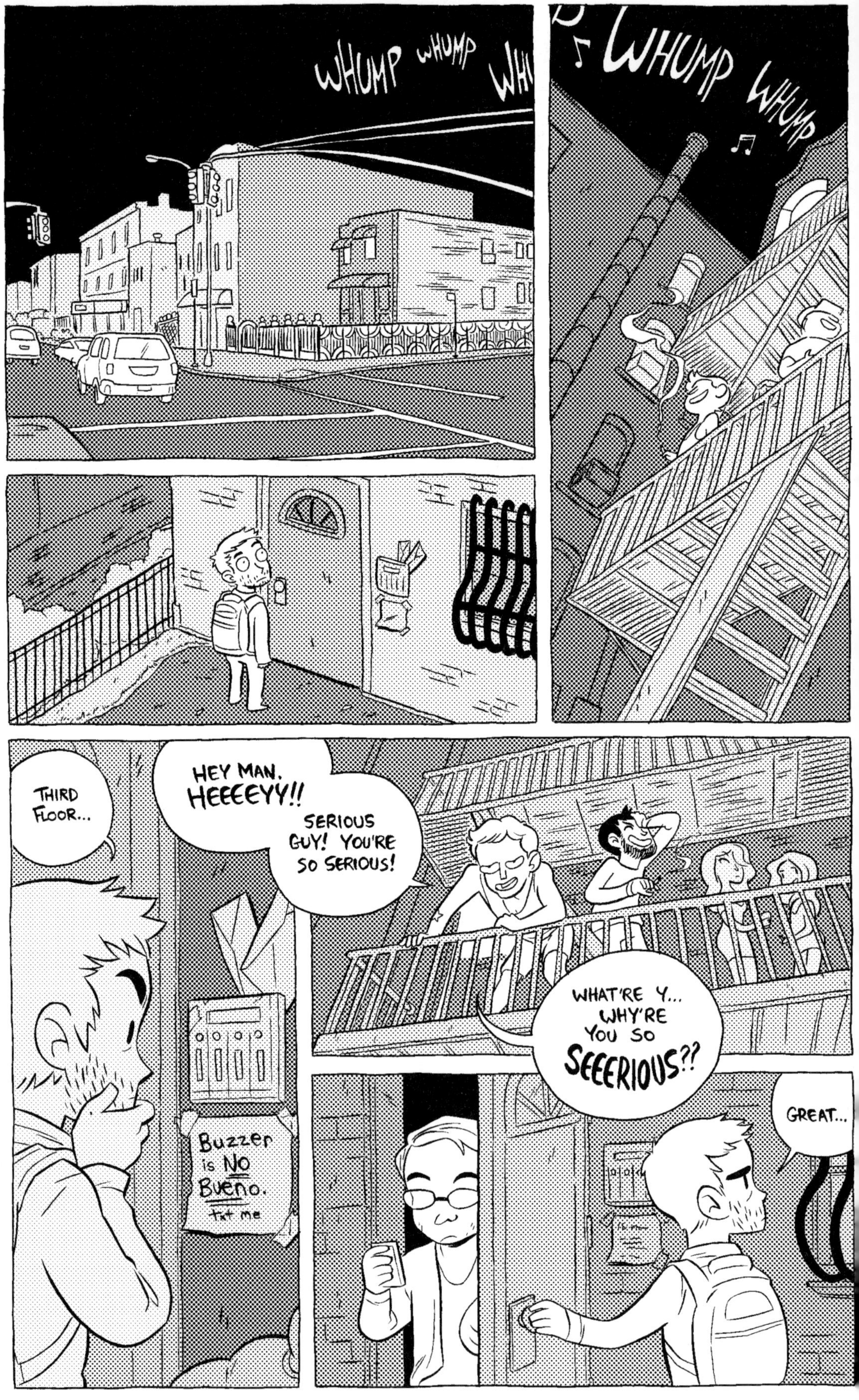
WHUMP WHUMP WHU
WHUMP WHUMP
THIRD FLOOR...
HEY MAN. HEEEEYY!!
SERIOUS GUY! YOU'RE SO SERIOUS!
Buzzer is NO Bueno. txt me
WHAT'RE Y... WHY'RE YOU SO SEEERIOUS??
GREAT...

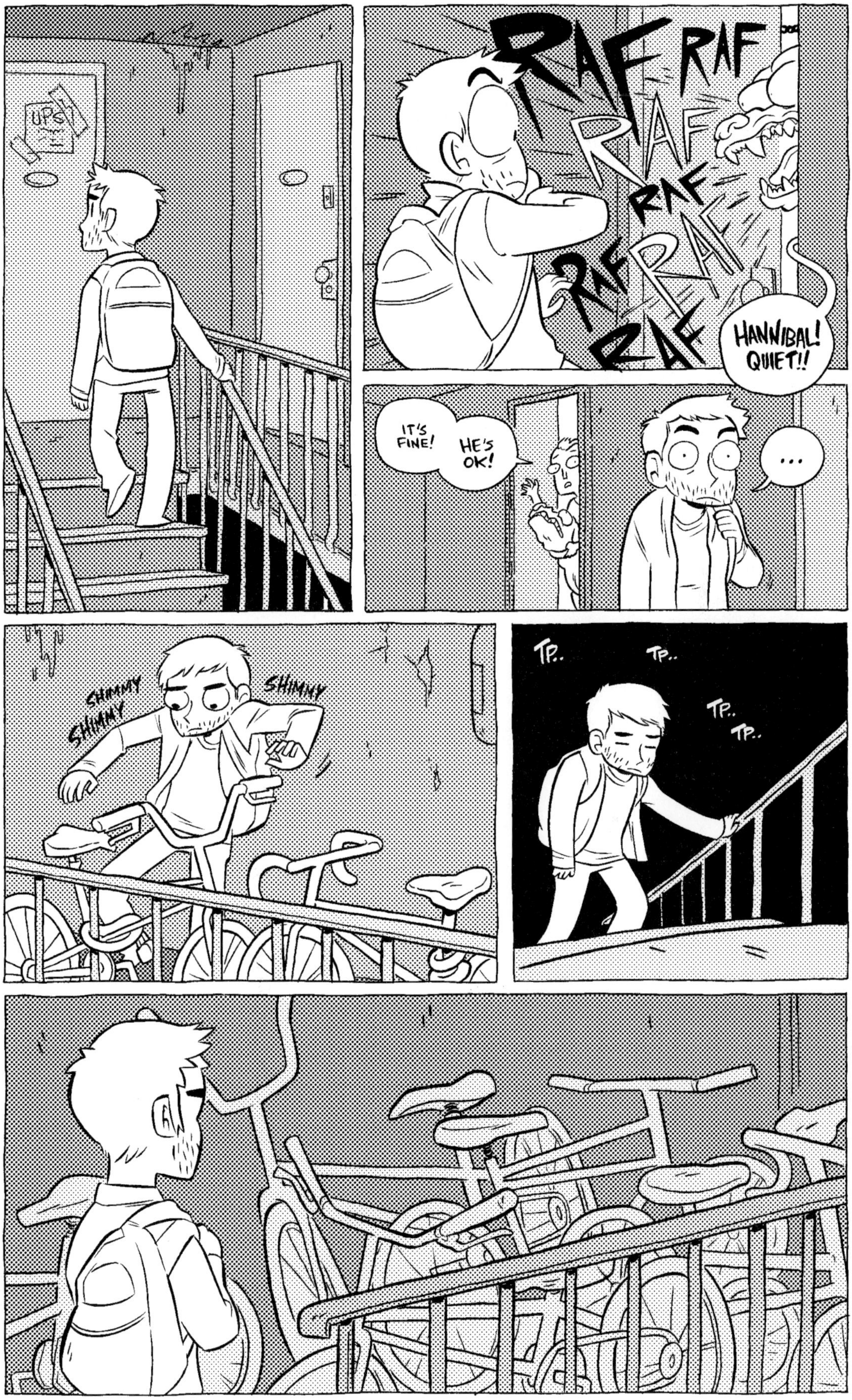
UPS
RAF RAF
RAF
RAF
RAF
RAF
RAF
HANNIBAL! QUIET!!
IT'S FINE!
HE'S OK!
...
SHIMMY SHIMMY
SHIMMY
TP..
TP..
TP..
TP..

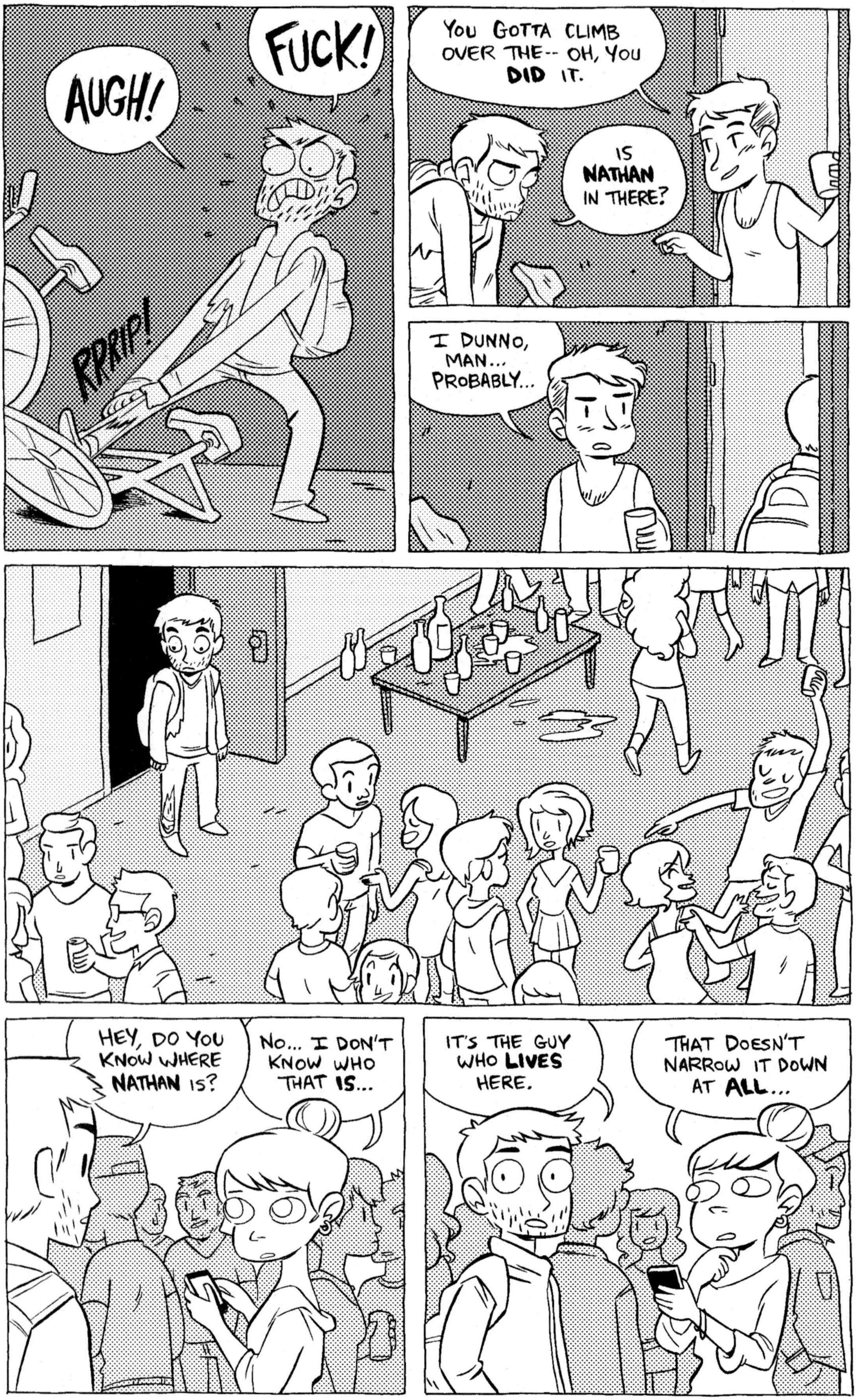
AUGH!
FUCK!
RPRIP!
YOU GOTTA CLIMB OVER THE-- OH, YOU DID IT.
IS NATHAN IN THERE?
I DUNNO, MAN... PROBABLY...
HEY, DO YOU KNOW WHERE NATHAN IS?
NO... I DON'T KNOW WHO THAT IS...
IT'S THE GUY WHO LIVES HERE.
THAT DOESN'T NARROW IT DOWN AT ALL...

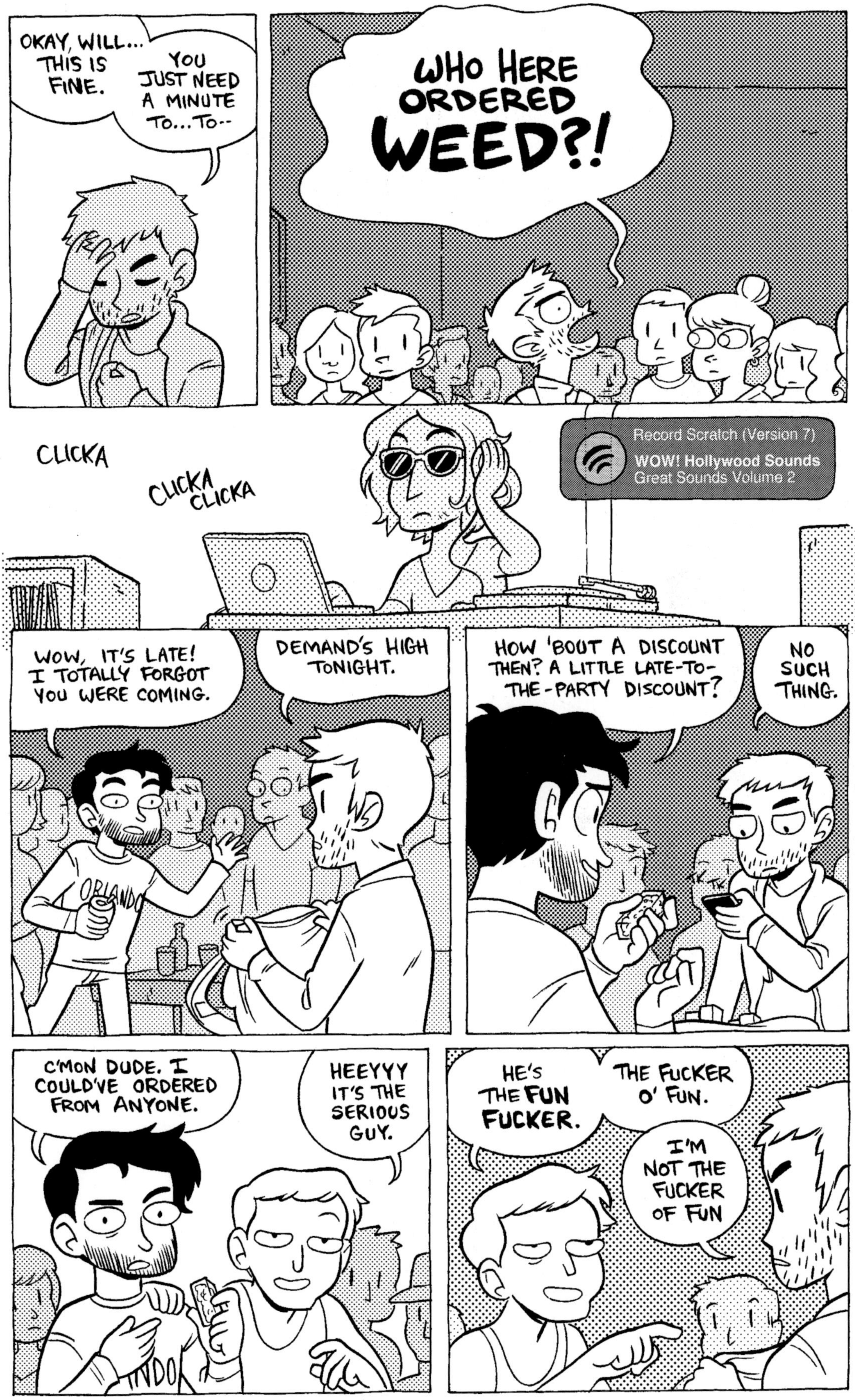
OKAY, WILL... THIS IS FINE.
YOU JUST NEED A MINUTE TO... TO--
WHO HERE ORDERED WEED?!
CLICKA
CLICKA CLICKA
Record Scratch (Version 7)
WOW! Hollywood Sounds
Great Sounds Volume 2
WOW, IT'S LATE! I TOTALLY FORGOT YOU WERE COMING.
DEMAND'S HIGH TONIGHT.
ORLANDO
HOW 'BOUT A DISCOUNT THEN? A LITTLE LATE-TO-THE-PARTY DISCOUNT?
NO SUCH THING.
C'MON DUDE. I COULD'VE ORDERED FROM ANYONE.
HEEYYY IT'S THE SERIOUS GUY.
HE'S THE FUN FUCKER.
THE FUCKER O' FUN.
I'M NOT THE FUCKER OF FUN

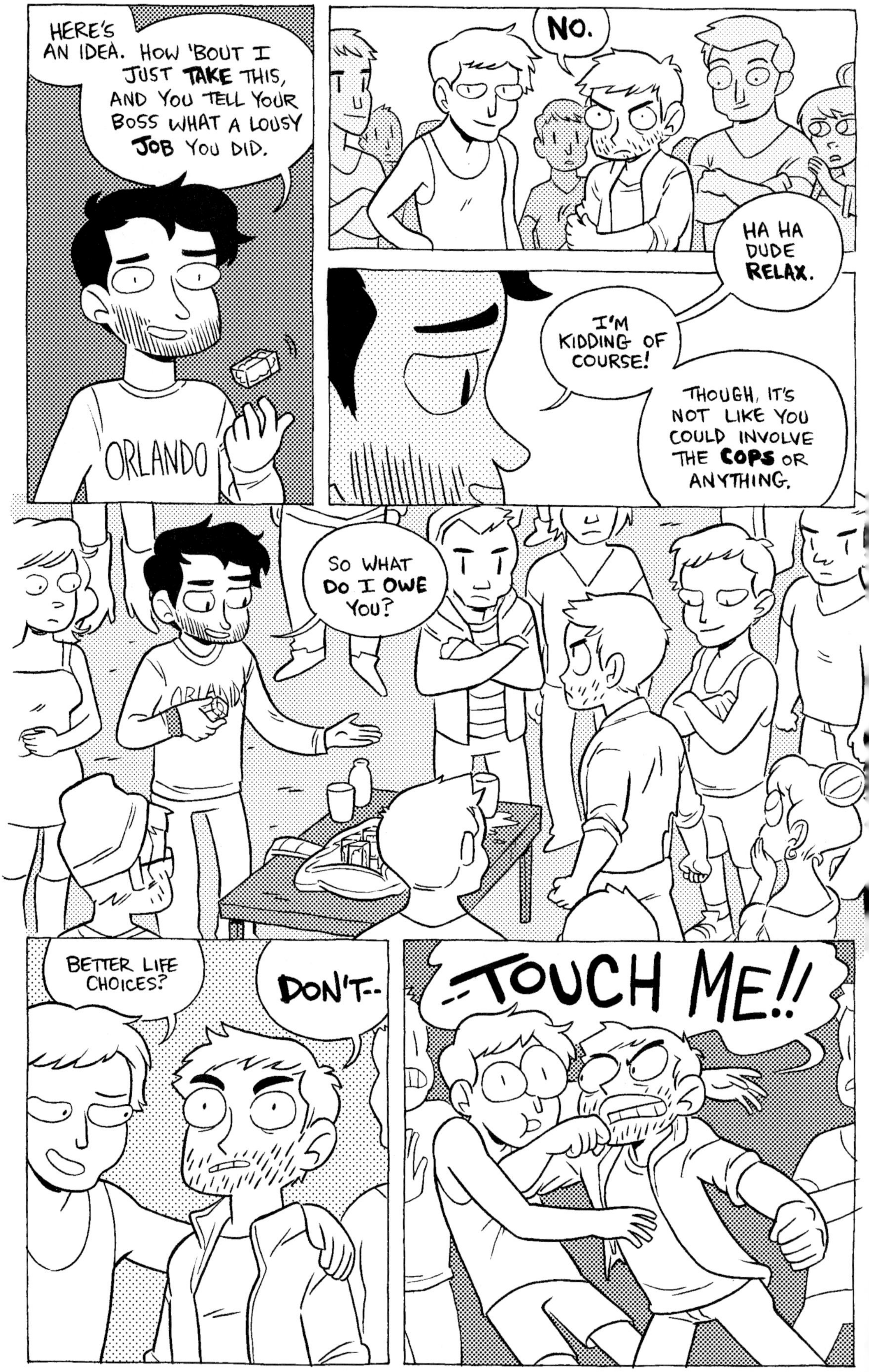
HERE'S AN IDEA. HOW 'BOUT I JUST TAKE THIS, AND YOU TELL YOUR BOSS WHAT A LOUSY JOB YOU DID.
ORLANDO
NO.
HA HA DUDE RELAX.
I'M KIDDING OF COURSE!
THOUGH, IT'S NOT LIKE YOU COULD INVOLVE THE COPS OR ANYTHING.
SO WHAT DO I OWE YOU?
BETTER LIFE CHOICES?
DON'T--
--TOUCH ME!!

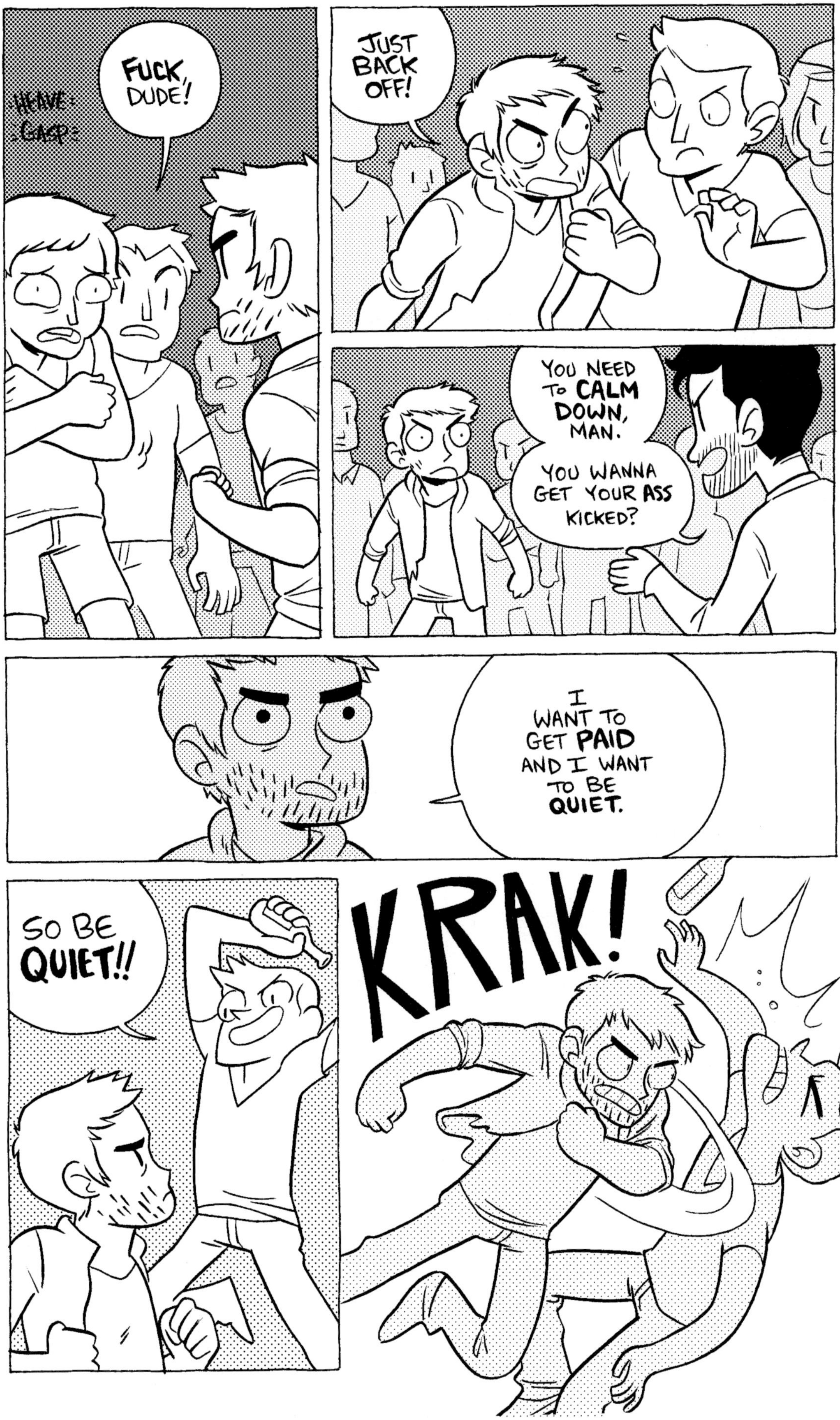

HEAVE
GASP
FUCK, DUDE!
JUST BACK OFF!
YOU NEED TO CALM DOWN, MAN.
YOU WANNA GET YOUR ASS KICKED?
I WANT TO GET PAID AND I WANT TO BE QUIET.
SO BE QUIET!!
KRAK!

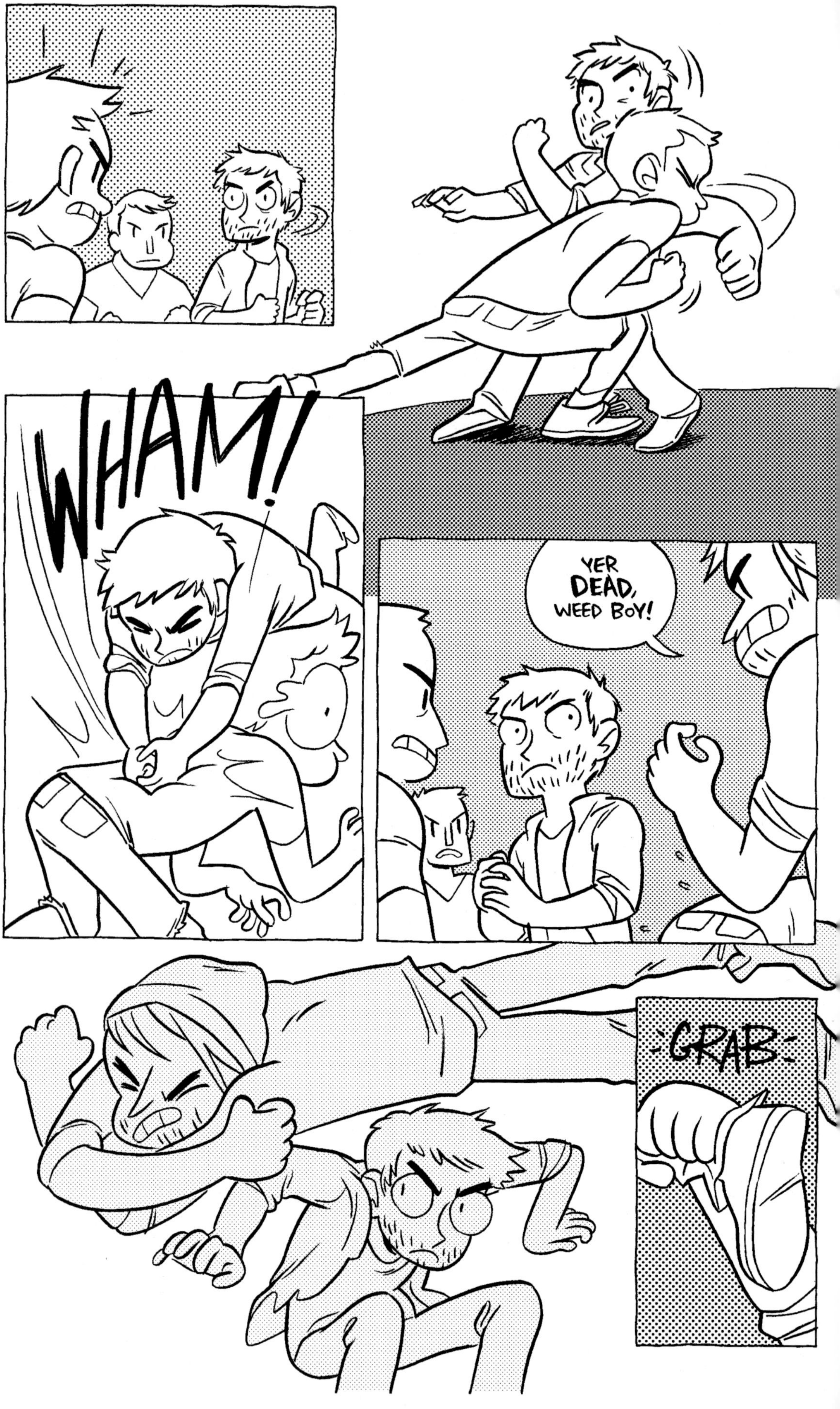
WHAM!
YER
DEAD,
WEED BOY!
GRAB

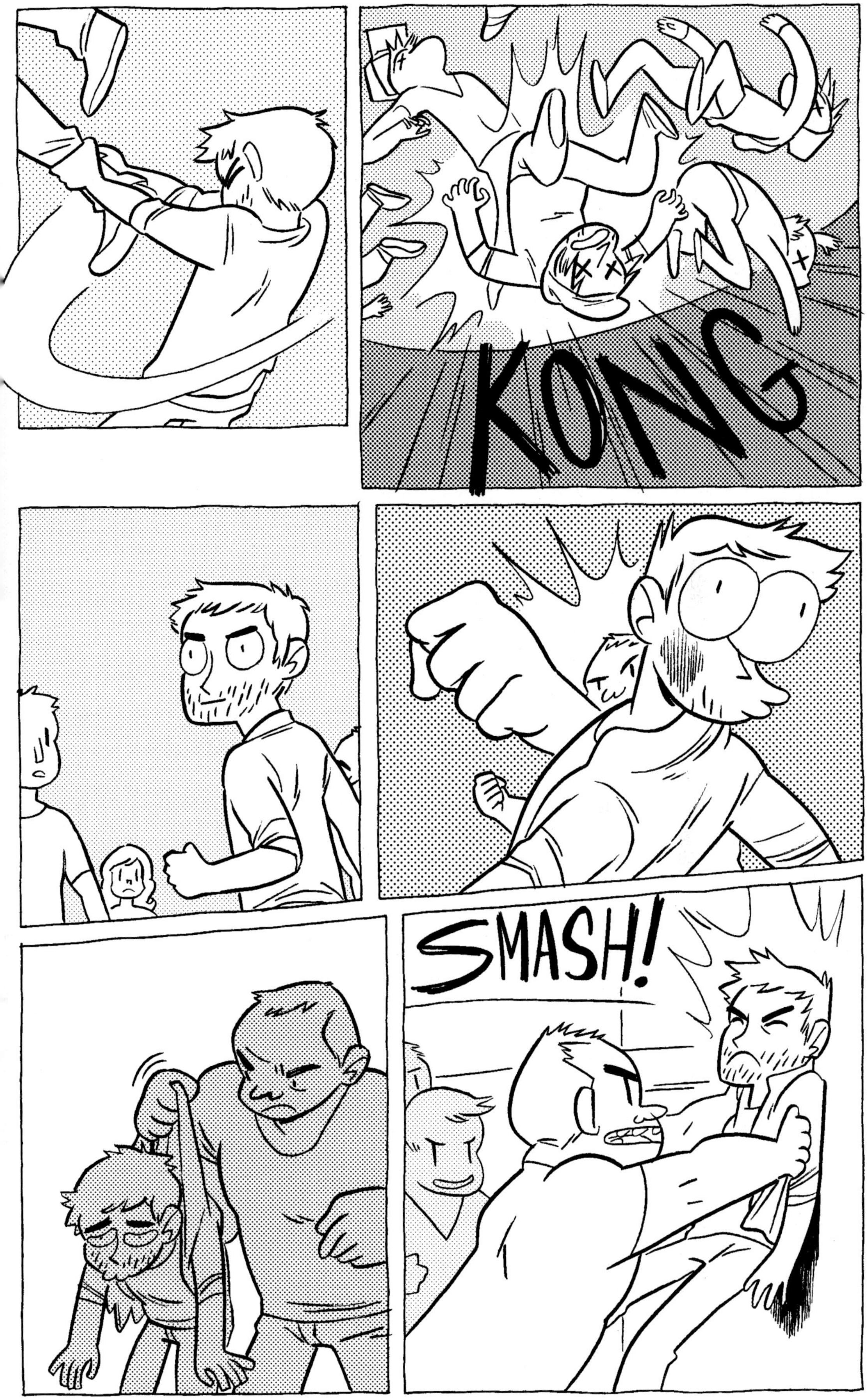
KONG
SMASH!

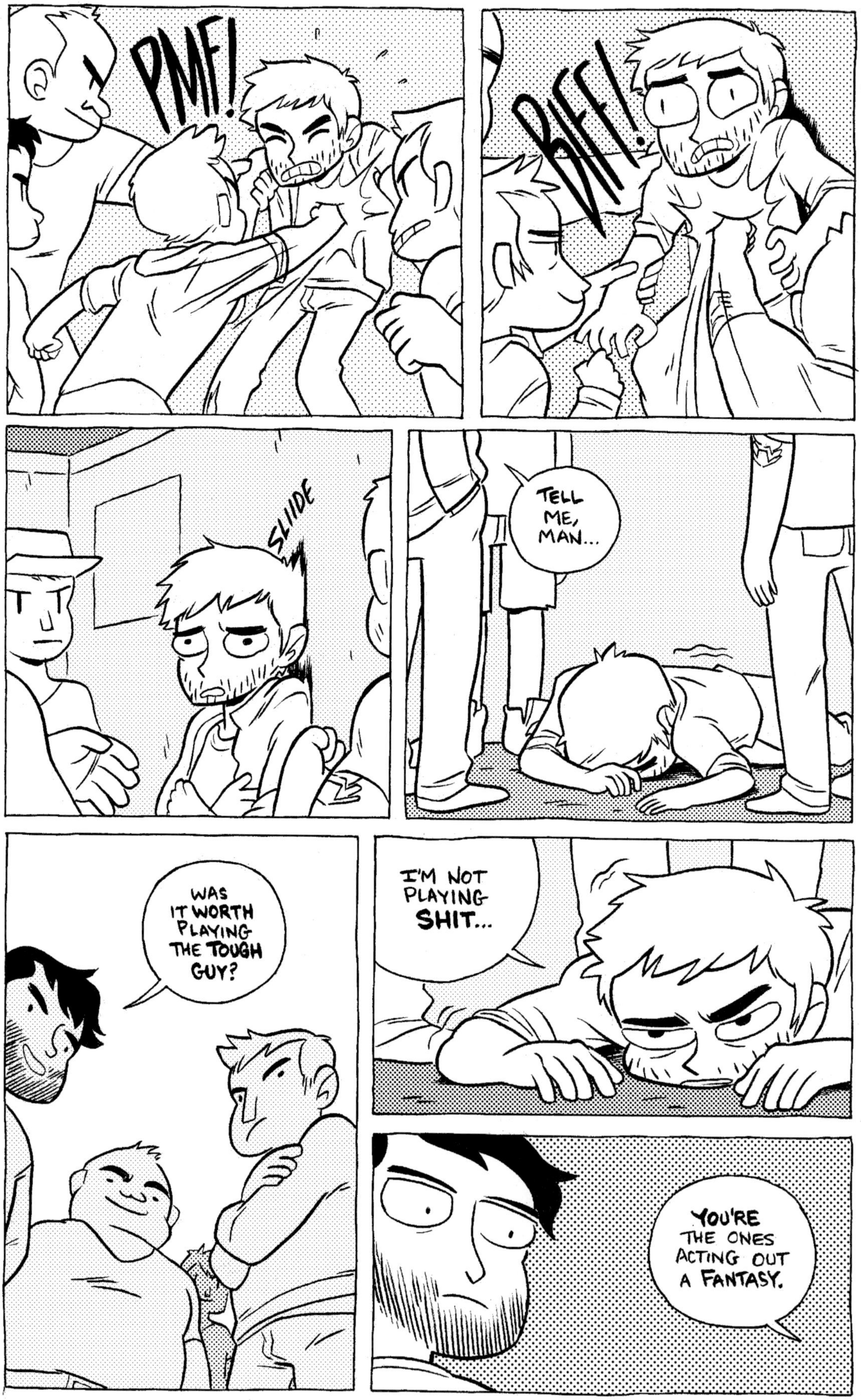
PMF!
BIFF!
SLIDE
TELL ME, MAN...
WAS IT WORTH PLAYING THE TOUGH GUY?
I'M NOT PLAYING SHIT...
YOU'RE THE ONES ACTING OUT A FANTASY.

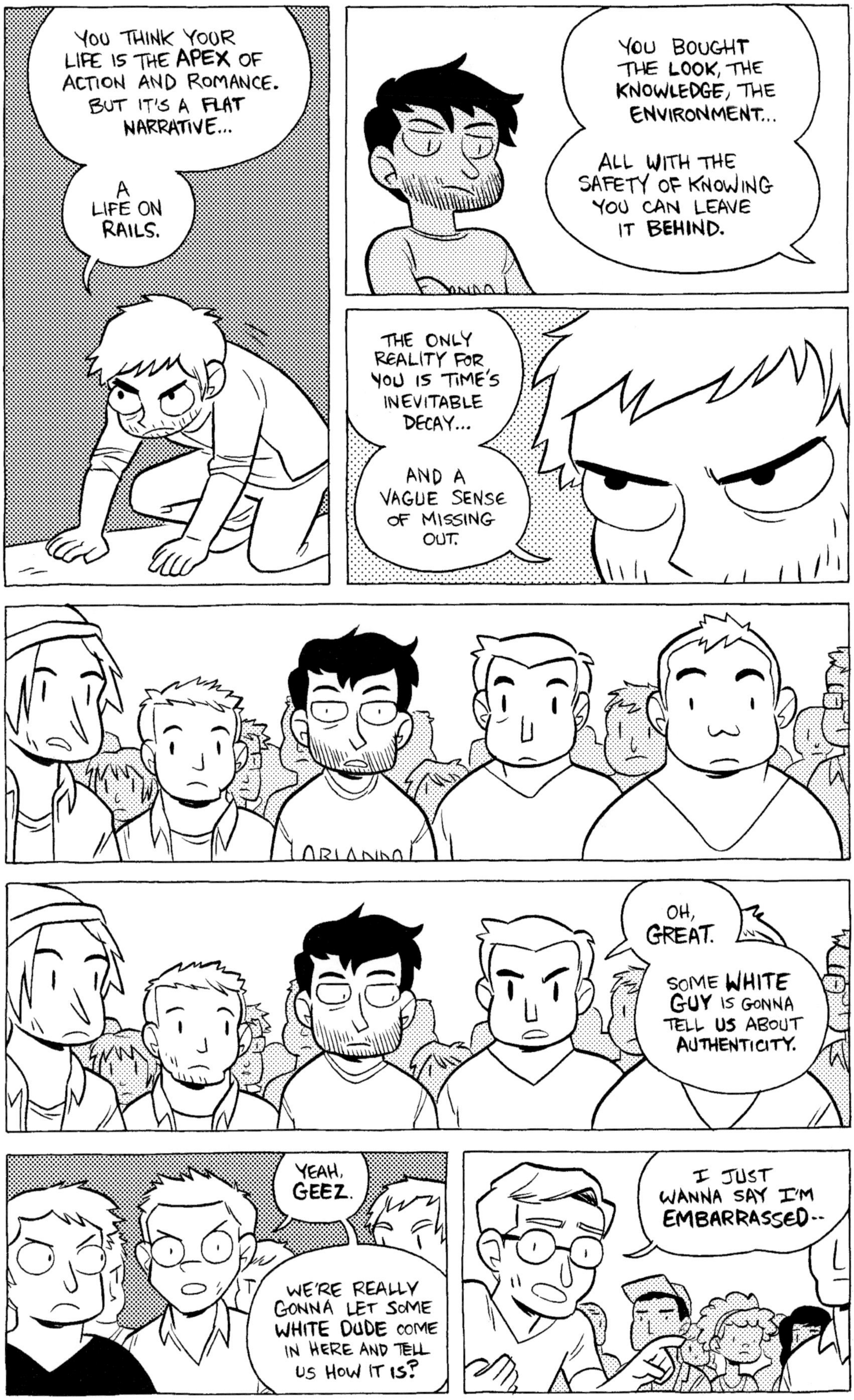
YOU THINK YOUR LIFE IS THE APEX OF ACTION AND ROMANCE. BUT IT'S A FLAT NARRATIVE...
A LIFE ON RAILS.
YOU BOUGHT THE LOOK, THE KNOWLEDGE, THE ENVIRONMENT...
ALL WITH THE SAFETY OF KNOWING YOU CAN LEAVE IT BEHIND.
THE ONLY REALITY FOR YOU IS TIME'S INEVITABLE DECAY...
AND A VAGUE SENSE OF MISSING OUT.
ORLANDO
OH, GREAT.
SOME WHITE GUY IS GONNA TELL US ABOUT AUTHENTICITY.
YEAH, GEEZ.
WE'RE REALLY GONNA LET SOME WHITE DUDE COME IN HERE AND TELL US HOW IT IS?
I JUST WANNA SAY I'M EMBARRASSED--

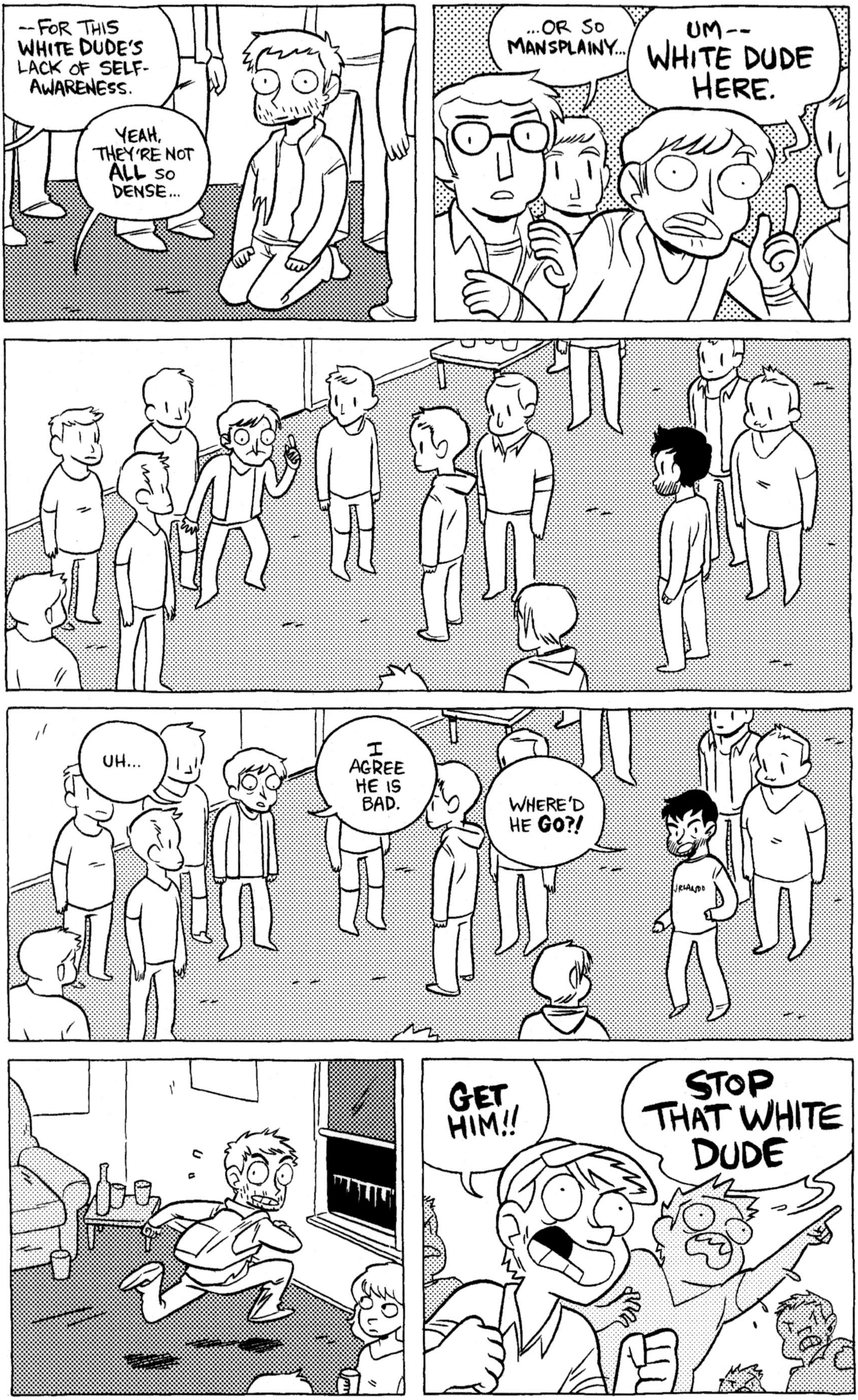
--FOR THIS WHITE DUDE'S LACK OF SELF-AWARENESS.
YEAH, THEY'RE NOT ALL SO DENSE...
...OR SO MANSPLAINY...
UM-- WHITE DUDE HERE.
UH...
I AGREE HE IS BAD.
WHERE'D HE GO?!
GET HIM!!
STOP THAT WHITE DUDE

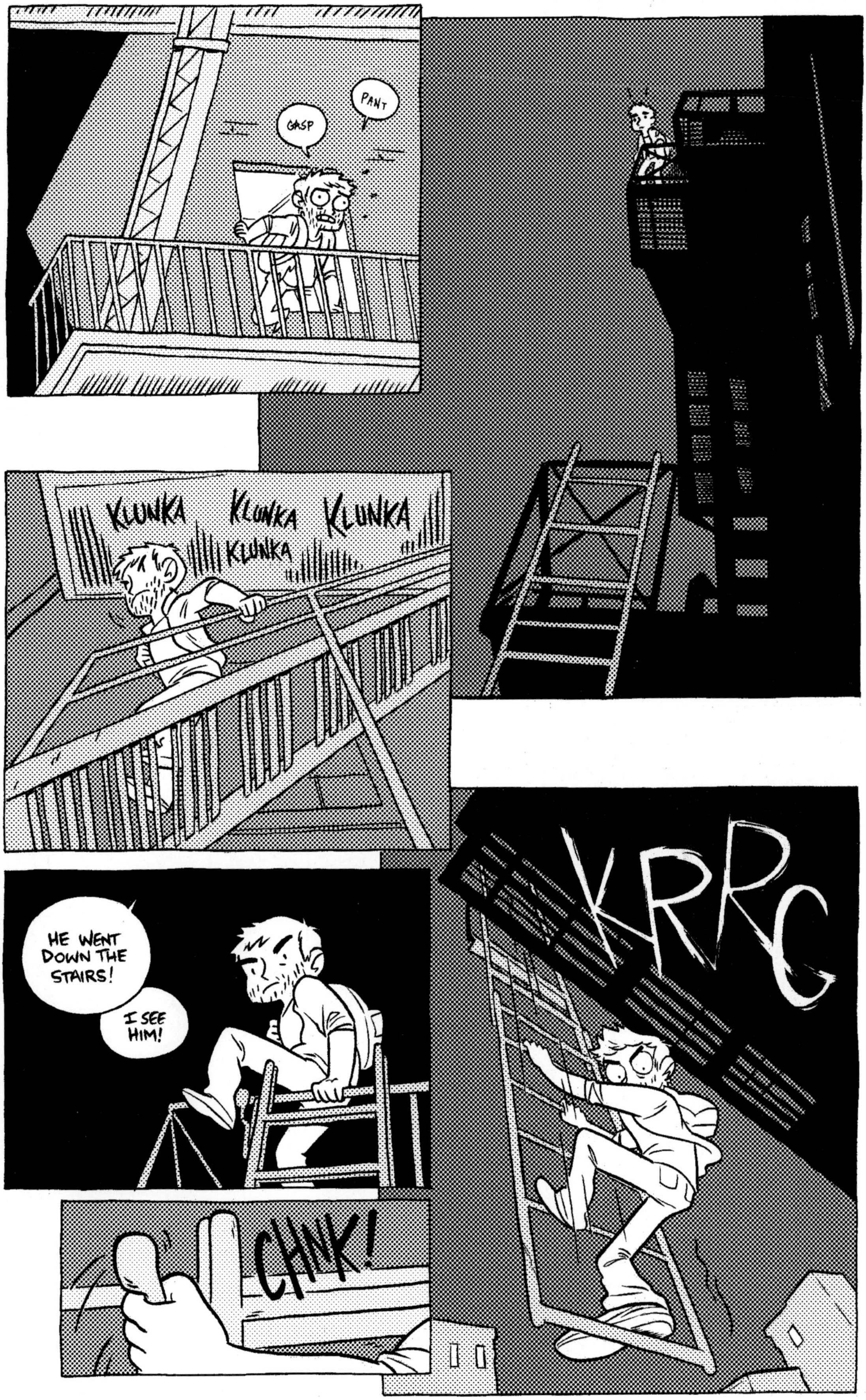
GASP
PANT
KLUNKA KLUNKA KLUNKA
KLUNKA
HE WENT DOWN THE STAIRS!
I SEE HIM!
KRRG
CHNK!

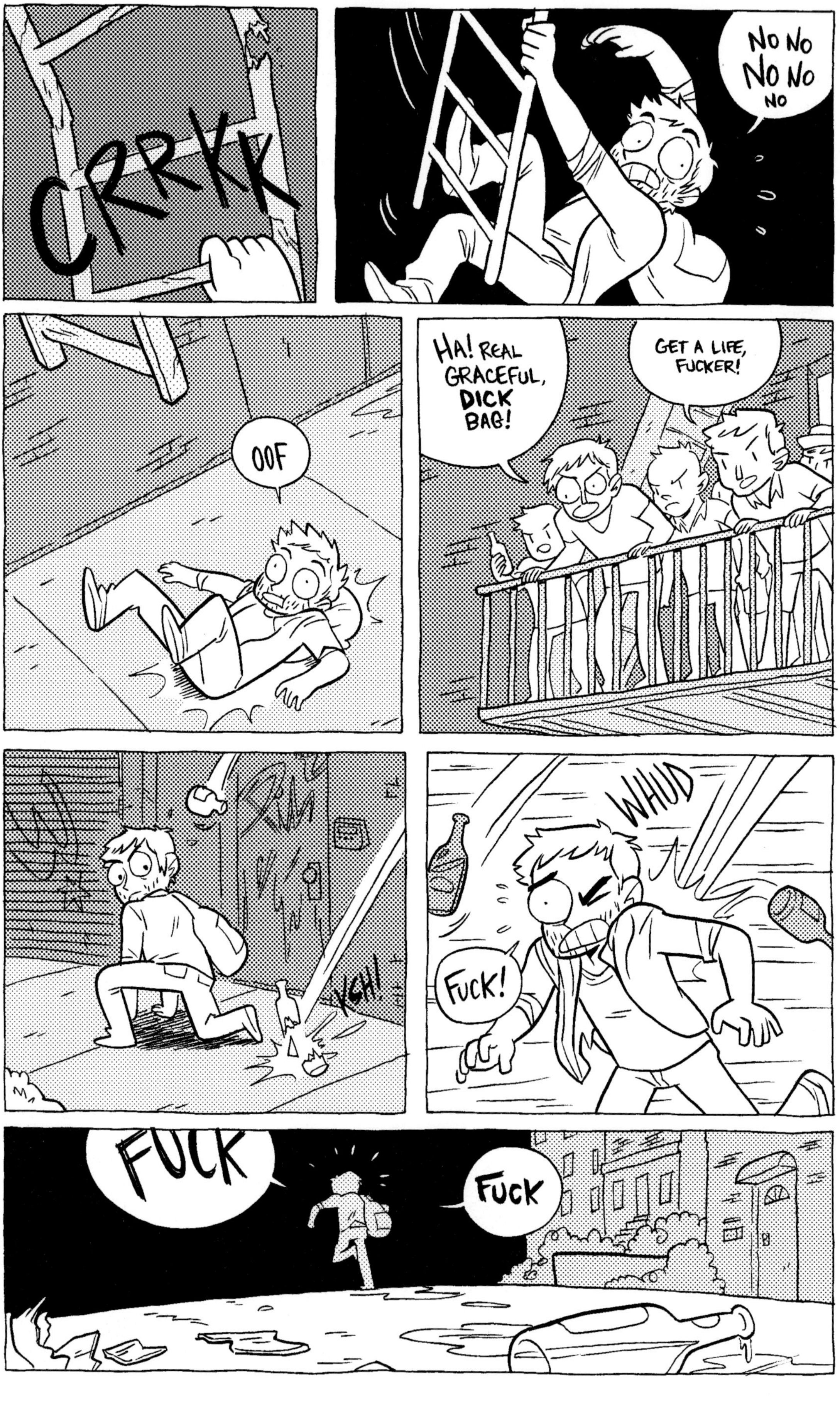
CRRKK
NO NO NO NO NO
OOF
HA! REAL GRACEFUL, DICK BAG!
GET A LIFE, FUCKER!
KSH!
WHUD
FUCK!
FUCK
FUCK

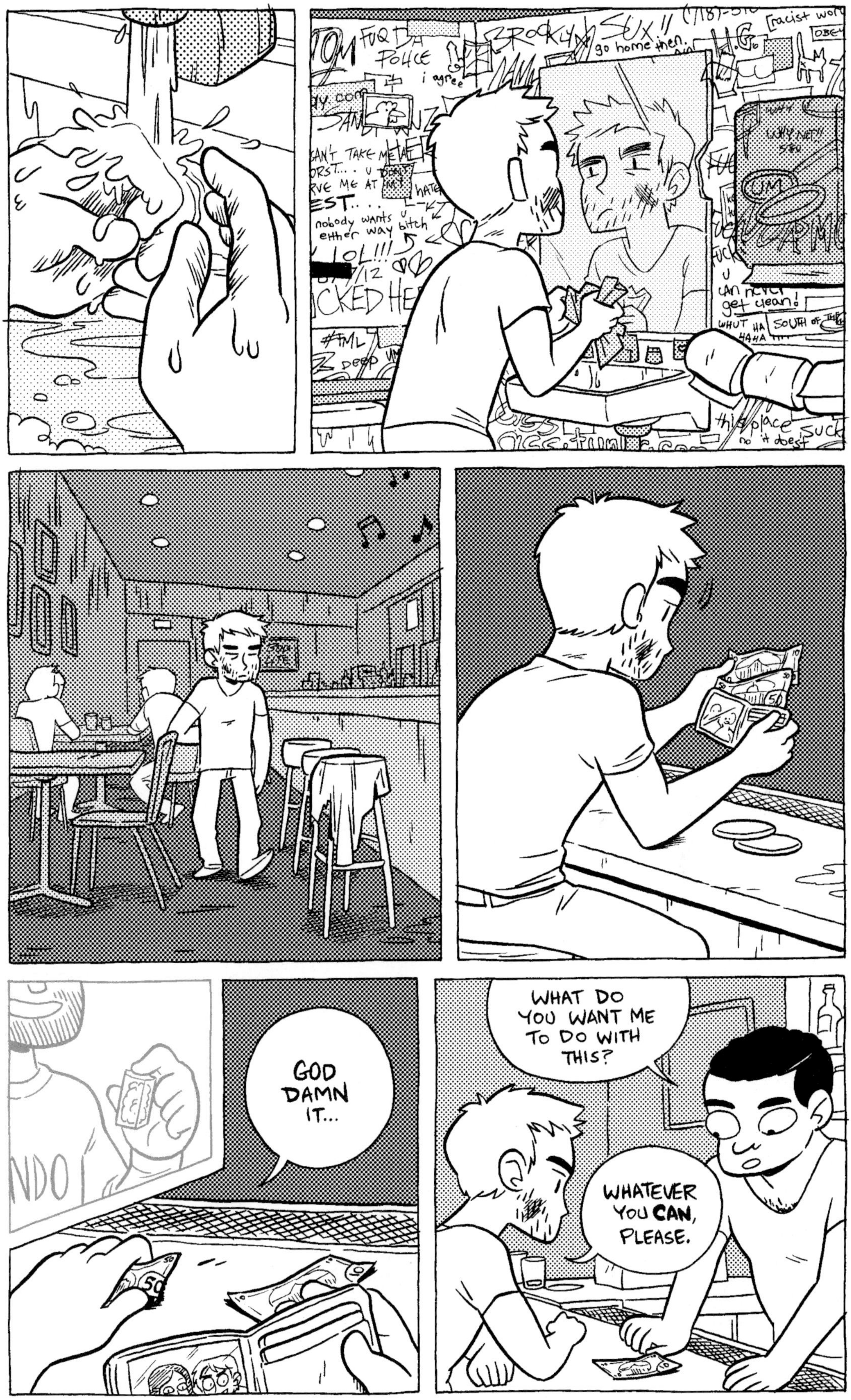
GOD DAMN IT...
WHAT DO YOU WANT ME TO DO WITH THIS?
WHATEVER YOU **CAN**, PLEASE.

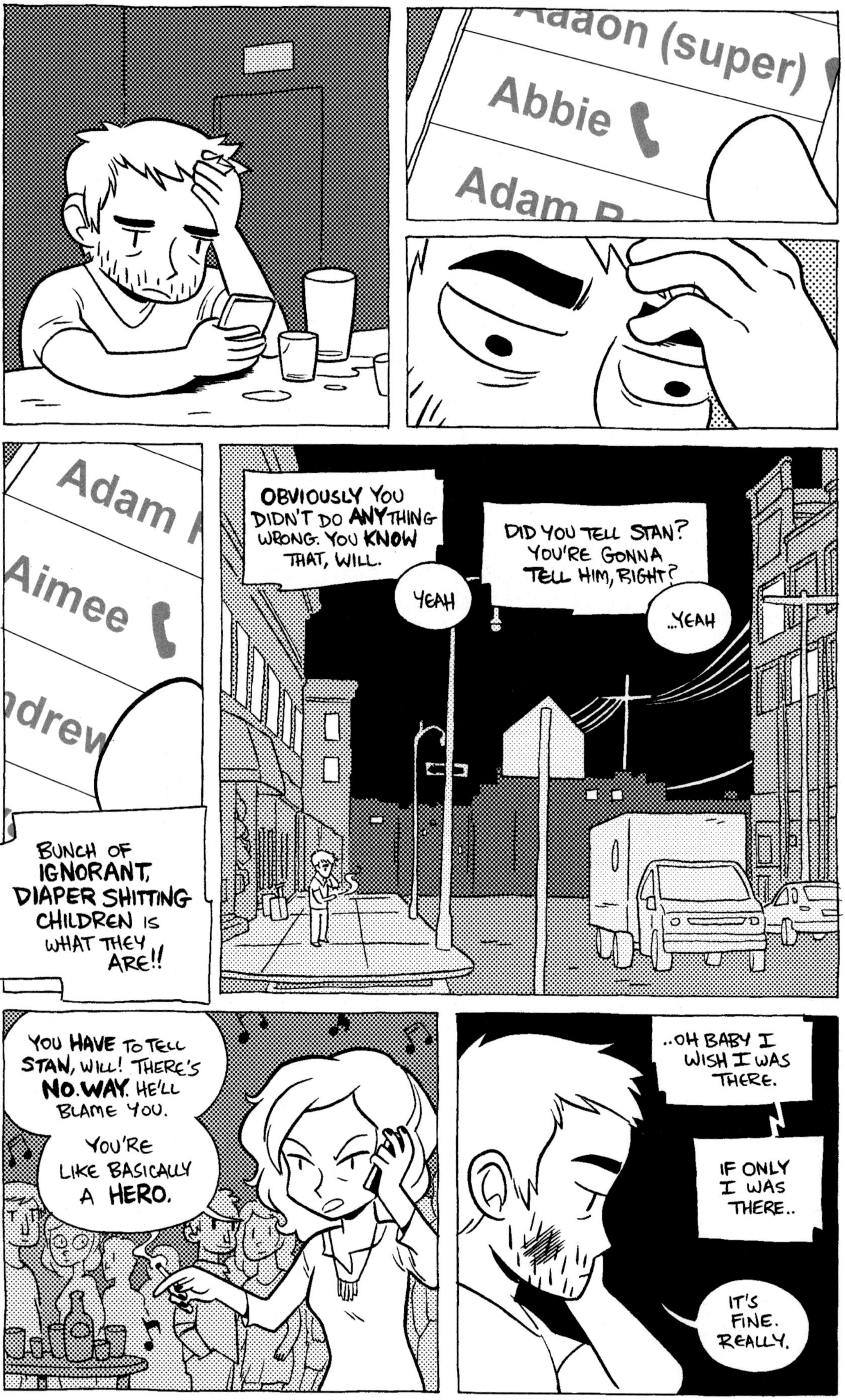

Aaaon (super)
Abbie
Adam R
Adam
Aimee
ndrew
BUNCH OF IGNORANT, DIAPER SHITTING CHILDREN IS WHAT THEY ARE!!
OBVIOUSLY YOU DIDN'T DO ANYTHING WRONG. YOU KNOW THAT, WILL.
YEAH
DID YOU TELL STAN? YOU'RE GONNA TELL HIM, RIGHT?
...YEAH
YOU HAVE TO TELL STAN, WILL! THERE'S NO. WAY. HE'LL BLAME YOU.
YOU'RE LIKE BASICALLY A HERO.
..OH BABY I WISH I WAS THERE.
IF ONLY I WAS THERE..
IT'S FINE. REALLY.

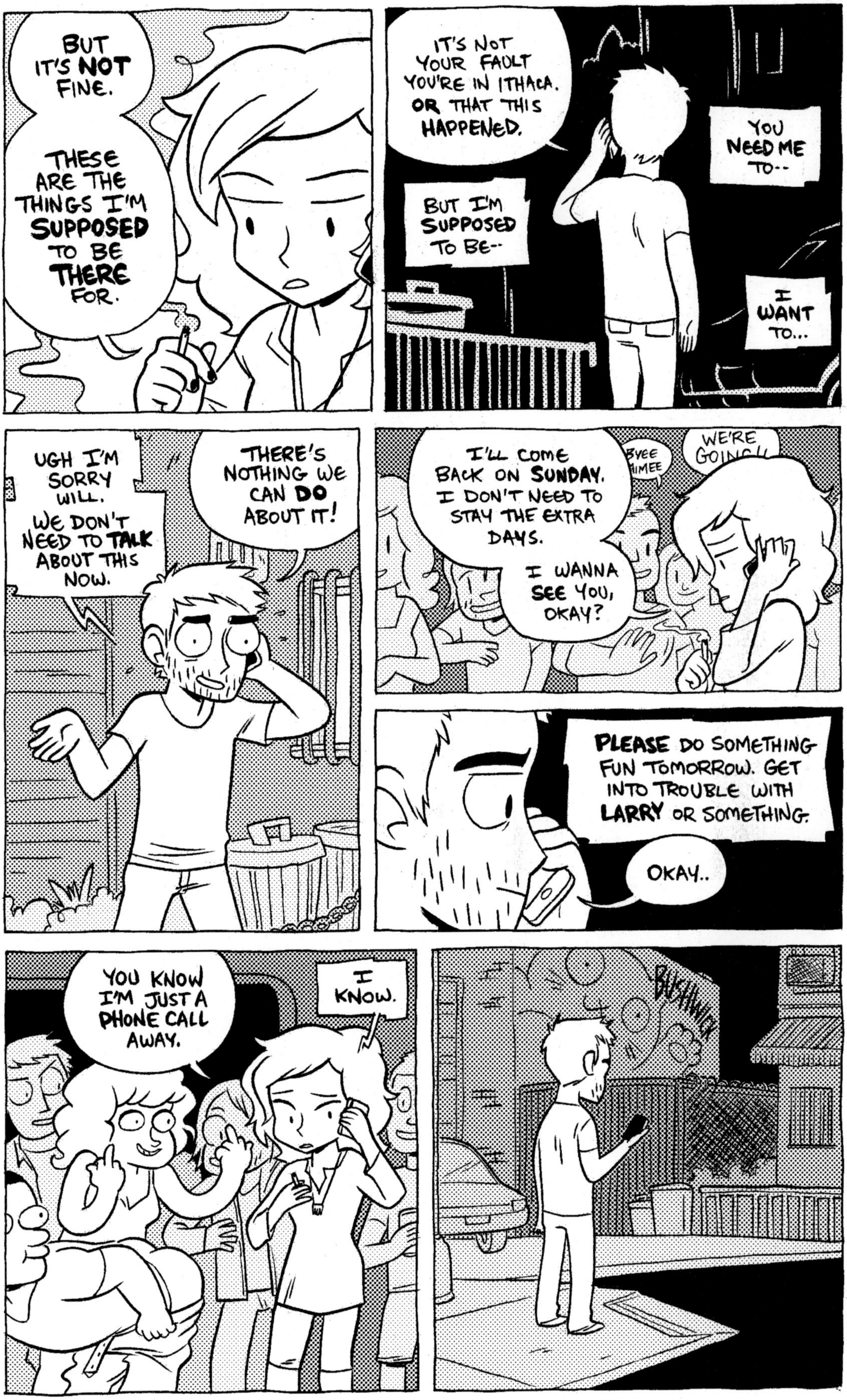
BUT IT'S NOT FINE.
THESE ARE THE THINGS I'M SUPPOSED TO BE THERE FOR.
IT'S NOT YOUR FAULT YOU'RE IN ITHACA. OR THAT THIS HAPPENED.
BUT I'M SUPPOSED TO BE--
YOU NEED ME TO--
I WANT TO...
UGH I'M SORRY WILL. WE DON'T NEED TO TALK ABOUT THIS NOW.
THERE'S NOTHING WE CAN DO ABOUT IT!
I'LL COME BACK ON SUNDAY. I DON'T NEED TO STAY THE EXTRA DAYS.
BYEE AIMEE
WE'RE GOING!!
I WANNA SEE YOU, OKAY?
PLEASE DO SOMETHING FUN TOMORROW. GET INTO TROUBLE WITH LARRY OR SOMETHING.
OKAY..
YOU KNOW I'M JUST A PHONE CALL AWAY.
I KNOW.
BUSHWICK

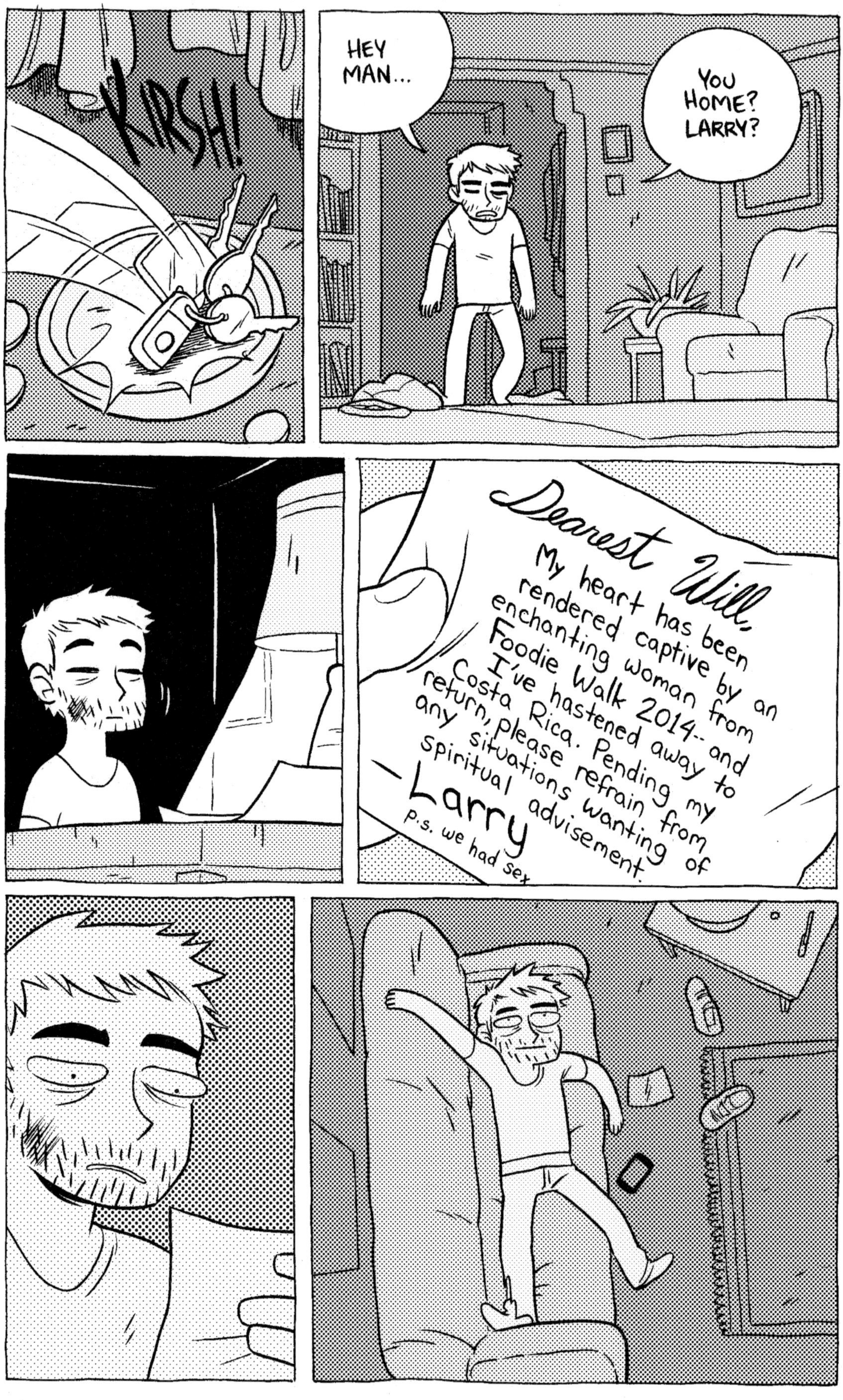
KRSH!
HEY MAN...
YOU HOME? LARRY?
Dearest Will,
My heart has been rendered captive by an enchanting woman from Foodie Walk 2014-- and I've hastened away to Costa Rica. Pending my return, please refrain from any situations wanting of spiritual advisement.
-Larry
p.s. we had sex

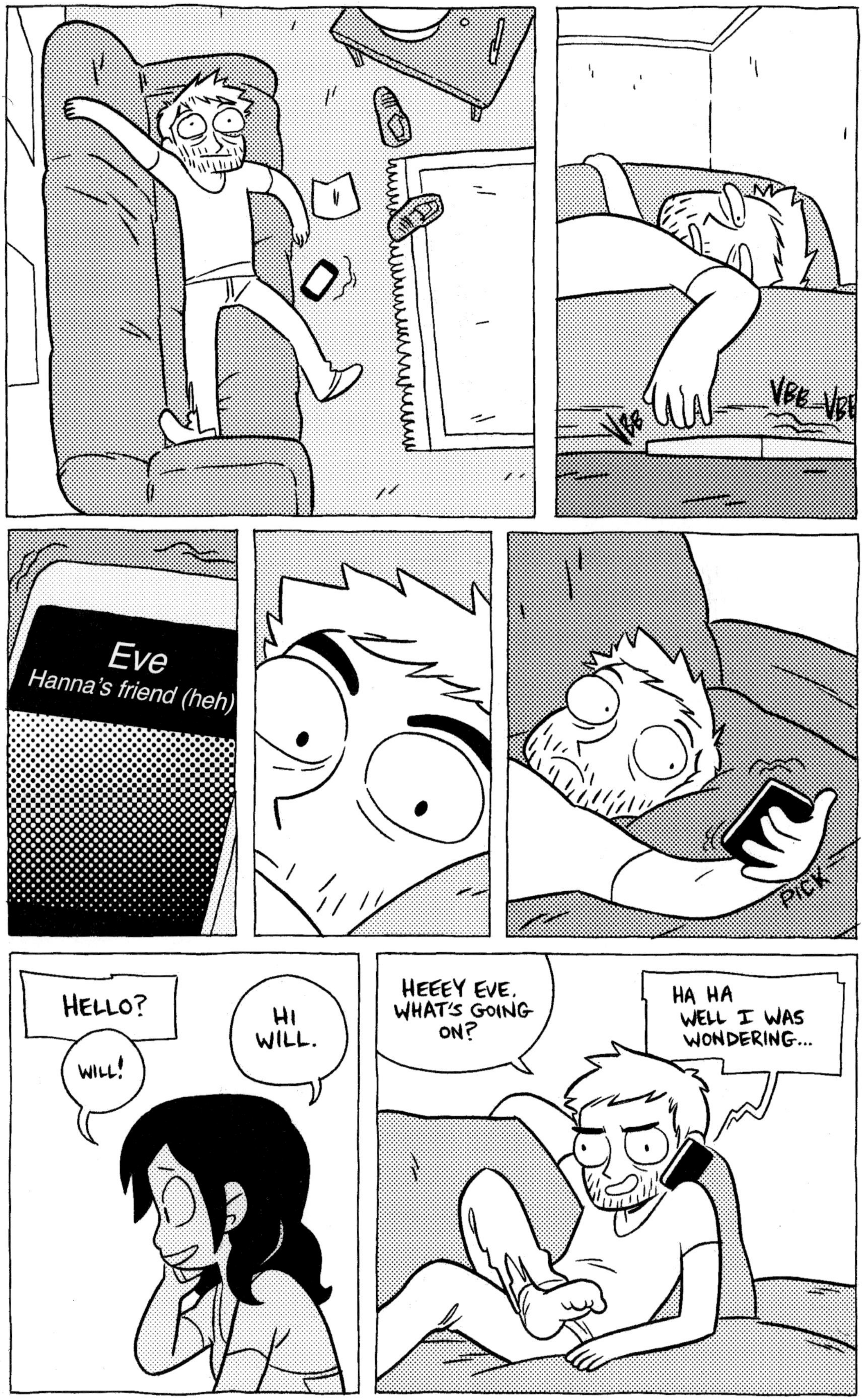
VBB
VBB VBB
Eve
Hanna's friend (heh)
PICK
HELLO?
WILL!
HI WILL.
HEEEY EVE. WHAT'S GOING ON?
HA HA WELL I WAS WONDERING...

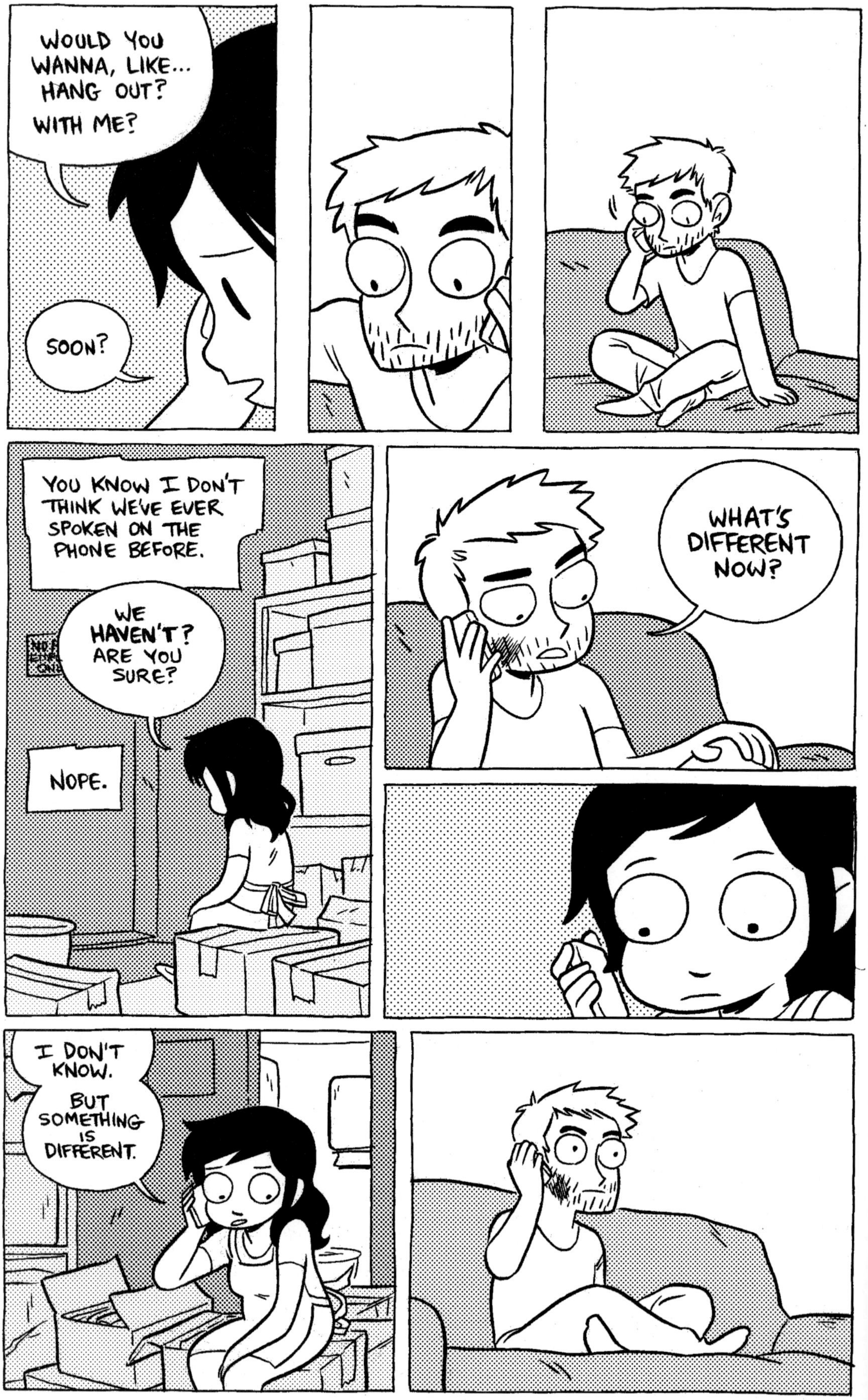
WOULD YOU WANNA, LIKE... HANG OUT? WITH ME?
SOON?
YOU KNOW I DON'T THINK WE'VE EVER SPOKEN ON THE PHONE BEFORE.
WE HAVEN'T? ARE YOU SURE?
NOPE.
WHAT'S DIFFERENT NOW?
I DON'T KNOW.
BUT SOMETHING IS DIFFERENT.

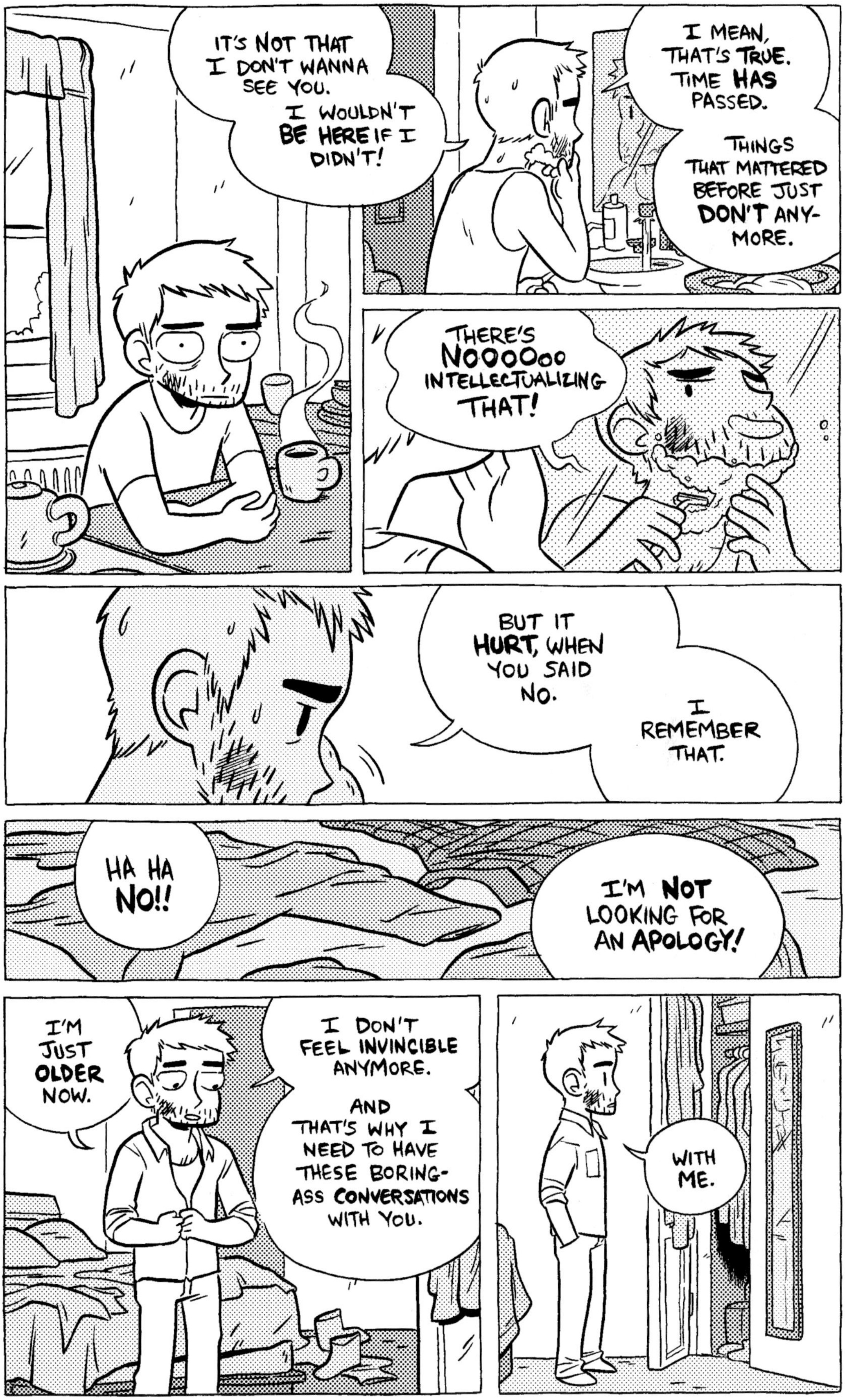
IT'S NOT THAT I DON'T WANNA SEE YOU.
I WOULDN'T BE HERE IF I DIDN'T!
I MEAN, THAT'S TRUE. TIME HAS PASSED.
THINGS THAT MATTERED BEFORE JUST DON'T ANY-MORE.
THERE'S NOOOOoo INTELLECTUALIZING THAT!
BUT IT HURT, WHEN YOU SAID NO.
I REMEMBER THAT.
HA HA NO!!
I'M NOT LOOKING FOR AN APOLOGY!
I'M JUST OLDER NOW.
I DON'T FEEL INVINCIBLE ANYMORE.
AND THAT'S WHY I NEED TO HAVE THESE BORING-ASS CONVERSATIONS WITH YOU.
WITH ME.

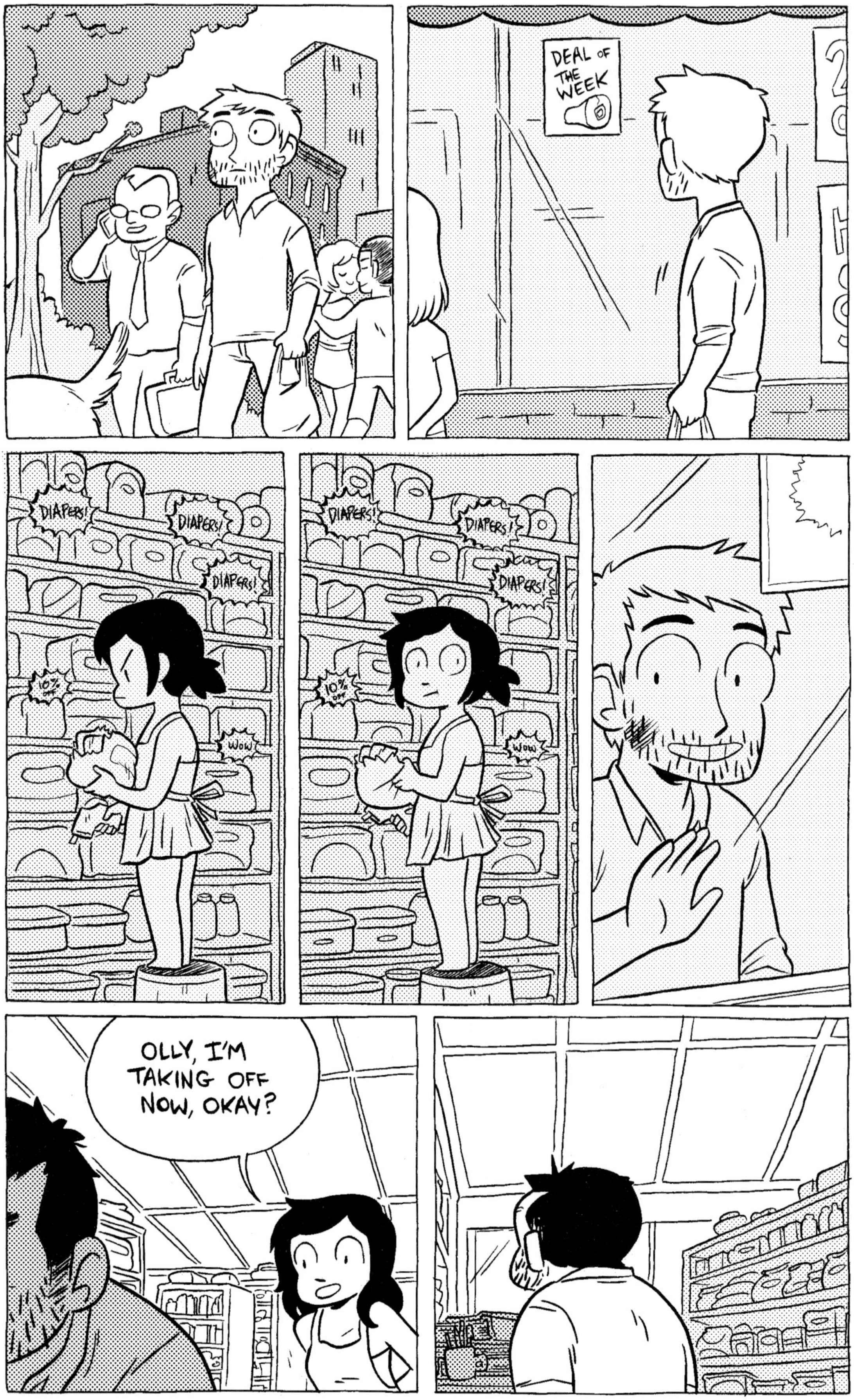
DEAL OF THE WEEK
DIAPERS!
DIAPERS!
DIAPERS!
10% OFF
WOW!
DIAPERS!
DIAPERS!
DIAPERS!
10% OFF
WOW!
OLLY, I'M TAKING OFF NOW, OKAY?

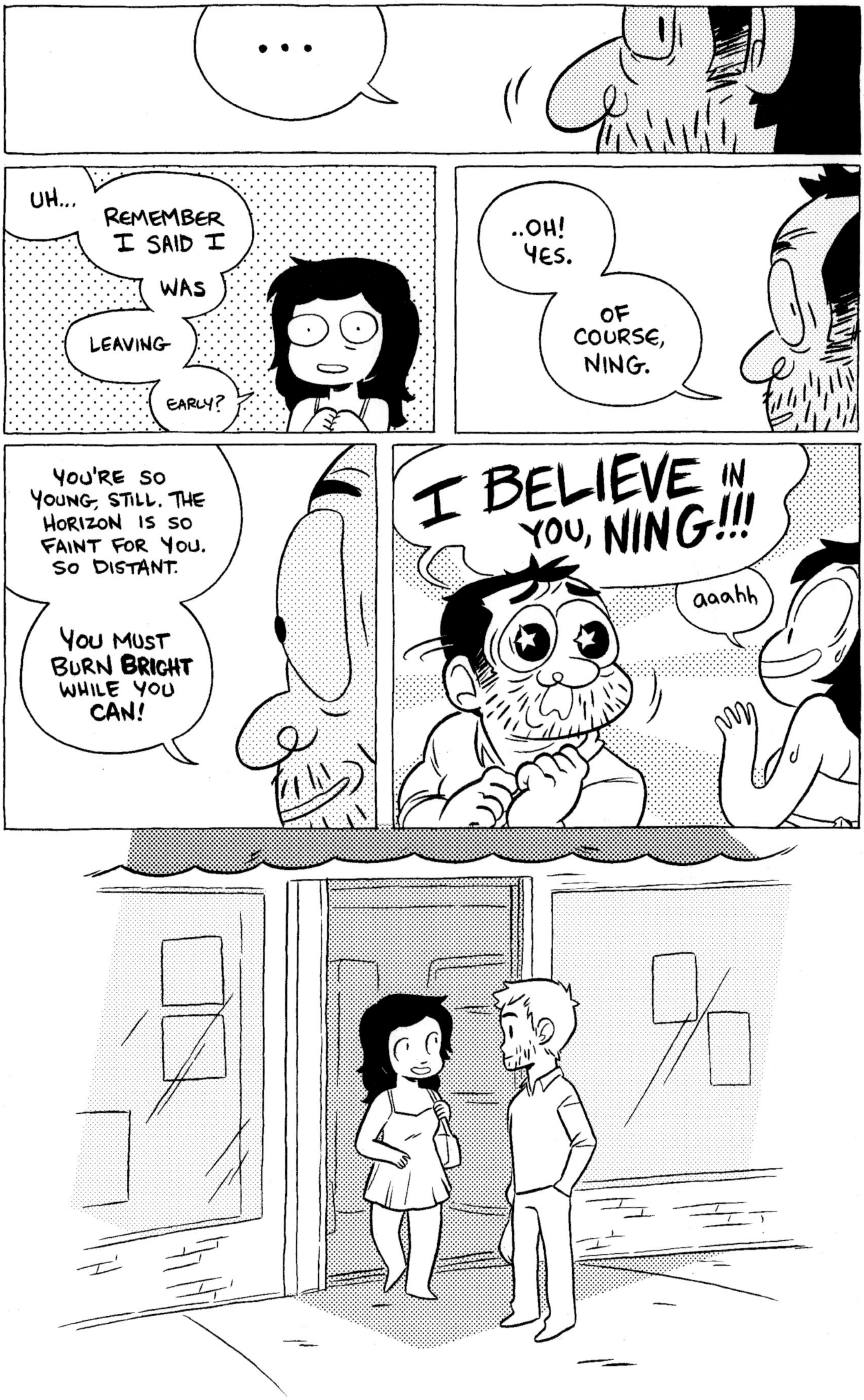
...
UH...
REMEMBER I SAID I WAS LEAVING EARLY?
..OH! YES.
OF COURSE, NING.
YOU'RE SO YOUNG, STILL. THE HORIZON IS SO FAINT FOR YOU. SO DISTANT.
YOU MUST BURN BRIGHT WHILE YOU CAN!
I BELIEVE IN YOU, NING!!!
aaahh

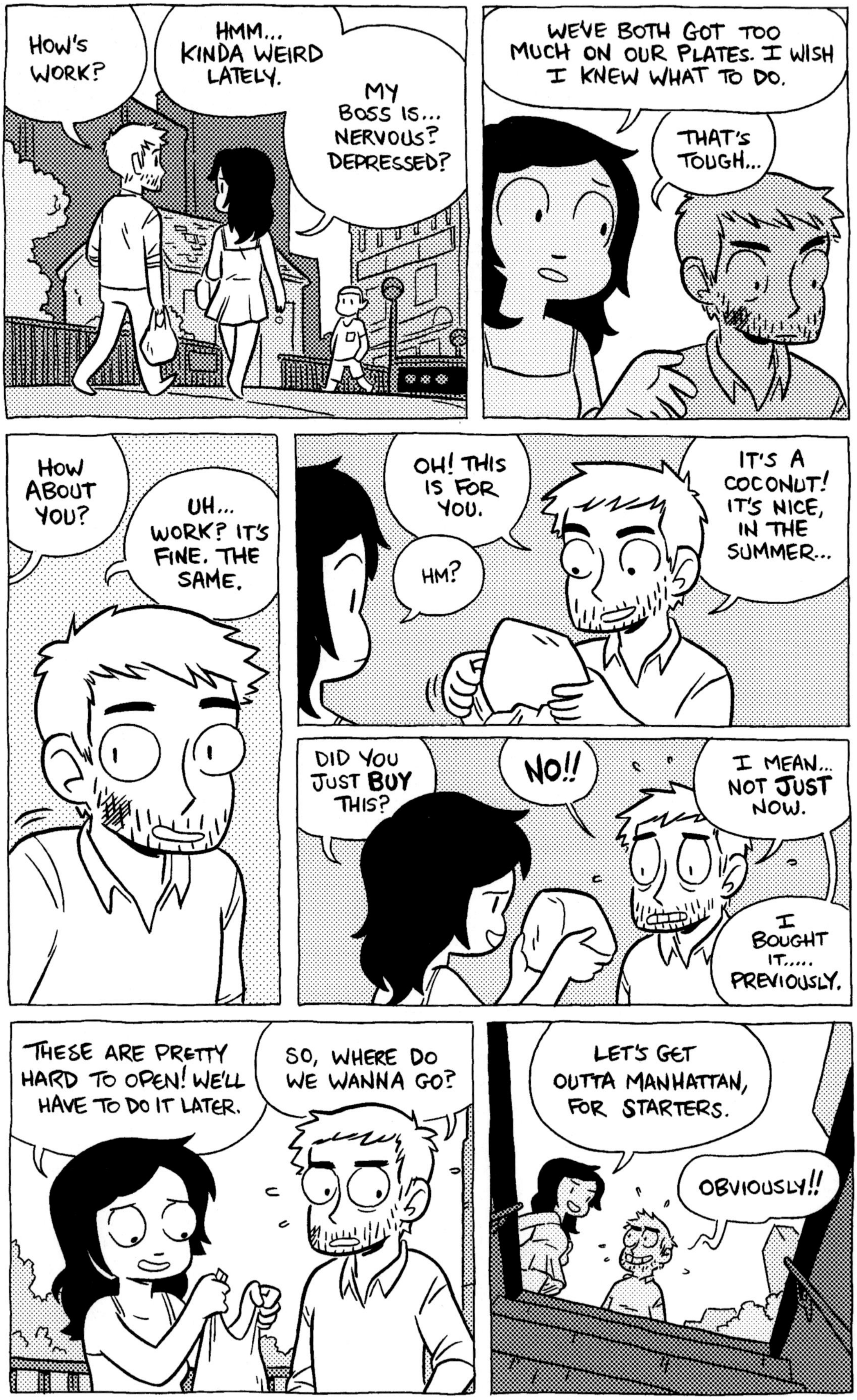
HOW'S WORK?
HMM... KINDA WEIRD LATELY.
MY BOSS IS... NERVOUS? DEPRESSED?
WE'VE BOTH GOT TOO MUCH ON OUR PLATES. I WISH I KNEW WHAT TO DO.
THAT'S TOUGH...
HOW ABOUT YOU?
UH... WORK? IT'S FINE. THE SAME.
OH! THIS IS FOR YOU.
HM?
IT'S A COCONUT! IT'S NICE, IN THE SUMMER...
DID YOU JUST BUY THIS?
NO!!
I MEAN... NOT JUST NOW.
I BOUGHT IT..... PREVIOUSLY.
THESE ARE PRETTY HARD TO OPEN! WE'LL HAVE TO DO IT LATER.
SO, WHERE DO WE WANNA GO?
LET'S GET OUTTA MANHATTAN, FOR STARTERS.
OBVIOUSLY!!

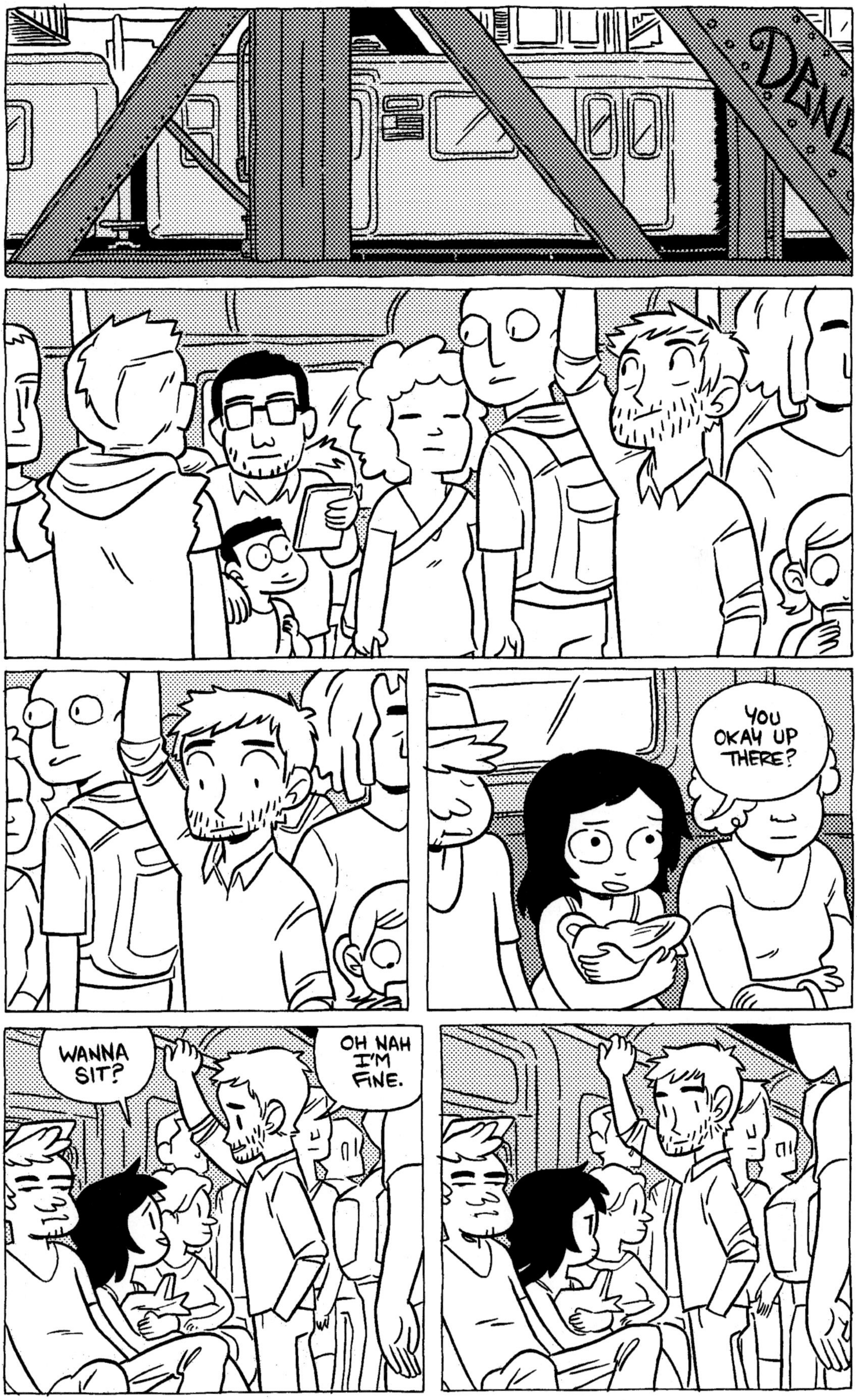
DENL
YOU OKAY UP THERE?
WANNA SIT?
OH NAH I'M FINE.

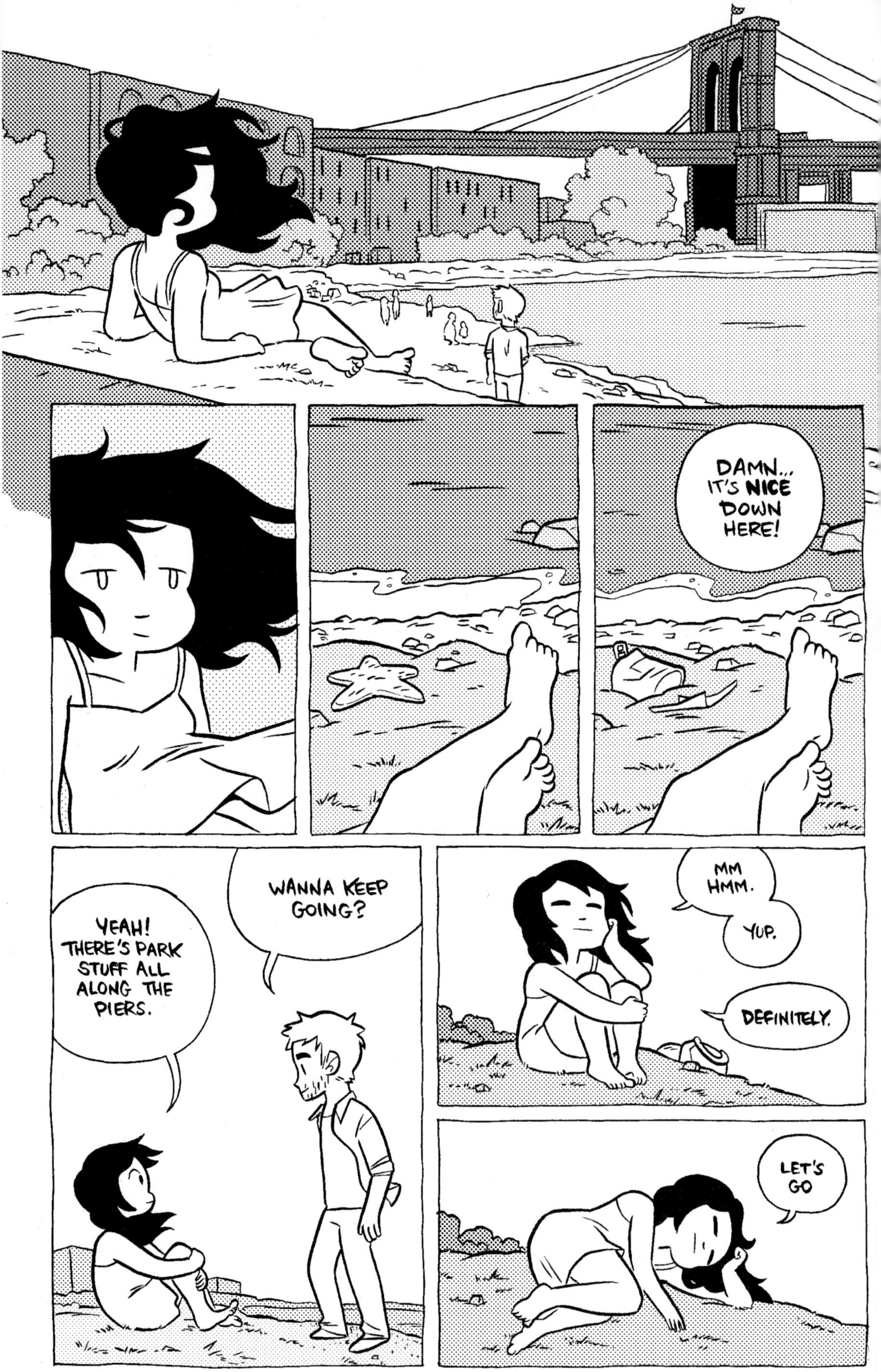
DAMN... IT'S NICE DOWN HERE!
WANNA KEEP GOING?
YEAH! THERE'S PARK STUFF ALL ALONG THE PIERS.
MM HMM.
YUP.
DEFINITELY.
LET'S GO

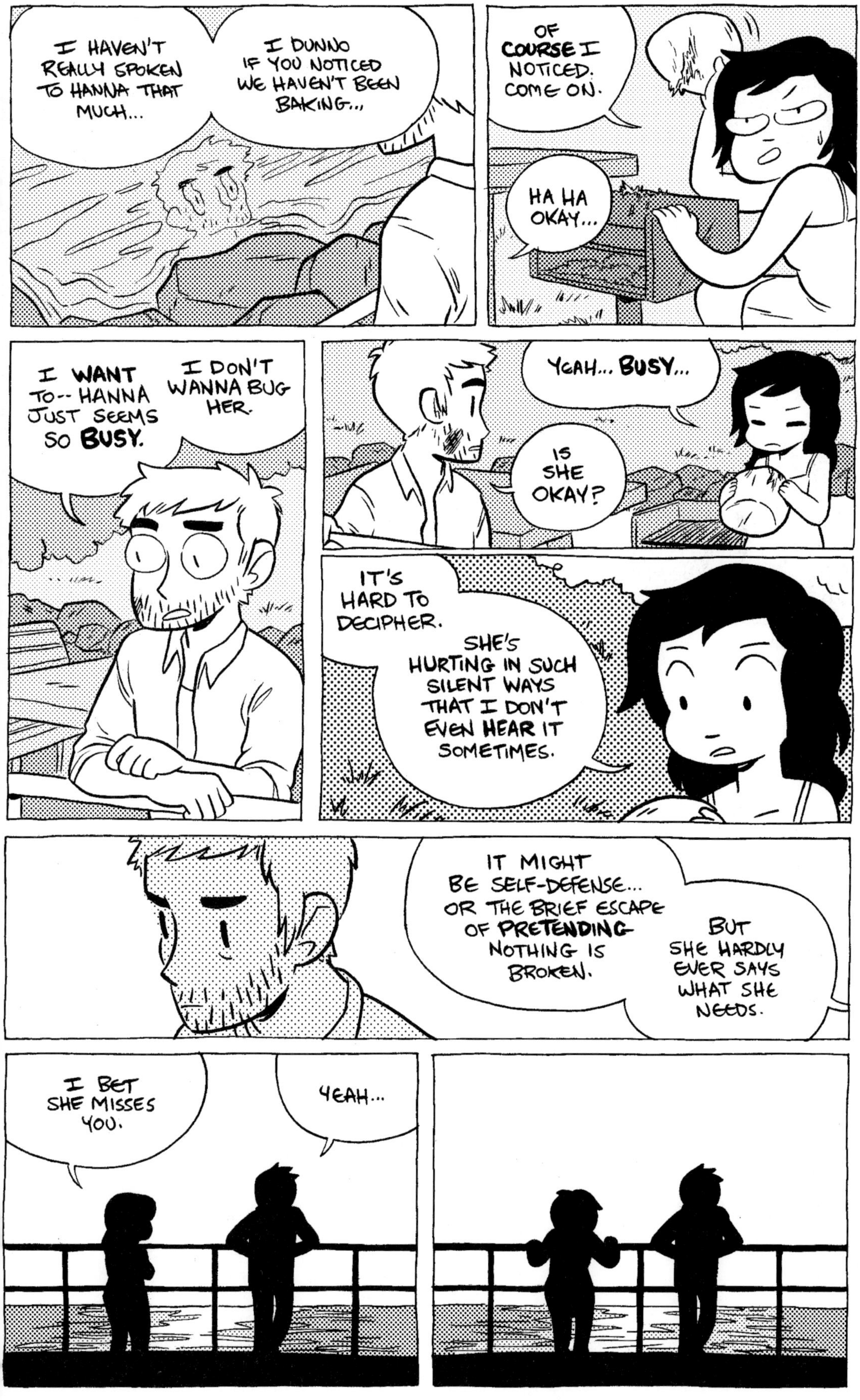
I HAVEN'T REALLY SPOKEN TO HANNA THAT MUCH...
I DUNNO IF YOU NOTICED WE HAVEN'T BEEN BAKING...
OF COURSE I NOTICED. COME ON.
HA HA OKAY...
I WANT TO-- HANNA JUST SEEMS SO BUSY.
I DON'T WANNA BUG HER.
YEAH... BUSY...
IS SHE OKAY?
IT'S HARD TO DECIPHER.
SHE'S HURTING IN SUCH SILENT WAYS THAT I DON'T EVEN HEAR IT SOMETIMES.
IT MIGHT BE SELF-DEFENSE... OR THE BRIEF ESCAPE OF PRETENDING NOTHING IS BROKEN.
BUT SHE HARDLY EVER SAYS WHAT SHE NEEDS.
I BET SHE MISSES YOU.
YEAH...

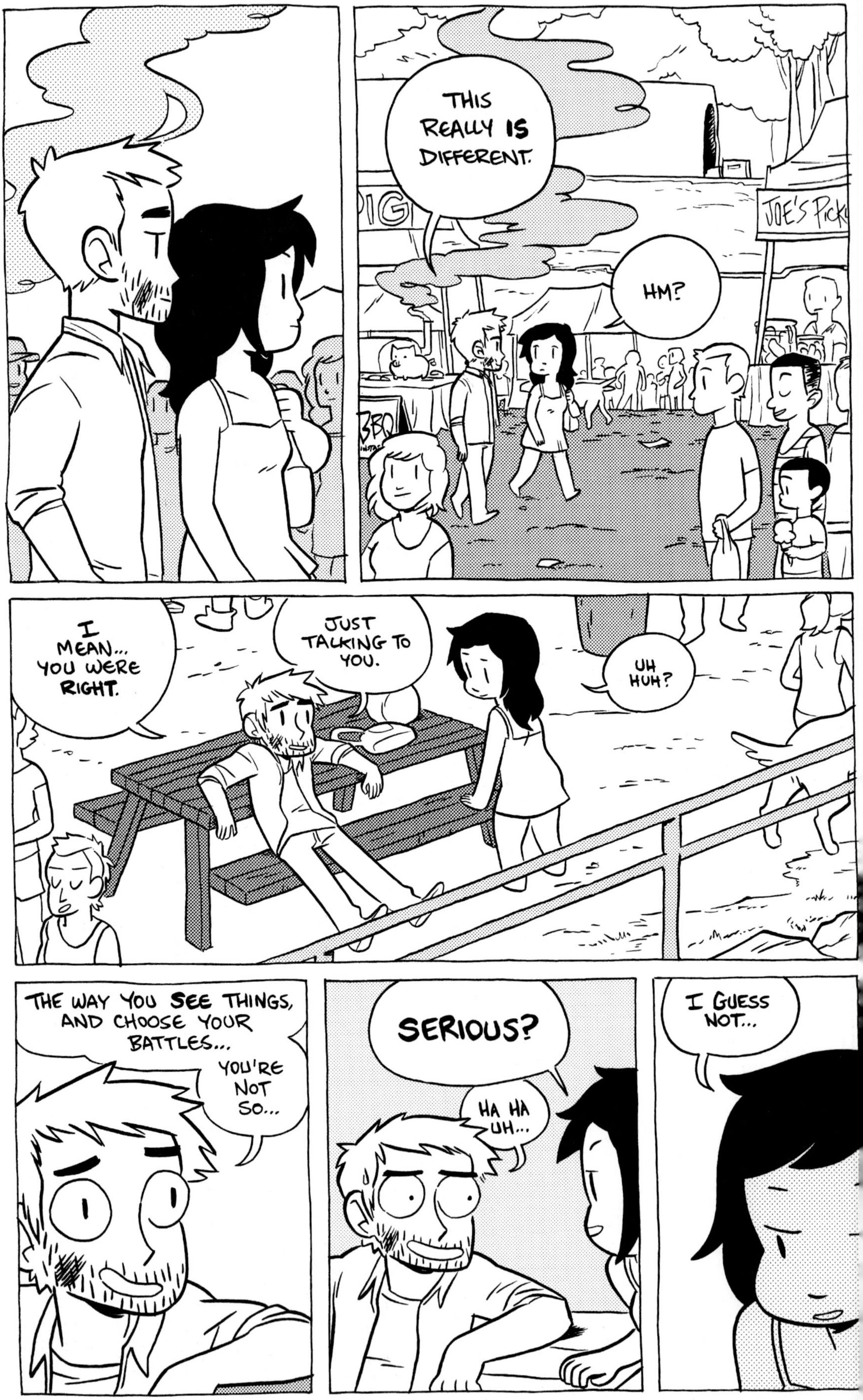
THIS REALLY IS DIFFERENT.
JOE'S PICK
HM?
I MEAN... YOU WERE RIGHT.
JUST TALKING TO YOU.
UH HUH?
THE WAY YOU SEE THINGS, AND CHOOSE YOUR BATTLES...
YOU'RE NOT SO...
SERIOUS?
HA HA UH...
I GUESS NOT...

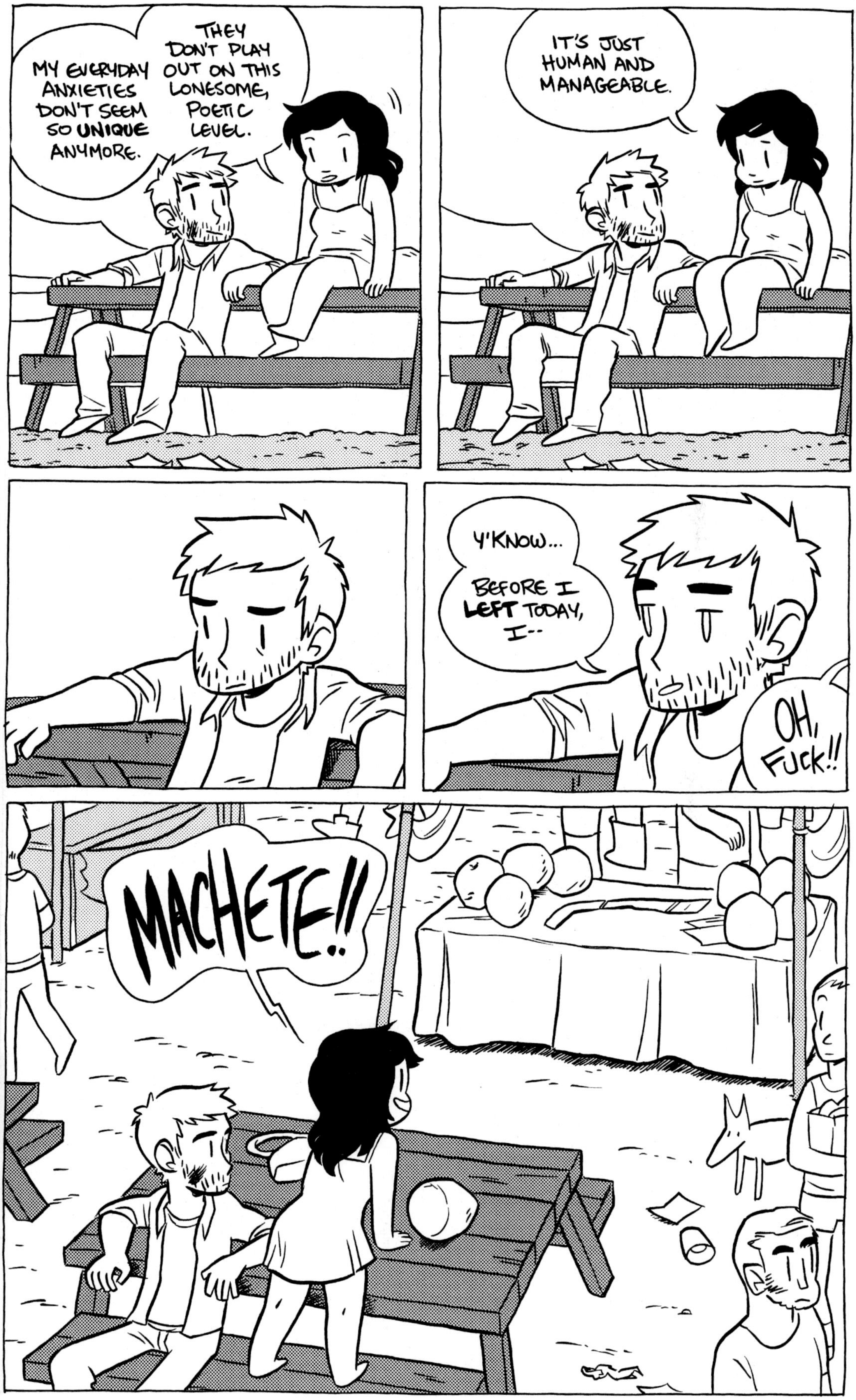
MY EVERYDAY ANXIETIES DON'T SEEM SO **UNIQUE** ANYMORE.
THEY DON'T PLAY OUT ON THIS LONESOME, POETIC LEVEL.
IT'S JUST HUMAN AND MANAGEABLE.
Y'KNOW...
BEFORE I **LEFT** TODAY, I--
OH, FUCK!!
MACHETE!!

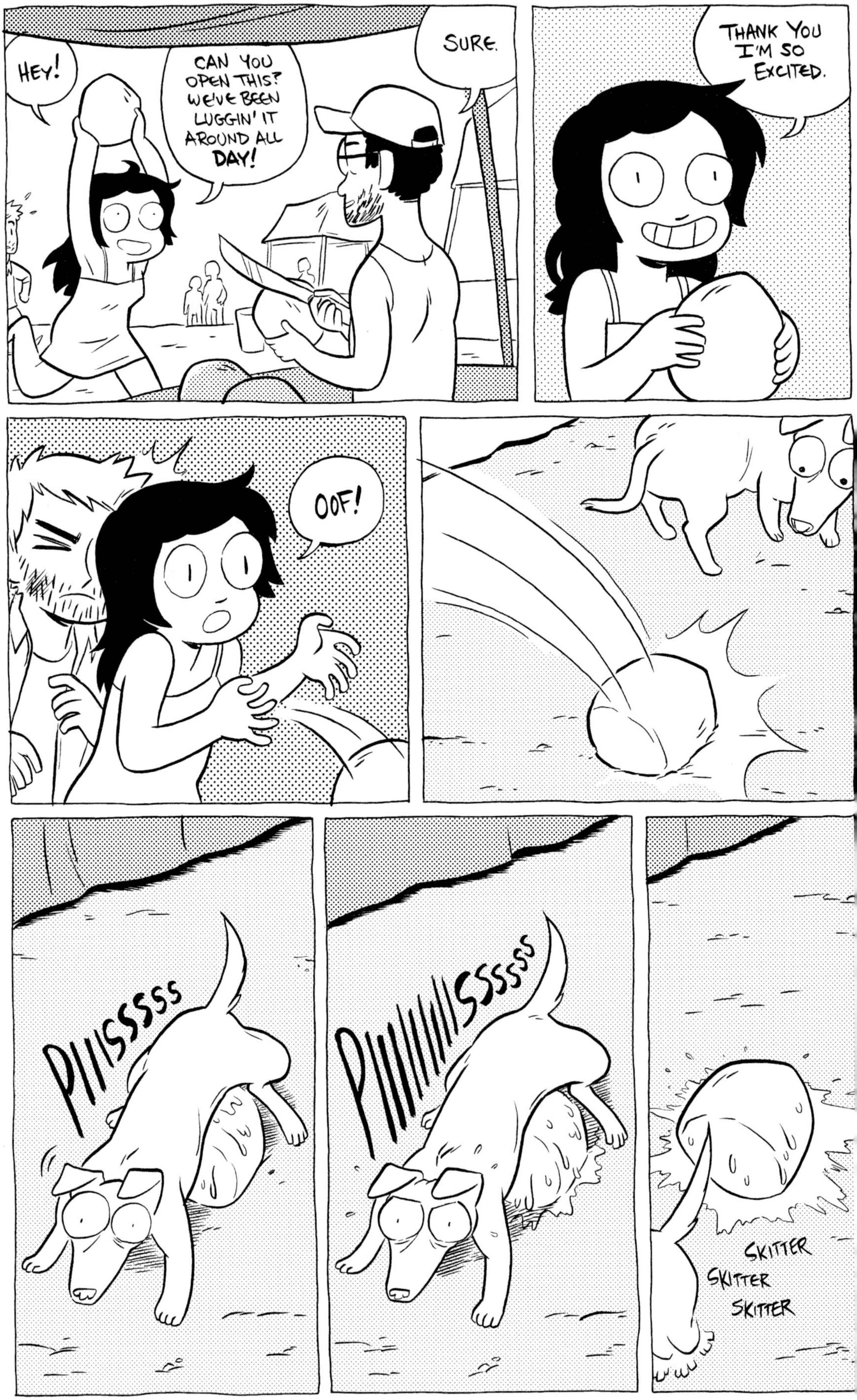
HEY!
CAN YOU OPEN THIS? WE'VE BEEN LUGGIN' IT AROUND ALL DAY!
SURE.
THANK YOU I'M SO EXCITED.
OOF!
PIIISSSSS
PIIIIIIIISSSSS
SKITTER
SKITTER
SKITTER

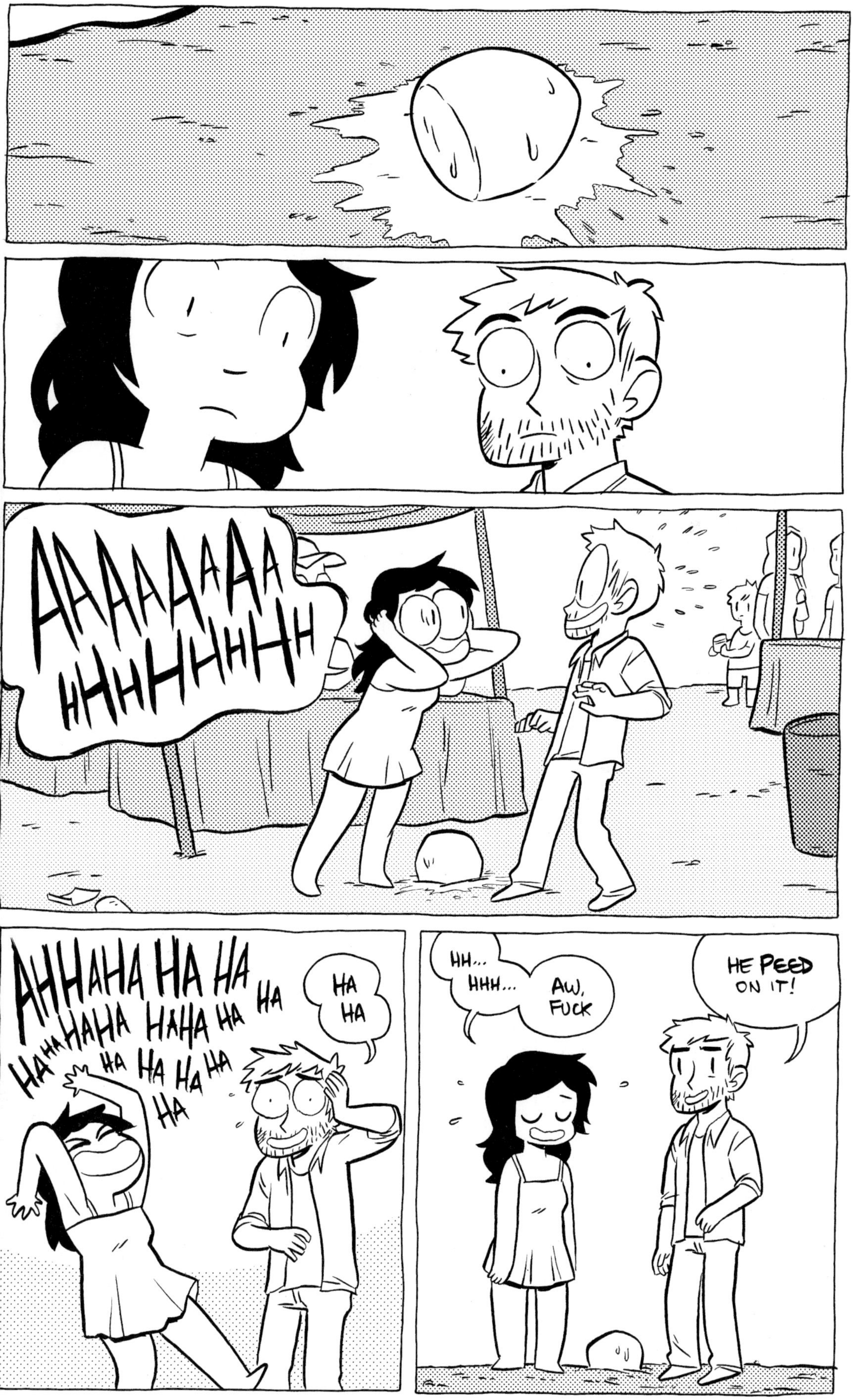
AAAAAAAA HHHHHHHHH
AHHAHA HA HA HA HAHAHAHA HAHA HA HA HA HA HA HA HA
HA HA
HH... HHH...
AW, FUCK
HE PEED ON IT!

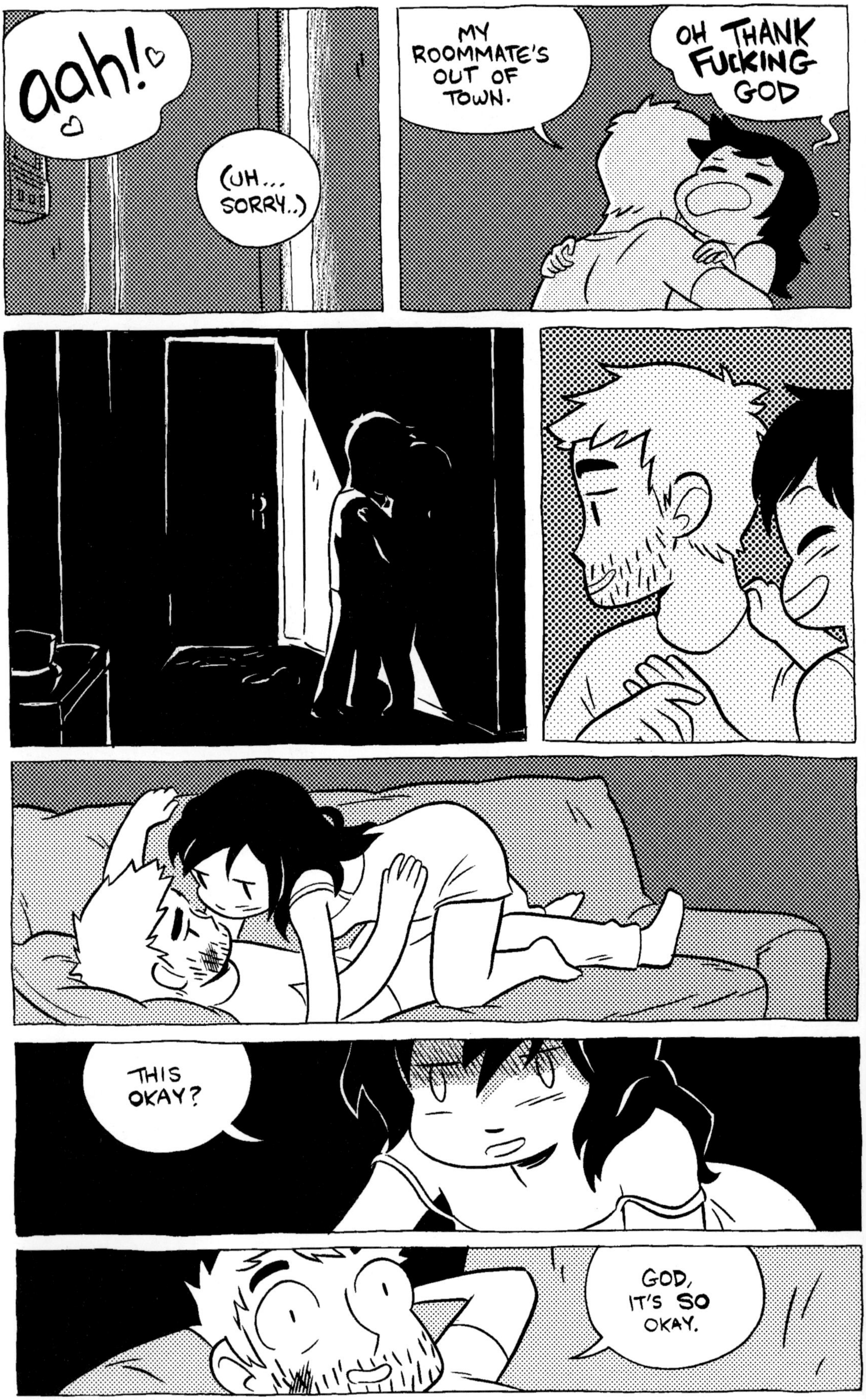
aah!
(UH... SORRY..)
MY ROOMMATE'S OUT OF TOWN.
OH THANK FUCKING GOD
THIS OKAY?
GOD, IT'S SO OKAY.

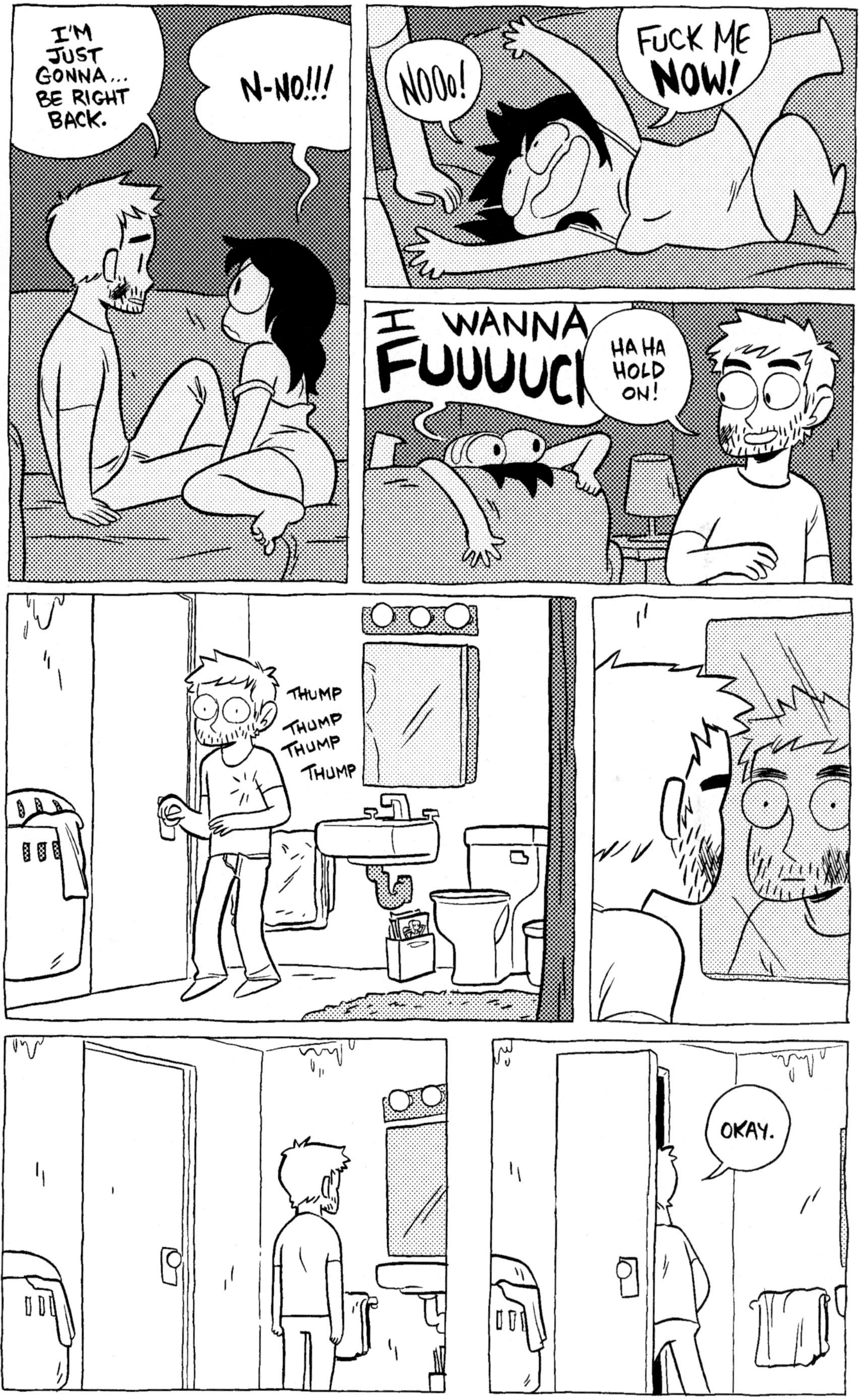
I'M JUST GONNA... BE RIGHT BACK.
N-NO!!!
NOOo!
FUCK ME NOW!
I WANNA FUUUUC
HA HA HOLD ON!
THUMP
THUMP
THUMP
THUMP
OKAY.

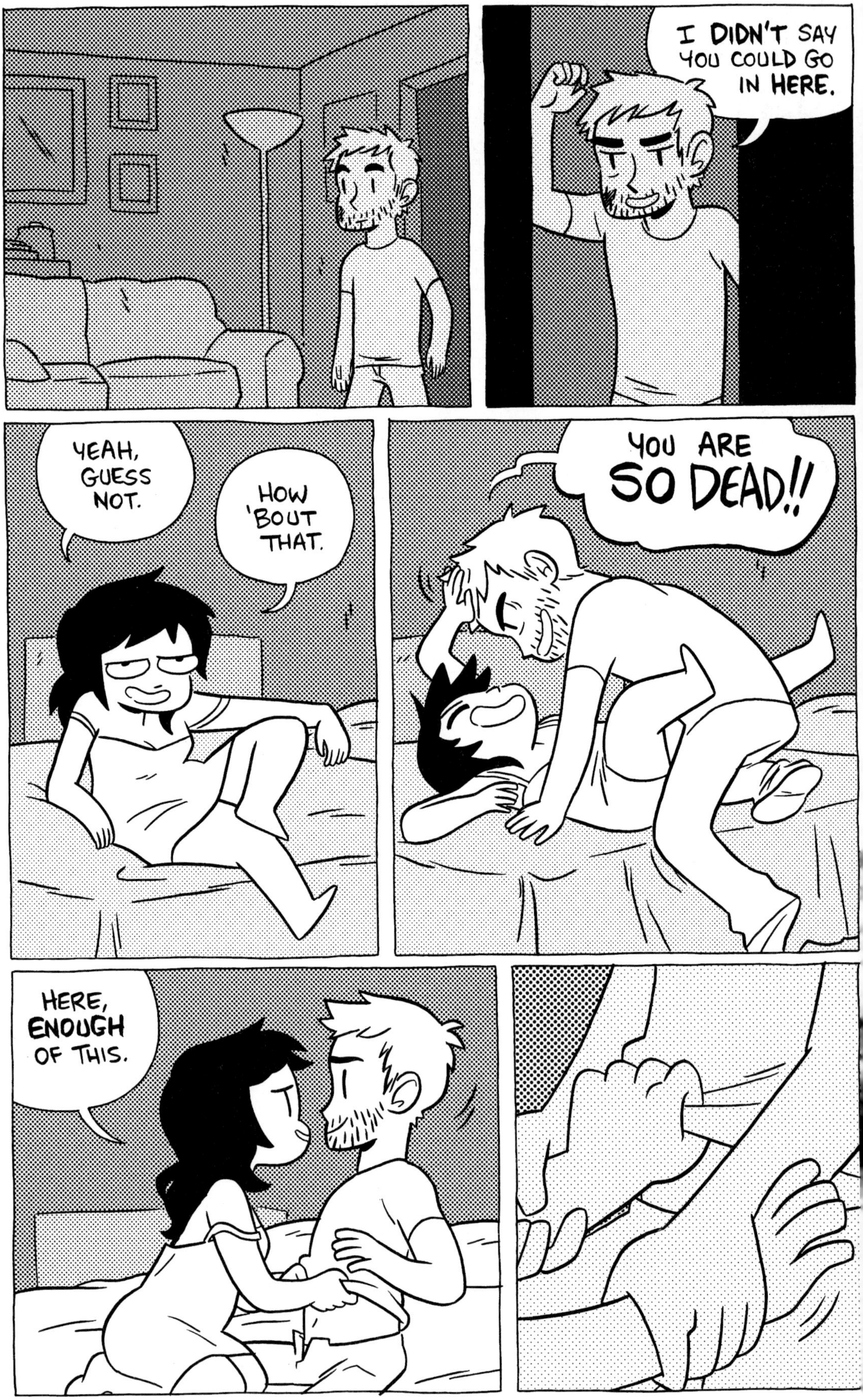
I DIDN'T SAY YOU COULD GO IN HERE.
YEAH, GUESS NOT.
HOW 'BOUT THAT.
YOU ARE SO DEAD!!
HERE, ENOUGH OF THIS.

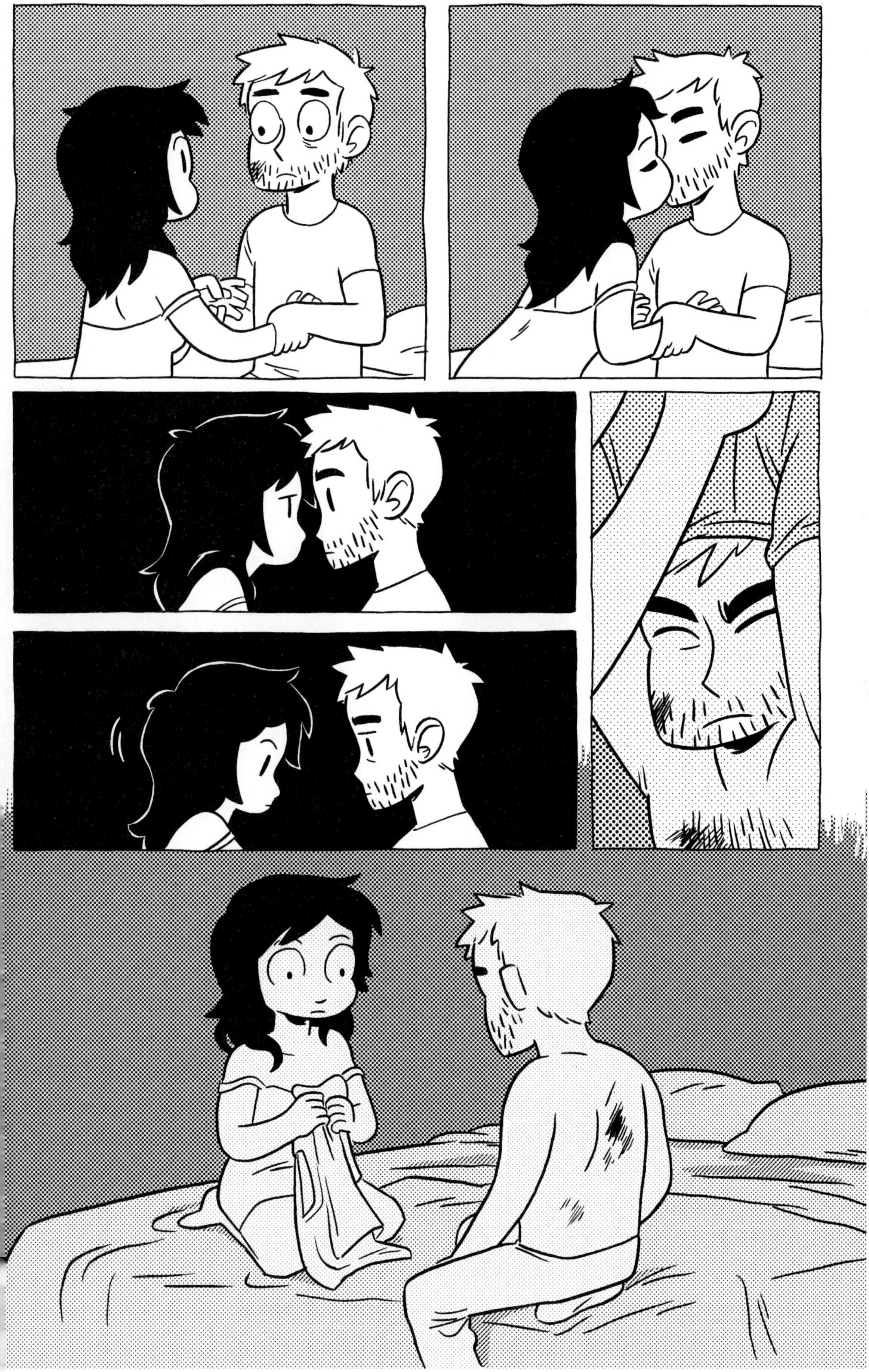

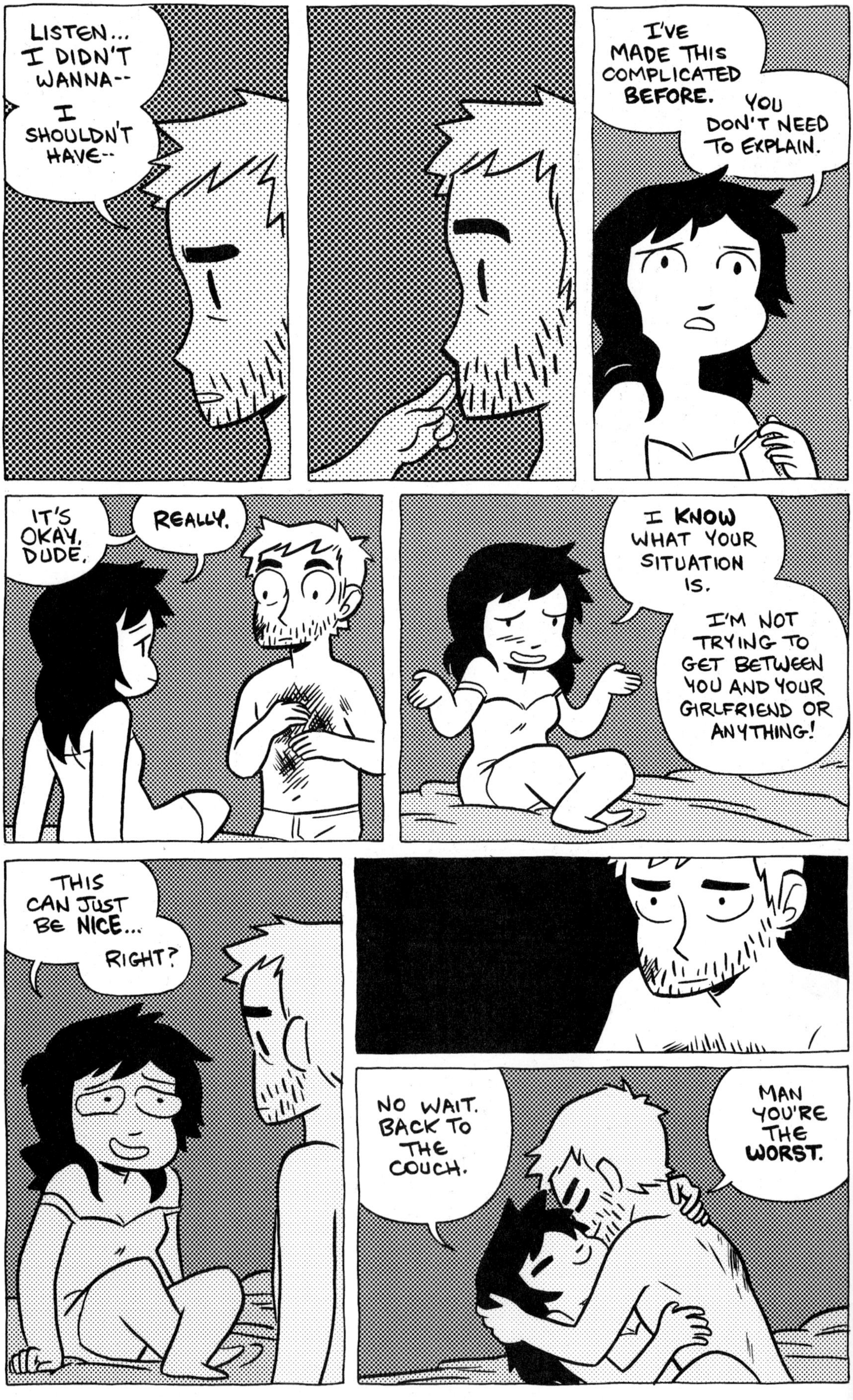
LISTEN... I DIDN'T WANNA--
I SHOULDN'T HAVE--
I'VE MADE THIS COMPLICATED BEFORE.
YOU DON'T NEED TO EXPLAIN.
IT'S OKAY, DUDE.
REALLY.
I KNOW WHAT YOUR SITUATION IS.
I'M NOT TRYING TO GET BETWEEN YOU AND YOUR GIRLFRIEND OR ANYTHING!
THIS CAN JUST BE NICE...
RIGHT?
NO WAIT. BACK TO THE COUCH.
MAN YOU'RE THE WORST.

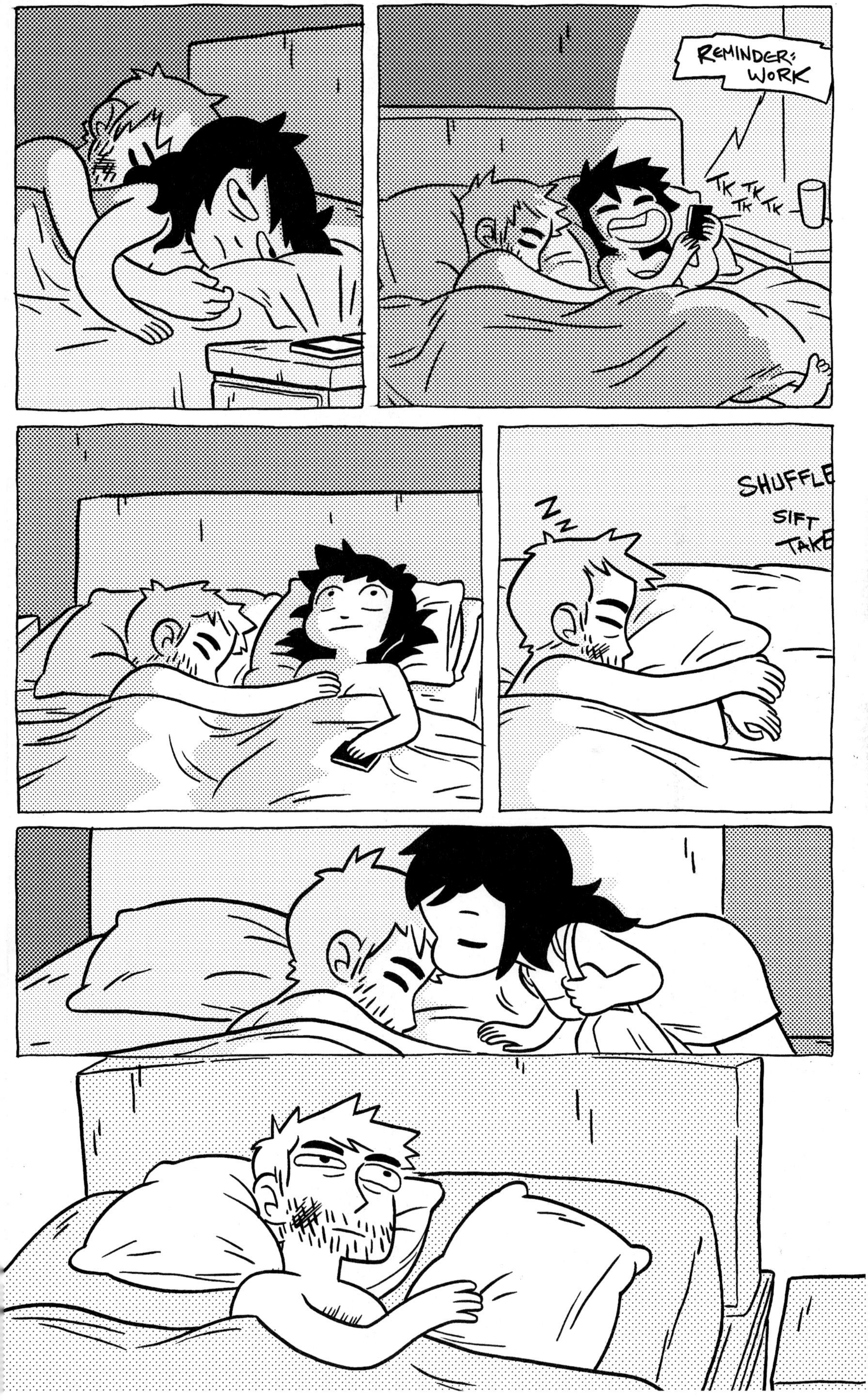
REMINDER: WORK
TK TK TK TK TK
Z Z
SHUFFLE
SIFT
TAKE

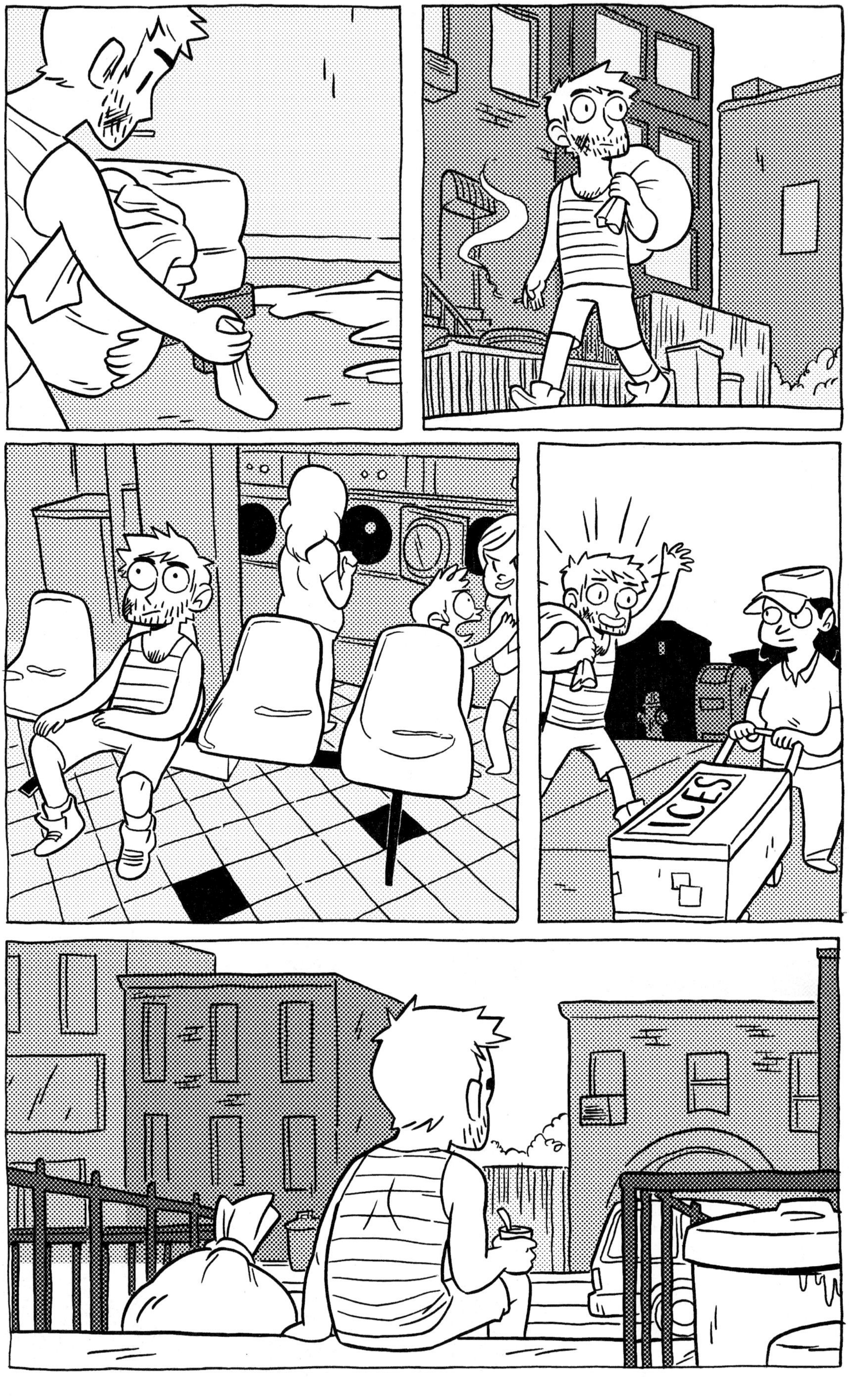
ICES

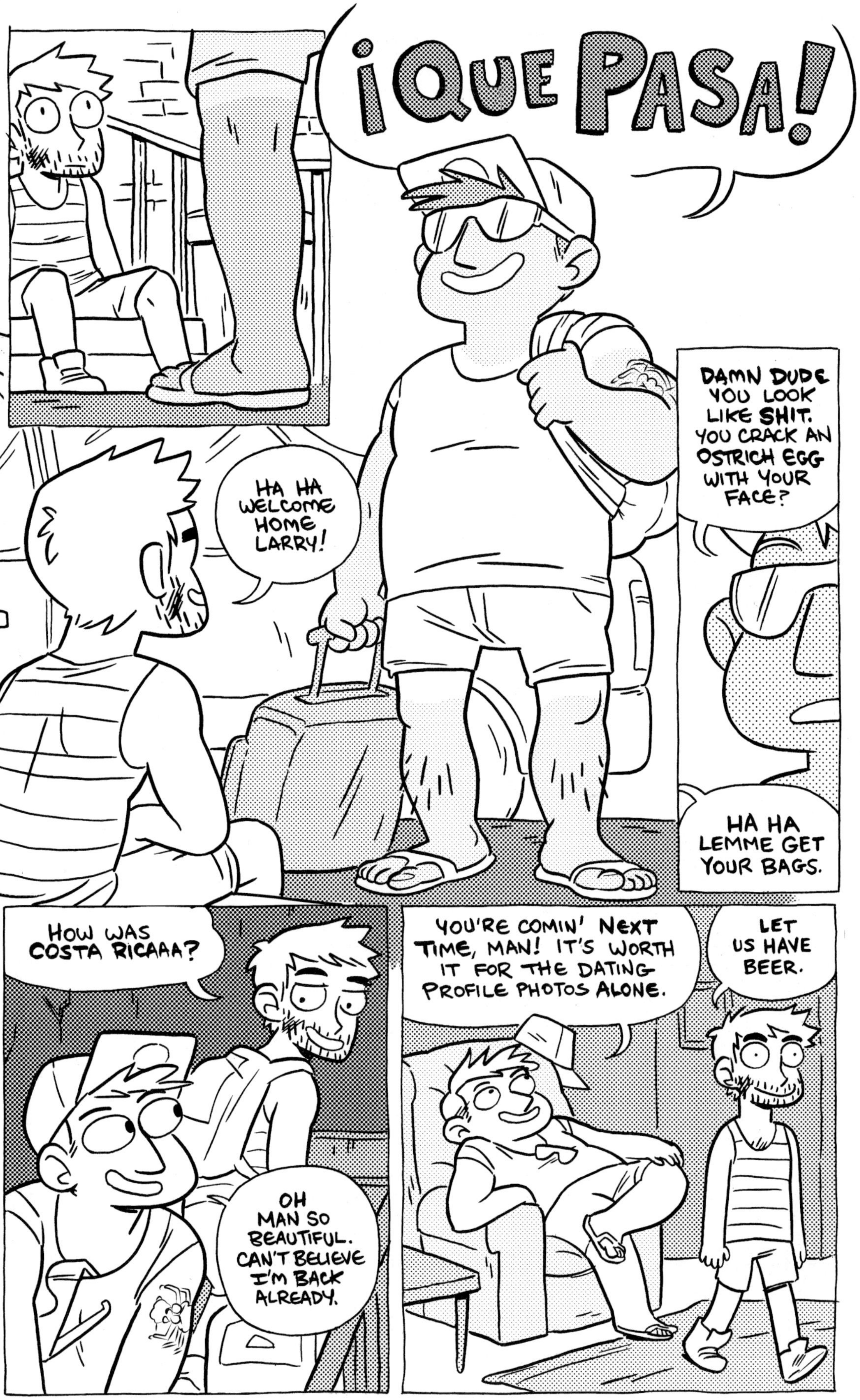
¡QUE PASA!
HA HA WELCOME HOME LARRY!
DAMN DUDE YOU LOOK LIKE SHIT. YOU CRACK AN OSTRICH EGG WITH YOUR FACE?
HA HA LEMME GET YOUR BAGS.
HOW WAS COSTA RICAAA?
OH MAN SO BEAUTIFUL. CAN'T BELIEVE I'M BACK ALREADY.
YOU'RE COMIN' NEXT TIME, MAN! IT'S WORTH IT FOR THE DATING PROFILE PHOTOS ALONE.
LET US HAVE BEER.

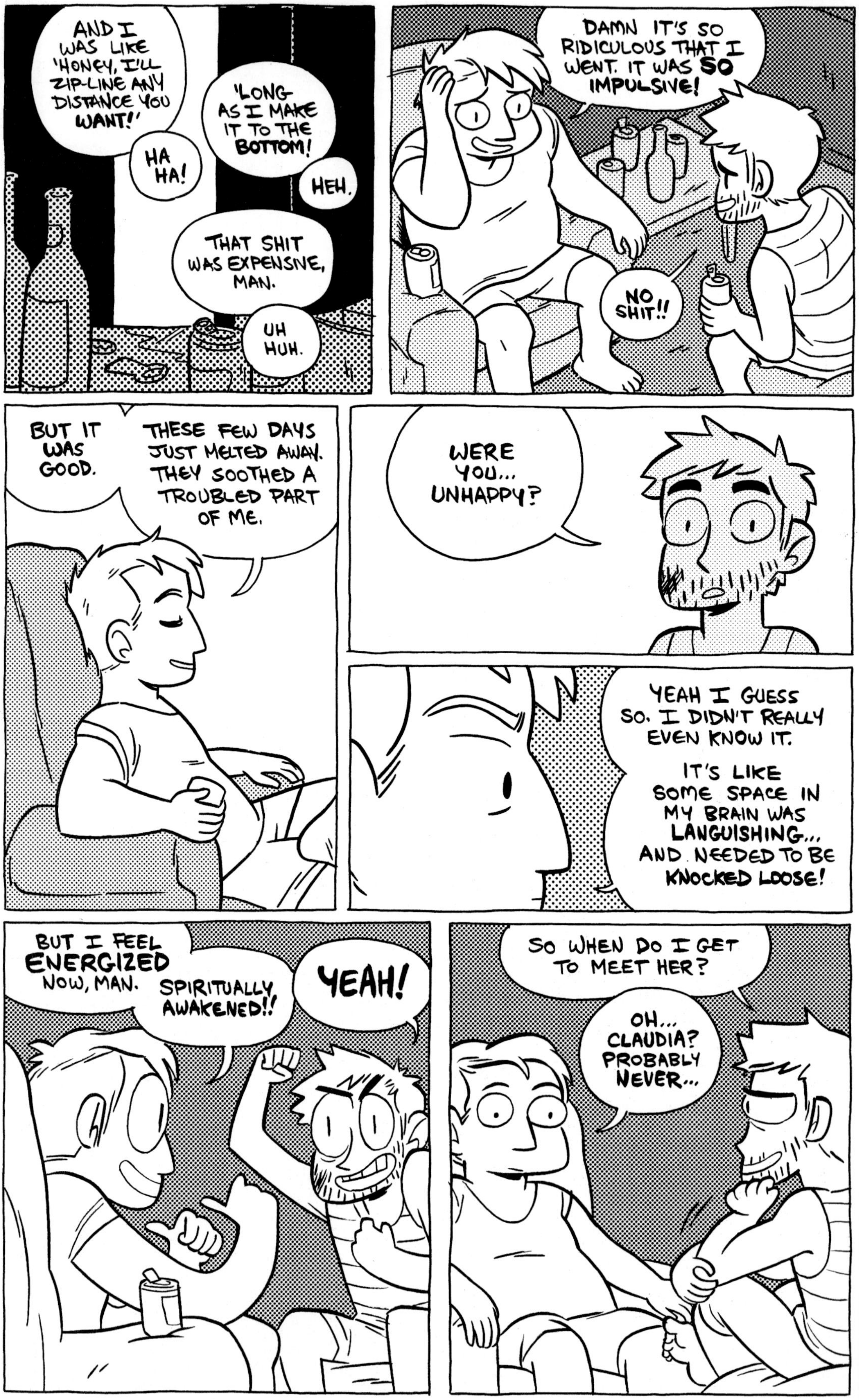
AND I WAS LIKE 'HONEY, I'LL ZIP-LINE ANY DISTANCE YOU WANT!'
HA HA!
'LONG AS I MAKE IT TO THE BOTTOM!'
HEH.
THAT SHIT WAS EXPENSIVE, MAN.
UH HUH.
DAMN IT'S SO RIDICULOUS THAT I WENT. IT WAS SO IMPULSIVE!
NO SHIT!!
BUT IT WAS GOOD.
THESE FEW DAYS JUST MELTED AWAY. THEY SOOTHED A TROUBLED PART OF ME.
WERE YOU... UNHAPPY?
YEAH I GUESS SO. I DIDN'T REALLY EVEN KNOW IT.
IT'S LIKE SOME SPACE IN MY BRAIN WAS LANGUISHING... AND NEEDED TO BE KNOCKED LOOSE!
BUT I FEEL ENERGIZED NOW, MAN.
SPIRITUALLY AWAKENED!!
YEAH!
SO WHEN DO I GET TO MEET HER?
OH... CLAUDIA? PROBABLY NEVER...

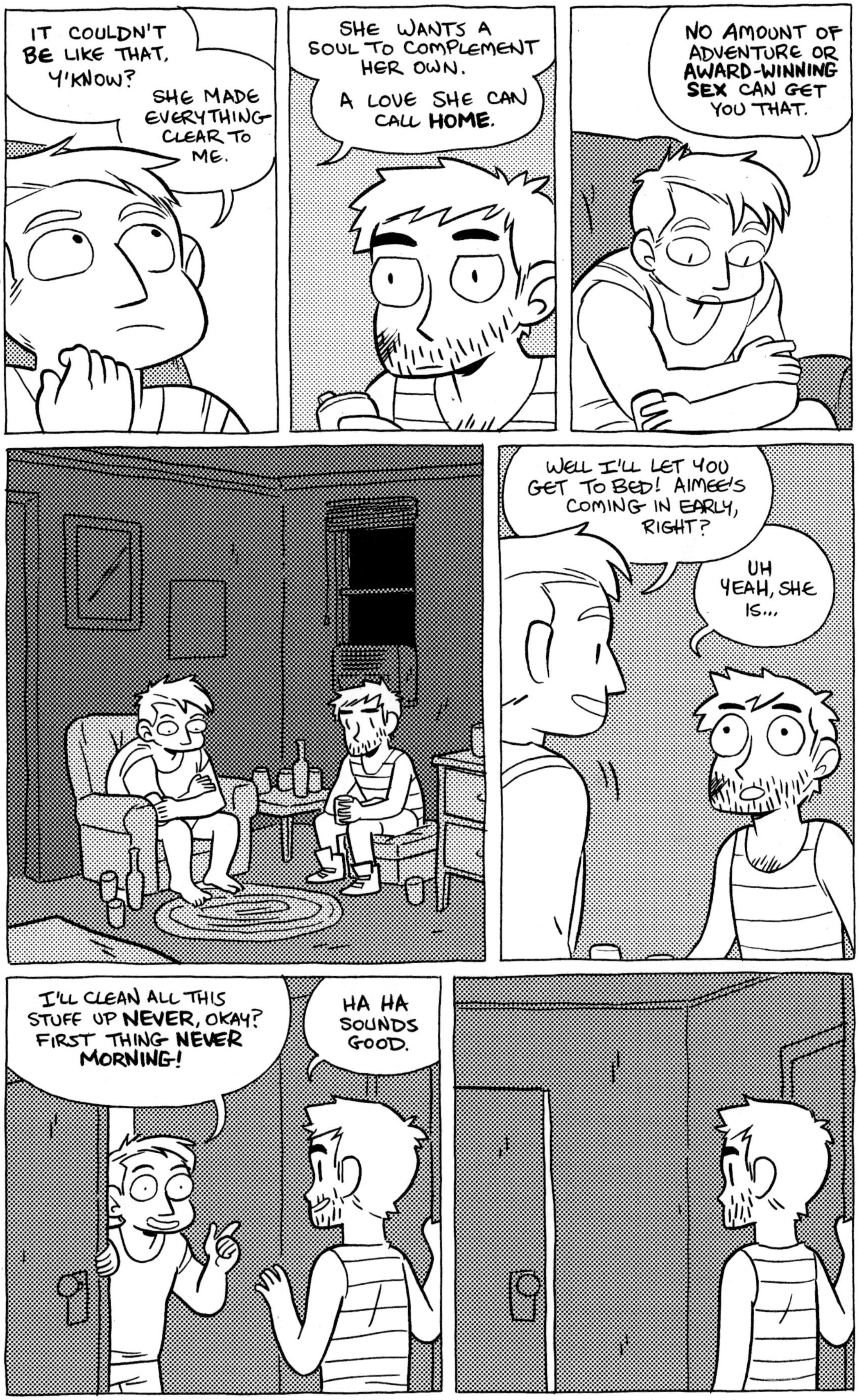
IT COULDN'T BE LIKE THAT, Y'KNOW?
SHE MADE EVERYTHING CLEAR TO ME.
SHE WANTS A SOUL TO COMPLEMENT HER OWN.
A LOVE SHE CAN CALL HOME.
NO AMOUNT OF ADVENTURE OR AWARD-WINNING SEX CAN GET YOU THAT.
WELL I'LL LET YOU GET TO BED! AIMEE'S COMING IN EARLY, RIGHT?
UH YEAH, SHE IS...
I'LL CLEAN ALL THIS STUFF UP NEVER, OKAY? FIRST THING NEVER MORNING!
HA HA SOUNDS GOOD.

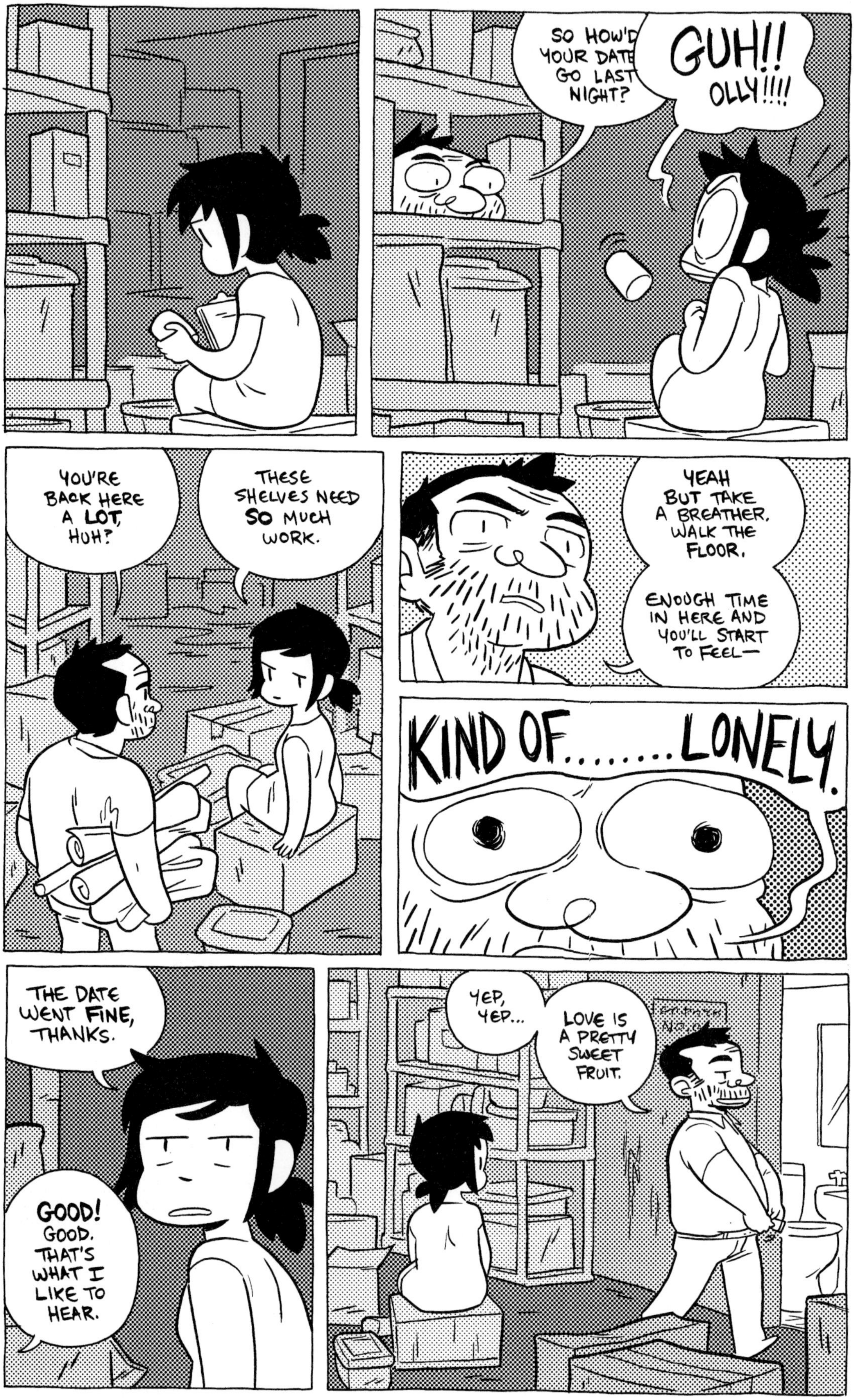

SO HOW'D YOUR DATE GO LAST NIGHT?
GUH!! OLLY!!!!
YOU'RE BACK HERE A LOT, HUH?
THESE SHELVES NEED SO MUCH WORK.
YEAH BUT TAKE A BREATHER. WALK THE FLOOR.
ENOUGH TIME IN HERE AND YOU'LL START TO FEEL—
KIND OF.......LONELY.
THE DATE WENT FINE, THANKS.
GOOD! GOOD. THAT'S WHAT I LIKE TO HEAR.
YEP, YEP...
LOVE IS A PRETTY SWEET FRUIT.

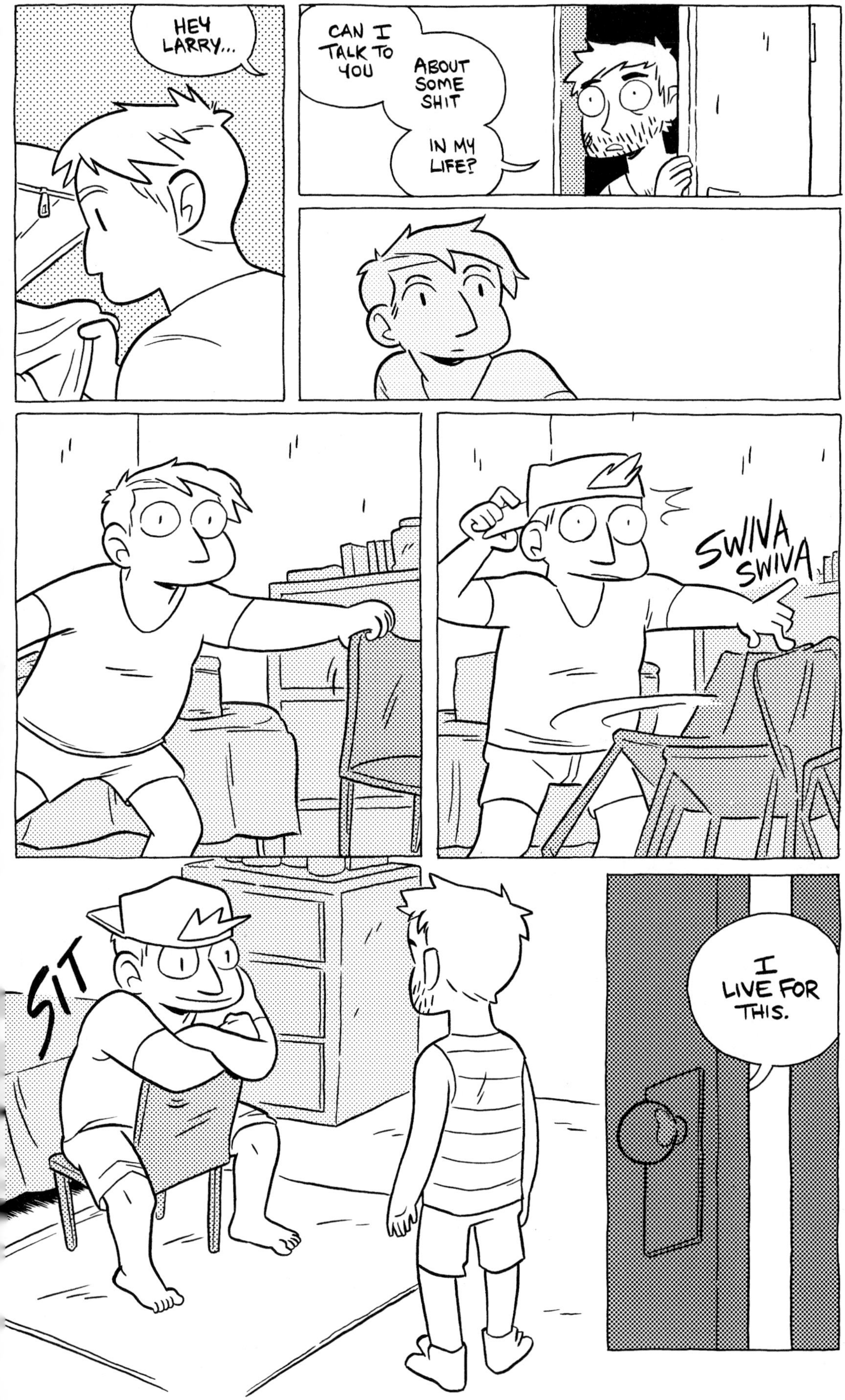
HEY LARRY...
CAN I TALK TO YOU
ABOUT SOME SHIT
IN MY LIFE?
SWIVA SWIVA
SIT
I LIVE FOR THIS.

46

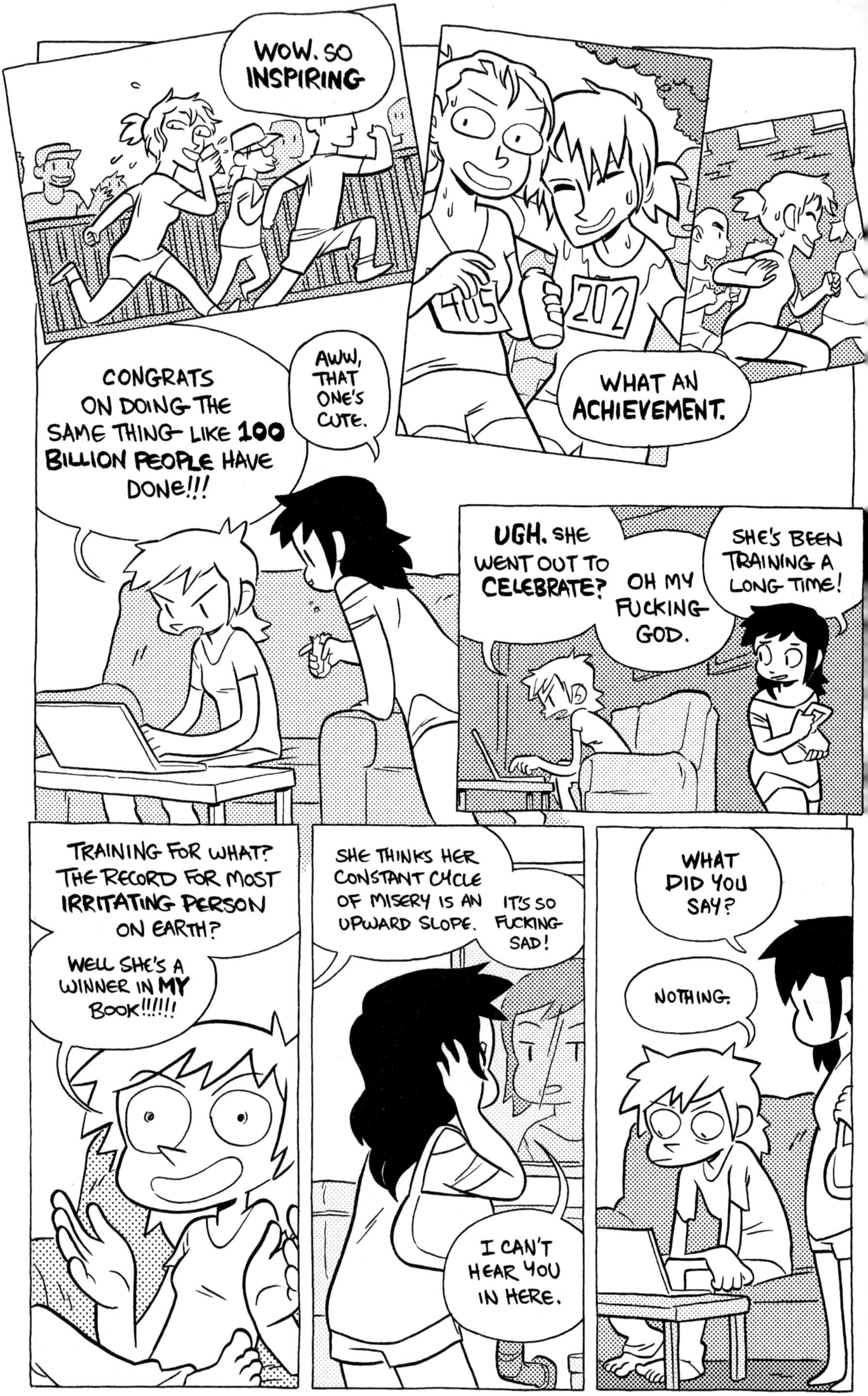
WOW. SO INSPIRING
405
202
WHAT AN ACHIEVEMENT.
CONGRATS ON DOING THE SAME THING LIKE 100 BILLION PEOPLE HAVE DONE!!!
AWW, THAT ONE'S CUTE.
UGH. SHE WENT OUT TO CELEBRATE?
OH MY FUCKING GOD.
SHE'S BEEN TRAINING A LONG TIME!
TRAINING FOR WHAT? THE RECORD FOR MOST IRRITATING PERSON ON EARTH?
WELL SHE'S A WINNER IN MY BOOK!!!!!!
SHE THINKS HER CONSTANT CYCLE OF MISERY IS AN UPWARD SLOPE.
IT'S SO FUCKING SAD!
I CAN'T HEAR YOU IN HERE.
WHAT DID YOU SAY?
NOTHING.

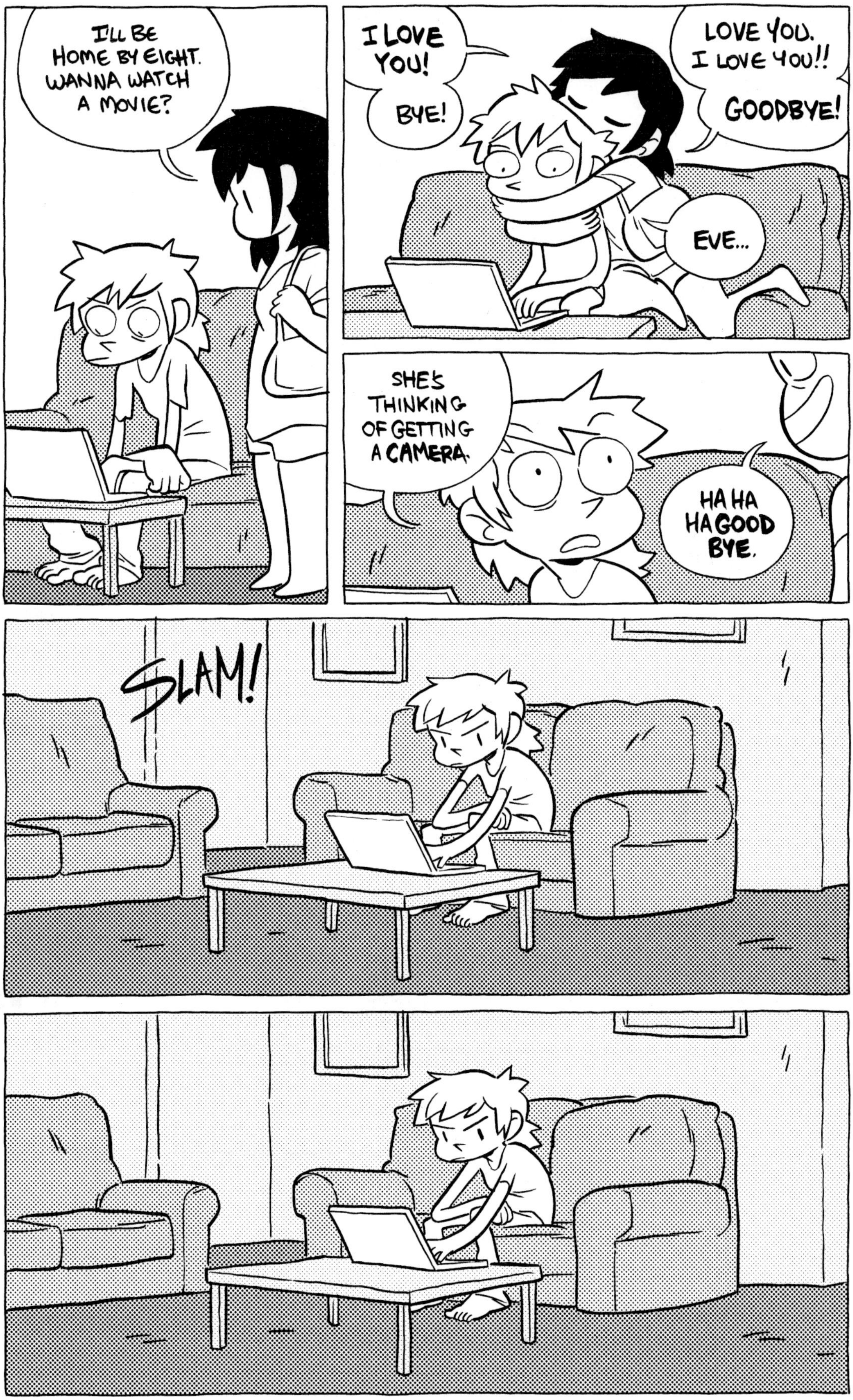

I'LL BE HOME BY EIGHT. WANNA WATCH A MOVIE?
I LOVE YOU!
BYE!
LOVE YOU. I LOVE YOU!!
GOODBYE!
EVE...
SHE'S THINKING OF GETTING A CAMERA.
HA HA HA GOOD BYE.
SLAM!

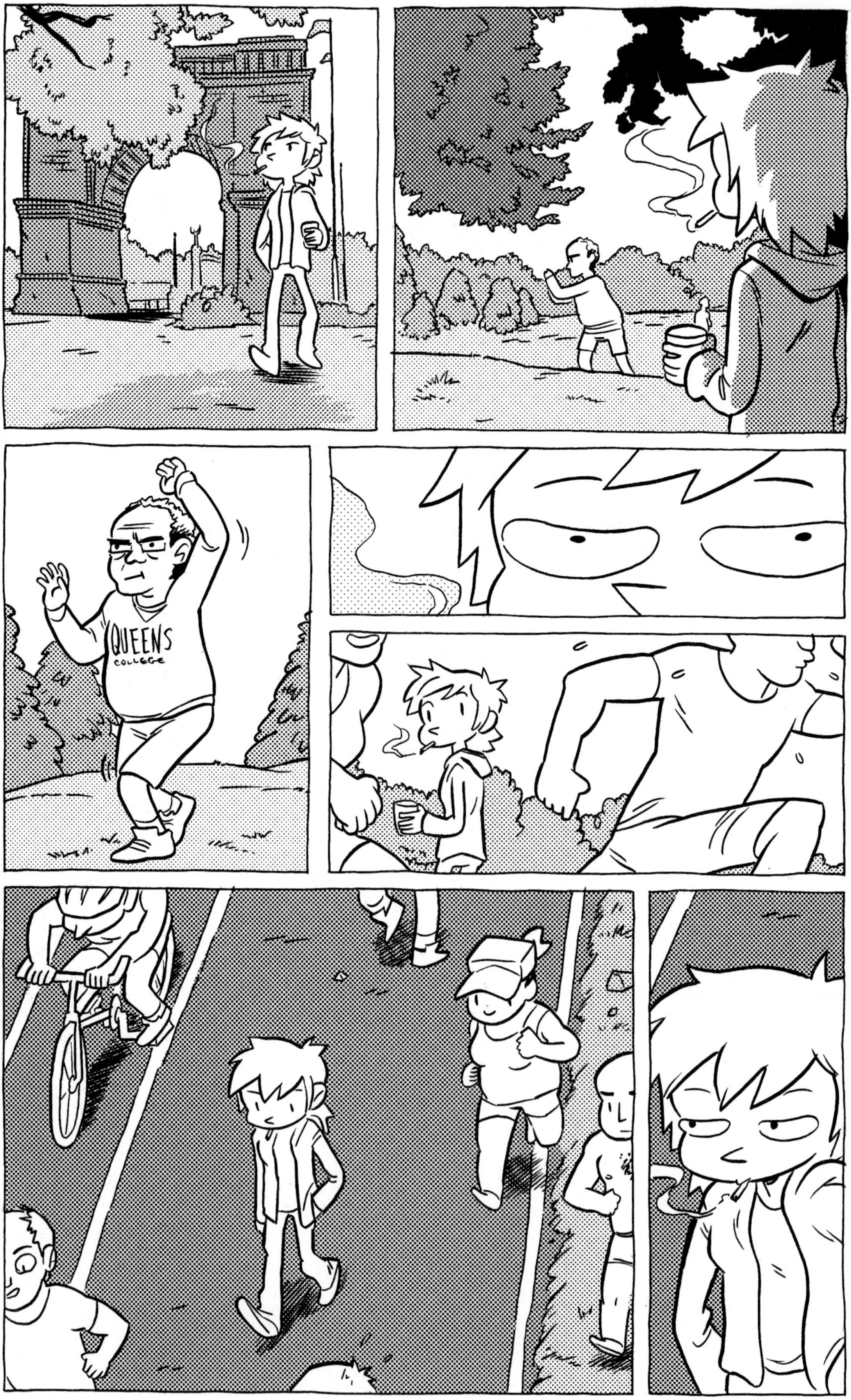
QUEENS
COLLEGE

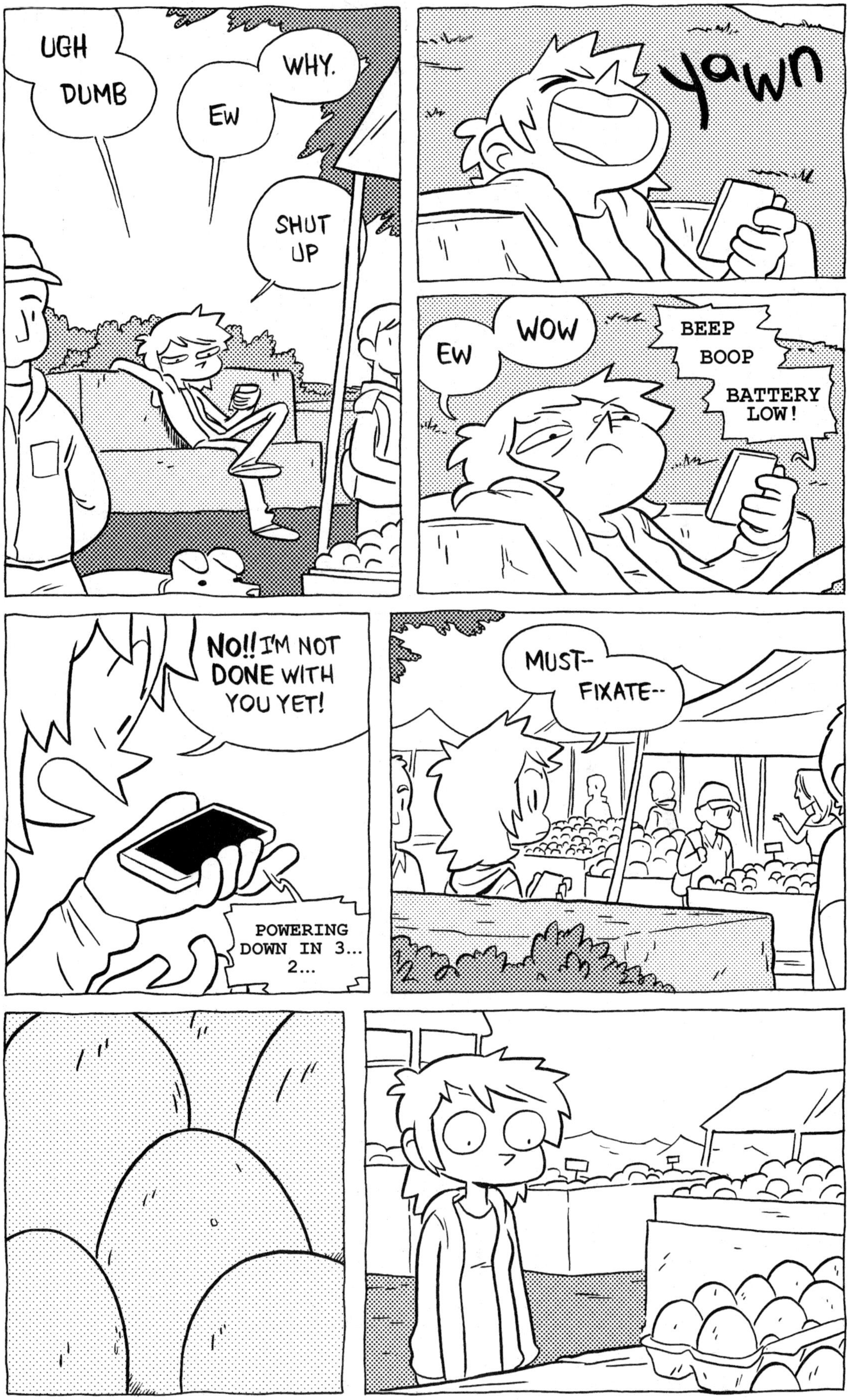
UGH
DUMB
EW
WHY.
SHUT UP
yawn
EW
WOW
BEEP
BOOP
BATTERY LOW!
NO!! I'M NOT DONE WITH YOU YET!
POWERING DOWN IN 3... 2...
MUST-
FIXATE--

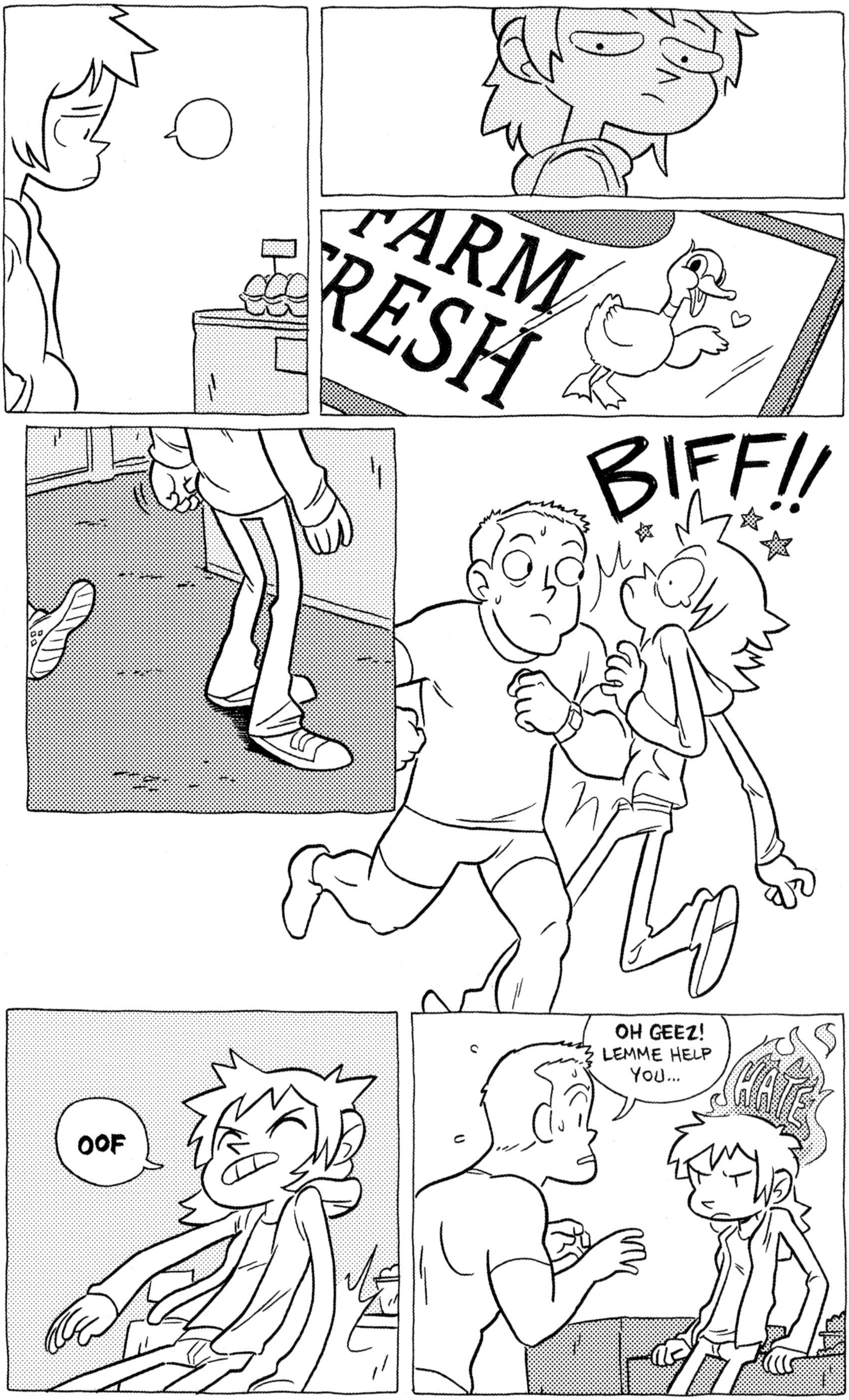
FARM
FRESH
BIFF!!
OOF
OH GEEZ! LEMME HELP YOU...
HATE

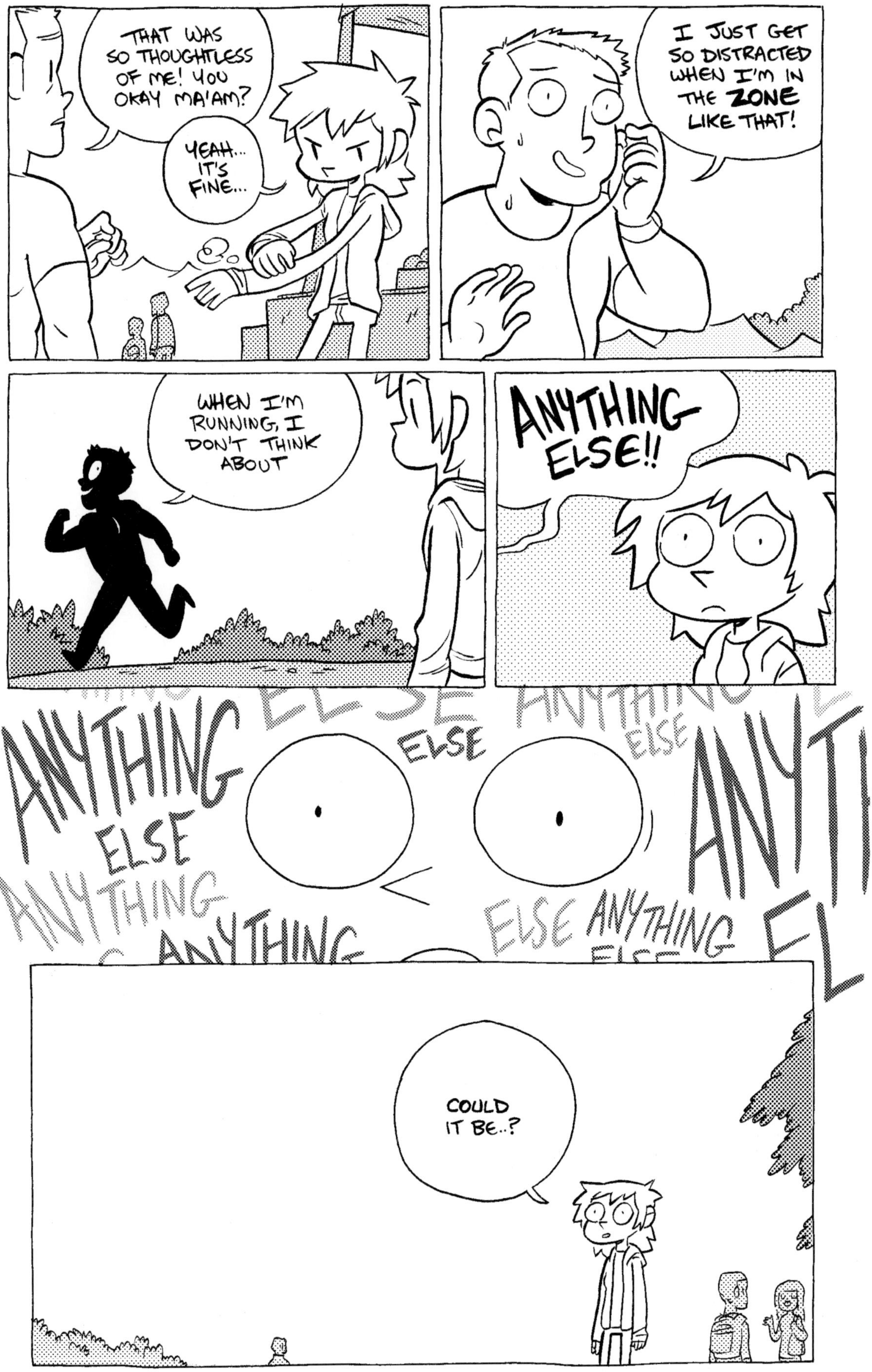
THAT WAS SO THOUGHTLESS OF ME! YOU OKAY MA'AM?
YEAH... IT'S FINE...
I JUST GET SO DISTRACTED WHEN I'M IN THE **ZONE** LIKE THAT!
WHEN I'M RUNNING, I DON'T THINK ABOUT
ANYTHING ELSE!!
ANYTHING ELSE
ELSE
ANYTHING
ELSE ANYTHING
COULD IT BE..?

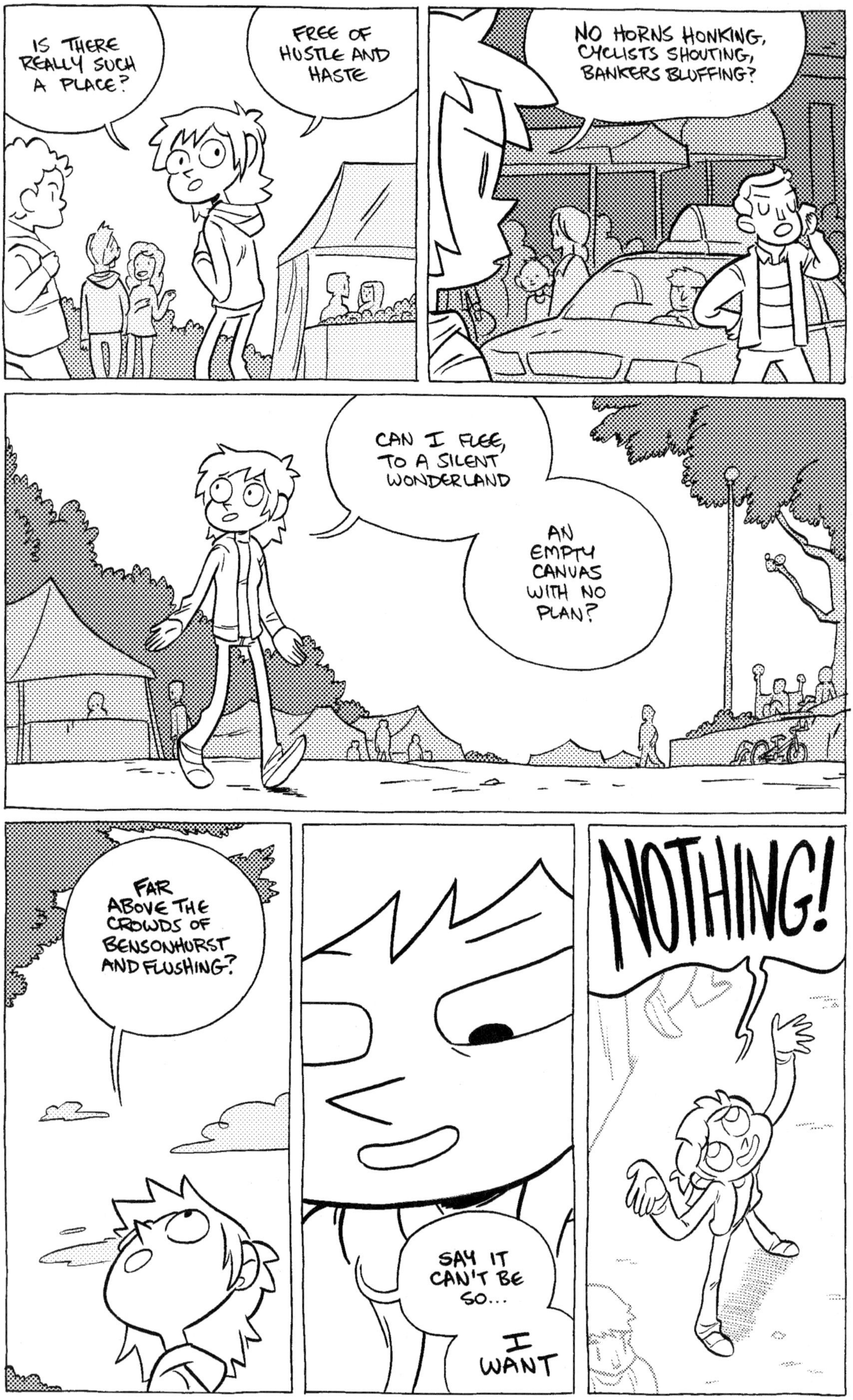
IS THERE REALLY SUCH A PLACE?
FREE OF HUSTLE AND HASTE
NO HORNS HONKING, CYCLISTS SHOUTING, BANKERS BLUFFING?
CAN I FLEE, TO A SILENT WONDERLAND
AN EMPTY CANVAS WITH NO PLAN?
FAR ABOVE THE CROWDS OF BENSONHURST AND FLUSHING?
SAY IT CAN'T BE SO...
I WANT
NOTHING!

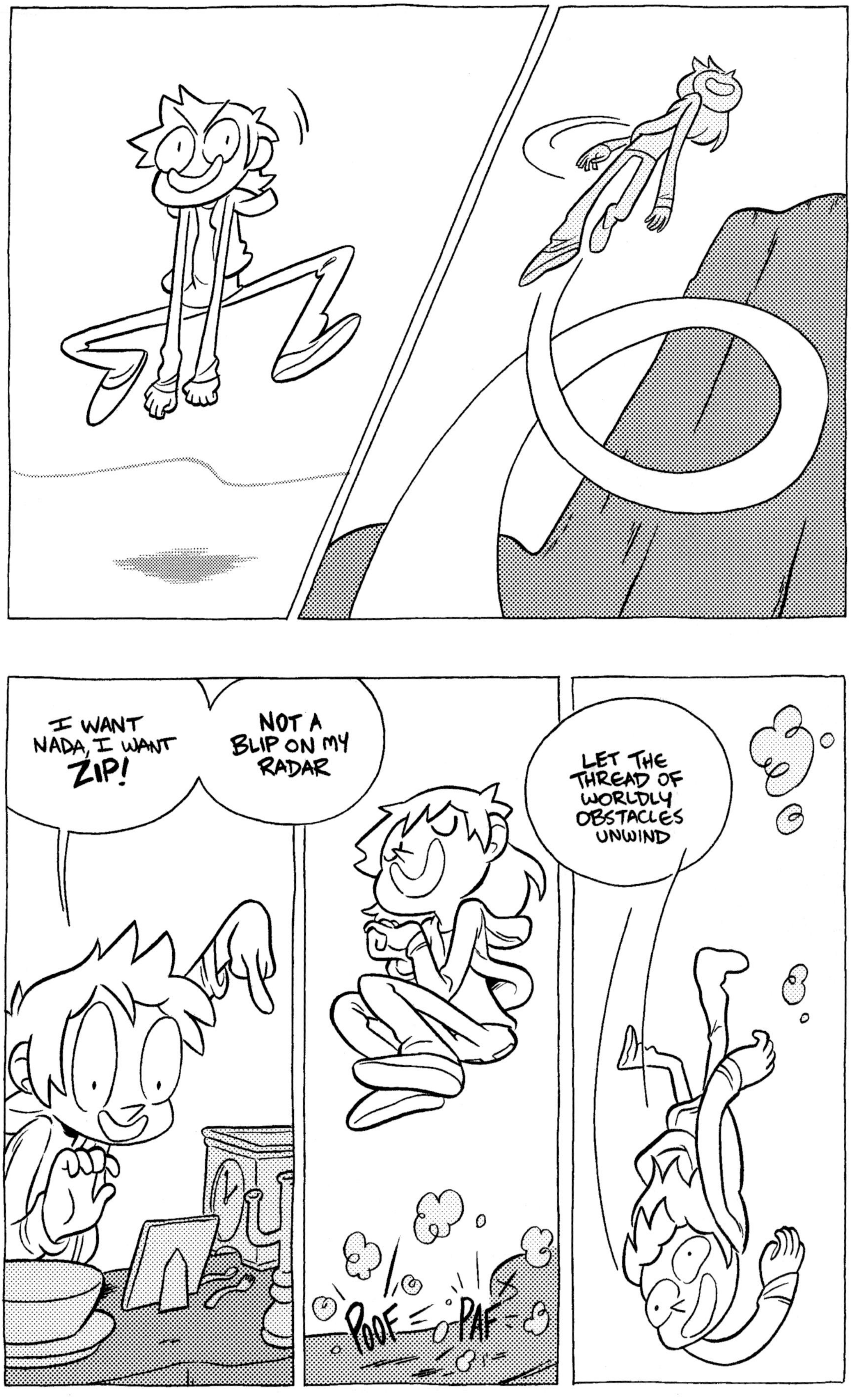
I WANT NADA, I WANT ZIP!
NOT A BLIP ON MY RADAR
POOF
PAF
LET THE THREAD OF WORLDLY OBSTACLES UNWIND

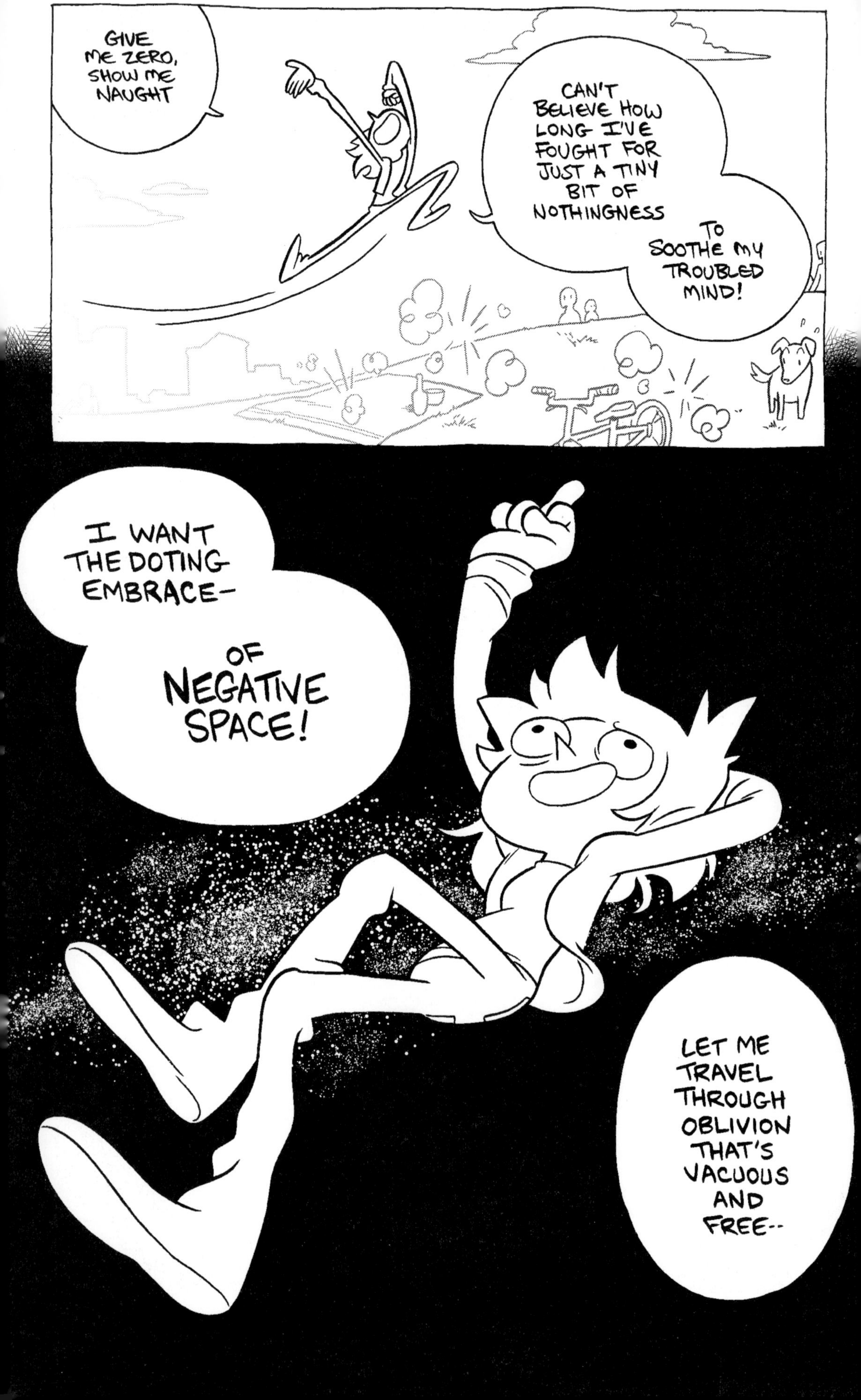
GIVE ME ZERO, SHOW ME NAUGHT
CAN'T BELIEVE HOW LONG I'VE FOUGHT FOR JUST A TINY BIT OF NOTHINGNESS
TO SOOTHE MY TROUBLED MIND!
I WANT THE DOTING EMBRACE–
OF NEGATIVE SPACE!
LET ME TRAVEL THROUGH OBLIVION THAT'S VACUOUS AND FREE--

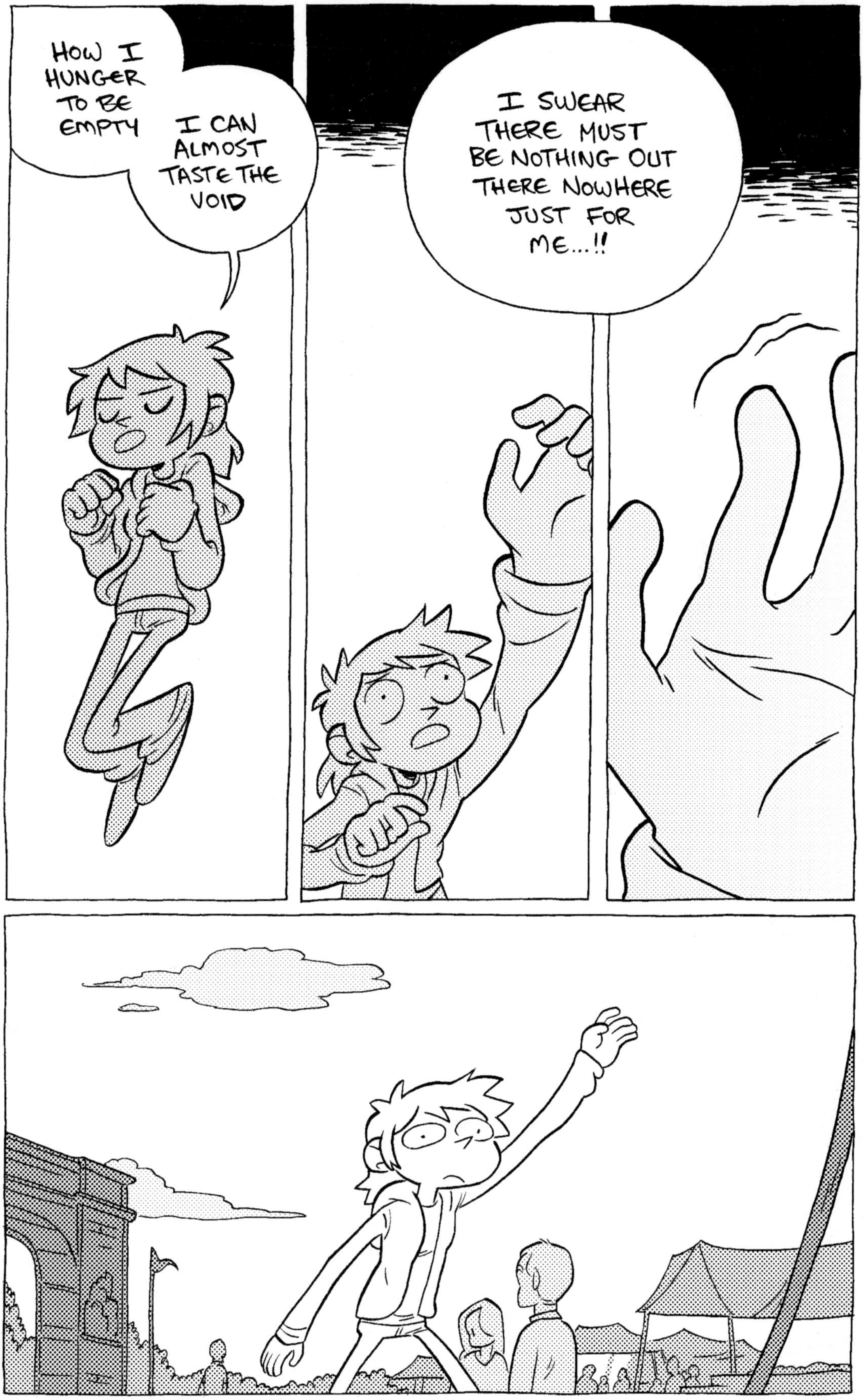
HOW I HUNGER TO BE EMPTY
I CAN ALMOST TASTE THE VOID
I SWEAR THERE MUST BE NOTHING OUT THERE NOWHERE JUST FOR ME...!!

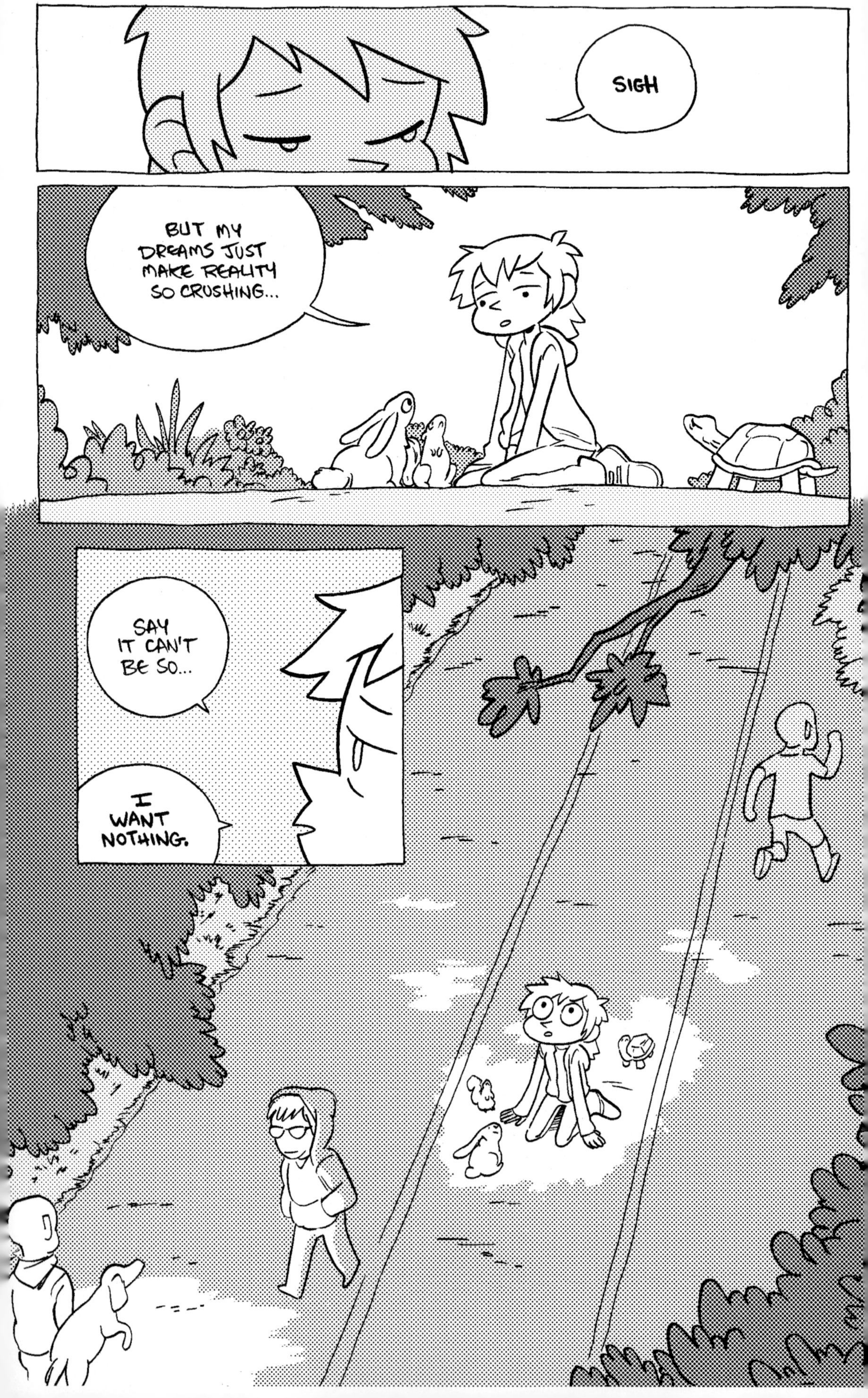
SIGH
BUT MY DREAMS JUST MAKE REALITY SO CRUSHING...
SAY IT CAN'T BE SO...
I WANT NOTHING.

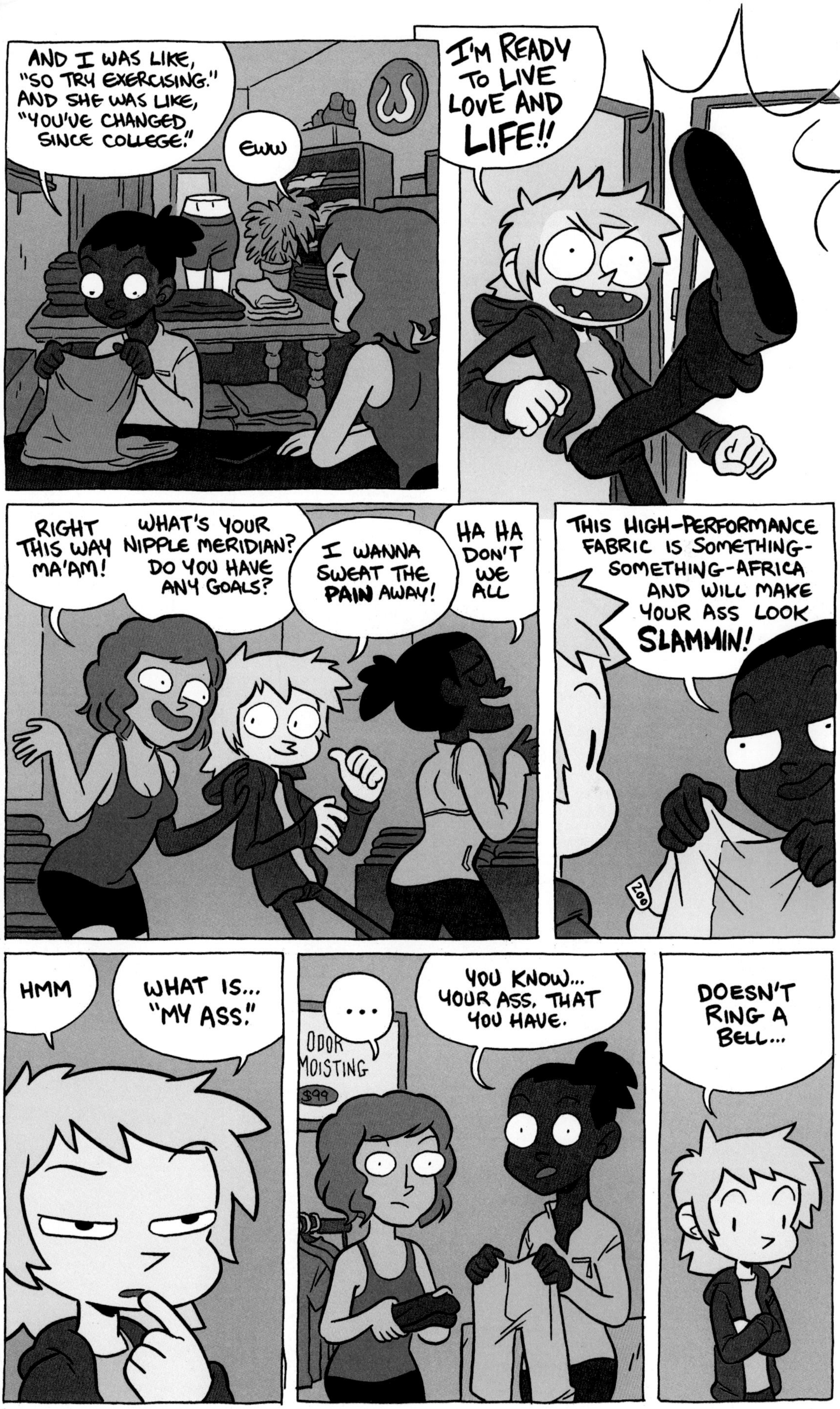

AND I WAS LIKE, "SO TRY EXERCISING." AND SHE WAS LIKE, "YOU'VE CHANGED SINCE COLLEGE."
EWW
I'M READY TO LIVE LOVE AND LIFE!!
RIGHT THIS WAY MA'AM!
WHAT'S YOUR NIPPLE MERIDIAN? DO YOU HAVE ANY GOALS?
I WANNA SWEAT THE PAIN AWAY!
HA HA DON'T WE ALL
THIS HIGH-PERFORMANCE FABRIC IS SOMETHING-SOMETHING-AFRICA AND WILL MAKE YOUR ASS LOOK SLAMMIN!
200
HMM
WHAT IS... "MY ASS."
...
ODOR MOISTING
$99
YOU KNOW... YOUR ASS, THAT YOU HAVE.
DOESN'T RING A BELL...

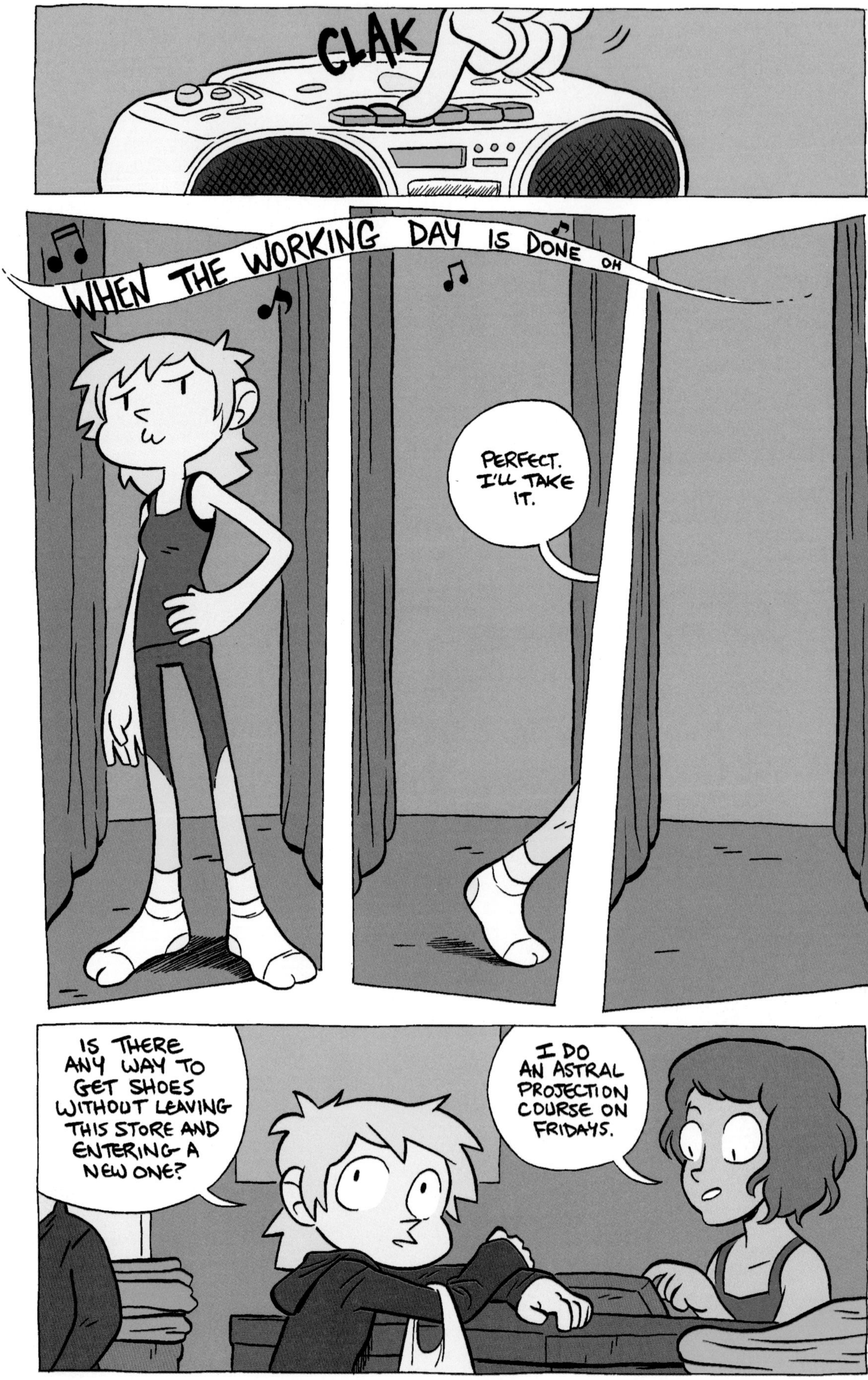
CLAK
WHEN THE WORKING DAY IS DONE OH
PERFECT. I'LL TAKE IT.
IS THERE ANY WAY TO GET SHOES WITHOUT LEAVING THIS STORE AND ENTERING A NEW ONE?
I DO AN ASTRAL PROJECTION COURSE ON FRIDAYS.

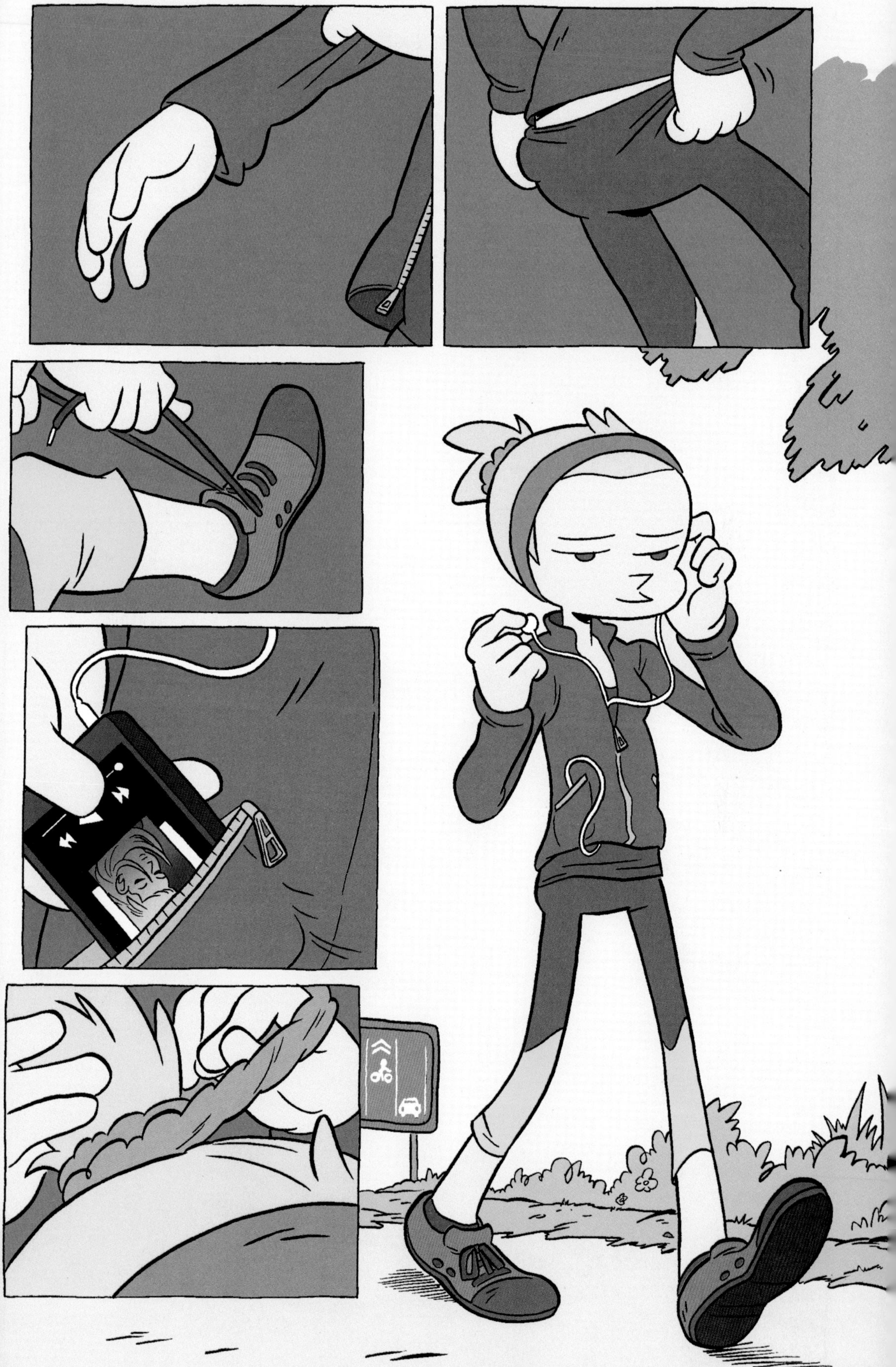

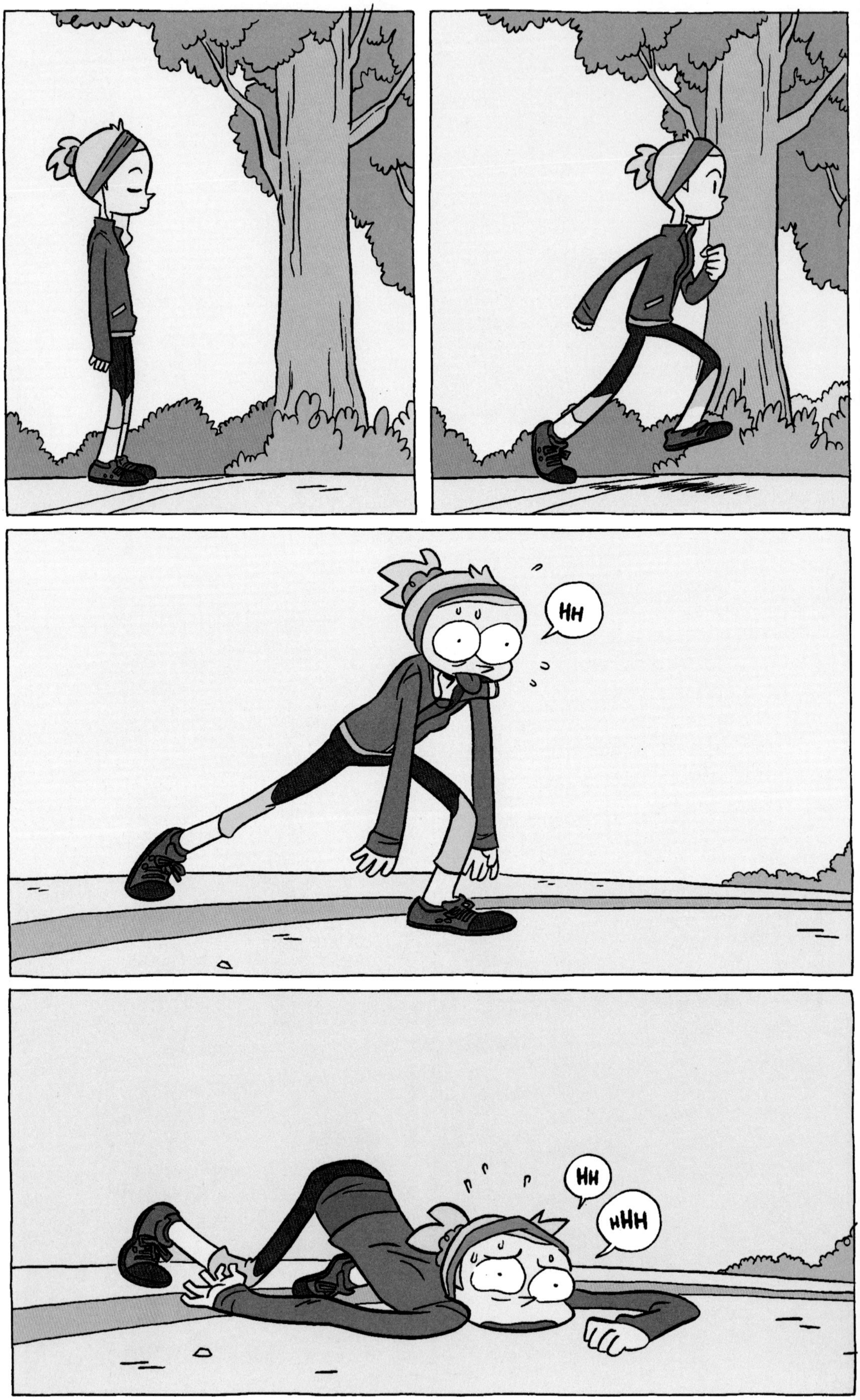
HH
HH
HHH

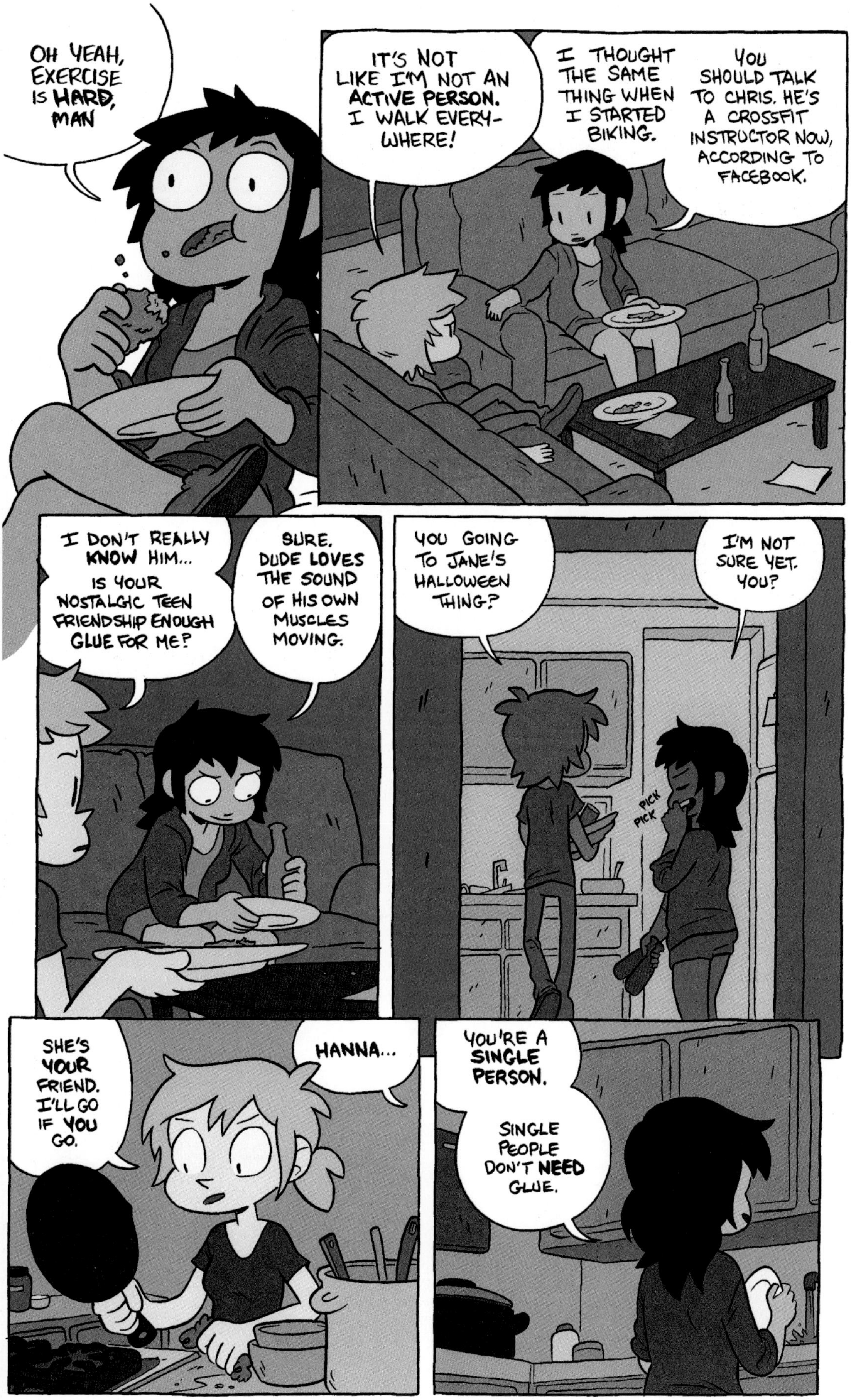
OH YEAH, EXERCISE IS HARD, MAN
IT'S NOT LIKE I'M NOT AN ACTIVE PERSON. I WALK EVERYWHERE!
I THOUGHT THE SAME THING WHEN I STARTED BIKING.
YOU SHOULD TALK TO CHRIS. HE'S A CROSSFIT INSTRUCTOR NOW, ACCORDING TO FACEBOOK.
I DON'T REALLY KNOW HIM... IS YOUR NOSTALGIC TEEN FRIENDSHIP ENOUGH GLUE FOR ME?
SURE. DUDE LOVES THE SOUND OF HIS OWN MUSCLES MOVING.
YOU GOING TO JANE'S HALLOWEEN THING?
I'M NOT SURE YET. YOU?
PICK PICK
SHE'S YOUR FRIEND. I'LL GO IF YOU GO.
HANNA...
YOU'RE A SINGLE PERSON.
SINGLE PEOPLE DON'T NEED GLUE.

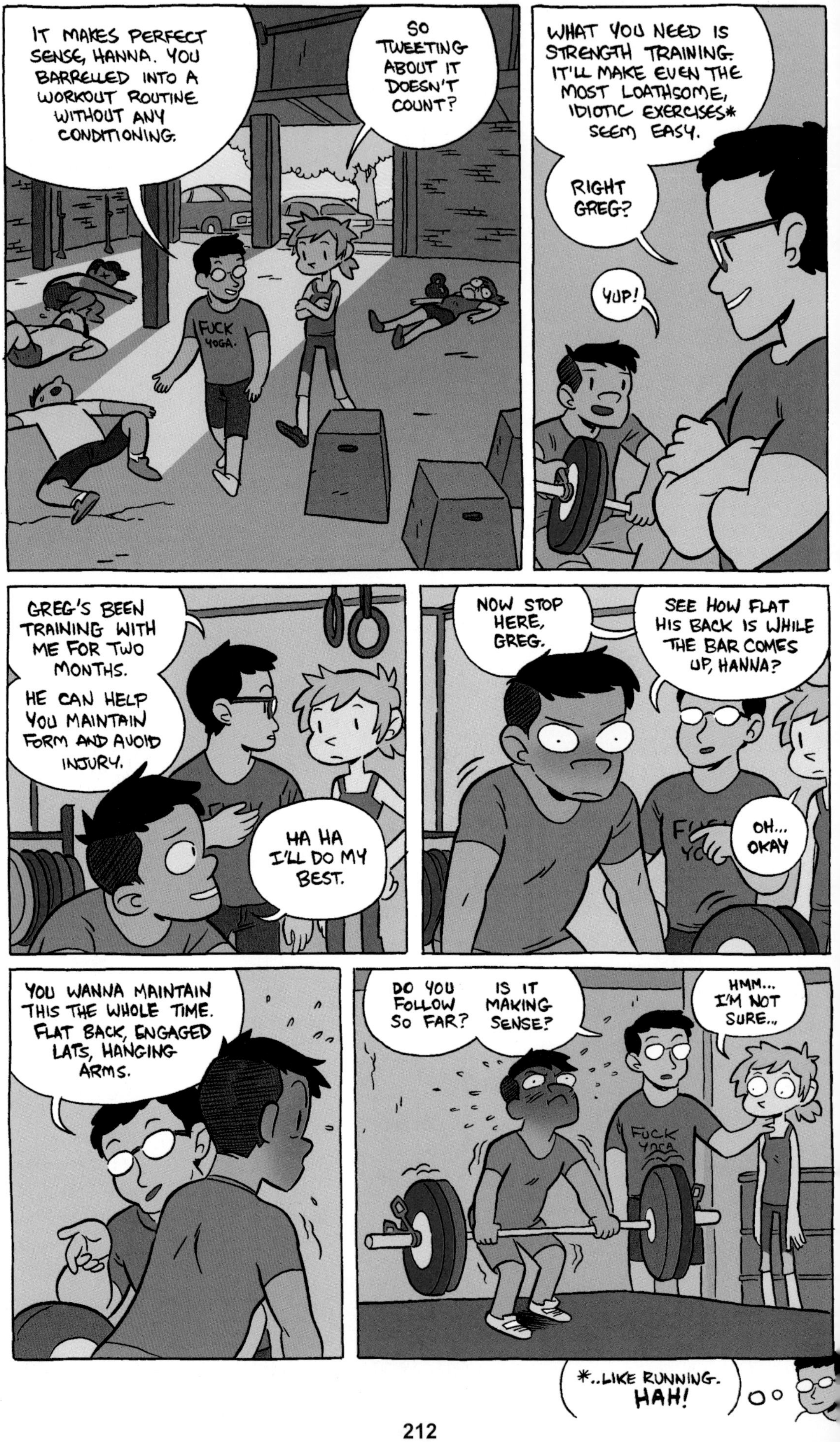
IT MAKES PERFECT SENSE, HANNA. YOU BARRELLED INTO A WORKOUT ROUTINE WITHOUT ANY CONDITIONING.
SO TWEETING ABOUT IT DOESN'T COUNT?
FUCK YOGA.
WHAT YOU NEED IS STRENGTH TRAINING. IT'LL MAKE EVEN THE MOST LOATHSOME, IDIOTIC EXERCISES* SEEM EASY.
RIGHT GREG?
YUP!
GREG'S BEEN TRAINING WITH ME FOR TWO MONTHS.
HE CAN HELP YOU MAINTAIN FORM AND AVOID INJURY.
HA HA I'LL DO MY BEST.
NOW STOP HERE, GREG.
SEE HOW FLAT HIS BACK IS WHILE THE BAR COMES UP, HANNA?
OH... OKAY
YOU WANNA MAINTAIN THIS THE WHOLE TIME. FLAT BACK, ENGAGED LATS, HANGING ARMS.
DO YOU FOLLOW SO FAR?
IS IT MAKING SENSE?
HMM... I'M NOT SURE...
*...LIKE RUNNING. HAH!

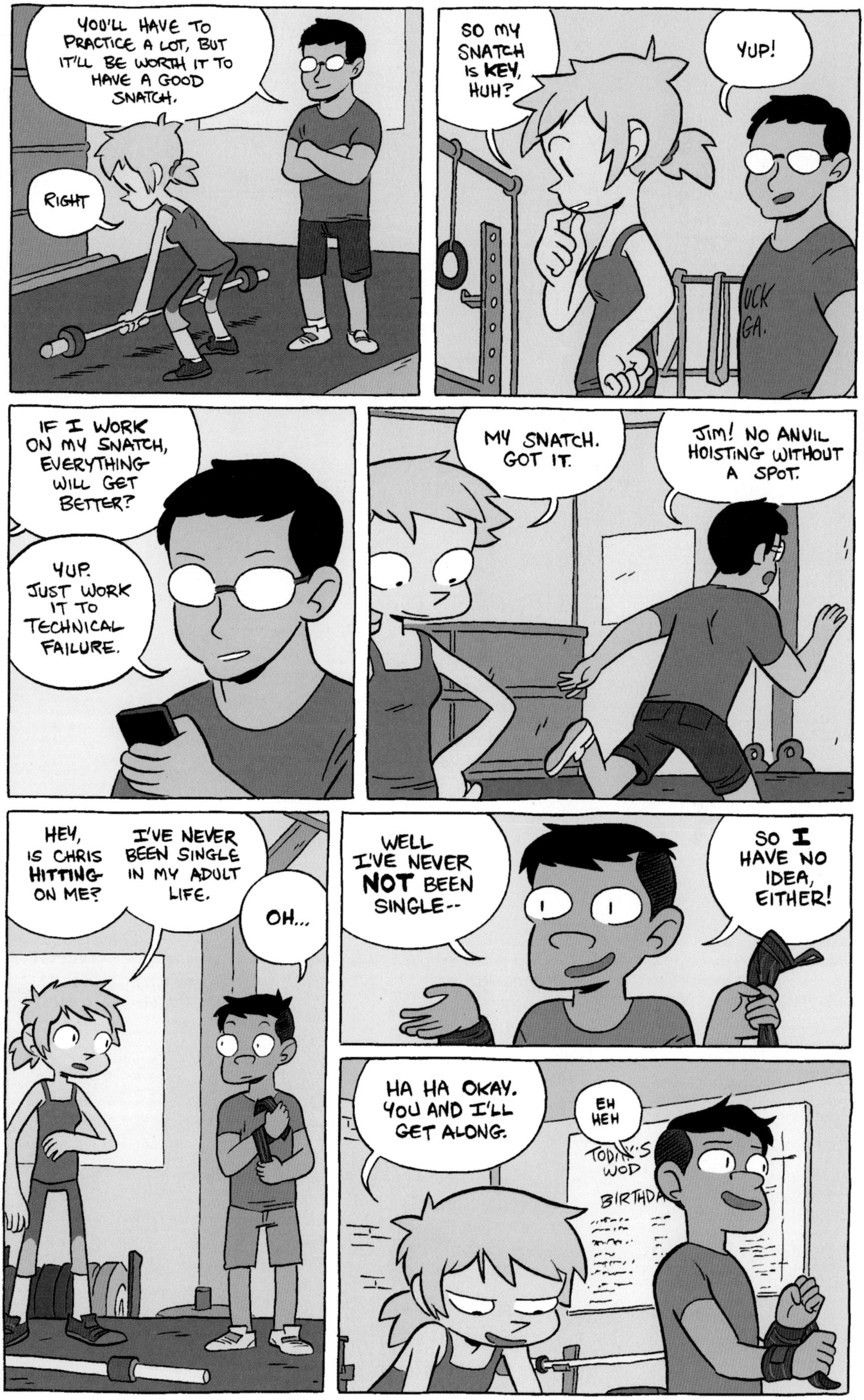
YOU'LL HAVE TO PRACTICE A LOT, BUT IT'LL BE WORTH IT TO HAVE A GOOD SNATCH.
RIGHT
SO MY SNATCH IS KEY, HUH?
YUP!
UCK
GA.
IF I WORK ON MY SNATCH, EVERYTHING WILL GET BETTER?
YUP. JUST WORK IT TO TECHNICAL FAILURE.
MY SNATCH. GOT IT.
JIM! NO ANVIL HOISTING WITHOUT A SPOT.
HEY, IS CHRIS HITTING ON ME?
I'VE NEVER BEEN SINGLE IN MY ADULT LIFE.
OH...
WELL I'VE NEVER NOT BEEN SINGLE--
SO I HAVE NO IDEA, EITHER!
HA HA OKAY. YOU AND I'LL GET ALONG.
EH HEH
WOD
BIRTHDA

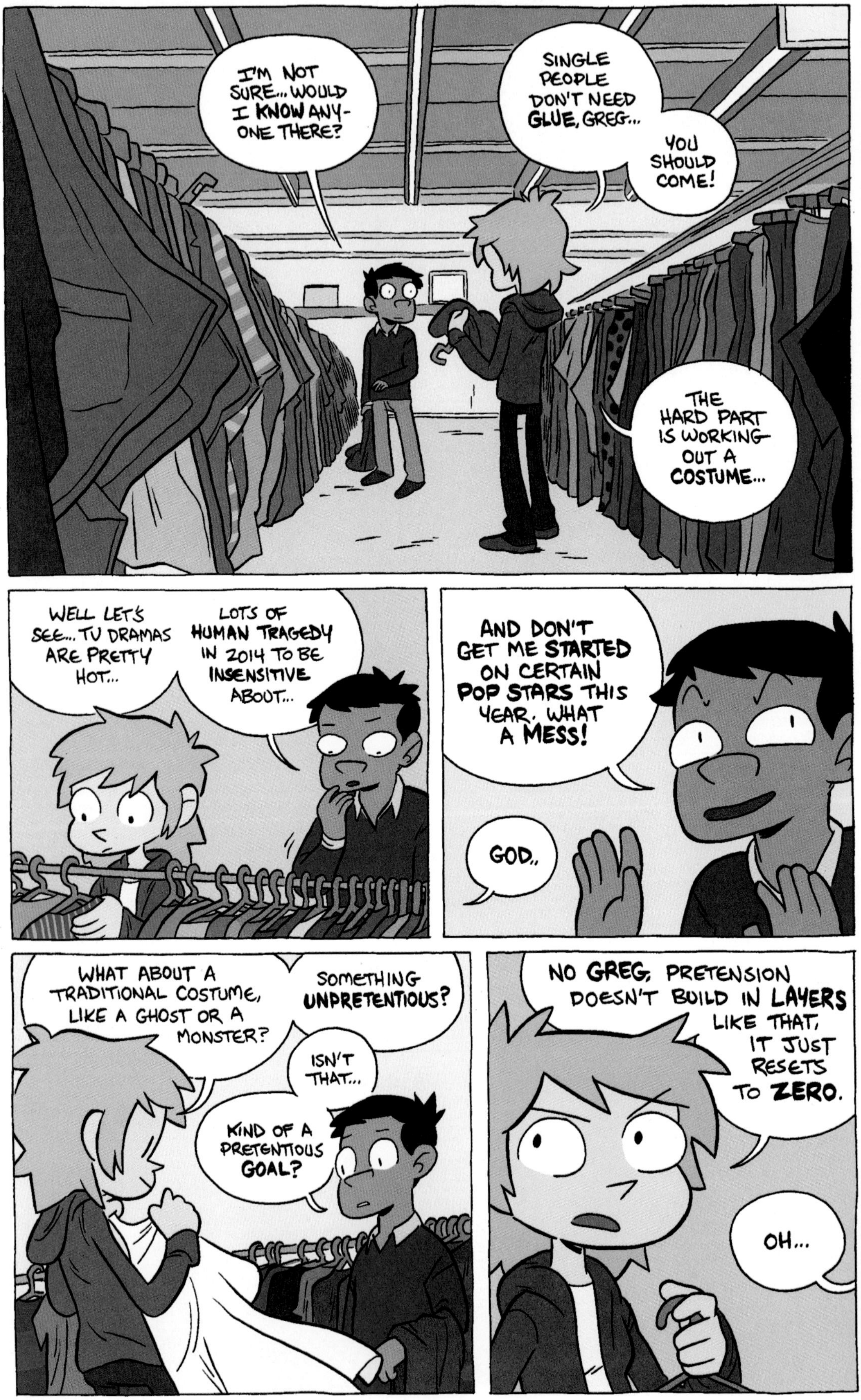

I'M NOT SURE... WOULD I KNOW ANY-ONE THERE?
SINGLE PEOPLE DON'T NEED GLUE, GREG...
YOU SHOULD COME!
THE HARD PART IS WORKING OUT A COSTUME...
WELL LET'S SEE... TV DRAMAS ARE PRETTY HOT...
LOTS OF HUMAN TRAGEDY IN 2014 TO BE INSENSITIVE ABOUT...
AND DON'T GET ME STARTED ON CERTAIN POP STARS THIS YEAR. WHAT A MESS!
GOD..
WHAT ABOUT A TRADITIONAL COSTUME, LIKE A GHOST OR A MONSTER?
SOMETHING UNPRETENTIOUS?
ISN'T THAT...
KIND OF A PRETENTIOUS GOAL?
NO GREG, PRETENSION DOESN'T BUILD IN LAYERS LIKE THAT, IT JUST RESETS TO ZERO.
OH...

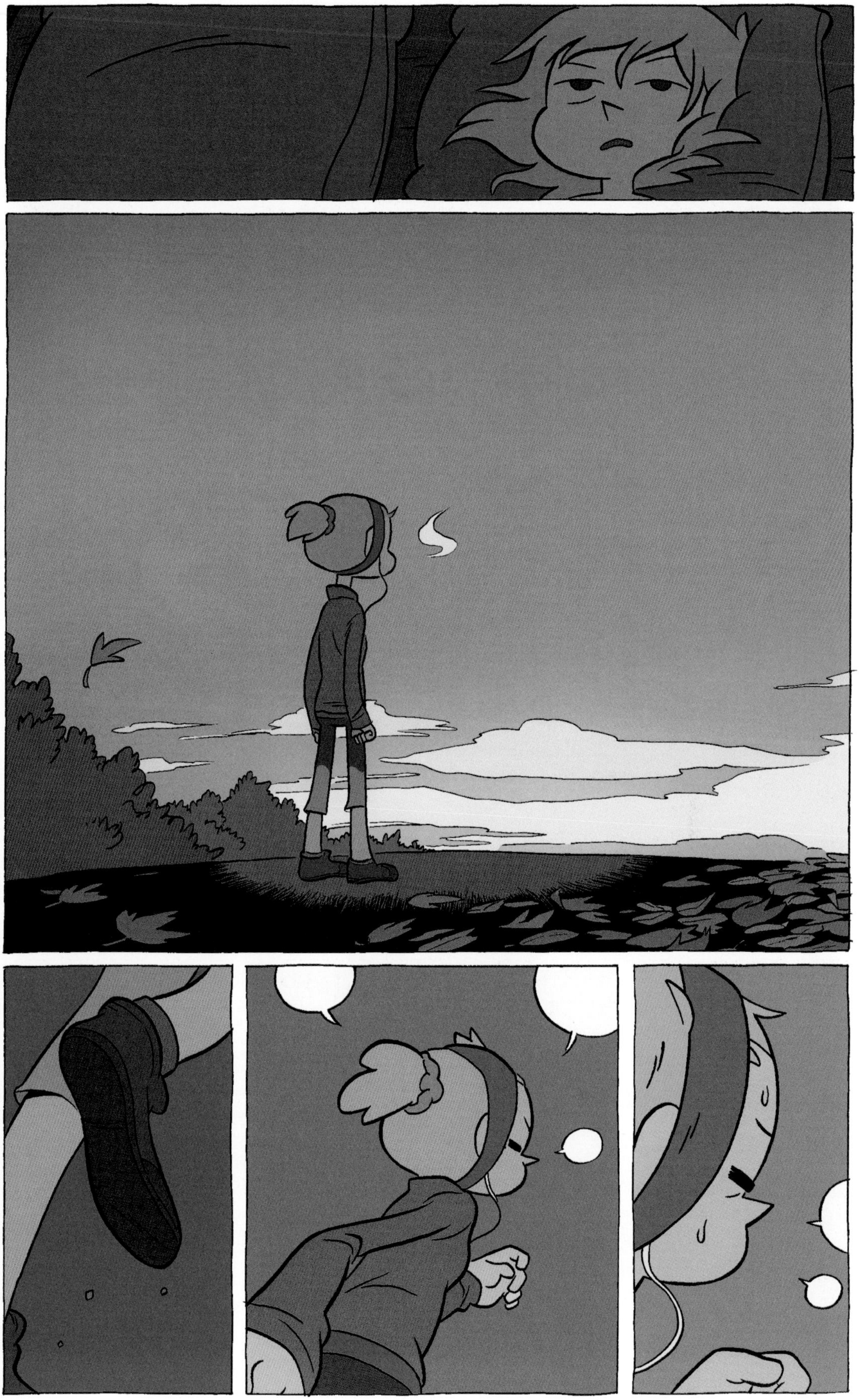

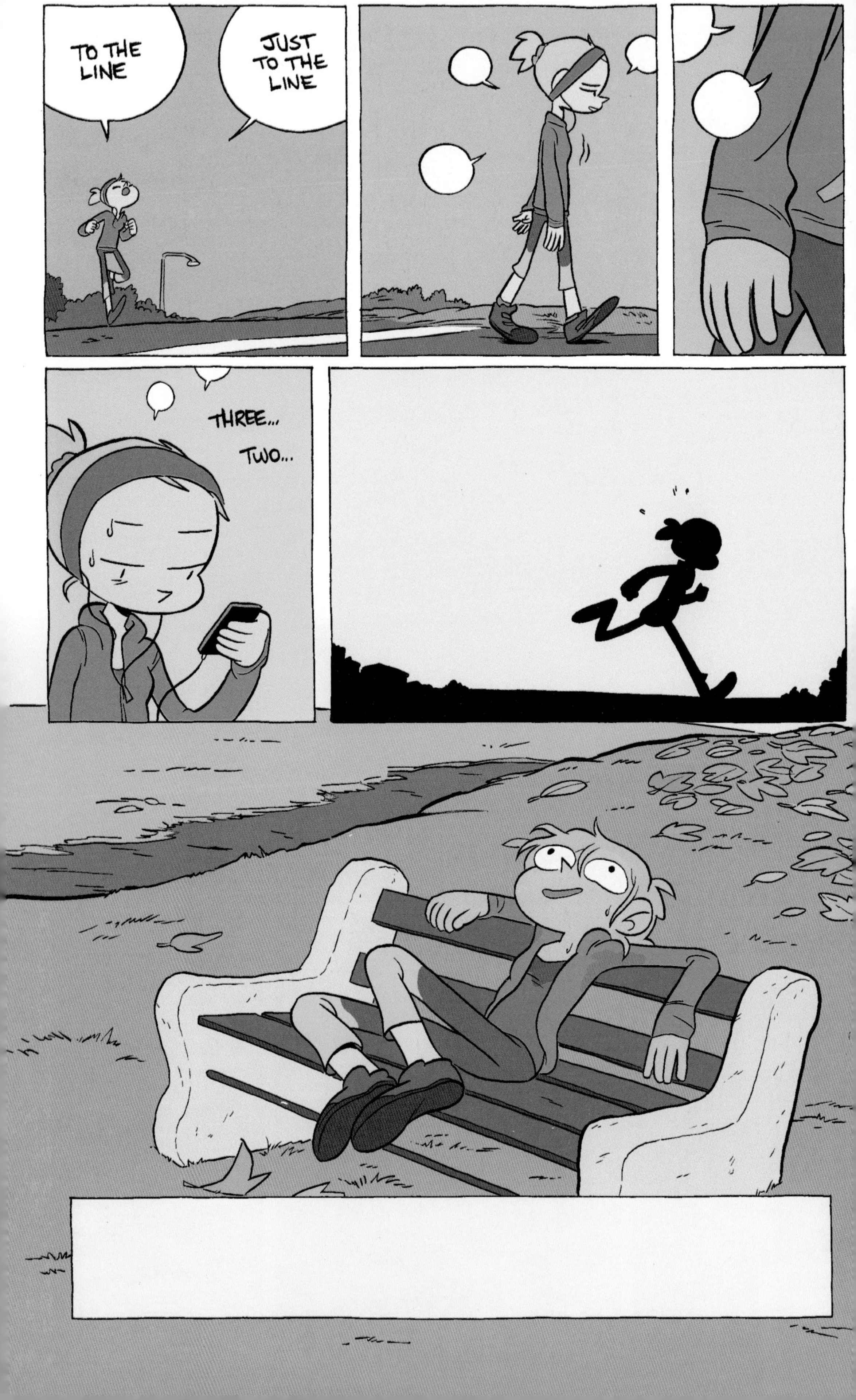
TO THE LINE
JUST TO THE LINE
THREE...
TWO...

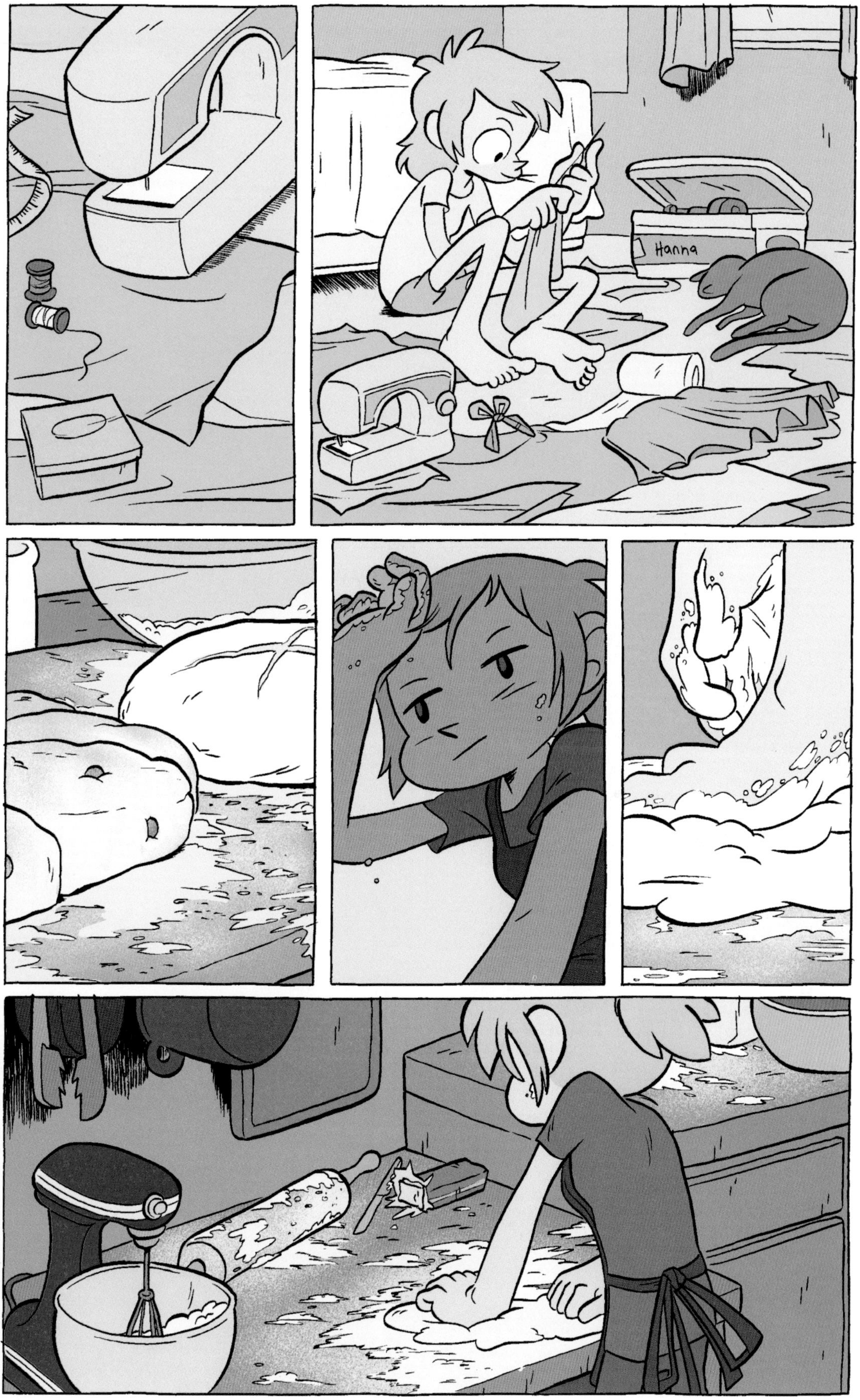
Hanna

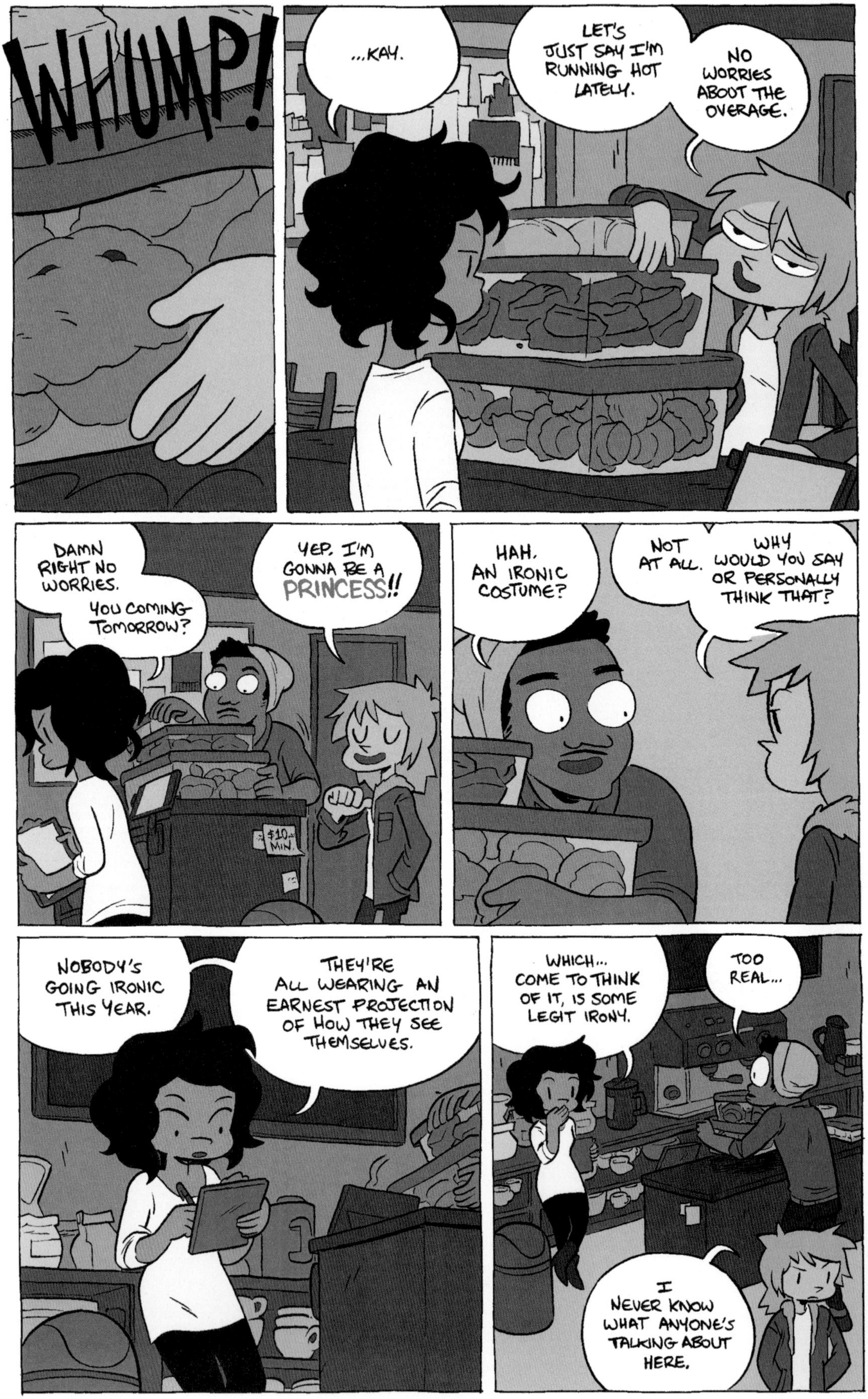
WHUMP!
...KAY.
LET'S JUST SAY I'M RUNNING HOT LATELY.
NO WORRIES ABOUT THE OVERAGE.
DAMN RIGHT NO WORRIES.
YOU COMING TOMORROW?
YEP. I'M GONNA BE A PRINCESS!!
$10 MIN.
HAH. AN IRONIC COSTUME?
NOT AT ALL.
WHY WOULD YOU SAY OR PERSONALLY THINK THAT?
NOBODY'S GOING IRONIC THIS YEAR.
THEY'RE ALL WEARING AN EARNEST PROJECTION OF HOW THEY SEE THEMSELVES.
WHICH... COME TO THINK OF IT, IS SOME LEGIT IRONY.
TOO REAL...
I NEVER KNOW WHAT ANYONE'S TALKING ABOUT HERE.

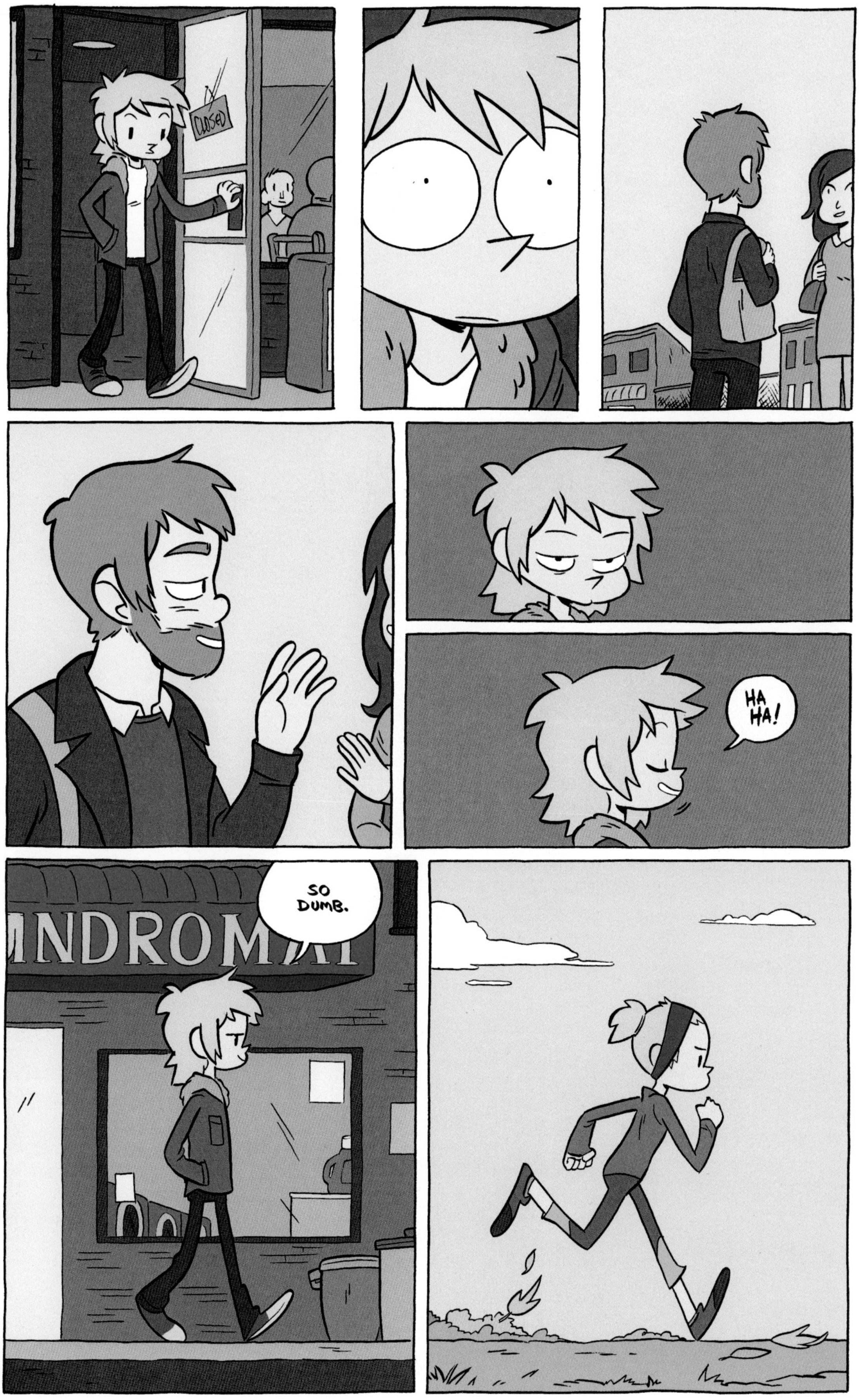
CLOSED
HA HA!
SO DUMB.
NDROMAT

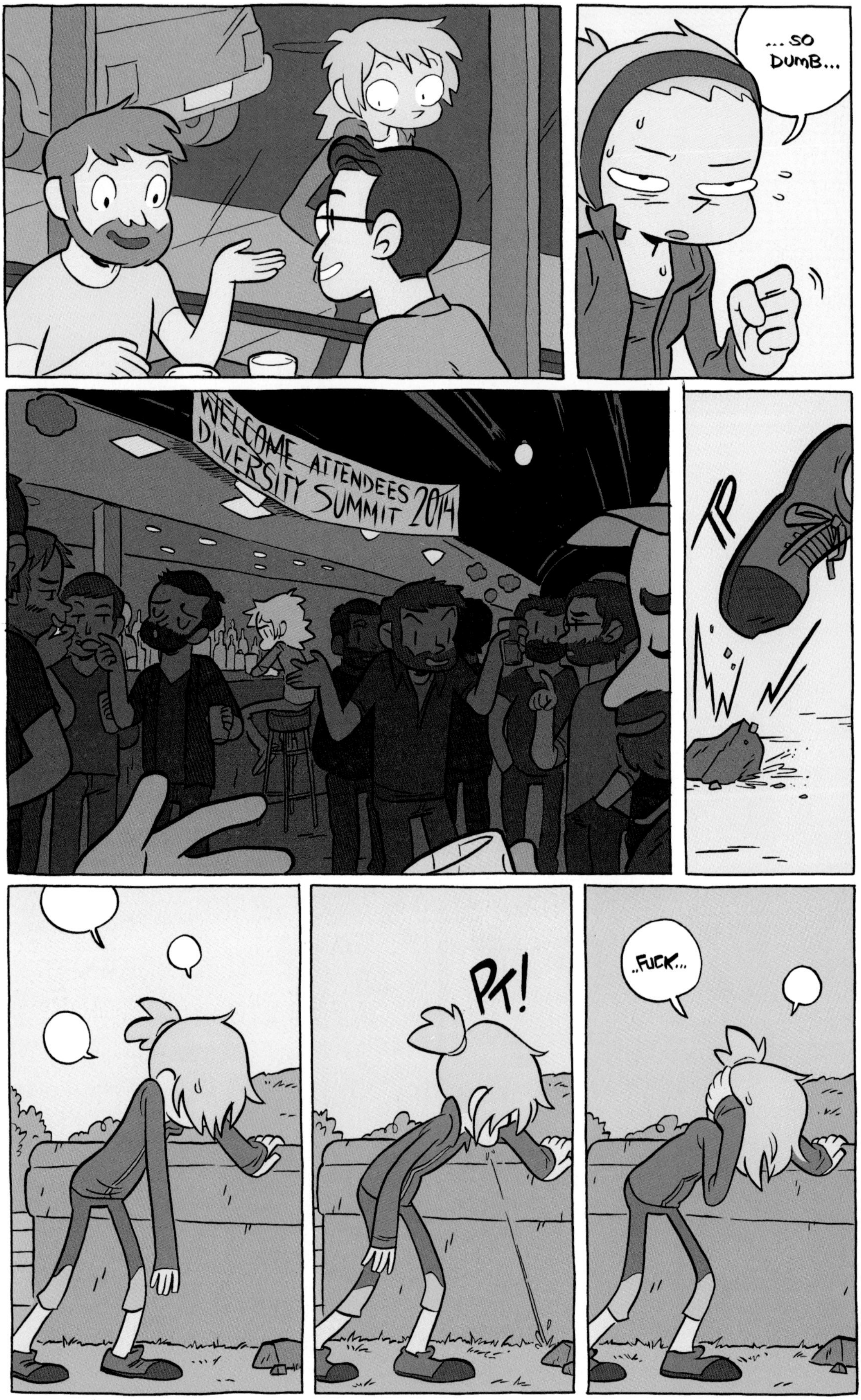
...SO DUMB...
WELCOME ATTENDEES DIVERSITY SUMMIT 2014
TP
PT!
..FUCK...

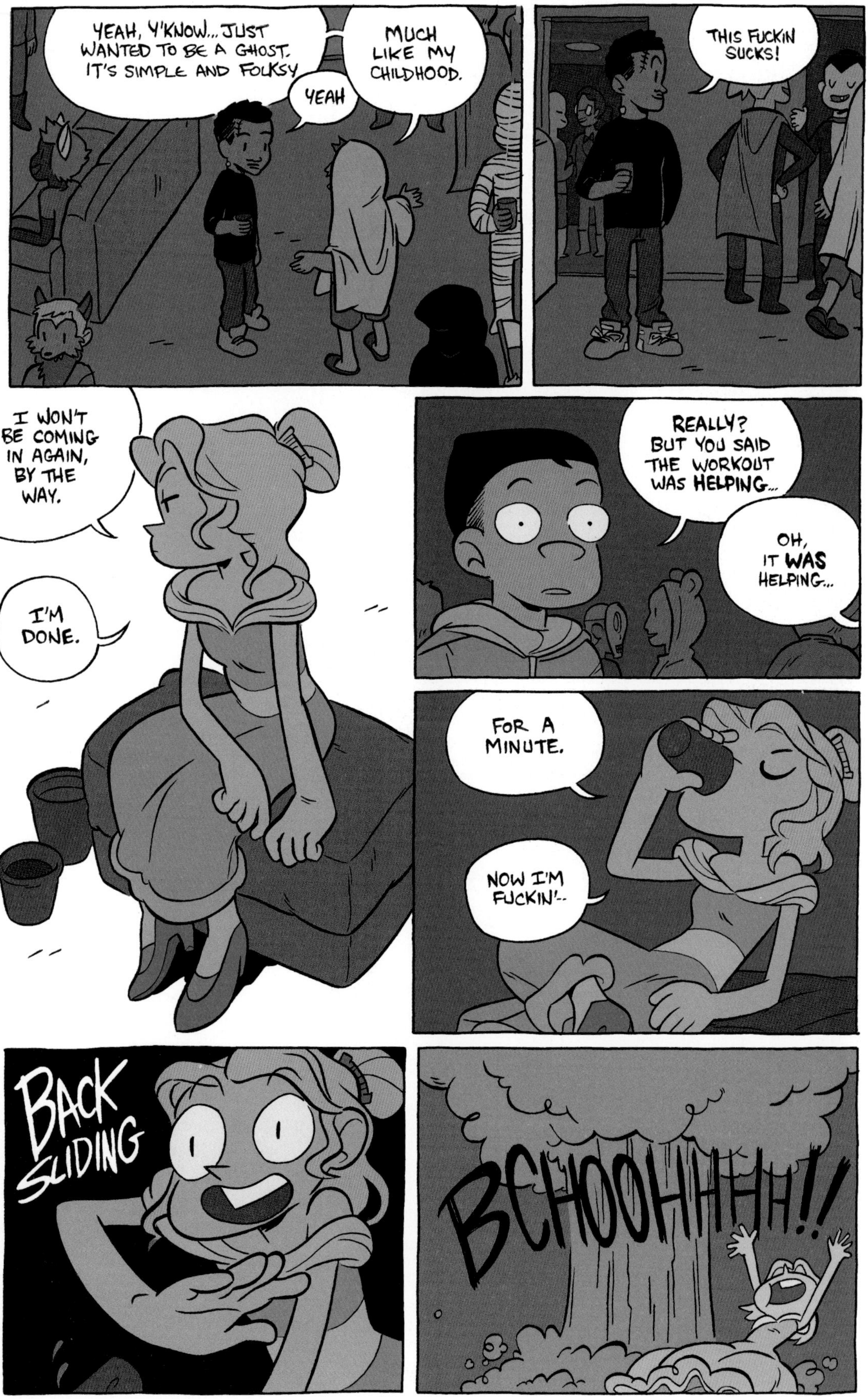
YEAH, Y'KNOW... JUST WANTED TO BE A GHOST. IT'S SIMPLE AND FOLKSY
YEAH
MUCH LIKE MY CHILDHOOD.
THIS FUCKIN SUCKS!
I WON'T BE COMING IN AGAIN, BY THE WAY.
I'M DONE.
REALLY? BUT YOU SAID THE WORKOUT WAS HELPING...
OH, IT WAS HELPING...
FOR A MINUTE.
NOW I'M FUCKIN'--
BACK SLIDING
BCHOOHHHHH!!

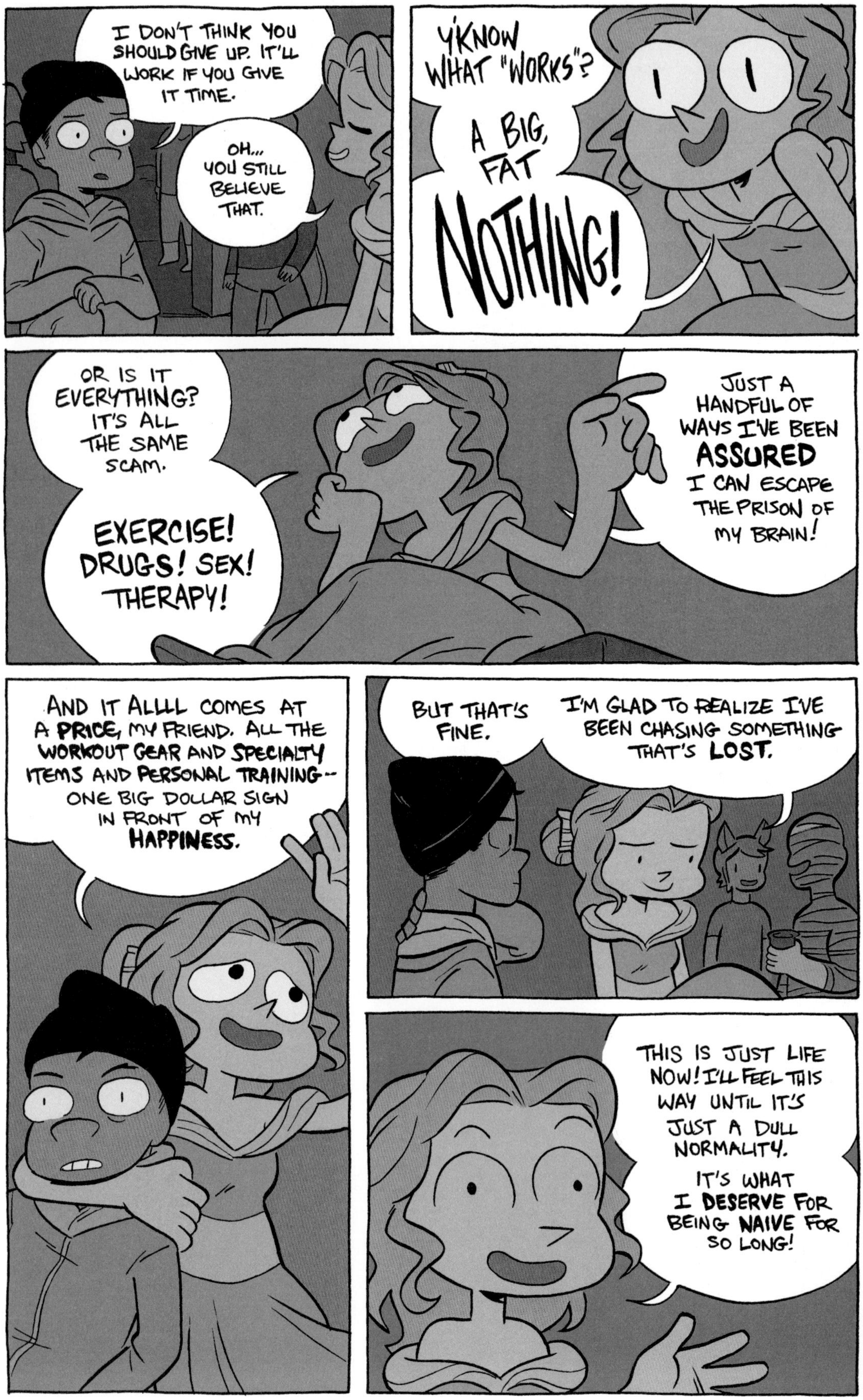
I DON'T THINK YOU SHOULD GIVE UP. IT'LL WORK IF YOU GIVE IT TIME.
OH... YOU STILL BELIEVE THAT.
Y'KNOW WHAT "WORKS"?
A BIG, FAT NOTHING!
OR IS IT EVERYTHING? IT'S ALL THE SAME SCAM.
EXERCISE! DRUGS! SEX! THERAPY!
JUST A HANDFUL OF WAYS I'VE BEEN ASSURED I CAN ESCAPE THE PRISON OF MY BRAIN!
AND IT ALLLL COMES AT A PRICE, MY FRIEND. ALL THE WORKOUT GEAR AND SPECIALTY ITEMS AND PERSONAL TRAINING-- ONE BIG DOLLAR SIGN IN FRONT OF MY HAPPINESS.
BUT THAT'S FINE.
I'M GLAD TO REALIZE I'VE BEEN CHASING SOMETHING THAT'S LOST.
THIS IS JUST LIFE NOW! I'LL FEEL THIS WAY UNTIL IT'S JUST A DULL NORMALITY.
IT'S WHAT I DESERVE FOR BEING NAIVE FOR SO LONG!

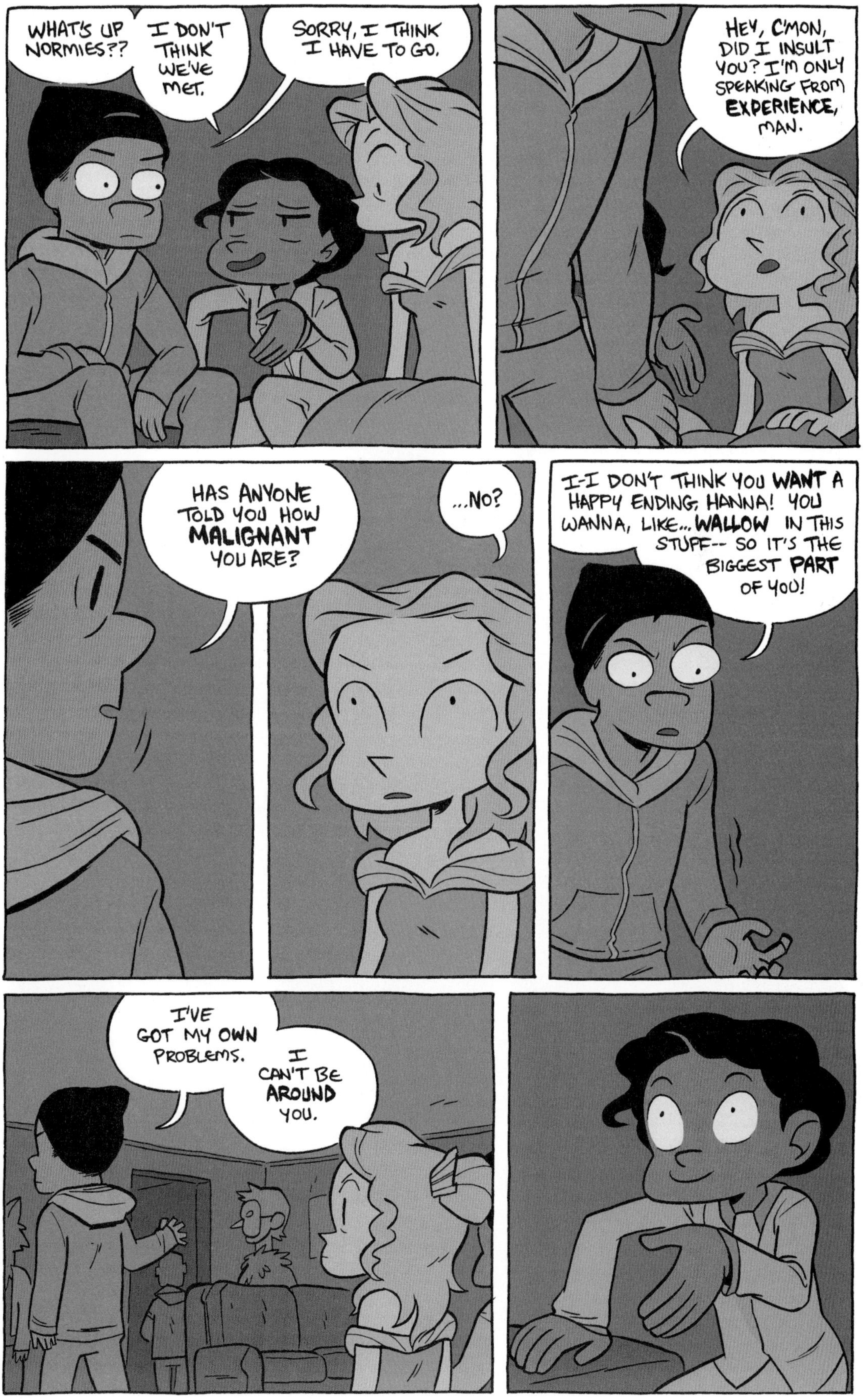

WHAT'S UP NORMIES??
I DON'T THINK WE'VE MET.
SORRY, I THINK I HAVE TO GO.
HEY, C'MON, DID I INSULT YOU? I'M ONLY SPEAKING FROM EXPERIENCE, MAN.
HAS ANYONE TOLD YOU HOW MALIGNANT YOU ARE?
...NO?
I-I DON'T THINK YOU WANT A HAPPY ENDING, HANNA! YOU WANNA, LIKE... WALLOW IN THIS STUFF-- SO IT'S THE BIGGEST PART OF YOU!
I'VE GOT MY OWN PROBLEMS.
I CAN'T BE AROUND YOU.

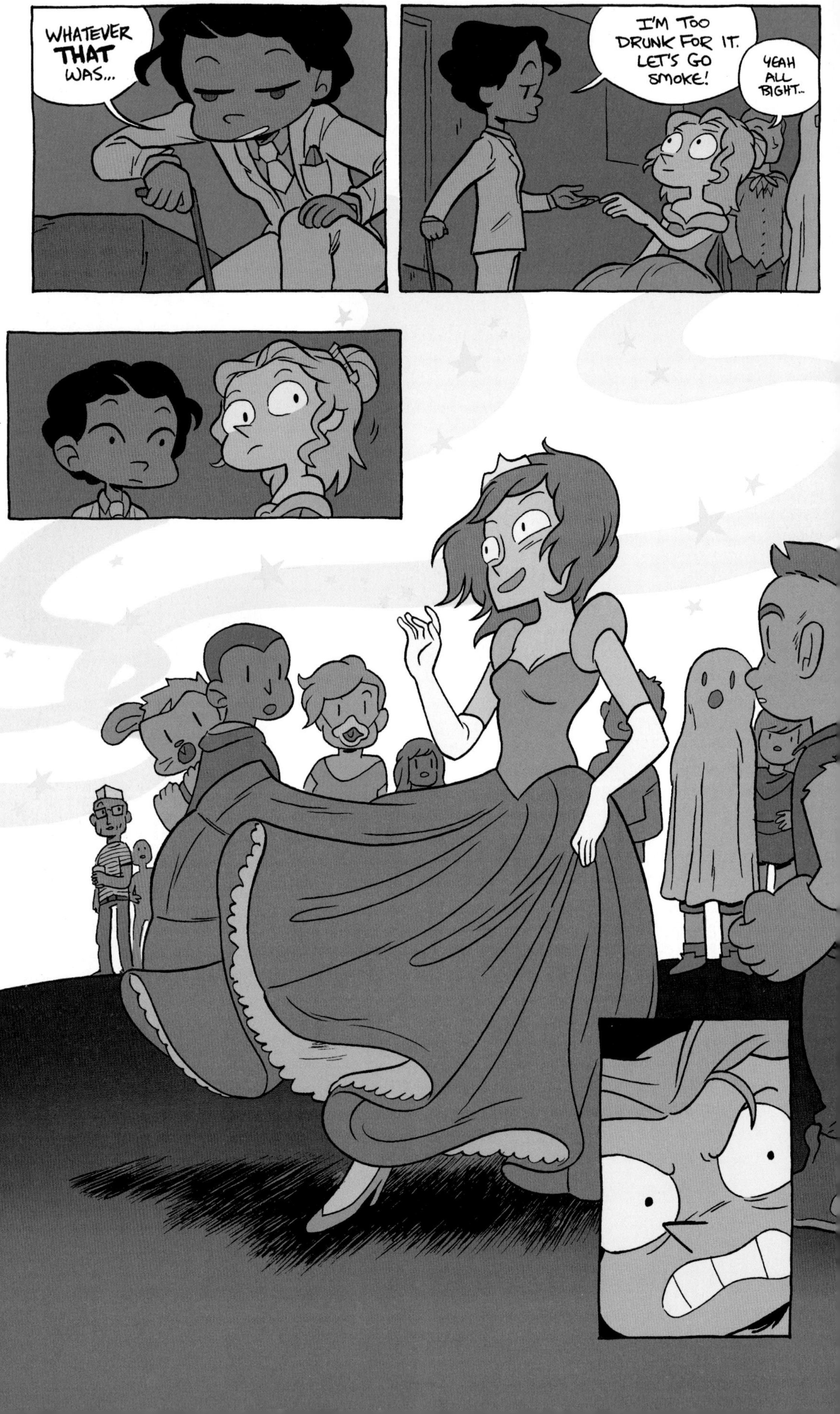
WHATEVER **THAT** WAS...
I'M TOO DRUNK FOR IT. LET'S GO SMOKE!
YEAH ALL RIGHT...

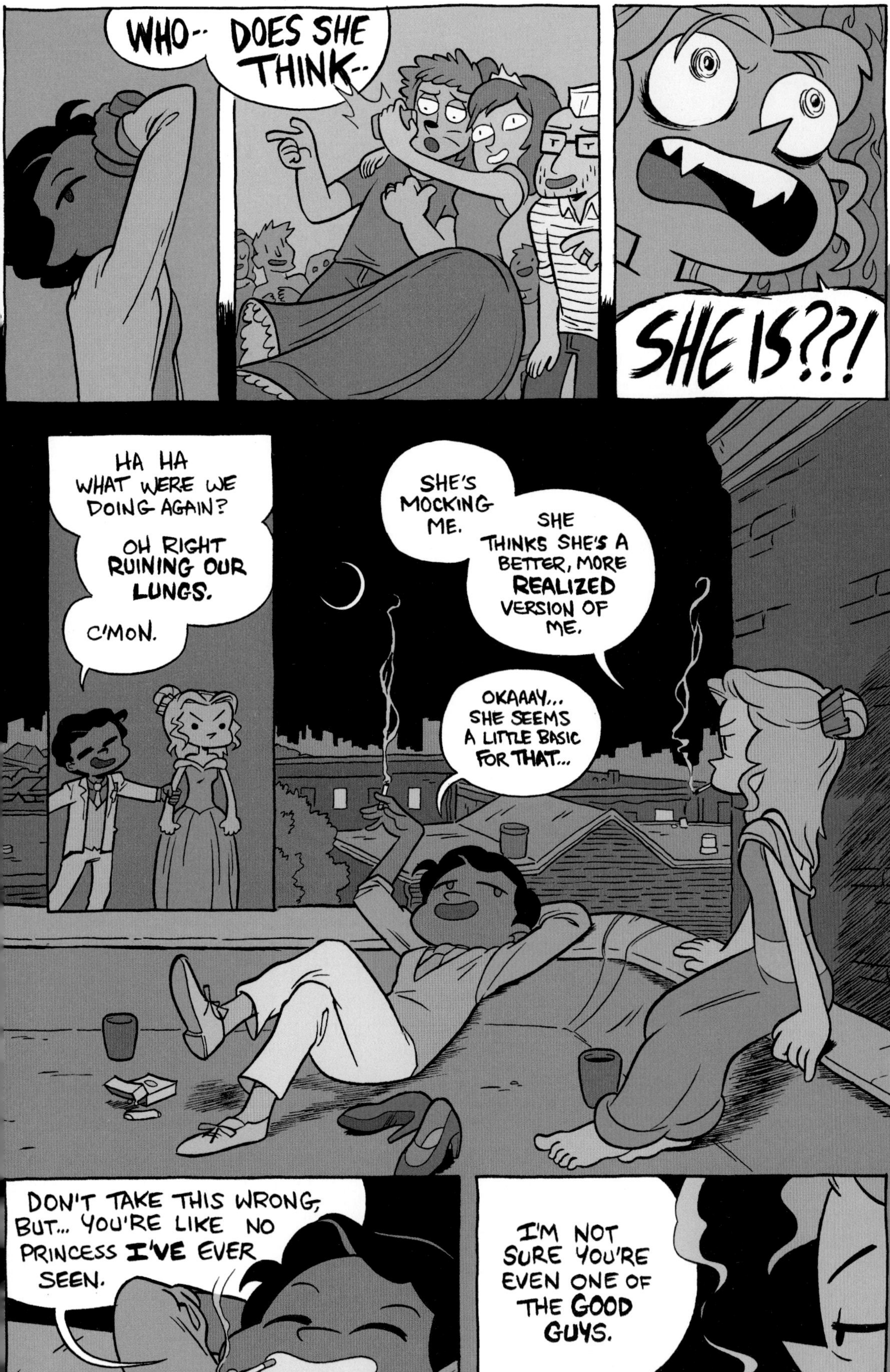
WHO-- DOES SHE THINK--
SHE IS??!
HA HA WHAT WERE WE DOING AGAIN?
OH RIGHT RUINING OUR LUNGS.
C'MON.
SHE'S MOCKING ME.
SHE THINKS SHE'S A BETTER, MORE REALIZED VERSION OF ME.
OKAAAY... SHE SEEMS A LITTLE BASIC FOR THAT...
DON'T TAKE THIS WRONG, BUT... YOU'RE LIKE NO PRINCESS I'VE EVER SEEN.
I'M NOT SURE YOU'RE EVEN ONE OF THE GOOD GUYS.

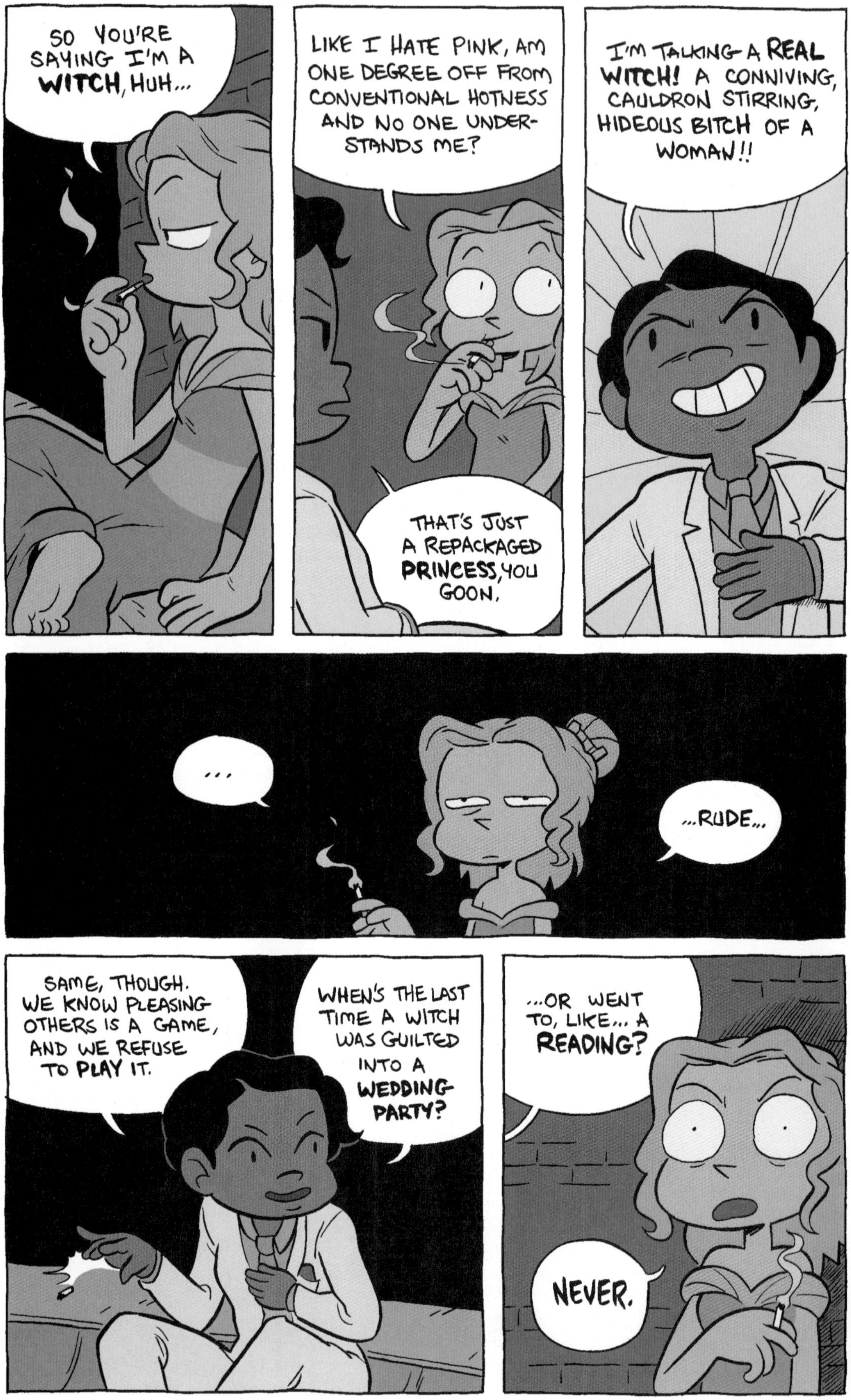
SO YOU'RE SAYING I'M A WITCH, HUH...
LIKE I HATE PINK, AM ONE DEGREE OFF FROM CONVENTIONAL HOTNESS AND NO ONE UNDER-STANDS ME?
THAT'S JUST A REPACKAGED PRINCESS, YOU GOON.
I'M TALKING A REAL WITCH! A CONNIVING, CAULDRON STIRRING, HIDEOUS BITCH OF A WOMAN!!
...
...RUDE...
SAME, THOUGH. WE KNOW PLEASING OTHERS IS A GAME, AND WE REFUSE TO PLAY IT.
WHEN'S THE LAST TIME A WITCH WAS GUILTED INTO A WEDDING PARTY?
...OR WENT TO, LIKE... A READING?
NEVER.

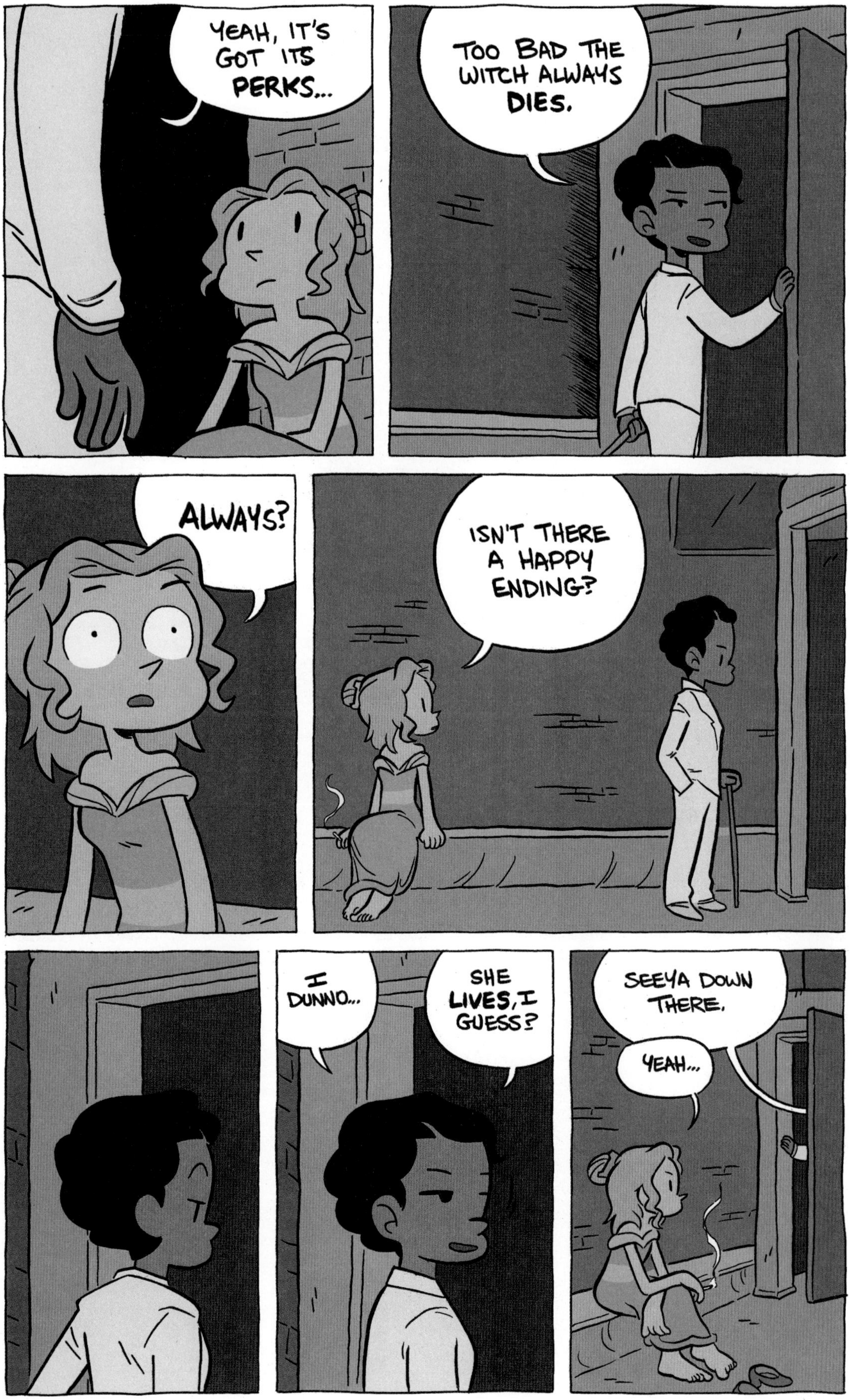
YEAH, IT'S GOT ITS PERKS...
TOO BAD THE WITCH ALWAYS DIES.
ALWAYS?
ISN'T THERE A HAPPY ENDING?
I DUNNO...
SHE LIVES, I GUESS?
SEEYA DOWN THERE.
YEAH...

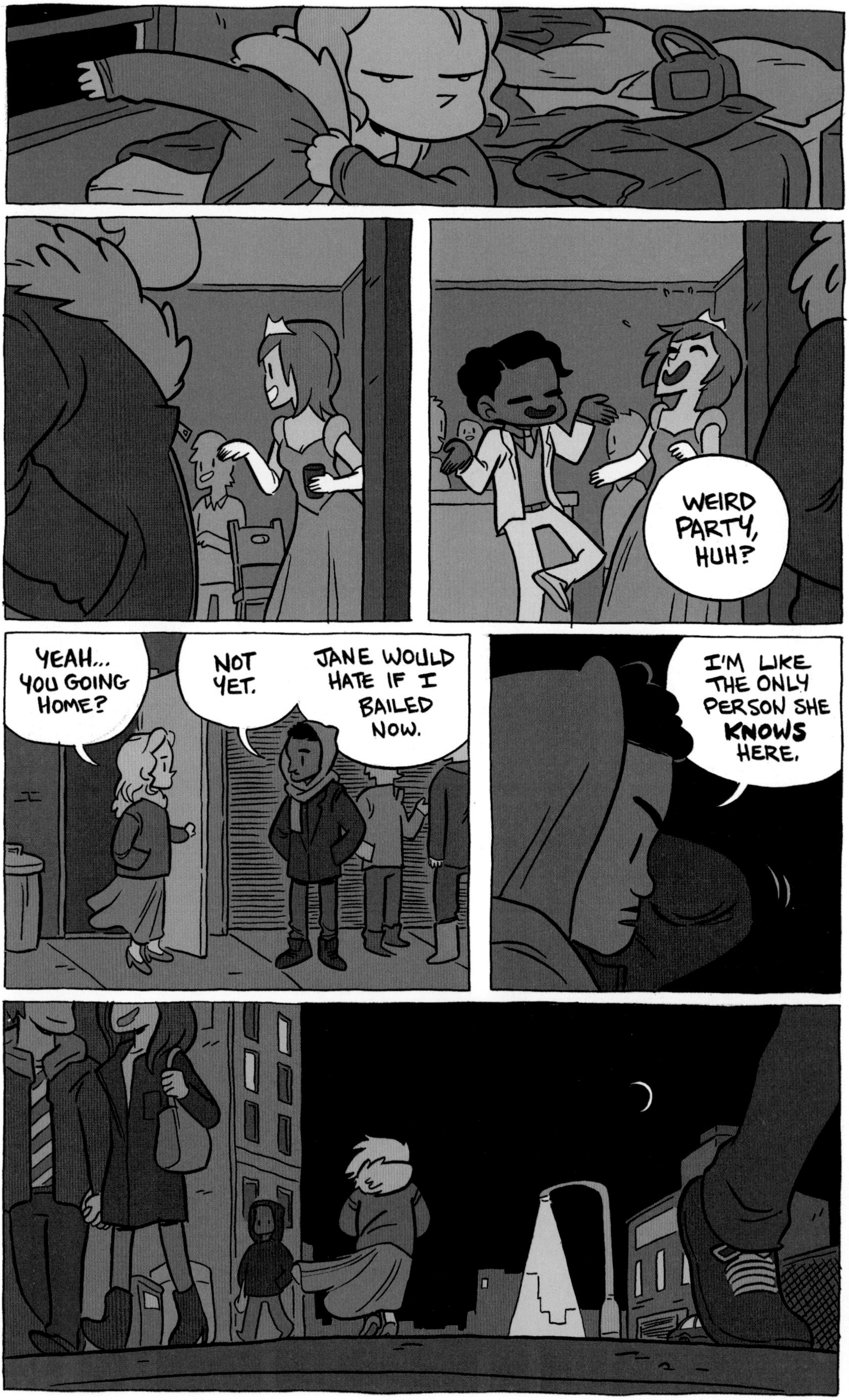

WEIRD PARTY, HUH?
YEAH... YOU GOING HOME?
NOT YET.
JANE WOULD HATE IF I BAILED NOW.
I'M LIKE THE ONLY PERSON SHE **KNOWS** HERE.

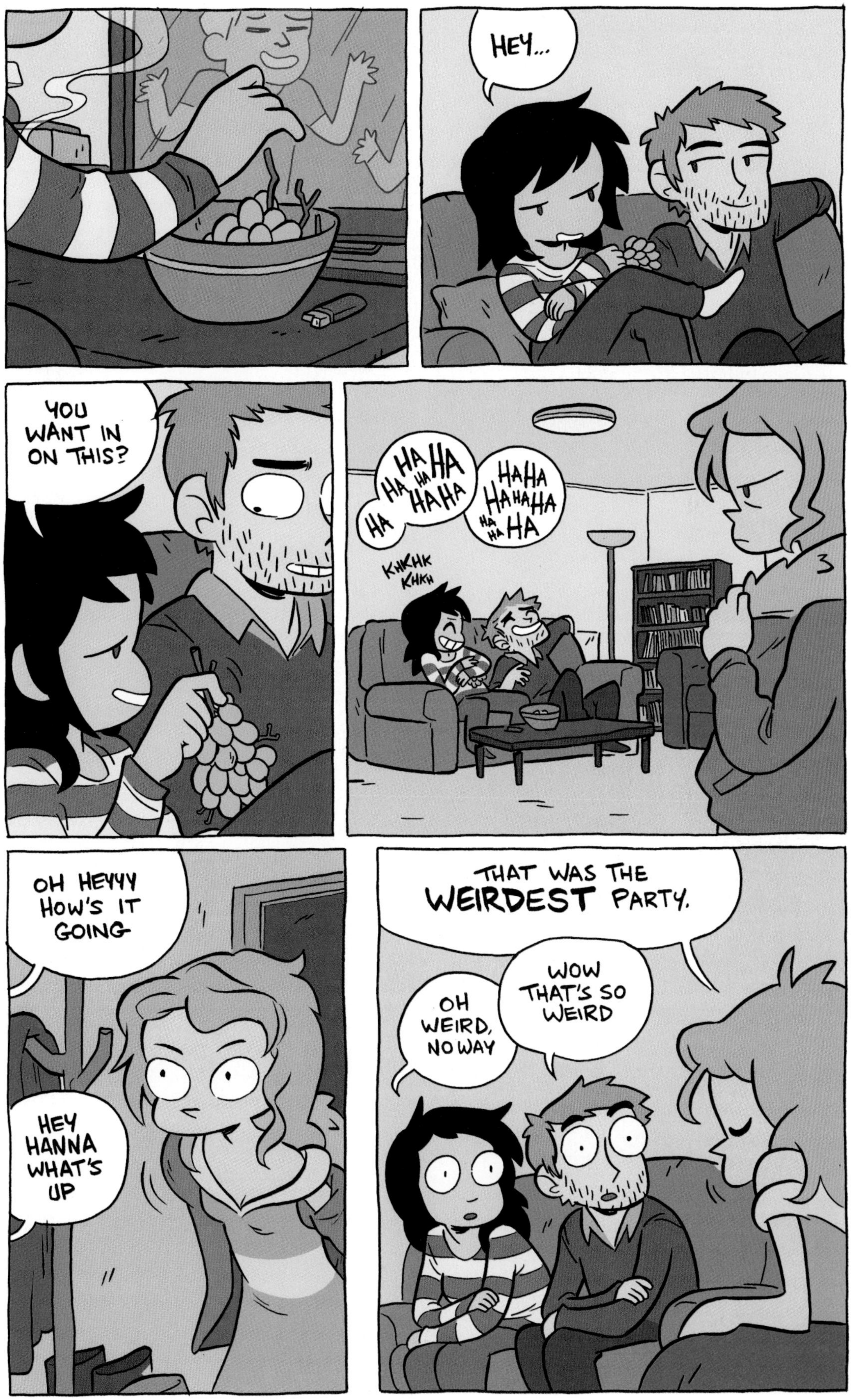
HEY...
YOU WANT IN ON THIS?
HA HA HA HA HAHA HAHA
HAHA HAHAHAHA HA HA HA
KHKHK KHKH
OH HEYYY HOW'S IT GOING
HEY HANNA WHAT'S UP
THAT WAS THE WEIRDEST PARTY.
OH WEIRD, NO WAY
WOW THAT'S SO WEIRD

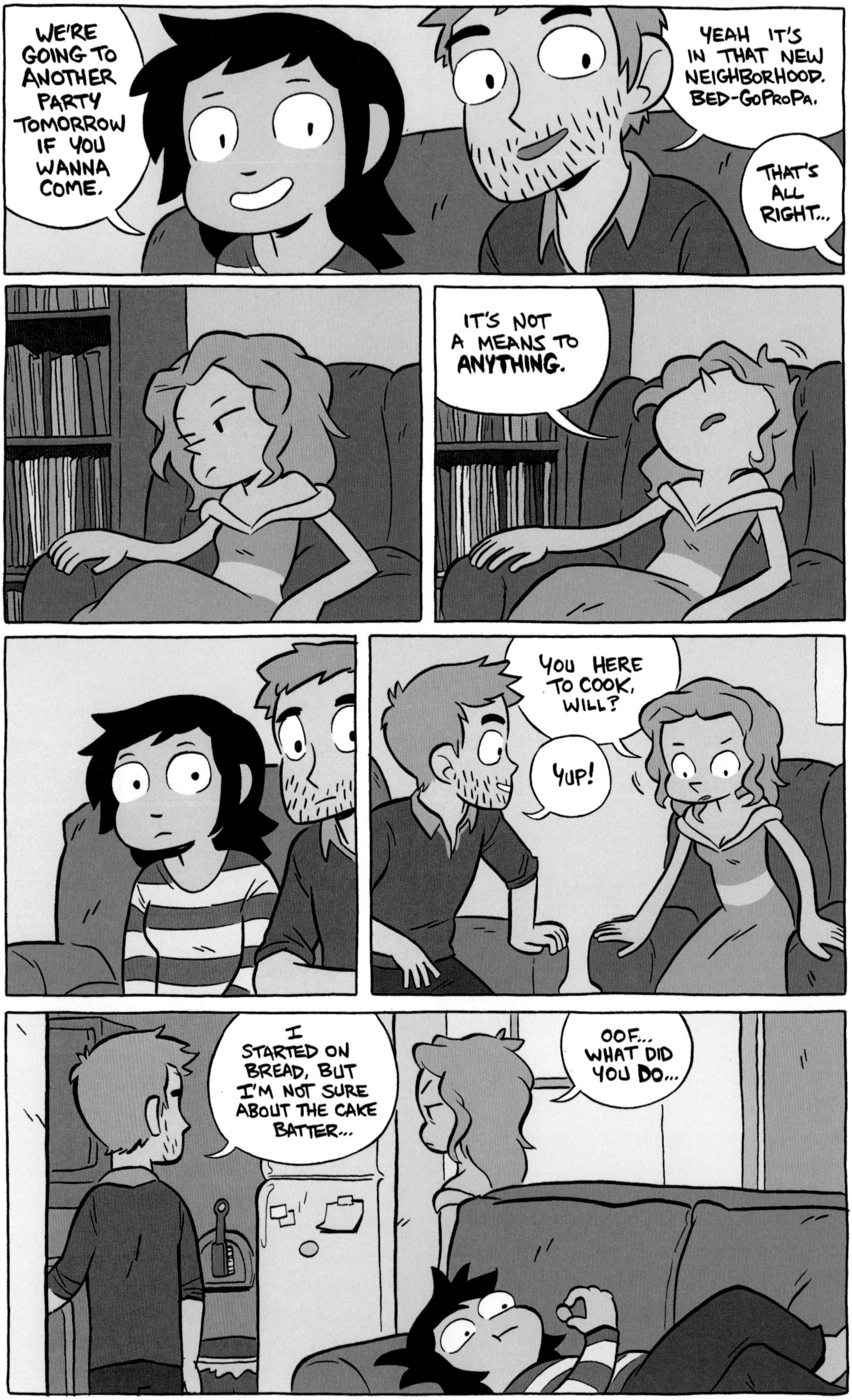

WE'RE GOING TO ANOTHER PARTY TOMORROW IF YOU WANNA COME.
YEAH IT'S IN THAT NEW NEIGHBORHOOD. BED-GOPROPA.
THAT'S ALL RIGHT...
IT'S NOT A MEANS TO ANYTHING.
YOU HERE TO COOK, WILL?
YUP!
I STARTED ON BREAD, BUT I'M NOT SURE ABOUT THE CAKE BATTER...
OOF... WHAT DID YOU DO...

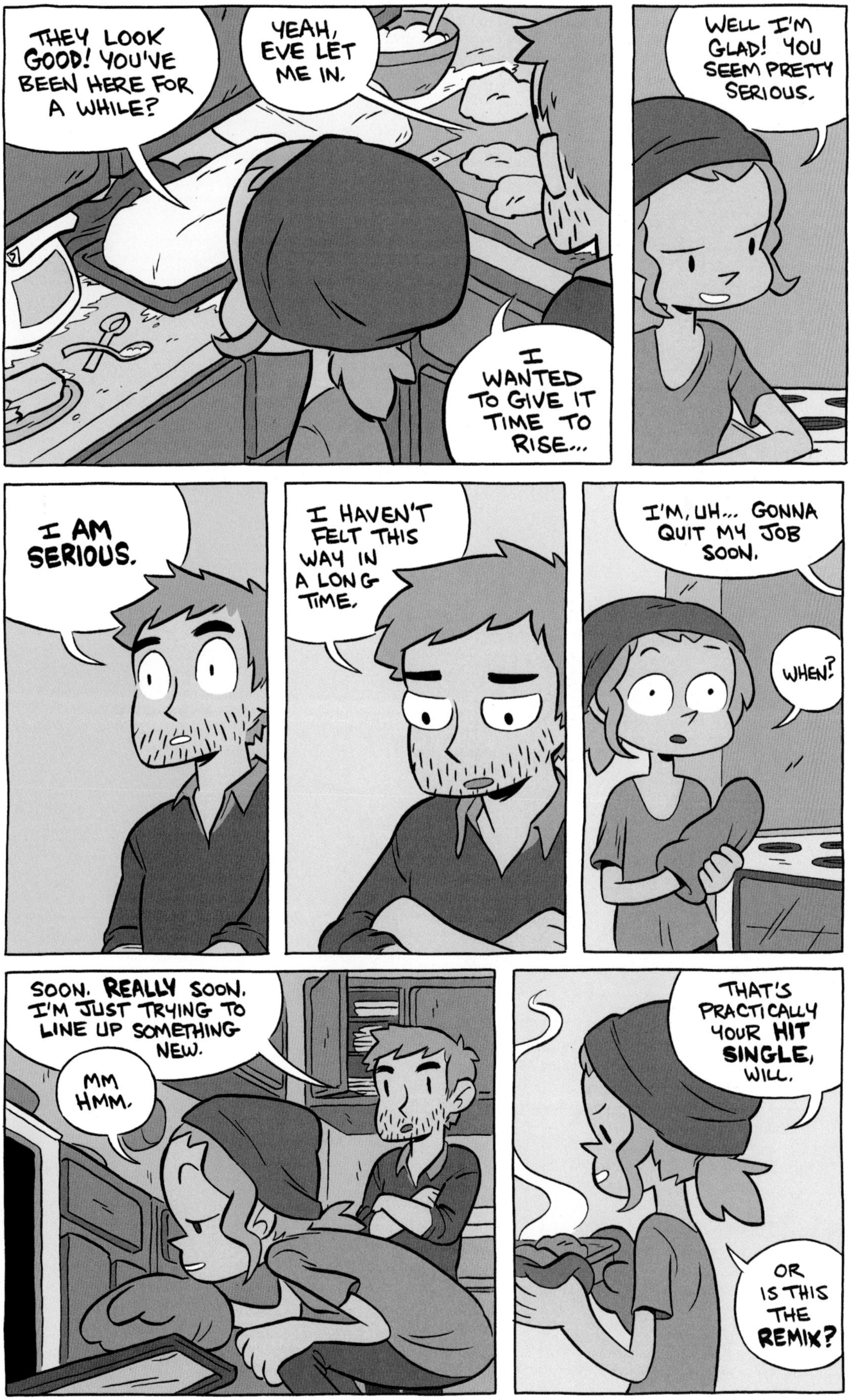
THEY LOOK GOOD! YOU'VE BEEN HERE FOR A WHILE?
YEAH, EVE LET ME IN.
I WANTED TO GIVE IT TIME TO RISE...
WELL I'M GLAD! YOU SEEM PRETTY SERIOUS.
I AM SERIOUS.
I HAVEN'T FELT THIS WAY IN A LONG TIME.
I'M, UH... GONNA QUIT MY JOB SOON.
WHEN?
SOON. REALLY SOON. I'M JUST TRYING TO LINE UP SOMETHING NEW.
MM HMM.
THAT'S PRACTICALLY YOUR HIT SINGLE, WILL.
OR IS THIS THE REMIX?

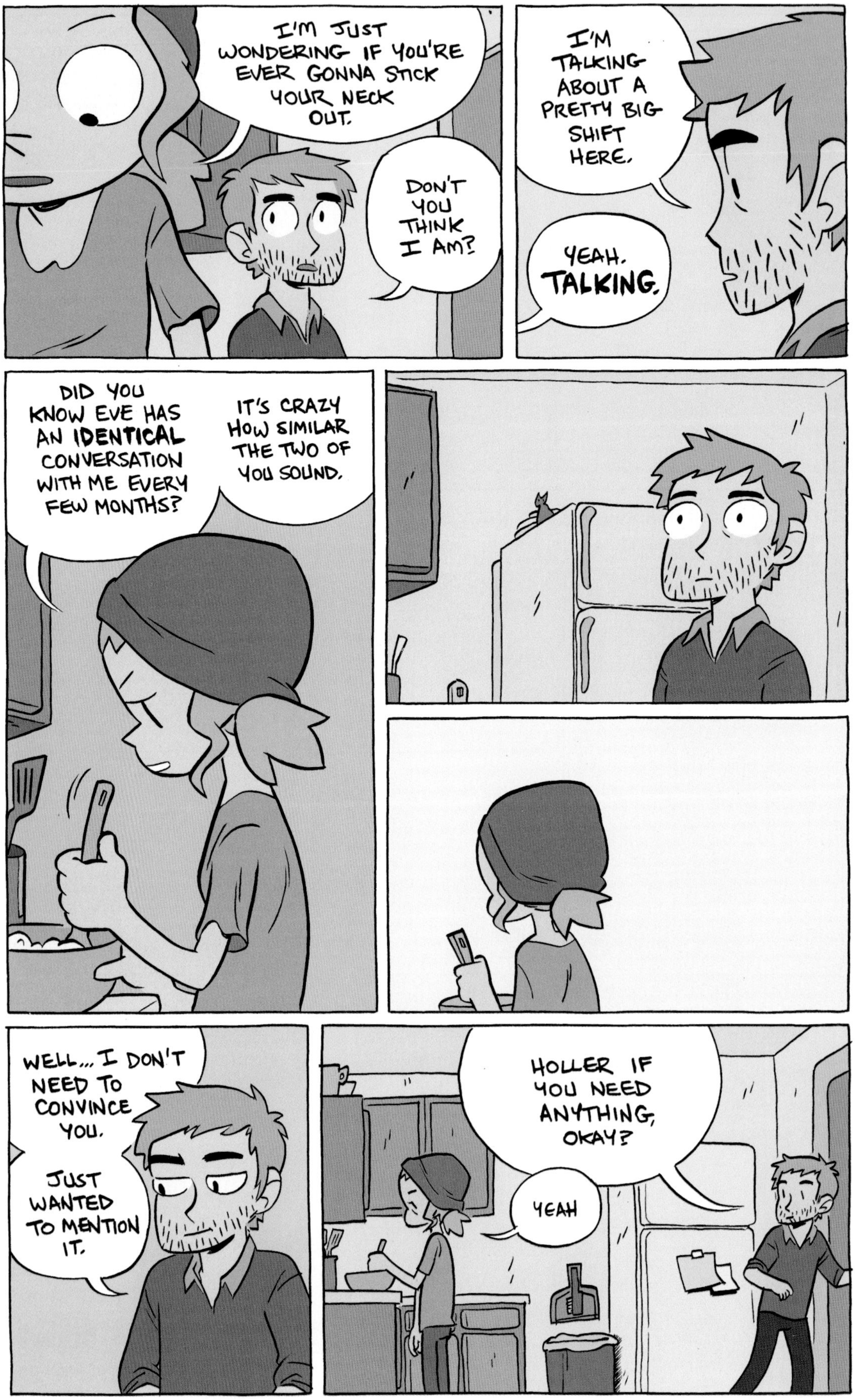
I'M JUST WONDERING IF YOU'RE EVER GONNA STICK YOUR NECK OUT.
DON'T YOU THINK I AM?
I'M TALKING ABOUT A PRETTY BIG SHIFT HERE.
YEAH. TALKING.
DID YOU KNOW EVE HAS AN IDENTICAL CONVERSATION WITH ME EVERY FEW MONTHS?
IT'S CRAZY HOW SIMILAR THE TWO OF YOU SOUND.
WELL... I DON'T NEED TO CONVINCE YOU.
JUST WANTED TO MENTION IT.
HOLLER IF YOU NEED ANYTHING, OKAY?
YEAH

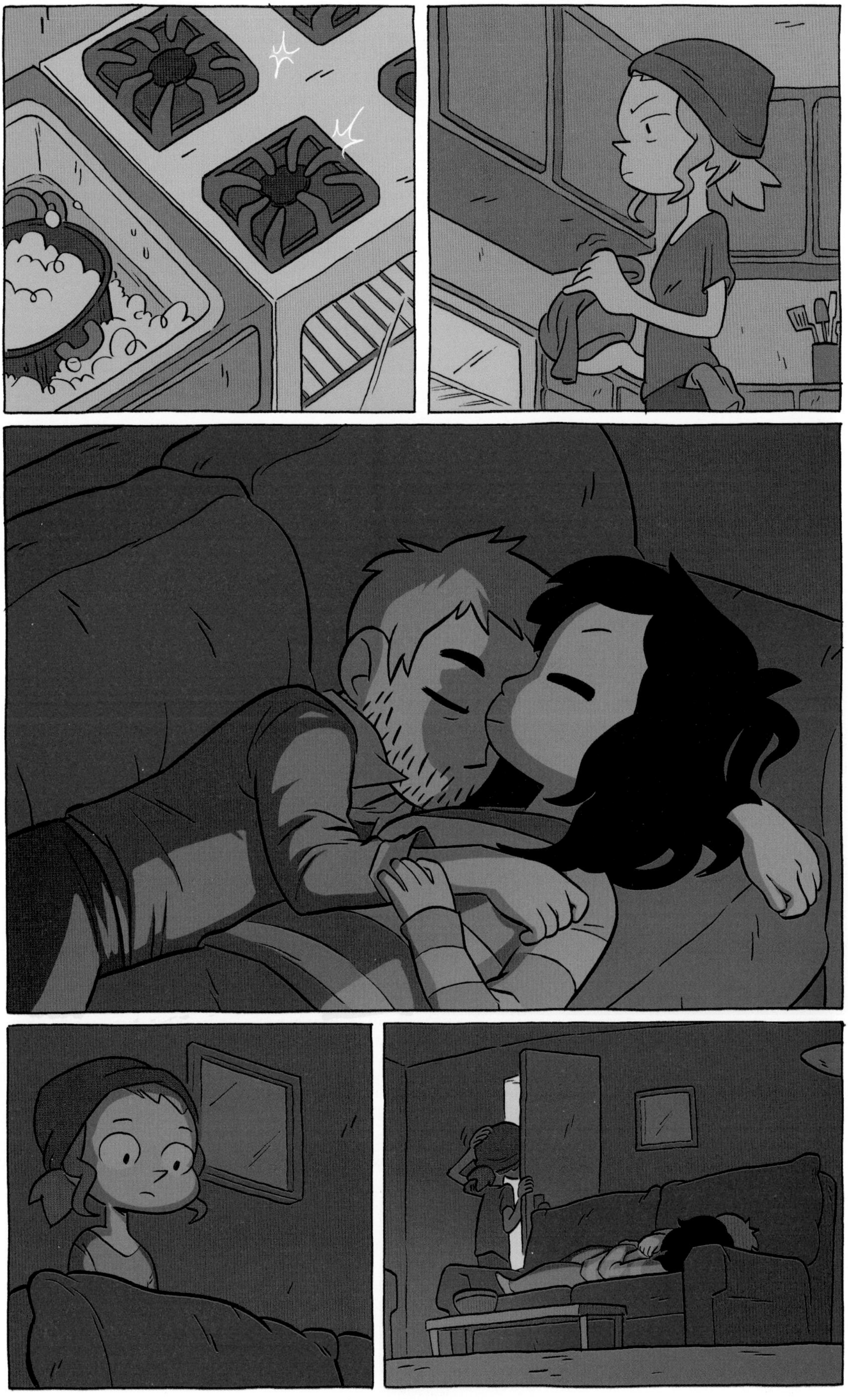

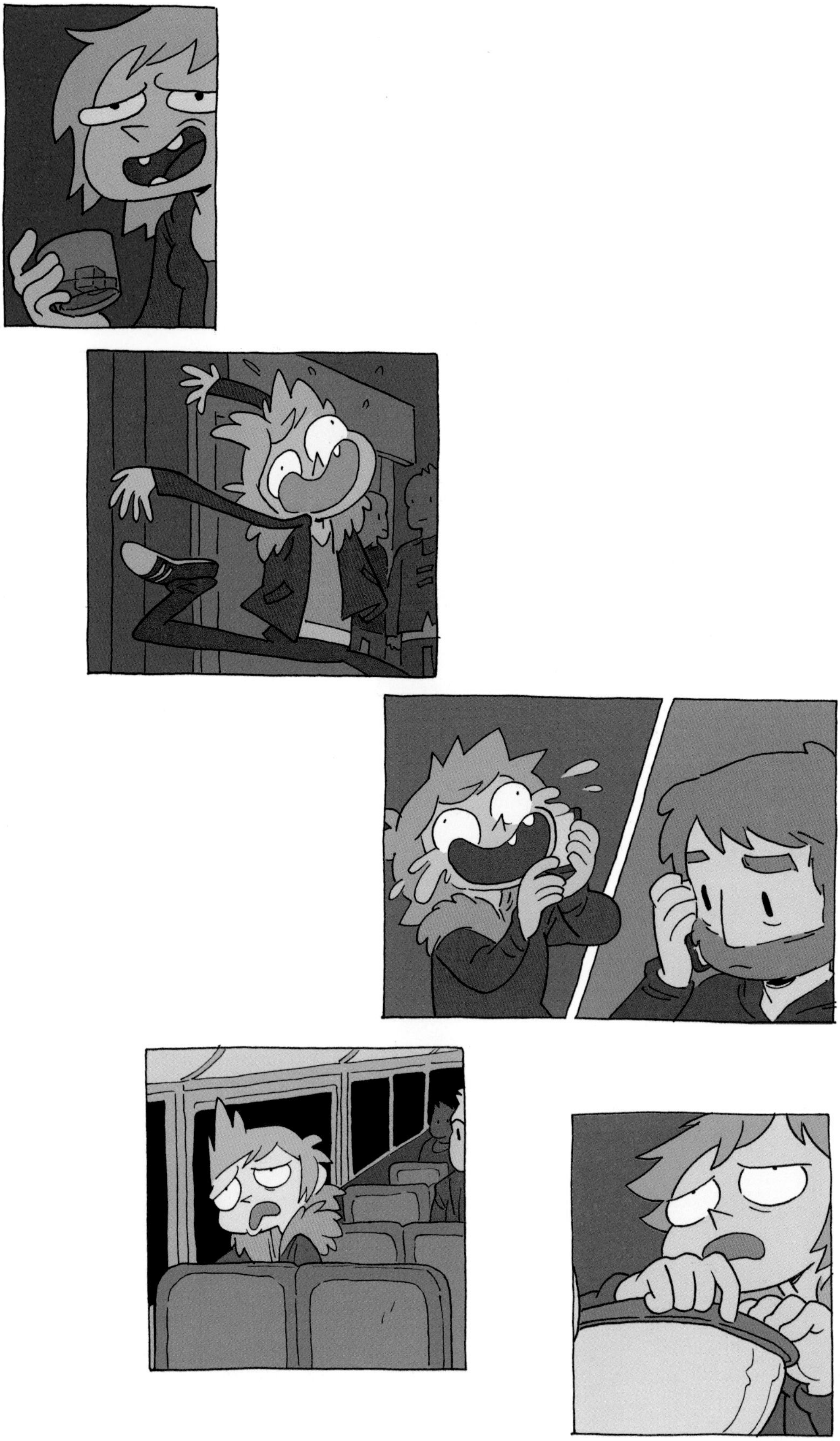

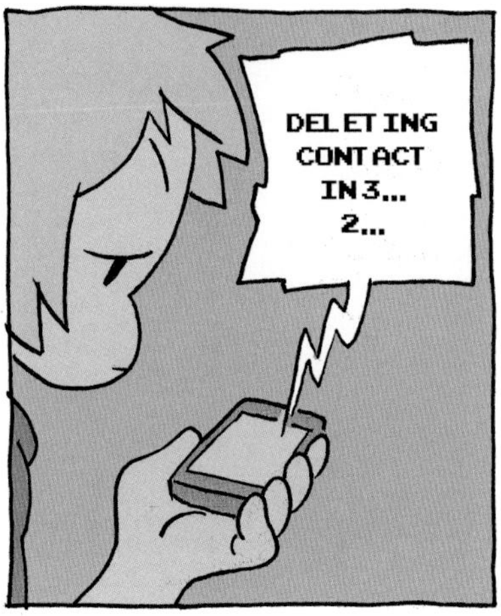
DELETING
CONTACT
IN 3...
2...

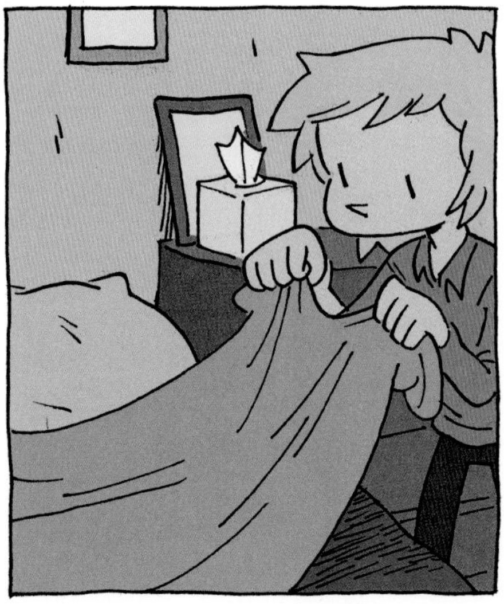

Meredith Gran makes comics and teaches at the School of Visual Arts. She lives in Brooklyn and has tried every vegan cheese, even the good ones.

Read more *Octopus Pie* online at:
www.octopuspie.com